Off-Trail Publications

Elkhorn, California

Acknowledgements
A frosty mug of thanks to the world's leading Harold Hersey authority, John Gunnison, for assistance in compiling this volume.

back cover illustrations
top: *Gangster Stories*, March 1931, by Tom Lovell
middle: *Racketeer Stories*, March 1931, by Walter M. Baumhofer
bottom: *Gangster Stories*, November 1932

OFF-TRAIL PUBLICATIONS
2036 Elkhorn Road
Castroville, CA 95012
offtrail@redshift.com

Printed in the United States of America
First printing: April 2008

CONTENTS
(Fiction titles in uppercase)

Glorifying the American Goon
By John Locke

LEGENDARY EDITOR, HAROLD HERSEY, rose through the ranks working for publishers Street & Smith, Clayton, and Bernarr Macfadden. In late 1928, he established his own company, Magazine Publishers, popularly known as The Hersey Magazines. He called it the "Easy Credit Era"; five-thousand dollars launched the line. Thirteen titles were introduced from October 1928 through May 1929. All but two were pulps. They covered the field, from aviation to western to crime to romance, a typical "hope-for-a-winner" strategy, as Hersey put it in his 1937 book, *Pulpwood Editor*.

The third title introduced, with a cover date of November 1928, was *The Dragnet Magazine*. An above-the-title banner on the cover advertised its contents as "Detective and Crook Stories." The cover painting was adapted from the 1928 Paramount film, *Ladies of the Mob*. December's cover adapted art from another Paramount entry, 1927's *Underworld*, the first in a new wave of popular gangster films. January's cover revisited *Ladies of the Mob*, after which the covers sported homegrown concepts. We should further note that another Paramount gangster film, *The Dragnet*, was released in May 1928. So it's quite apparent that Hersey, in New York, was attempting to mirror Hollywood's success.

Another crime title, *The Underworld*, was obtained from the Eastern Distributing Corporation after its publisher, J. Thomas Wood, experienced financial difficulties. Renamed *The Underworld Magazine*, it debuted under the Hersey swastika seal with the issue of December '28. Wood's version had not been a gang pulp, however. It reprinted detective and mystery fiction from the likes of Arthur Conan Doyle and Arthur B. Reeve.* Under Hersey's hand, it presented "new detective, gangster, and mystery stories," the "new" assuring readers that the reprint policy was dead.

Both *Dragnet* and *Underworld* included healthy doses of gangland stories from authors like Henry Leverage, an ex-con who started his writing career in Sing Sing, Anatole Feldman, and Armitage Trail, author of the novel *Scarface*, basis for the 1932 gangster film. In *Pulpwood Editor*, Hersey barely mentions *The Dragnet*, but says of *Underworld*:

> I was asked to take over *The Underworld Magazine*, a periodical that had been on the newsstands for sometime. Having been aware (weren't we all?) that the public fancy was engrossed with the amazing spectacle of racketeers enjoying a fabulous prosperity in the

---

* The first issue of Wood's *The Underworld* was dated May 1927. *Underworld*, the film, released in August '27, may have been announced as in-production earlier in the year, but connections between the magazine and the film, other than the title, aren't apparent.

period of The Noble Experiment, when the newspapers made heroes
out of the great gangsters, I decided to concentrate on this theme in
The Underworld Magazine.

He omits Hollywood's influence from his account. It dignifies the editor
to be seen as reflecting Life itself in his work, when in fact popular culture
trends were as large a calculation in creating the product.

THE MOTIVATIONS are murky (*Writer's Digest* called it "agreeing to disagree"),
but by the end of the summer, 1929, Hersey had resigned from Magazine
Publishers, leaving it in the hands of his co-founders. Aron Wyn, an editor
at Dell, was brought in to run the magazines. The chain, with about half the
Hersey-created titles surviving, became known as the Ace magazines. *The
Underworld*, still owned by Eastern Distributing, returned to the editorial
control of J. Thomas Wood who continued it as an original fiction magazine.
Both *Dragnet* and *Underworld* continued Hersey's editorial policies, at least
at first.

Hersey, presumably with financial backing from Macfadden, started
the Good Story Magazine Company, known also as the Red Band or the
Blue Band magazines for the diagonal stripe running through the cover
background. In a ridiculously abbreviated time, he had the company up
and running. Twelve new titles hit the newsstands with cover dates ranging
from October to February 1930. Admittedly, most of the new magazines
turned out to be notable obscurities: *Western Outlaws, Love and War
Stories, Thrills of the Jungle.* Some were started as experiments, with low
expectations. But in November debuted one of his greatest career successes,
the first pure gang pulp, *Gangster Stories.* The seed he'd planted in *Dragnet*
and *Underworld* now bloomed in full. Gone was the mix of conventional
detective and mystery stories. *Gangster* gave the reader a wall-to-wall, floor-
to-ceiling underworld. Hersey had ceded the mainstream, preferring to look
for his fortune on the margins. With *Gangster*, at least, the strategy worked.
The pulp sold well—apparently about 40,000 copies per issue initially. The
formula, and the success, was quickly repeated with *Racketeer Stories*, with
a cover date of February. (For the record, a racketeer runs a bootleg liquor
operation, a speakeasy, or some other illegal operation; gangsters supply
the muscle.) Hersey had finally found the independent success he'd been
pushing toward for nearly two decades. But life can't be that sweet—can
it—in the early days of the Depression? Something had to go wrong—and
it took the form of a backlash against *Gangster* and *Racketeer.* As quickly
as Hersey had gotten the magazines onto America's newsstands, the censors
pushed back.

In the remainder of this essay, we'll explore the nature of the gang story;

we'll examine what happened, how Hersey responded, and how the pulps were affected. Additionally, the book collects nineteen stories from the first year of the gang pulps, from both before and after the controversy left its mark.

HERSEY GAVE FEW editorial guidelines for the gang titles in the writers' mags, making him unlike, on the other extreme, science-fiction editor Hugo Gernsback who provided a lengthy, detailed outline of do's, don'ts, and philosophy. Numerous authors appear regularly in Hersey's gang pulps, a stable of reliable wordsmiths who could deliver the highly-specialized product on schedule. Hersey would have given prospective freelancers the standard advice: read a couple of issues to get an idea of what's required. Today, we must follow in the footsteps of the outsiders, but, still, it's difficult to draw a line between Hersey's dictates and the inventiveness of his authors.

In a letter published in the June 1933 *Writer's Digest*, Ralph Daigh, editor of the new (and short-lived) *Nickel Detective*, wrote: we don't "care for the 'in the groove' gang story. That does not mean that stories with gangdom as a background are barred." His remarks came well after the period in question, but get at the main idea. The pure gang story took *gangland* out of the narrative background, and made it the foreground. The main characters became gang members or close associates. The gang story broke the mold of good guys versus bad guys, by sliding the moral spectrum all to the dark side. The conflict became merely bad guys versus really bad guys. The merely bad guy played the role of the hero, of course, and claimed his dubious moral high ground through toughness, loyalty to fellow gang members, kindness to his moll. The really bad guy was the squealer, the double-crosser, the coward, the rival who violated territorial boundaries—the rat.

Gangland didn't exist in a complete vacuum. The "civilian world" provided a stage for gang dramas to play out on; but ordinary victims of crime were rarely shown. Members of law enforcement wandered in and out of the stories. But when gangland moved to the foreground, law enforcement got shunted to the background. Often it was treated as an annoyance; the police and the detectives—the "bulls" and the "dicks"—are mere hurdles on an obstacle course. The permanent existence of the gangs was taken for granted. "Gangster's Revenge" (*The Dragnet Magazine*, December 1929), for example, treats the law with brazen disregard (quoted stories are included in this collection unless otherwise noted):

> [Czar Rohan, chieftain of the west side] had had little to worry about from the law. [He] knew all the cops throughout his domain personally, and they knew of him and his activities. They recognized his power and let him alone.

. . .

On several occasions one or more of [Rohan's] lieutenants had sought to rebel. Their fate had been certain and swift. Outraged citizens demanded that the law do something about bringing their murderers to justice. The police had protested that no hint had been given as to the identity of the killers.

They were right. None had been given. But they knew. The press knew. The average man in the street could guess. But nothing was done.

In "When China Jo Lost His Woman" (*Gangster Stories*, November 1929), our hero, Dude Jim, instigates murder and mayhem on a grand scale at the "chop suey dive" of his rival gang boss, China Jo. Dude's object is Jo's girl, the alluring Half-Breed Rose. The story ends with Dude triumphant:

They were all on the street. The gang scattered. Rose and Dude sauntered on down the block. Rose started a little as a cop rounded the corner.

"Evenin', O'Neil." Dude was casual.

"Evenin', Dude. Livin' peaceable?"

"Me? Sure! Just spendin' a quiet evenin' with the girl friend!"

And life goes on with the law blissfully oblivious.

Occasionally, law enforcement characters played a central role. But not as honest servants of society. They were either taking bribes, expropriating ill-gotten gains for personal enrichment, or looking the other way. They were, in essence, de facto gang associates, making law enforcement just another racket. In "Racketeer Wages" (*The Dragnet Magazine*, December 1929), Detective McCarthy walks a corrupt beat:

McCarthy swaggered over to Hardy's table. . . . He grinned at the racketeer. "Making the rounds, Hardy. Get me?"

"Sure, Mac. This baby never slips up on his payments." With that Hardy again pulled out his heavy wallet, selected several crisp bills and passed them to the detective.

Pocketing the hush money, McCarthy rose to his feet. He refused Hardy's offer to have a drink. "Not tonight, Hardy. If I took a glass at all the places I gotta stop tonight I'd be as pie-eyed as hell. S'long."

Later, McCarthy, acquiescing to "Broadway racketeer" Hardy's entreaty, is a willing accomplice to murder:

"Take it easy, Mac, it's on the up and up. Now listen. In about an hour Tony is gonna take some Tommy guns and get a guy in a blue sedan up at the next corner. Never mind who the punk is. Let him shoot the guy. Then you and the two carloads of dicks jump Tony. Easy, ain't it? You got the punk that was killed and the guy that did it. How's it sound, Mac?"

"It's a go, Hardy."

Thus we have a broad outline of gangland, a dark, inverted fairy-tale world where crime is the law, and the law-keepers contribute to crime. But there are many other elements to the formula:

▪ Not surprising, the typical setting was New York City, with Chicago coming second. Some stories played up rivalries between New York and Chicago gangs, like "The 'Eyes' Have It," (*Gangland Stories*, August-September 1930), wherein the Chi Kid comes into New York and murders the "first lieutenant to [the] overlord of New York racketeers." Sometimes the urban setting went unnamed. Outlying settings were infrequently used, such as the Bay Area, which was accurately described in "The Singing Kid" (*Gangland Stories*, November 1930). A common hybrid was the air-gang story (none of which are included here) which tapped into the incredible popularity of the air pulps. Examples include "Night Clubs of the Air" (*Gangster Stories*, December 1929) and "A Racket in the Clouds" (*Racketeer Stories*, June-July 1930).

▪ One of the most glaring elements, since it conflicts with contemporary standards, is the treatment of ethnic groups. It becomes immediately apparent that there are few actual human beings in gangland. Instead, we get familiar stereotypes. One of the main gangs is Italian:

> There were those who hinted that Italian Joe had framed Big Red Regan. The olive-skinned, oily haired wop and Big Regan had clashed on several occasions.
> ("One Hour Before Dawn," *Gangster Stories*, December 1929)

Another central group is the Irish, although they come off pretty well in descriptions. Red Regan, in "One Hour Before Dawn," is "the big, good natured Irishman." Chinese gangs—tongs—were popular in the pulps before and after the gang pulp era, and they get the expected condescension:

> With all the oily, subtle grace of his race, China Cholly extended the hospitality of his house to Sadie when she called on him the following afternoon. At a clap of his hands, tea and rice cakes were served to them by a mute Oriental who bowed deferentially to the white woman.
>
> China Cholly, grinning devilishly, swept forward with his

villainous crew of Chinks.

("Rough on 'Rats'," *Gangster Stories*, December 1929)

Jewish characters make occasional appearances: Little Hymie Zeiss ("Rough on 'Rats' ") ("Now when a Jew is tough and a bad egg—he's just that. Wicked."); and "Izzy the Yid over in Brooklyn" ("The 'Eyes' Have It"). Black characters appear seldom, typically in menial roles, e.g. "the nigger elevator boy" ("Guns of Gangland," *Gangster Stories*, December 1929, not included).

Stereotypes were as likely to be found in descriptive passages as in dialogue, removing the defense that it was the characters speaking and not the authors themselves. In truth, it was the times talking.

• The moll, the gangster's girlfriend, or even crime partner, proves to be a major theme. Nearly all the stories feature them. Sometimes they were edgier than the men:

> Floss O'Connor's small white face was within an inch of his own. Gone now was the happy, careless girl that had been Big Red Regan's moll. In her powdered face her eyes were dark as the night. Her nervous, highly polished fingers twitched. But her voice was low and well under control.
>
> ("One Hour Before Dawn")

> Shifty Al looked back at her with a sheepish grin. He could hold his own against a skirt's temper, better than face that cold hard stare from her eyes. He looked her over slowly and critically. The emerald green dress she was wearing was a little shabby. But she had told him she had been against her luck lately. The dress didn't matter anyway. Sal was about his speed—small, well-rounded, seductive. Devastating might have been the word used to describe her, but that word was not in Shifty's vocabulary.
>
> ("A Long Chance," *Racketeer Stories*, June-July 1930)

> On the threshold stood a tall, beautifully dressed woman. She was clad in a tight fitting red velvet dress, that creased in soft folds as she entered the room. Marie was Dirk's moll, his tiger moll as she was known, for she was tall and sinuous. Her walk was the cat-like gliding step of the denizen of the jungle. And she was like her ferocious namesake. She had a great love for her man, and an implacable hatred for her enemies.
>
> ("Racketeer Revenge," *Racketeer Stories*, March 1930)

They could be every bit as coldblooded, like the unforgettable Kate from "Blood Thirst" (*Gangland Stories*, June-July 1930):

Suddenly, from below, came the sound of a heavy door slammed back on its hinges. Kate leaned far over the rail. . . . The lolling men at the tables below were on their feet, their necks thrust forward toward the entrance, their hands bristling with guns.

"At 'em, boys!" yelled Kate, but her voice was lost in the volley of shots that came from the doorway. Instantly, the room below was a hell of shattering sound. Kate swung her body far out over the railing, striving to peer through the curling smoke of guns that cut the blue haze of tobacco.

"They've dropped," she screamed, "four of 'em, at the door! At 'em, boys!" She was shrieking now, heedless of the man beside her, heedless of everything but the smell and sound of battle . . .

Her face was burning with mounting blood, her painted lips loose, her white bosom heaving.

▪ Violence, of course, was a large part of the bargain. Sometimes it was the all-out mayhem of machine guns blasting from speeding automobiles. At other times, the violence was personal and psychopathic:

"Go back to Fat's place and you'll find him all tied up like you left him—but I slit his throat, the big stoolie. You'll find your fuzztailed guard beside him. He ain't so damn pretty neither. I moved the front of his face back an inch or two with a piece of pipe."

("The 'Eyes" Have It")

Sometimes the stories built toward a violent confrontation, then delivered it with brief, and oddly poetic, passages:

With a quick jerk of his right wrist [Eddie the Dope] swung an ugly looking automatic into view. Before Big Red or Floss could make a move to stop him the automatic went into action. The crashing slug tore straight into the Italian's head. The wop went down. Eddie the Dope did a dance of rage, pumping slug after slug into the body at his feet.

("One Hour Before Dawn")

Ace squirmed past the gear shifting lever into the seat Mike had vacated. Even before he could voice a protest . . . there came the terrifying realization that the business end of the automatic in Mike's steady hand was aimed at his heart. Ace saw the flash, felt the cruel stabbing pain of death.

("The Highway to Hell," *The Dragnet Magazine*, January 1930)

His face livid with fear, he flung himself at her and she pressed the trigger twice. His body fell against her, almost knocking her from her

feet, and there were twin holes in the center of his forehead.
("Hair-Trigger," *Racketeer Stories*, March 1930)

▪ Gangsters needed equipment to conduct business; for starters, a high-performance automobile:

> The roaring sedan avoided a fireplug, scraped an iron railing, swerved with its right wheels on the sidewalk, tore off the bumper of the truck, and spun the corner at full speed.
> ("Glycerined Gangsters," *Racketeer Stories*, November 1930)

Weapons of all sorts came in handy: sawed-off shotguns, Tommy guns; handguns, often referred to as "rods" or "gats." High-performance was an issue here, too:

> In a flash a grim, blunt nosed automatic appeared in his hands. There was a terrific roar; another, coming so suddenly on the first it seemed but an echo, two piercing flashes of orange flame, and then the acrid smell of burnt powder.
> ("Racketeer Revenge")

> Machine guns thrust their blunt, ominous nozzles from the windows of the cars and splattered a murderous rain of hail into the middle ranks of the gangsters.
> ("Rough on 'Rats'")

▪ A central theme of the stories was revenge. It's a convenient way of introducing murderous intent into the proceedings. It's also inherent in the gang structure: to kill one gang member is to invite response from the entire gang. A number of the stories advertised the theme upfront in their titles: "Gangster's Revenge," "Racketeer Revenge." Revenge was treated with such solemnity, it became a near-religious experience:

> ... in back of Sam's chow house the men of the mob sat assembled, in expressions that conveyed but one message to the on-looker—the insatiable desire for revenge, and the need, the overwhelming need for action.
> ("Limehouse Blues," *Gangster Stories*, June-July 1930, not included)

> Red was at the wheel, driving fast. The moon was full, and the road lighted by its reflection flashed by swiftly. There was little talk in the car. Each man concentrated grimly on their single motive. Revenge.
> ("Racketeer Revenge")

A half hour later a weird and terrible scene was being enacted in a dirty, musty room of Little Hymie's warehouse. The three rats had been strung up by their wrists to a raftered beam in the ceiling and their ankles manacled together. Then the terrible revenge of the underworld began!

("Rough on 'Rats' ")

▪ A critical element, present in every story, and also the source of much amusement today, was the heavy use of gangland lingo.

"Fade before the bulls come."

("Rod Rule," *The Dragnet Magazine*, December 1929)

"Geese, do you take me for a sap?" Tony wanted to know. "Cripes! your checks are too damn gummy to suit me. Wait up! No hard feelings, bozo. This is business!"

("Triple Cross," *The Dragnet Magazine*, February 1930)

"You think you've got something on her. You've been out to get something on her ever since she turned you down for me. Let's have your little rat tale. I don't want to seem impolite to an acquaintance of the old days, but the perfume you slather on yourself is abominable."

("Blood Thirst")

"Maybe you're right, Chimp, but there's enough lads going for one way rides without sacrificing a lot of our best guns just because the Big Noise in Chicago thinks he's fast enough to cut in here. Damn it all! For a plugged nickel I'd hop a rattler for Chicago tonight, hunt this troublemaker up and shoot it out with him on his own dunghill."

("The 'Eyes' Have It")

Needless to say, these randomly selected samples barely scratch the surface.

Some of the lingo found a foothold in the wider language, as this excerpt from a syndicated editorial reveals:

In this [new, violent] literature there is a hint of what the public attitude of the new generation is toward law and order. The jargon of the gangster and the racketeer is on the lips of . . . youngsters. . . . The high school lass of today who wants a pineapple sweet at a soda fountain asks for a Chicago sundae because everybody knows that a pineapple is a bomb.

("Gangster Stories of Today Are Successors of the Dime Novels," *The Haskin Letter*, May 20, 1931)

• Lastly, as writers' mag analysts were quick to point out, the gangster story was as closely related to the adventure story as to the mystery or detective, emphasizing action over crime detection.

SO THAT'S the layout of gangland, more or less, and what's wrong with that? It's easy to view the stories today as a "guilty pleasure"—they *are* fun to read—or as an unclouded window onto the past. But, in their time, they carried, though not the accomplishment of literature, the power. It's inherent in fiction that taking a character's point of view makes that character sympathetic to some degree; as practiced by true artists of the written word, a great degree. Fiction allows us to be someone else momentarily, to live in another place or time, to see the world from an alien point of view, and thus gain understanding and a greater sense of humanity. But these gang stories represent a perversion of those purposes. By bringing gangland into the foreground, and flattening "the civilian world" to a ghosted background, gangland is redefined as the standard of normality. We hear only the voices of the gang members. The worst of us can justify any behavior, and the justification can be discovered in the argument both for and against some action. "I had to steal. I was hungry." "I had to shoot him. He questioned my manhood." True enough. In the pulp story, if acting out the argument in favor produces the most exciting story, then arguments against dwindle to insignificance.

This is neither to praise or condemn these stories for their socially redeeming value, or lack thereof—they've scarcely been read since original publication—but to get a sense of how the society of the time, other than the thrill-seekers who found the magazines entertaining, might have perceived them. Which brings up the next question: what happened?

IN FEBRUARY 1930, Hersey's Good Story Magazine Company was threatened with prosecution by the New York Society for the Suppression of Vice (NYSSV). The vice that need be suppressed: *Gangster Stories*, which had been appearing for a few months, and *Racketeer Stories*, which had its first or second issue on the newsstands.

The NYSSV, with its grandiose title, sounded like a holdover from the Victorian era, which in some sense it was. Charted in 1873 by the state legislature, its mission, as stated in its annual report for 1928, was "to enforce certain laws intended to strengthen and perpetuate American standards of morality and to discourage the dissemination of publications or other matters whose effect would be to break down those standards." The key figure in the NYSSV was executive secretary John S. Sumner, who had led the organization since 1915, succeeding its founder, Anthony Comstock. In an interview with the *New York Times* (October 9, 1932), Sumner described how his office operated:

> . . . we initiate no complaints on our own initiative. I choose to regard the Society as an unofficial adjunct of the District Attorney's office. When a citizen sees something which he feels is contrary to our State laws he complains to us. We investigate the complaint and if we discover that it is well founded we take our findings either to the police or to the District Attorney's office. . . . I am not carrying out the ideas of our society in any spirit of a reformer. I am only trying to have laws which exist on our statute books enforced. . . . We are only concerned with the violation of that statute which makes it wrong to display or sell indecent objects.

Sumner's authority was real. An October 5, 1929 report in the *Times* describes the seizing of 3,000 books from several New York City book dealers. The titles included books by eminent authors James Joyce, D.H. Lawrence, Oscar Wilde, and even a writer who appears in this collection, Clement Wood. In his groundbreaking study of censorship of the so-called "sex magazines," *Uncovered: The Hidden Art of the Girlie Pulps*, Douglas Ellis describes the many-years' war of Sumner against magazine publishers. Magazines were seized by the truckload and incinerated to heat police departments. The Catholic magazine, *America*, described the magazine problem in appropriately dramatic terms (as quoted in a *NYT* article, October 29, 1929):

> The news stands of the metropolis, which ten years ago offered nothing more deleterious than newspapers devoted to athletic contests, now fairly groan under a weight of pamphlets and magazines, of which the best are suspicious and the worst utterly degraded.

America praised Sumner and the Society for their valiant efforts in combating the problem.

To sum up, Sumner was likely acting on a citizen complaint against *Gangster* and *Racketeer*; and Hersey had reason to fear. But what possible law was he breaking? There were some frighteningly glamorous molls in the gang pulps, but no real sex.

Sumner had "exhumed," in the terms of Lemuel F. Parton's syndicated report (February 21/22, 1930), a thirty-year old state law that banned "magazines devoted to or chiefly made up of bloodshed, lust or crime." Sumner's description of the problem was that "Gangsters always triumph at the end of the adventures described in both magazines"; adding, "I especially resent the women who lead the gangs." So maybe it was about sex. . . . In all probability, there was much more about the stories that bothered Sumner, but these brief quotes are what percolated into the public record.

Good Story's attorney, Joseph Schultz, conceded that the gang pulps met the law's definition, but that the law was unconstitutional. He was probably right, though we can only speculate as to how 1930's courts might have ruled. But right or wrong, challenging the law was an expense Hersey likely never seriously considered.

The magazines were distributed nationally, and the story of Sumner's threat received national coverage, although of a minor sort. Hersey made it one-day news by pulling the magazines out of New York state—or promising to. Schultz pointed out that there was no Federal equivalent of the New York statute, the magazines would continue, and that New York "does not mean much in the bulk of their circulation." The last part sounds like bravado. There's no reason to believe that America's most populous city (and state) would not have been a significant market for magazines with, essentially, New York stories.

We should also note that Hollywood suffered its own "crime problem" in early '29. The industry dug into its deep pockets and produced a criminological study authored by a former governor of Maine, which demonstrated that the villain in films always got what was coming to him. Schultz echoed the argument: "In these [gang pulp] stories, the villain always gets the worst of it—as all villains should." As you will discover in reading through these collected stories, Schultz was sugarcoating his client's problem—as all lawyers should. The censors may have been tilting against windmills, but they weren't inaccurate in their charges.

UNDERLYING THE backlash was a widespread fear that gang pulps promoted criminal behavior among the young; the same argument being made about video games today, violent movies in the '60s, rock and roll in the '50s, sharpened sticks in the Pleistocene, etc. The attitude is reflected in this humorous item from Joseph Van Raalte's syndicated column, *Bo Broadway* (February 16, 1931):

> A settlement worker asked one of the youthful prisoners in the Tombs to write down the names of the periodicals he bought from the magazine vendor, allowed in the North Annex, reserved for young offenders. The list included: *The Underworld*, *Gun Molls*, *Gangster Stories* and *Detective Fiction*.
>
> Those who think that a minute a Rough Guy finds himself in "the can" he forswears his habitual mental gait and turns for solace to Thomas à Kempis and *The Lives of the Saints*, has another guess coming.

In a September 1930 *Writer's Digest* piece, "The NEW Gangster Story,"
Joseph Lichtblau sided with the analysis of the censors (the article is reprinted
in full in this volume):

> Fashions in fiction change with the times. When Prohibition came
> into being, it was orthodox and accepted technique to have crime
> punished in the ending of any story dealing with criminal leading
> protagonists. Then the wave of crime all over the country following
> the bootlegging racket exploitation by gunmen gave writers nifty
> new ideas for crook yarns, and a flood of sensational gangster stories
> swept these United States.
>
> The kids who used to read dime novels seized on the new type
> of magazine with whoops of joy. The stories far exceeded in danger,
> suspense, thrills and excitement the most gory dime novel yarns they
> had ever read! But they grew up, these youngsters; they became
> adolescents and young men, and many of them got dangerous ideas
> from the racketeer and gangster stories. Many a prison warden can
> tell you, grimly, that plenty of his "cons" are in "stir" now because
> they got the idea of becoming gangmen and racketeers solely from
> these stories, which pictured crime and organized rackets and mobs
> so alluringly.

Lichtblau suggests a historical sweep not justified by magazines that had
been on the newsstands less than two years at the time of his writing; not
quite enough time for masses of youths to pass from wide-eyed boyhood to
corrupted incarceration. But Lichtblau raises the question of what Hersey's
target age group might have been for the gang pulps. One doesn't read these
delectably vile stories and think, "great entertainment for kids!"; but at the
same time it's extremely difficult from a modern perspective to determine
what an average educated adult, a working-class reader of the pulps, or an
adolescent, might have considered acceptable entertainment in 1930.

In *Pulpwood Editor*, Hersey confirms that he considered young readers
part of the audience, and addresses the corruption question:

> The same objections that were voiced against my making heroes
> out of hoodlums in *Gangster Stories* were heard on every hand in
> the yellowback weekly days. I have yet to hear of an instance where
> a reader turned to a criminal career after buying this or any other
> pulpwood magazine. The earnest, well-meaning critics forget always
> that the normal youngster or oldster who devours these adventure
> tales, takes it all out in the reading. It is the proverbial water on the
> duck's back, so far as harm to him is concerned.

Hersey also addressed the age-group question from an oblique angle:

> As a rule it is the older reader who points to misspelled words, split infinitives or errors in fact. Boys seldom criticize grammatical mistakes; girls even less.

We introduce this quote because Hersey's gang pulps rank among the worst-edited, most ungrammatical fiction in all of the pulps. For all his fame as an editor, Hersey seemed to apply little or no effort to smoothing out what is often execrably rough prose. Sentences are poorly constructed; sometimes the narrative meanders for paragraphs before the action becomes apparent; often, the irrational punctuation wouldn't pass a third-grade exam. And, to make it even harder on the reader, there are the kind of errors that can be attributed to the drinking habits of the typesetter. We've exercised a light touch in cleaning up the stories for reprint, simply to improve readability problems; but some stories were considered too laborious to decipher and rejected for inclusion (we *do* have standards).

At any rate, a direct link between gang pulps and youth crime will not be proven nor disproven here, or anywhere else—which makes it a perfect subject to argue over—and we'll leave it at that.

NOT EVERYONE took Sumner seriously. While the New York *Herald Tribune* made the attack on *Gangster* and *Racketeer* a front-page item, *The Hartford Courant* consigned the story to a humor column, *The Lighter Side* (February 20, 1930):

> *Gangster Stories* and *Racketeer Stories*, two recent additions to the news stands, are to be withdrawn from publication. . . .
> Now this is all very well, but is Mr. Sumner going to stop here? What, for instance, does he intend to do to the publishers of E.W. Hornung's stories about that super-crook, "Raffles"? Will he take no action, in the case of Louis Joseph Vance's "Lone Wolf," and what, if anything, is to be done about that other evil character, the "Grey Seal," a product, as we remember, of Frank W. Packard's nimble brain? And if Mr. Sumner takes action against all these immoral fellows, can he consider his job finished until he has rooted out from the library shelves of New York the last scrap and vestige of that French felon whom Gaston Leroux gave to an innocent world—Arsène Lupin?

There's no question that the gang pulps had crossed a threshold, but the *Courant* highlighted the challenge facing any censor, that of defining the problem so that it targets only the offending material, and not some similar, inoffensive material. Could New York's law have been amended to add a "lovable rogue" exception?

In *Pulpwood Editor* (1937), Hersey defended the gang pulps. He neglected to mention Sumner, but contradicted his main objection:

> I was careful never to permit an underworldling to triumph over justice. He got his deserts—and no mistake—in the end. It is true that I rather passed over the details of the hero's mob and was unsportsmanlike in the manner in which I detailed the criminal activities of the opposition; and I did not have the stories based on law and order, but in those days I would have been out of step with the masses had I done so. My hero was not usually permitted to go through reformation at the close *à la* Mr. Dombey; not at all; this would have made the stories monotonous. Generally speaking, he was associated with a gang against his will, to right a wrong, avenge a friend's injury or death (just as so many soldiers went berserk in the War), save the heroine from the villain's clutches, or, as a sleuth in disguise, run untold risks by joining some mob and learning its secrets from the inside. You couldn't fool the public by setting up conflict between officialdom and the racketeers; they knew too well that in many large cities the two were one and the same under their tough hides.

His defense, as we've already determined, is definitely not applicable to the stories published *before* the controversy hit. Underworldlings *did* triumph over justice. Perhaps the purest example is "One Hour Before Dawn" (*Gangster Stories*, December 1929). Mob boss Jim Regan is doing time in the Big House. Meanwhile, his associate, Italian Joe Mercurio, has taken Regan's moll, and obtained a small fortune from a crime Regan had carefully planned. Regan bribes his way out of prison, and reclaims the girl and the money. At the end of the story, the happy couple looks forward to living on "easy street," on "the continent," with no expectation that the law will ever catch up to them.

Hersey's defense, however, does apply to stories published immediately post-controversy. He chose to adjust the product rather than battle New York's anti-bloodlust law in court. Apparently, some accommodation was reached with Sumner. The explicit terms of the agreement are not available to us but the deal itself was mentioned, for instance, in Lichtblau's article: "in New York City, particularly, [Hersey's] magazines were forbidden on the stands until he agreed to change them radically." Hersey described the stakes in *Pulpwood Editor*: "I faced a legal battle that could be renewed with every succeeding issue which would cost me far more than I could make by selling the magazine in New York City." Neither *Gangster* nor *Racketeer* missed a monthly issue during this period; whether the magazines were distributed in New York without interruption is a separate issue.

Theoretically, we could read stories from multiple issues and determine the dateline that separates pre- and post-censorship issues. Fortunately, we don't have to do that—fortunately, because the differences between pre- and post- stories are sufficiently ambiguous to provoke a lot of head scratching. There are clearer indications in the magazines. In the February 1930 issue of *Gangster*, Hersey ran a one-page feature titled, "Editorial by the Publisher," which justified the stories, and spoke about them in elevated terms:

> In the pages of this magazine you meet a cruel race of humans; people who move through the dark alleys of crime and terror. They are but the creations of the writers' minds, however, and are only reflections of actuality. One has but to pick up any newspaper in order to read the actual accounts of gangsters and racketeers. This magazine would indeed be of little worth were it to portray the racketeer as "he isn't." We must show him in his true colors, in his real environment. We must go to the depths of his twisted heart and soul. Yet, in spite of all this, these pages are but figments of the imagination. They are only true in their balance of actuality and fancy. The characters you meet are only a continuation of the imaginative line of literature produced by such masters of underworld life as Balzac and Charles Dickens.
>
> You can gain much from these pages in truth; you can guard your own hearthstone from these modern brigands by understanding them and their ways. Knowledge is power, power is truth, and the truth will set you free. Knowing of these crooked byways of crime, and the people who walk there in darkness, you will be forearmed and forewarned about the pitfalls that are on all sides. But look only upon these pages as stories—the creations of our writers' fancies—and if you gain valuable knowledge through entertaining reading, then indeed we have fulfilled a real purpose in publishing this periodical.

Not only was *Gangster Stories* in a class with the classics, it was educational, and might even protect the reader from denizens of the underworld! The February *Racketeer* had a similar editorial titled, "A Page From the Publisher's Notebook," featuring this passage:

> Many of the characters seem to triumph in crime, but if we could go on with them beyond the ends of these stories, we would read of their eventual downfall. Glittering as they seem crime can never pay, in the long run.
>
> Crime is the product of weakness. And weakness is a disease of the mind and body. Therefore, in reading of the underworld, one must remember always that these pitiful children of evil are only red shadows in the shadowy realm of unreality. Let us read of them, but believe in them—no!

It's clear that this editorial was written *after* the one in *Gangster*. First, Hersey zeroes in on Sumner's objection—the triumph of the criminal—and addresses it. The earlier editorial in *Gangster* suggests that Hersey knew trouble was brewing, and anticipated that merely depicting racketeers and gangsters was the problem. Second, all issues of Hersey gang pulps into the late summer carried an editorial titled "A Page From the Publisher's Notebook." That the first entry in *Gangster* carried a generic title suggests a feature in embryo.*

In general, a pulp, like most magazines, would come out with a cover date from one of the two following months, so that they would never appear outdated on the newsstand. Good Story had nine titles with February dates (three titles were already defunct). But Hersey would have issued the nine over several weeks, so the precise date a particular title came out is almost impossible to determine without access to the publisher's or distributor's records which, needless to say, we don't have. The timing is critical because Sumner's threat to prosecute hit the newspapers on February 20.

The March issue of *Gangster* did, in fact, address Sumner's objections, as we would expect:

> The glittering people about whom you read in these rapid-action stories are a weird lot. . . .
> A forlorn yet fantastic army of the underworld!
> To believe in their reality would be stupid. . . .
> These characters are along the fringe of things. They live in shining splendor for a short time. They appear healthy. However behind them always are shadows sinister and weird: Death, Disease and Retribution!
> Sooner or later, mostly sooner, their fantastic hours are over. They go forth to rot in prison cells. They are shot down by their enemies, their bodies left in alleyways and open lots. Their wealth is lost by gambling and reckless living. The haunts they once knew, no longer know them—in fact they are completely forgotten.
> They pay dearly for their moments of high speed. Let us read of them but bear in mind that this army of the underworld is only a shell that glitters under the spotlight, but which is being crushed like a giant worm as it winds through the spotted darkness.

Going by plausible dates, Hersey had to have reacted in advance of the actual problem. In *Pulpwood Editor*, he confirms he'd been warned ahead of time. So, putting it all together, this may be what happened: Hersey caught

---

* We reprint the majority of Hersey's editorials in this book. That wouldn't have been necessary to demonstrate his response to the censorship, but the editorials proved to be as lurid as the stories, and entertaining in their own right.

wind of the trouble coming in January. He added the editorial to the February *Gangster* at the last minute, not only to head off Sumner, but to inoculate the magazines against potential copycat complaints in other states (though laws like New York's proved to be rare). He learned what Sumner's objections were in time to add the modified editorial to the February *Racketeer*. He withdrew both pulps from distribution in New York until the crisis was resolved, which it was not on February 20, according to the news coverage. He entered into negotiations with Sumner. Sumner does not prefer a court battle since he, too, has a budget, and bigger fish to fry. He may even have shown flexibility, allowing Hersey to use up his purchased inventory of stories in return for a good-faith promise to comply with the law thenceforth. Under this scenario, both titles would have missed at least one month of New York distribution, and there will be no distinct line separating the pre- and post-censorship stories.

Hersey's editorials became increasingly melodramatic in tone, such as this passage from *Racketeer*, March 1930:

> Tinsel children of the darkness are the characters in these stories—wayward children—yet spawn of the Devil himself!
>
> They dance—marionettes in dazzling finery—in the white spotlight our authors throw upon them. They dance the dance of death. Their thin faces smile, but it is only a set grin of pain when you examine them closely.
>
> Their finery is as gay as their laughter sounds, yet we see that there are patches; their jewels only paste. Their lives are rapidly being snuffed out; they soon pay their debts to nature and to Humanity in full.

At times he sounded more Catholic than the Pope in his distaste for gangland (*Gangster Stories*, April 1930):

> The restless army of the underworld waves its tattered banners in a wind of newspaper words. The world stands aghast as this terrible cavalcade goes by our front doors. What can be done about it?
>
> The police and the secret service are working day and night to protect our fireside from these beasts of a jungle that come to our very hearthstones—a jungle where the cries of the lost are like the drone of a myriad tropical insects humming through the menace of a fungus darkness.

As time went by, Hersey seemed stuck for new ways of expressing the same idea. By the August issue of *Racketeer*, the editorials had run their course. In that issue, Hersey talked up the new expanded size of the magazines, then added his "crime does not pay" comments as a coda. After that, the editorials disappear, as Hersey must have considered the crisis over.

Another feature was added to *Gangster* with the April issue. It was a column, titled *Gangland*, that reprinted news stories about gangsters getting caught up with the law or coming to a bad end. Like the editorials, it was counter-programming for people offended by the stories; perhaps part of a legal defense strategy, in case needed. *Gangland* ran as a regular feature, then showed up in *Racketeer* with the November issue. We reprint the entire April column here as a representative sample.

THEN, OF COURSE, there are the stories to consider in evaluating Hersey's actions. An odd one is "Kid Dropper Plays It Alone," from the February *Racketeer*. By virtue of the editorial, this should be considered a post-censorship issue. The story uses a bulletproof vest as a gimmick. The vest saves the Dropper in a shootout. But he's picked up by the cops wearing the vest. Irony of ironies, the vest that saved him will now be the evidence that dooms him. But the cops confiscate his weapons, never see the vest, and inexplicably set him free. End of story and—*huh*? The ironic and natural conclusion would have satisfied Sumner's objections, but that's not the conclusion we get, even though the ending could have been Sumner-proofed with little effort. That shows the blurry line between the pre- and post-, and further suggests that this issue was not distributed in New York.

In "City of Bullets" (*Gangster Stories*, April 1930), gang leader Mike Regan lethally vanquishes his rival mobsters. The story ends with him raising a toast to his moll. It sounds like it would be offensive to the arbiters of morality, but this may actually be a "legal" post-censorship story. There were very few published guidelines for gang stories from any publisher, but according to a September 1930 *Writer's Digest* freelance solicitation for *Detective-Dragnet* (formerly *The Dragnet Magazine*): "The gangster must not triumph over the law. However, when gang meets gang—either may win." This may have been the core of Hersey's agreement with Sumner. Aron Wyn, the listed editor of *Detective-Dragnet*, would have been all too aware of the controversy. In fact, *The Dragnet* changed title to *Detective-Dragnet* with the April 1930 issue, undoubtedly to shed some of Hersey's taint. It also dropped the "Detective and Gangster Stories" banner from the front cover, though it retained it above the table of contents.

Gangster and *Racketeer* sold well enough that Hersey added two more gang titles in the summer of '30, both debuting with June-July issues. He was apparently determined to guarantee that supply met, if not exceeded, demand. He may also have been concerned with competition from the new Popular Publications, which had promised that a gangster pulp would be among their initial titles. Hersey's two new titles were *Gangland Stories* and *Mobs*, which were essentially similar. (*Mobs* ran only two issues, while *Gangland* continued into 1932. Our theory is that Hersey wanted one new gang pulp but couldn't decide on a title. He tested the market with two and stayed with the best seller.)

That bit of background aside, *Gangland's* second issue (August-September) contains one of the best examples of a story that seems rewritten to comply with the law, the sadistic "The 'Eyes' Have It." The New York gangs have established Fat Siler's speakeasy as a no-warfare zone. Into this oasis of peace wanders a "congenital killer" called the Chi Kid, from the other gang capital. He murders a drunk and belligerent racketeer who all the New Yorkers know to ignore. This starts a violent contest between the Chi Kid and the boss of bosses, Martin Farrell. A gun duel provides a fitting climax. The natural narrative thrust of the story is that because he broke the peace, the Chi Kid will come to a bad end at the hand of Farrell, a happy end to bracket the happy opening. Paradise regained. However, after the call to "fire" during the duel, the story cuts away to a news story which reports that that both men were shot and killed simultaneously, and that Farrell's gang was quickly rounded up. The ending may have satisfied the censors, but it betrays the narrative and thus leaves a bad taste.

By contrast, "The Singing Kid," in the November *Gangland*, integrates the police presence through the length of the narrative, so that when the Kid is brought to justice at the conclusion, it feels like a natural, not forced, event. It reads like a story that was written with the editorial and legal requirements firmly in mind. A similar example is "A Long Chance" (*Racketeer Stories*, June-July 1930). A detective is well-entrenched in the narrative; he eventually brings the protagonist-thieves to justice, closing with the observation, "All crooks are so damn dumb." The only catch is that the detective is crooked, using his badge to coerce the female thief, and confiscating stolen money for himself. He doesn't come to justice, but apparently, that wasn't a problem.

Did the censors have a long-term effect? "Glycerined Gangsters" (*Racketeer Stories*, November 1930) recounts another mob war, with one gang prevailing after creating horrendous public mayhem and a trail of carnage. At the end, the gangster and his moll embrace in their car, while a passing beat cop warns them, "No petting parties allowed! Move on!" It's a light, comical follow-up to some very heavy violence, and strongly implies the law's impotence, quite similar to the pre-censorship story, "When China Jo Lost His Woman." It raises the question of whether Sumner's threat made a permanent difference.

WE CAN POINT to a ripple effect through the industry. Publishers were put on guard. As mentioned, when Hersey came under fire, Ace quickly changed the title of *The Dragnet* to *Detective-Dragnet* and de-emphasized gangster stories on the cover. *The Underworld* retained the same mix of detective and gangster stories, but we weren't able to examine any issues for further details. A February 1932 solicitation blurb for *Underworld* in *Writer's Digest* read: "We do not want stories that glorify the gangster. It is best to observe the rule of 'Crime Doesn't Pay.' "

Black Mask is the best-remembered crime pulp of the day, and in a September 1930 letter in *Writer's Digest*, editor Joseph Shaw weighed in on the gang-story question and showed himself to be the anti-Hersey:

> . . . as far as I have any knowledge, *Black Mask* has published only one story in which the gangster was in any sense the "hero," and that story is the great novel by Dashiell Hammett, which recently was published by us serially under the title of "The Glass Key." This was a story of modern gangsters, a seriously written and highly dramatic presentation of the present day alliance between corrupt politicians and public officials and organized crime—which alliance is the sole reason for the profitableness of crime as a profession.
>
> Even in this story, virtue comes out on top—the crook who has ruled a city is defeated, his gang is broken up, the corrupt politicians who have made his career possible are swept out of office by the voters. . . . If you have read this story, or will read it, you will agree with me, I am sure, that publication of it, and of all stories like it, is a public service. Not until the general public realizes that modern crime, modern gangs, cannot exist without the collusion of corrupt and equally criminal police and public officials, will it be possible to cure what is undoubtedly one of the most serious illnesses, to put it mildly, that our body politic has ever suffered from.
>
> *Black Mask* never has and never will make money or attempt to make money by appealing to the appetite for stories which present crime and criminals in a prepossessing and alluring light: our policy is and always will be the exact opposite—to appeal to those who hate crime and criminals and who get pleasure from reading stories in which they can identify themselves with the detective or other officers who are solving crimes, and capturing criminals.

Another pulp that eschewed the pure gang story was *The Shadow*, as revealed by this excerpt from a May 1933 *Writer's Digest* solicitation blurb: "Gangster stories are not wanted—that is, stories which center about gangsters themselves. The officers can match their wits against gangsters, but the gangsters must always be shown up for unlawful citizens, and fittingly punished."

The paucity of examples demonstrates how difficult it is to get a clear picture of behind-the-scenes editorial policy.

On April 4, 1930, while on a cross-country trip to check up on business,

Hersey stopped in Denver to visit his friend, Willard E. Hawkins, editor of *Author & Journalist*, which had published a number of articles by Hersey in 1927 and '28. Soon after arriving, his hotel room was accosted by reporters asking about the *Gangster Stories* controversy. Hersey later visited the *A&J* offices, then attended a luncheon where he addressed a gathering of local writers. His talk was interrupted by two officials from the District Attorney's office who determined that he was the publisher of *Gangster Stories*, then whisked him away, ostensibly to see the D.A. Instead, he was taken to the jail, stripped, searched, and put into a cell. A deeply regretful Hawkins came to visit him, and offered to procure a lawyer. After three hours of incarceration, Hersey was ushered into a courtroom. The judge charged him with publishing magazines that corrupted the young. *Gangster Stories* was the evidence. Witnesses testified to damage inflicted upon youthful readers in their charge. As a result, Hersey was held over for trial with bail set at $25,000. As he left the courtroom, he was approached by western pulpster, Ray Humphries, whose day-job was in the D.A.'s office. Upon his greeting the assemblage burst into laughter. It had all been an elaborate practical joke planned by Humphries. Court officers, the D.A.'s office, the jail warden, were all in on it, though many of the spectators were not. The complete story is far more detailed; Hersey recounts it in Chapter XIII of *Pulpwood Editor*. It's all part of Hersey's brief notoriety.

The gang pulp era continued several years for Hersey. After he added

---

GANGSTER STORIES

needs novelettes from 10,000 to 20,000 words in length and novels between 35,000 and 60,000 words in length. Such novels must have high emotional pressure; sharp, exciting characterization; easily understandable plots and lots of local color. Payment is made on acceptance. The gangster must lose out, either through the law or through his own undoing. No novels wanted where the gangster is a detective in secret. We are pretty well fed up on newspaper stories. We want glamorous, swiftly-moving and tremendously interesting novels written by those who are no longer amateurs in experience but not necessarily professionals in writing.

Address communications to 25 W. 43rd St., N. Y. C.

P. S. Our other magazines are:

Gangland   Racketeer Stories   Outlaws of the West   Prison Stories
Quick Trigger Stories of the West   Ghost Stories   The Dance Magazine

HAROLD HERSEY, PUBLISHER, GOOD STORY MAGAZINE
COMPANY, INC.

Gangland Stories and *Mobs*, he inaugurated *Prison Stories* with the November 1930 issue. It lasted six issues. *Compete Gang Novel Magazine* was introduced in March 1931. It produced ten issues over little more than a year. Another gang-variant was *Speakeasy Stories*, "strictly on the side of the law but laid in the haunts of the underworld," inaugurated April-May 1931. It lasted four issues. In November-December 1931 came *New York Stories*, which was not about gangsters but marginally in the same class, featuring the same authors as the gang pulps. Three issues. In 1932, two of the pulps merged to form *Racketeer and Gangland Stories*—the beginning of the end. Starting in May, it lasted three issues. *Gangster's* last issue was November 1932, but that followed a four-month gap. In February 1933, Hersey issued *Greater Gangster Stories*, which reprinted old *Gangster* stories before returning to original material. It lasted thirteen issues, its last dated May 1934.

Other publishers got into the act. Popular Publications, as promised, issued *Gang World*. They published 25 issues from October 1930 to November 1932. Eventually, another company published it for seven issues spanning 1933 and '34. In late '31, Popular experimented with *Underworld Romances*, "clean stories of love and adventure in the world of crime." It only produced four issues. *Gun Molls Magazine*, from Real Publications, zeroed in on what really mattered in its choice of subject matter. It lasted 19 issues, from October 1930 to April 1932. There were other stragglers in ensuing years, but they fall out of the late-Prohibition gang-pulp era. Prohibition was officially repealed in 1933. This is often blamed for the demise of the gang pulps, but they'd really run their course as a viable entertainment medium before then. As in any narrowly-defined genre, the challenge is in maintaining variety, and the gang pulps certainly didn't attract the most creative writers.

Even as the gang pulps slowly became irrelevant, opposition reared up on occasion. In the May 1931 editorial, "Gangster Stories of Today Are Successors of the Dime Novels" (cited above re: Chicago sundaes), columnist Frederic J. Haskin shares his disdain for the form:

> The successor to the dime novel of the Nineties and the Nineteen Hundreds . . . is found blazoned forth on all news stands, publicly displayed and in the unashamed hands of the boys and girls of the hour. . . . Scores and scores of magazines are being published; some weekly, some monthly, and some bi-monthly, but all of which have taken up the torch once borne by the relatively inoffensive dime novels.
>
> . . . currently, [there is] a periodical publication the very title of which is *Speakeasy Stories*. . . . the leading story, heralded on the magazine cover, was entitled "Gangsters' Poorhouse." . . . [In] the Nineties . . . none but the wildest dreamer could have conceived the

idea of such a magazine or such a story. The idea of a poorhouse was an idea of an institution, eleemosynary in character, maintained for the benefit of the under-privileged. The idea of a gangster was an idea of an absolute outlaw, an enemy of society, universally condemned. That a poorhouse should be maintained for gangsters would have been considered, in the Nineties, by a wide margin, too wild for even a fiction magazine editor. . . . The very title . . . assumes violation of the law to constitute a normal part of every day American life.

. . . Today's maid may step out to any news stand and pick up a copy of *Gun Molls*, for instance. These publications are found in the hands of youthful readers, not hidden behind sheltering copies of the *Youth's Companion* or a geography book, but openly read on street cars, busses, subway trains. [The news stand] . . . displays literally dozens of magazines devoted to the glorification of the underworld. The characters in the tales are lawbreakers and the settings unthinkable in terms of what was regarded as polite literature only yesterday. Why there is a magazine called *Underworld!*

. . . No softness is tolerated in the magazine called *Gang World*. *The Black Mask* wants stern tales and so does *Gangland Stories* and *Gangster Stories*. *The Racketeer* [sic], another periodical magazine, would disappoint its readers if the hint of Victorian decency were permitted to creep in.

. . . nowadays a different definition of virtue is found. Virtue is indeed glorified in such publications as *Prison Stories*, *Speakeasy Stories* and *Gangster Stories*, but it is virtue of a different order. The hero is the type of criminal who does not expose his pals, does not double cross his associates, but is true to the code of the gang. The gun moll who goes to the chair or faces the machine guns of a rival gang without squealing is accorded the same title of heroism as the girl who took such strenuous measures to prevent curfew from ringing tonight.

. . . Violence is the order of the day. . . .

On July 28, 1932, the Chicago City Council introduced a resolution urging the suppression of crime magazines:

At the outset, we are confronted by a tremendous and never-ceasing amount of suggestions for murderous crimes. Detective stories, gangster stories, gun moll stories and racketeering stories by the millions and millions of copies, week after week, encourage those who are mentally defective to contemplate murder and execute the crime as opportunity offers.

Hersey could only have dreamed of circulations into seven figures. No doubt, the resolution went the way of most resolutions: into the noble memories file. Gangster pulps may have fizzled out, but detective and crime pulps remain with us in one form or another.

IN THE GRAND HISTORY of censorship in the 20th Century, the attack on the gang pulps barely merits a footnote (the footnote you're now reading). The original magazines are extremely scarce, and precious few of the stories have ever been reprinted. Thus, there has been only a vague notion of what the magazines contain, among the relatively few people who even know they existed. So how could we regret losing, because of censorship, that which we barely remember?

In an interesting coincidence, the infamous Hollywood Production Code (PC) was adopted by the film studios on March 31, 1930, a variance measured in weeks from when Hersey reached his accommodation with Sumner. Hersey's agreement, like the PC, was a form of self-censorship: We agree to restrict ourselves in order that retribution is not delivered upon us. The PC is best-remembered for its restrictions on sexual issues, adultery, nudity, rape, deviance, and sex itself. But it also addressed crime scenarios. Its restrictions in that category are a virtual catalog of what could be found in the gang pulps: "criminals should not be made heroes"; "brutal killings should not be presented in detail"; "killings for revenge should not be justified"; "law and justice must not by the treatment they receive from criminals be made to seem wrong or ridiculous"; "crime need not always be punished, as long as the audience is made to know that it is wrong." The PC, though, was skirted as quickly as it was adopted; thus creating the "pre-Code era" that lasted into 1934, when the Code was finally observed in earnest. We wonder if Hersey's agreement with Sumner did not, in its own way, produce a half-hearted standard, giving the reader the same product of revenge and violence bundled up in a chaste wrapping; analogous to a later generation of pornographic books advertised as "marriage manuals." The "packaging" may pacify outsiders, but the true consumers know better.

Reading these gang stories, and looking for evidence of pre- and post-censorship content, can be a puzzling experience, at times the imperfect science of reading tea leaves. The distinctions can be subtle to the modern eye, as jaded as we are to depictions of violence in print, film, or on television news. But understanding the cloud of scrutiny the stories were published under gives them another level of intelligibility all the same (assuming the rocky prose cooperates).

In 1930, Harold Hersey elected not to defend his constitutional rights—for perfectly understandable reasons. Though the Bill of Rights grants freedom freely, enforcing it can be very expensive, indeed. When Hersey reduced the conflict to a one-day news story, he guaranteed that the affair would soon be forgotten and that its inner details would never be public. That allowed him, whether from intent or selective memory, to claim in *Pulpwood Editor*: "I was careful never to permit an underworldling to triumph over justice." Because the magazines themselves were unavailable, his brief account became the prism through which future historians of the pulps would characterize his gang-story magazines. We hope, with this volume, to have corrected the record to the extent possible.

Bibliography

"Ban on Crime Story Magazines Is Sought in Chicago Council." (Associated Press) *New York Times*, July 29, 1932.

Doherty, Thomas. *Pre-Code Hollywood: Sex, Immorality, and Insurrection in American Cinema*, 1930-1934. Columbia University Press, 1999.

Ellis, Douglas. *Uncovered: The Hidden Art of the Girlie Pulps*. Adventure House, 2003.

" 'Gang Stories' Magazines To Be Withdrawn." *The Bee* (Danville, Virginia), February 21, 1930.

Gunnison, John P. "Let's Try Strange Courtroom Suicide Stories." *The Pulp Collector*, Summer 1988.

——. "Hersey, Revisited." *The Pulp Collector*, Fall 1991.

Haskin, Frederic J. "Gangster Stories of Today Are Successors of the Dime Novels" (in *The Haskin Letter* column of May 20, 1931). *The Independent* (Helena, Montana), May 25, 1931.

Hawkins, Willard E. Untitled, unsigned editorial. *The Author & Journalist*, May 1930. Account of Hersey's "arrest" in Denver.

Hersey, Harold. *The New Pulpwood Editor*. Adventure House, 2002. Reprint of *Pulpwood Editor* (Frederick A. Stokes Company, 1937).

"John S. Sumner, Foe of Vice, Dies." *New York Times*, June 22, 1971.

Lichtblau, Joseph. "The NEW Gangster Story." *Writer's Digest*, September 1930.

"The Lighter Side" (column). *The Hartford Courant*, February 20, 1930.

"Magazine Attacks Newstands' Wares." *New York Times*, October 29, 1929. Report of article in Catholic weekly, *America*.

"Magazines Stopped Here." *New York Times*, February 20, 1930.

Parton, Lemuel F. "New York Revives Old Law to Stamp Out Gang Stories." *Appleton Post-Crescent* (Wisconsin), February 22, 1930. Syndicated article.

"Reports on 1928 Vice War." *New York Times*, May 12, 1929. Describes mission and scope of activities for the New York Society for the Suppression of Vice.

"Seize 3,000 Books as 'Indecent' Writing." *New York Times*, October 5, 1929.

Van Raalte, Joseph. *Bo Broadway* (column). *Olean Evening Herald* (New York), February 16, 1931.

"Volte Face." *Writer's Digest*, April 1930. News item on Hersey's censorship problem.

Woolf, S.J. "A Vice Suppressor Looks at Our Morals." *New York Times*, October 9, 1932. Interview with John S. Sumner, executive secretary of the New York Society for the Suppression of Vice.

About the Authors

A NUMBER OF THESE NAMES may seem unfamiliar, even to diehard pulp fans. The natural conclusion to make is that a few writers produced the bulk of the stories, which the publisher issued under pseudonyms to conceal the lack of variety. However, few of the below names are pseudonyms; on the contrary, the majority seem to be real. Some of these writers, however, did sell regularly to Hersey and, perhaps, had less luck elsewhere.

The online *FictionMags Index* was mined for publication history, when available.

Archibald, Joe [1898-?] ("Gangster's Revenge"): Archibald's name is well-known in the pulps. He was a prolific producer of short stories from about 1928 through the end of the '50s. One rumor has it that Archibald graduated to the pulps out of newspaper sports reporting. Early on, western, war and aviation stories dominated his output. Later, he turned up increasingly in detective and sports pulps. Many of his stories were humor pieces, although "Gangster's Revenge" demonstrates he could be quite tough. In the March 1943 *Writer's Digest*, he wrote, "I've written approximately 60,000 words a month for twelve years and have sold every word, which goes to show you I have a strong back and a freak mind. . . . Success hasn't gone to my head because I haven't had any to speak of. I've been content, too long perhaps, to scrape along on a yearly income that matches that paid the president of the bank in my town. But he has to get up at eight o'clock every morning and work until three. I get up at nine and knock off when I droop."

Beaufort, Howard ("Racketeer Revenge"): *No information.*

Beyer, Bill ("A Long Chance"): An occasional name in the gang pulps.

Compton, Jack ("Racketeer Wages," "Triple Cross"): Also wrote under John H. Compton. He seems to have had a short but varied career as a pulpster in the '30s, appearing in magazines as diverse as sports and adventure, in addition to his many appearances in the gang pulps. He wrote under the Street & Smith house name Rand Allison for *Pete Rice*. He collaborated with Ed Witter and Off-Trail favorite, Thomas Thursday, for a short in the September 1, 1930 *Top-Notch*. In the early '40s, he appeared in early Marvel comic books like *Daring Mystery Comics* and *Marvel Mystery Comics*.

Dunn, Tim ("Blood Thirst"): *No information.*

Feldman, Anatole ("Rough on 'Rats' "): Feldman was a prolific producer for the gang pulps, penning many of the long novelettes. Later ones featured a Chicago mobster, Big Nose Serrano. He appears to have started his writing career around 1920. The October 1920 *Drama Magazine* referred to him as "a new American author" for his play *The Red Thirst*, which sounds like a title he could have recycled for *Gangster Stories*. He also wrote under the pseudonyms Anthony Field and A.F. Fields. Other genres he tapped include adventure and aviation. In 1931, he was involved in the management of the ill-fated pulp, *Far East Adventure Stories*. His wife, Hedwig, wrote pulp fiction under the name Beech Allen. His career seems to fade out through the '30s.

A profile in the December 1929 *Gangster Stories* said: "Tony is over in Lisbon right now. He is a great traveller and has been all around the world many times. He's gone all ways: by tankers, tramps, schooners, and big liners. He's found out a lot about the underworld in Paris—the sewers and the underground cafes, and the Limehouse District in London."

Gerard, John ("City of Bullets"): Seems to have been published primarily in Hersey aviation and gang pulps. Joined the American Fiction Guild in 1933.

Kiswold, Robert ("The Squealer"): *No information.*

Leverage, Henry [1885-1931] ("Glycerined Gangsters"): In Chapter IX of *Pulpwood Editor*, Harold Hersey writes of meeting Leverage in prison in 1916, and starting a long-term relationship. Hersey had been an executive with the Authors' League of America and received a request for membership from Leverage, the editor of Sing Sing's magazine, *The Star of Hope*. Hersey went to visit. Leverage "had pictures of Joseph Conrad, Kipling, and other well-known authors on the walls. There was a small library on a shelf over the tiny table where he kept his typewriter. He had special permission to write by candlelight after hours." He was selling to pulps and slicks from prison. "The Twinkler," a realistic story of underworld and prison life, was made into a five-reel film (1916).

Leverage had been convicted in 1914 of car theft and sentenced to three years, nine months as reported in the *New York Times* ("Graduate Engineer Sentenced as Thief," December 12, 1914), giving him a release date in late 1918. At the sentencing, it was revealed that Leverage was a graduate engineer, a member of the Royal Society of Engineers of London and the American Institute of Electric Engineers. The harsh sentence was based on three previous convictions which led to him serving sentences in Washington, Baltimore, and Philadelphia. Leverage told the court: "I admit that I have been an ocean card sharp and a general crook, and that I did not have to steal. When I wanted to I could always earn a good living in my profession. After I got started on the wrong road it was hard to get back again. I have tried several times, but all in vain."

One story published in *The Saturday Evening Post* (May 25, 1918), "Whispering Wires," was turned into a long-running play, and eventually a movie (1926). Of the serialization, the *Kansas City Star* wrote (December 28, 1918): "In this newest type of [scientific] detective story Mr. Leverage writes of new inventions, such as the war has brought out. Being an electrical engineer with an imagination, Mr. Leverage combines his abilities in both lines successfully as he builds one of the really gripping mysteries of the season." Hersey never asked him why he had been incarcerated but wrote, Leverage "let fall hints about experiences in China and Europe, anecdotes of sailing before the mast and adventures in the far West." In his February 14, 1926 syndicated column, *Curtain Calls*, Wood Soanes wrote: "Leverage . . . is a London-born American, who ran away from his Denver home and spent a winter on the San Francisco waterfront. He tried the sea for a while, hunted for gold in Alaska, worked in a railroad office in Denver and then went to New York to write. He had written about 150 stories before 'Whispering Wires' brought him fame and fortune, as the Alger books have it."

Leverage, "famous author, war correspondent and playwright," was quoted in a 1924 ad for Corona typewriters: "I took [my typewriter] to England during the war and had it up in one of the Royal Air Planes used in defense of London."

During his career, Leverage sold to Bob Davis at Munsey, Street & Smith, Clayton, *Blue Book*. His main genres were adventure and detective. Hersey reminisced: "He was a most charming, entertaining fellow. I miss him often when I go to make up an issue. He never failed to come in with just the right yarn for the right place."

McNeil, William ("One Hour Before Dawn"): *No information.*

Plunkett, Cyril ("Rod Rule"): Plunkett was primarily a detective-mystery writer who appeared regularly through the '30s and '40s, selling to most of the big pulp houses.

Poindexter, William E. [?-1932] ("Hair-Trigger"): According to obituaries syndicated on March 15, 1932, Poindexter was the pseudonym for Merry Ruth Mader, who died at her home in Corpus Christi. She was described as a "former Chautauqua entertainer with the late William Jennings Bryan"; "she served overseas as an entertainer with the Y.M.C.A. during the World War." The obits identify her as writing aviation, detective and western fiction, which the *FictionMags Index* confirms, an odd set of specialties for a woman. To confuse matters, the *Index* shows consist appearances by Poindexter through the late '30s, mostly in air pulps, both in Thrilling, Popular, and other company's pulps. We can only conclude that the stories were reprints or that the obituaries were incorrect. It's a mystery.

Reeve, Lloyd Eric ("A Regular Moll"): Reeve was best known as a prolific western pulp writer, appearing consistently in the '30s and '40s. He was well-known in the Oakland-Berkeley area where he occasionally lectured on the subject of writing. The August 1935 *Writer's Review* reported: "Lloyd Eric Reeve, told to cut down on his ciggies, did just that. He uses a razor blade to make five out of one, and catches a couple of puffs every thousand words or so at the end of a long holder. . . ."

In his introduction to *This Is the Way It Was: The Best Western Stories of Ryerson Johnson* (Ohio University Press, 1990), Johnson told this tale:

> I should mention an alternative way of writing stories. Good old Bill Mowery was . . . coaching two of my friends, Lloyd Eric Reeve and George [Armin] Shaftel, introducing them into the pulp world. The three of us would gather at Lloyd's apartment sometimes. Lloyd's wife, Alice, poured tea and listened quietly while we pitched the virtues of the Mowery Method.
>
> It became increasingly apparent that she was antagonistic to it. "It kills your creativity" she insisted. "Bill's making automatons of you all!"
>
> This was sacrilege. We argued with her—three against one.
>
> We couldn't budge her. "Bill's way allows no expression of verve, spontaneity, freshness . . . No human warmth—"
>
> "Yes, it does! All of that's structured into the outline—"
>
> "You can structure emotion?"
>
> "Sure . . . sure . . . sure. Look at the record. We're selling."
>
> But then Lloyd's record became not so good. He ran into a spell where nothing was selling. He dropped in at my place one day, gloomy and discouraged. "I've got the promise of a job driving a truck," he said. "I start tomorrow."
>
> But Lloyd's truck driving career never wheeled out. In that afternoon's mail he received two story checks.
>
> And Alice?
>
> Soon afterwards she sat down at the typewriter, and just out of her head and feelings—no outlining, no conscious striving—wrote a pleasant little story about some people with problems, and sold it to *Good Housekeeping* for $900. And she kept on doing this!

Alice's story sold in 1934, which dates the end of this anecdote. Reeve's writing career obviously started several years earlier, so Johnson must have compressed events in his memory.

Rivers, Vernon ("When China Jo Lost His Woman"): *No information.*

Stueber, William H. ("The Highway to Hell"): Stueber's (known) career runs from 1929-36. He wrote gang fiction both for Hersey and Popular's *Gang World.* He also wrote western stories and appeared in the rare one-shot, *Popular Engineering Stories.* He was a member of the American Fiction Guild as of March 1, 1933.

Wood, Clement [1888-1950] ("Kid Dropper Plays It Alone"): Wood was born in Tuscaloosa, graduated from the University of Alabama in 1909, and received a postgraduate degree from Yale in 1911. He was best known as a poet, and wrote several books on the subject. His poetry was collected in 1936 in *The Glory Road.* He also dabbled in the pulps with the occasional short.

Wrigley, Chuck ("The 'Eyes' Have It"): *No information.*

Young, Dan ("The Singing Kid"): *No information.*

The Squealer

By ROBERT KISWOLD

A stool—an ironic detective—and between them a brutal avenging underworld to hold the scales of justice.

A WIZENED RAT—A STOOL—A COPPER'S SNARK—A PUNK! All ugly words and every one at one time or another had been used to describe that most unlovely individual—Nosey Snedden.

For a long time now, the underworld had suspected him. Just give them a proper tip-off and, well, Nosey Snedden's wagging tongue would be silenced forever with a splash of hot lead through his guts.

First there was Topsy; piquant, defiant little Topsy. Good kid, Tops. Playing the lookout on a safe-cracking job she was snitched by the police and railroaded. Something queer about that lay.

Then the Monk was run down coming out of a nocturnal visit to a Post Office. The Monk was plugged—plugged dead with .45's.

Two or three other of the boys had mysteriously run into poison at the hands of the bulls. And Nosey Snedden, well, somehow he always came through with an unpunctured hide.

The underworld wondered; and fingers itched around the butts of heavy automatics.

Night. Nigger Mike's—the joint where booze and bullets mixed. Nosey Snedden lifted the mug of beer to his dry lips. His hand trembled slightly and two dark brown splotches slopped onto the oily table at which he sat. He drained the beaker without pausing for breath and set it down again with a defiant bang.

"To hell with Cassidy," he muttered to himself; but the clutching devils of fear in his heart belied his words.

He lifted his head toward the bar for a moment to order the whiskey that his system cried for, but hesitated half way through the gesture. Booze was no good on a job like this. Better shaky nerves than a fuddled brain.

The swinging doors of the bar were suddenly filled with a bulky black figure. Nosey Snedden's eyes straying in that direction reflected the fear that crept through his veins.

"The damn fool," he muttered. "If he speaks to me I'll kill him—"

Slowly the big shape in the doorway strode through the bar room. He surveyed the groups at the tables with an amused cynicism in his eyes.

The drinkers stared back at him, with lips set in grim red lines and hands conspicuously above the tables.

For Detective Sergeant Tim Cassidy was the quickest and most relentless rod that the Police force boasted.

The hand of Nosey Snedden tightened about the handle of his stein. Sweat congealed on the thick glass of the vessel as Cassidy continued his round of insolent scrutiny. For a fleeting second he paused before the table of Nosey Snedden.

Snedden inhaled quickly and kept the breath in his lungs for a full ten seconds. Slowly Cassidy raised his brows and indicated the door. Then suddenly he turned and walked out of the saloon.

Nosey Snedden's breath blew from his bursting lungs and his hand relaxed on the glass. Hastily he looked around the room. Quizzical inquiring glances were cast in his direction. He smiled nervously and fought with the tremor in his throat.

"Beer, Joe," he called loudly, masking his emotions in a bellowing roar. "Beer! Pronto!"

He drank but half the second glass. The empty sensation at the pit of his stomach had somehow killed his thirst.

A half hour later Nosey Snedden, with a swift, surreptitious glance behind him entered police headquarters. Straightway he made for the detective's room. Cassidy looked up from the depths of a racing sheet.

"Hello, Rat," he greeted affably.

Snedden's teeth jammed together and yellow hate flamed from his eyes.

"What's the idea?" he demanded. "What the hell's the idea of coming near me in Nigger Mike's? Christ! If that gang knows I'm talking to you, they'll croak me quicker than you'd cross me."

"What do you expect?" returned the other. "That's all part of your racket. Now listen, Nosey. I gotta tip, see? I know the Mullins mob is going to pull something tonight. I wanna know what it is and where!"

The hate in Nosey Snedden's eyes was chastened by a haunting fear.

"I don't know, Cassidy. Honest to God, I don't know. This is the first I heard of it!"

"Yeah," drawled the other. "I said I want to know what and where."

The venom on Nosey's face was conquered by the terror that gnawed at his heart. His voice cracked to an alto whine.

"Honest to God, Cassidy. Honest to God—"

"You wanna burn?"

"Honest to God—"

"Shut up. I can send you to the chair, Rat! And I'll do it. I'm not asking you again." He placed a thick hand on the telephone. "Come through."

Nosey Snedden's lips trembled. A single bitter tear streaming down his cheek, he came through.

"Get out!" said Cassidy and the contempt in his voice was vitriol. "You're lower than I thought. I had to have the info. It's my job. But I know and every mob in this town knows that Mullins dragged you out of the gutter when your name meant murder in this town. And now you rat on him!"

"Honest to God, Cassidy—"

"Screw!" said Timothy Cassidy.

The underworld was actually shocked. Mullins the Great was gone! The midnight Post Office robbery had ended in utter rout. Mullins was lying in the morgue his carcass riddled with police bullets. Shannon was laid out in the parlor of the Catholic home that he had left long ago, his face an unrecognizable bloody mass. Vittri was in the Police Hospital as the internes probed his abdomen for a .45 bullet. Nosey Snedden alone had escaped unharmed.

Nosey walked slowly into Nigger Mike's. His face was drawn and pale. His narrowed eyes darted nervously here and there.

He started toward an occupied table with a greeting, but stopped half way. In response to his forced laugh, he found a duo of hard, unsmiling faces. He turned to an empty table and sat down.

This time he ordered double whiskey. The burning liquor poured his throat and surged through his veins. The screaming of his nerves was somewhat quieter.

He glanced again about the room and flushed uneasily at the suspicious looks that came his way. The third drink aroused a measure of defiance.

"To hell with them!" he muttered. "They can't prove anything. Let 'em think. They won't give me the works till they're sure."

He drummed nervously on the table. His wandering eyes shot toward the door and remained fixed upon what he saw.

A dry flame licked his throat, and the familiar form of Cassidy loomed through the entrance. Nosey Snedden stared at him as he entered. His heart hammered against his thin chest. His toes tightened against the soles of his shoes. His jaw tensed as his teeth came together.

Every eye in the house followed Cassidy. Usually he sauntered, strolled aimlessly through the bar, but tonight he walked direct—a purposeful walk.

Nosey Snedden gripped the whiskey glass. An almost palpable shadow of fear hovered over him. Closer and closer came Cassidy. Was he? No, he couldn't!

The bulky form stopped and stretched out a hand.

"Howdy, Nosey," said Cassidy. "Howza boy?"

He slapped him heartily on the back and then was gone. Nosey Snedden watched him stride toward the door. Each footstep marked off the time that Nosey Snedden would live. For a moment he was physically chained. Paralyzed. The awful intelligence that his brain had received was not yet translated to his rigid muscles. Cassidy's pudgy hand was on the swinging door.

A brittle silence fought with the screech of the door hinge. Nosey Snedden's muscles broke the spell. The glass dropped, shattered to the floor; the table banged over, as Snedden, his eyes distended marbles, his fingers clawlike, saliva slobbering his jaws, sprang to his feet.

"Honest to God—" he shrieked. "Honest to God!"

The swinging door obscured Cassidy's body.

Snedden's hazy stare saw merciless eyes, thin bloodless lips. A score of hands flashed below the table.

"Honest to God—" screamed Nosey again. "Hon—"

A thud in his breast like a hammer blow! He screamed again in fear. He felt no pain. His mind was a searing flash of lightning. A roar sounded in his ears. His mouth framed words that were never uttered.

"Honest to—"

But a bursting bubble of blood drowned the end of his words.

When China Jo Lost His Woman

By VERNON RIVERS

The Dude liked skirts—played around with them. But no matter what Hell they dragged him to, his guts and his 45's carried him through.

MANY OF NEW YORK'S UNDERWORLD frequented China Jo's chop suey dive. That was on a second floor, off Mott Street. But nobody had ever been up the next flight of stairs, not even the police. That is, nobody but Jo's henchmen, spying, sneaking, crafty devils; and, of course, China Jo himself. And Half-Breed Rose.

At the foot of that flight of stairs, a sleepy looking Chink sat smoking, smoking all the time. In reality, the slits of eyes were watching, watching continually.

But now, someone else reclined on a low divan covered with rare embroidered silks in the front room on the third floor. It was Dude Jim, the head of a rival gang.

"Women's sure gonna be Dude's finish," the gang had decided long ago and it looked like it now.

But Dude didn't think so. A hard man with his mob, he was soft with a swell looking dame. He knew it. What did it matter if he was a softy and talked too much when a jane's arms were around his neck? He didn't think then.

But let the jane blab! He could rely on himself to get out of any scrape. He thought fast. He shot straight. His muscles were iron. And then he had a sweet revenge doped out for all stools.

It was a woman who led him on this foolhardy adventure now. He had seen Half-Breed Rose dance downstairs several times. Tonight he had fallen and fallen hard. Tiny, voluptuous lips she had that looked soft and moist. Eyes that promised much if you looked into them—alone.

"But why do these Chink kids wear those damn long kimonas?" he said to one of the men at the table with him. "Can't even see as far as their shoulders and I'll bet they're knockouts. I'd give both my gats to see her do that dance with no more clothes on than an American burlesque queen."

Rose saw Dude looking at her and understood the look. It doesn't take a girl of the underworld long to know that she is wanted. She knew he wanted her bad. And did she care? What woman failed to turn and look at him with the dark handsome head, muscular powerful flesh which she sensed beneath the neat blue suit. The look in his eyes made her warm. She moistened her lips.

But she belonged to China Jo. She turned away. Her mother had given her to China Jo when she was sixteen. She belonged to China Jo bodily. There were spying eyes that followed her everywhere, spying eyes that Jo sent. She belonged to that puny, brutal, sinister Jo always. Damn it! If it were only for herself, she might attempt an escape even though it would mean death, but it would mean sure death for the man she went with.

Warm with anger, now that she had seen to-night the reason for a desire to escape, she paused at the foot of the stairs before going on. She stopped to speak to the smoking guard. She saw that Dude had followed her to the hall. She saw nothing more. She must stop with the guard a minute to calm her anger. Jo might be met upstairs.

Unseen by her, unseen by even the keen-eyed guard, for Rose was in front of him, Dude had climbed to the banister, pulled himself up and over and silently and swiftly climbed to the third floor.

Rose did not see Jo as she ascended. She did not see him in the passage above. She reached the door that led to her apartment and entered. There was Dude. She stifled her surprise and rapidly closed the door behind her.

They were face to face now. He could reach out and grab her. The dare devil nerve of him thrilled her, as he lay on the divan and smiled up at her. The warmth she had felt downstairs during the dance returned, only more insistent. Yet there was dread. Better a rendezvous anywhere but here. Well she knew that the very walls of her room had ears, human ears, concealed even she did not know where.

He started to speak. She hushed him with a quick and imperative gesture. She bent low that he might whisper what he wished to say. His warm breath caressed her ear and neck.

"Rose," he whispered, "I had to see that swell dance you were doing, again. Will you? Only not with that Chink mother hubbard."

"I heard you say you'd give both your gats for that kind of a sideshow," she whispered in return.

Was she trying to get him unarmed? After all, she belonged to China Jo's tong. But he had made the proposition and he would stand by it. Two guns were flung into a heap of pillows opposite.

Half-Breed Rose rushed for the guns. He was alert again. But she brought them to him as she glanced fearfully around. She knew well the peril he was in, she did not think of her own danger. She begged him to pocket the gats again.

"I tell you I'll stand by what I said." His voice was low but jaunty, taunting. "Now, your part of the bargain."

Rose looked at him again and almost forgot his danger. She was no quitter. She would come through with the dance.

The kimona had covered her well. When she removed it to begin the dance, she felt almost naked. Dude reclined in blissful expectation, watching the waving of white arms, the flash of the rounded ivory flesh of perfect thighs.

"And to think some dumb guys don't think a show like this is worth a little risk!" he breathed in her as she passed him.

He half rose and touched her . . .

The dancing limbs tensed. The knob of the door had been turned. It had not yielded.

But without a pause, before Dude could reach the mass of pillows where his rods lay, an expert aim had smashed the door square at the lock and two Chinamen were in the room. The first covered Dude Jim with a gun. Behind him, safe, walked a short Chink in an elaborate mandarin coat of silk. He waved a fan slowly as he looked through two slits at his half-breed courtesan. The look was brief. He would settle with her later.

The cold, expressionless slits travelled to Dude. He looked at him long. As another gangster prying into the racket of Jo's tong, he could be dispensed with quickly. There were strong chemicals known among his people that ate the heart's blood quickly and destroyed the flesh with it.

But they would not do now. This white man deserved worse treatment— much worse.

He had approached China Jo's woman.

China Jo did not have to pause to think out a scheme. His plans for vengeance were carefully thought out beforehand. A smile of immeasurable cruelty formed on the impenetrable mask of his face as he selected the revenge best fitted to the man before him. With a slight turn of the head he addressed the henchman with the gun.

"Down the shaft with him, to the red dungeon, Hip Sing."

But Dude's mind had been working, too, even faster than China Jo's. His swift conclusion was, "I ain't over anxious to investigate none of this Chink's torture instruments in the cellar."

But he would if he didn't move quickly! One of the men in front of him was armed, but only one. His own gats were at least four yards away.

But there was a thick glass decanter on a stand nearby. He measured the distance without seeming to do so. He could reach it without making a step.

In a flash, he had seized it and had hit the one gun that covered him. The gun crashed to the floor. There was a shrill cry from the Chinaman as the decanter crashed on his hand. China Jo reached like a flash for the gun on the floor. Dude beat him to it, gripped him by the shoulders and flung the tiny shaking form against the wall. It slumped down and stayed there.

But the other Chink who had fallen back when the glass came hurtling at him, had seized a priceless vase of the Chinese Rain God from a low altar and was at Dude with it. Dude raised his left arm to ward it off. It smashed and splintered. Before the blood showed, before the other had raised an arm again, Dude shot in his right. It had to be sure. There would be others to Jo's aid any minute. The sharp knuckles met the Chink's chin with a brittle sound. The Chink fell.

And just in time! Swift feet were heard in the passage beyond the splintered door. Dude looked at Rose.

"So long, cutie! Be back soon!"

He made for the window. He smashed it with a chair he grabbed on the way and was on the sill. Could he make the roof? Just above the corner window where he stood, a huge green dragon formed the eaves and sloped up to the roof.

But it was the only way, anyway, and he heard men in the room behind him. He jumped. He caught a foot of the dragon. Thank God there had been some projection to grip! The thing was metal and slippery. But once he had pulled himself up, he could grasp the coping of the roof. He was on it in a flash, so quickly that he had not even been seen from the street. Maybe the Chinks hadn't reached the roof yet. He looked and saw no one.

One swift look back. Rose was at the window. "Take me!" she screamed, "or Jo will!"

"Soon, kid," he called back and was on over the roof, four roofs. The fifth had a loose hatch. He pulled it up and was down the stairs. So far so good. The Chinks were not on the roof yet. Then the thought flashed on him, "Maybe they stayed to shoot the works to Rose." And he paused a second. "No, that damned Oriental will make it long and lingerin' and I'll be back before then."

And he hurried on down the three flights and peered out into the street. He was safe. People walked the streets. A cop lolled across the way. No one would dare fire at him.

He adjusted his coat, wiped the blood from the arm where the Chinese idol had crashed, and sauntered out into the street. He stopped when he had crossed to the officer.

"Walkin' my way, O'Neil?" he asked.

"Yeh. I guess so. Ain't up to anything, are you, Dude?"

"Do I look it?" was Dude's reply as he started on down the street past China Jo's and back to his room on the second floor at Poker Maud's.

He had lost his jaunty air now. He bounded up the stairs and into his room. Fortunately, Pete was there. So far, so good! He wasted no time.

"Get the gang together and follow me to China Jo's," was his order. He thought that enough and rushed for the door.

"What are you goin' to do at Jo's? Eat?" drawled Pete.

"We're goin' to get Half-Breed Rose." And Dude started for the door again.

"Don't be a damn fool," Pete laughed. "You can't get Rose out of that joint. There's as many doors in that dive as New York's got cops."

Dude had his shoulders in a grip of steel.

"Get this straight, you dumb yegg. We're gonna get her. We gotta get her now. And what's more, it's either Jo's tong or our gang now. I already been up on that third floor. Get me now? If we don't get them first, they'll be here and we ain't ready. Get the men."

"A skirt again!" grumbled Pete. But he shook himself loose and beat it for the door. They both dove down the stairs.

"Guess the Chink'll shoot her the same works he wanted to shoot me. Make for the red dungeon, Pete."

"Where's . . .?"

"How do I know?" growled Dude as he yanked open the front door. "Sounds like some side show rigged up in the basement. Find it, where ever it is, see?"

Dude was off alone down the street.

As he neared China Jo's, he walked slower. What was his next move? He could wait for the fellows to arrive and walk into the restaurant backed safely by his gang. Nothing could happen then. The chop suey joint was still too crowded with people for any rough stuff. He could reach as far as the second floor that way. But what could he do then? He could not get beyond. A move farther and then the blazin' would start.

"Blazin'," he laughed to himself. "Guess the Chink is too clever for that! He's got other and less noisy means of sendin' a guy to hell."

Dude took the other side of the street and slunk past Jo's and up as far as the house from which he had made this exit from the roof just a short time before. He waited in the vestibule a minute, hands on his gats.

Had a look-out at Jo's seen him and followed? He waited another minute, watchful, ready. He was safe so far. They had not seen him. They didn't expect him back so soon—and alone.

He started up the stairs. Then he paused. He would not try the roof again. Best not try the same thing twice. They might be waiting for him there.

He came back down the stairs, turned, and walked slowly along the dark, smelly hallway, and out the back door. He was over fence after fence like a cat. Finally, the lights on the second floor showed him he was at the back entrance of China Jo's. Best go easy now! That door was never unguarded. He hugged close to the wall and noiselessly reached the door. He flattened himself against the wall next the door and made a sound with his foot.

As he expected, yellow ears had caught the sound. It had worked. A latch slipped. The back door flung open and a head appeared. He brought his billy down and a body fell across the threshold.

Still he was wary. He would not enter that way. He pulled the inert body clear out and closed the door. A window next to the door yielded noiselessly to his jimmy and he was in the back room of what was supposedly a Chinese grocery. He would not trust himself to use a flash. He crept around the wall, feeling with his sensitive fingers. He could glide without a sound.

"If there's a secret shaft down to the basement," he figured, as he continued along the wall, "it's not in the hall. That's too easy for the bulls. It would have to stick out from the rest of the wall some. And it ain't in the grocery in front or anybody could see it. I'm in the room with it now, unless that damn Chink was just tryin' to throw a scare into me."

His hand met a joining. It was not the corner. In the darkness he could make out the wall two feet beyond. He had struck the shaft!

Now his real difficulty began—to get into that shaft and down it. He continued to feel around. If he attempted to remove plaster and lath he would be heard. Maybe even the shaft was lined with steel. And above all, it would take at least a quarter of an hour. Too long, much too long. One of his spread fingers sunk a little in the plaster!

"Luck for the first time to-night," was his thought. "China Jo ain't so damn clever."

He pushed his finger again, harder. The entire side of the shaft, as high as the ceiling, had opened almost half an inch. He pushed harder. It would open no more. This entrance to the shaft was evidently little used. He tugged at the open half inch. There was a grating noise. No time for delicate operations now. He may have been heard.

Dude ripped it open the rest of the way. He was sure that noise had been heard outside. In a second he had grasped the cable in the shaft, slid to the cellar and crouched against the brick wall in the darkness.

No sound above. Maybe the Chinks knew the dangers of the cellar and did not think it necessary to follow. He dared not move without his flash now. The ray of light revealed a long, dark passage. And thank God he had turned on the flash!

Directly at the entrance to the passage was a pit in the floor—a long drop. Dude trained the flash down—a sheer wall down of—he could not see how many feet.

He shivered as he pictured his mangled body at the bottom. He made the jump across and was about to start up the dark passageway when there were lights behind and above. Voices! Not one—several.

Dude was back at the pit. He grasped the edge and lowered himself. His head was below the floor level. Only the tips of clutching fingers above. Maybe they would pass over him and not see him. It was a chance.

He could hear the voices more plainly now.

"A cinch, so far," one whispered.

"There's some trap," another insisted. "Never knew a tong guard to fall asleep at a door before and leave a trap door open. Good we didn't have to sink some lead through him and bring on the cops."

"You dumb gunman, you"—Dude recognized the voice as Pete's—"that tongman wasn't asleep. He's out for the count. Must have been the same way Dude came, see? Watch out here. A pit. Jump it!"

"Damn you! Get off my fingers," and as Pete jumped back and leveled his rod, Dude pulled himself out of the pit, shaking his bruised hand.

Orders were fast now. They crept on along the passage. A blind alley. No door at the end. Suddenly, a scream! A woman's scream of fear.

"It's somewhere on this wall on the left," said Dude.

A search revealed no door. They were about to try the other wall when a streak of light showed on the wall they had searched. The streak widened. A tongman came out. Dude had his throat. Pete trained the flash on him. Tango's silencer clicked. The Chink smashed on the concrete floor.

A louder scream. The door was closing. Dude jumped quick. He was inside the door, both guns drawn. The door closed fast behind him. His gang was on the other side, pounding. Their blows were useless against tested steel. He was alone in China Jo's stronghold.

But there were only three other men in the room. With one gun, Dude had covered the cringing tong leader Jo, as he sat enthroned on a high carved chair against the wall. The other was ready to fire at either of the two henchmen opposite.

They had hold of Half-Breed Rose and were dragging her, bound, terrified, naked, to a colossal image, an enormous porcelain furnace in reality. From the god's gaping mouth shot tongues of flame. Marble steps led from the floor to the greedy, fiery jaws.

"No such delicious morsel," said Dude, indicating with a nod of his head Rose's figure stretched on the floor; "No such delicious morsel ain't goin' into yon big god's pot belly. Now, open this door!" he commanded.

"I will do so"—China Jo reached for a button.

"No," came a shriek from the floor. "Jump, Dude!"

He did, just in time, but his guns never shifted their aim. The floor had opened where he stood. A quick glance down showed darkness.

Dude's nostrils expanded in fury.

"Get over with the other two, you damn Chinaman," he yelled. "Now, let the girl loose."

Rose stretched her cramped arms. Immediately, she was conscious of her naked flesh, and reached for a silken cloth at the foot of the idol.

"Come here, Rose. I want you to let my men in. They're back o' this door."

Even China Jo's scowling eyes did not prevent her from obeying. Dude's voice carried authority. She reached to press a spring under the arm of the chair in which the tong leader had sat. The steel door began to open. Dude's gang was behind him.

But China Jo had seen his opportunity. When the door began to open, he pressed a lever in one of the great god's feet. From inside came two of his men who had tended the fire in a compartment underneath. They were armed. Shots rang.

"Hit the floor, Rose!" shouted Dude. "At 'em boys!" And both of Dude's guns flashed. Two of the Chinamen fell. There was a yell of pain from Pete, but he stood his ground.

A volley of shots from China Jo's side. Dude had slid behind a chair.

"Save China Jo for me!" he yelled into the din of ringing shots.

He picked off another Chink and Tango's silencer listed another casualty.

"The last of 'em! Now, me for Jo!" And Dude shoved his rods in his pockets as he strode swiftly across to the crouching figure of China Jo. Dude yanked him to his feet.

"Now, you little baby he-devil, you, I'll settle with you." His voice was low in the Chink's ear. "It was either me or you, Jo, and I kinda guess it's you."

"Time, please, time! Prayer—I make prayer!"

"Prayer," sneered Dude. "You want time to push another button."

"No, no! Prayer!"

"Oh, yeh? O.K. with me." He was carrying the whimpering writhing form up the marble steps.

"I got a great idea, Jo," Dude was saying. "You want to pray. Well now, where's there a better place than in the great big belly of your great big heathen god. See the point, Jo?"

Dude was at the top of the marble staircase. His powerful arms stretched the body into the air. Jo's slant eyes looked in terror. His scream was muffled as he fell through the flaming mouth below.

Rose gave a little cry of pity.

"Don't waste any tears on that yellow scoundrel," said Dude. "It might have been you or me or both of us!"

Dude was the softy again as he held Rose's yielding form in his arms.

"It's good for us, boys," he said, "that China Jo had sound proof walls in this hole, or we'd have had the cops here before this. And if there's anything annoys me, it's a lot of flat feet buttin' in."

Soon Rose was dressed again in the clothes that had been taken from her at the idol's feet.

They were all on the street. The gang scattered. Rose and Dude sauntered on down the block. Rose started a little as a cop rounded the corner.

"Evenin', O'Neil." Dude was casual.

"Evenin', Dude. Livin' peaceable?"

"Me? Sure! Just spendin' a quiet evenin' with the girl friend!"

Racketeer Wages

By JACK COMPTON

Boss of his mob, racketeer, hi-jacker, cold-blooded killer—he baited a double-cross trap. Then grim Fate flashed her fiery gat of revenge.

"I'll put Tony Scilli on the spot," muttered Steve Hardy to the little man seated across the bare wooden table from him, "and you'll bump him off!" With a hasty glance about the frowsy speakeasy, Hardy turned back to watch the effect of his words on his companion.

Slim Withers, a frail little fellow in an ill-fitting suit quickly looked at the big perfume-reeking Hardy. "Gese, boss, quit yer kiddin'. Nobody can get Scilli. He's a red-hot!"

"Take a drink, kid." Steve Hardy shoved a gin bottle across the table. "I've got everything set," he went on hurriedly. "Cripes—it's in the bag!" The Broadway racketeer frowned as the little man ignored the gin. "This wop is peddlin' stuff in my territory. I gotta give him the works. See?"

"But," put in Slim, his face suddenly serious, "I ain't no gun-toter. I—"

"Who says you ain't?" demanded Steve harshly. "Guess you clean forgot about the bull you rubbed off at the Brooklyn wharf, the one they fished out of the Red Hook canal last week. You got a poor memory, kid."

"Gese, Steve," blurted out Slim, his lips twitching nervously, "you—you got that bull. Not me!"

Hardy stiffened in his chair, quickly looking around the partially-filled speakeasy. No one was within earshot. He heaved a sigh of relief. "Listen, you little mutt, another crack like that and I'll turn you over to the dicks. Do you think they'd believe *you*? Haw! Haw! Like hell they would!"

"No! No!" pleaded the cowering little man. "We're pals, boss, an' we stick together. Ain't we pals, Steve?" he asked timidly.

"Sure, kid." Hardy grinned from ear to ear. "Now about gettin' Scilli. Tonight he's gonna leave his dancin' joint at four o'clock—"

"But—"

"Keep your shirt on, kid," growled the big man, "and let me finish. It's on the up and up. Can't go wrong. His rods will be tight and foolin' around with broads. Then when he staggers out in the street you ride by and give him both barrels of a shotgun. Easy." The racketeer raised his eyebrows wisely and pulled out a stuffed wallet. "The job is worth a grand to me. I'll give you two hundred now and the rest when Tony is getting flowers he can't smell. See? Then you take a train out of this burg till I give the dicks something else to worry about."

Slim Withers pocketed the money resignedly. Spilling out a stiff drink, he squared his drooping shoulders. Then he took out a big gold-plated watch and fingered it lovingly. Suddenly Slim started. "Gese, boss, tonight's the—"

"For cripes sake, get going!" Steve Hardy was looking uneasily at the door, which now framed the figure of a man. The newcomer's baggy suit, derby hat and broad shoes had "dick" written all over them. Hardy whispered behind his gin glass to Slim. "Here's that damn snoopin' McCarthy. G'wan, get out before he starts asking embarrassin' questions."

"But, boss," insisted Slim pointing to his watch, "they—"

"*Get out!*" Hardy hissed from the side of his mouth.

Under the threat of that harsh command Slim did go out; but there was a worried look on his drawn face.

McCarthy swaggered over to Hardy's table. Pushing his derby over one eye he slid into the chair that Slim had vacated. He grinned at the racketeer. "Making the rounds, Hardy. Get me?"

"Sure, Mac. This baby never slips up on his payments." With that Hardy again pulled out his heavy wallet, selected several crisp bills and passed them to the detective.

Pocketing the hush money, McCarthy rose to his feet. He refused Hardy's offer to have a drink. "Not tonight, Hardy. If I took a glass at all the places I gotta stop tonight I'd be as pie-eyed as hell. S'long."

When the detective had left the speakeasy, Hardy slipped over to one of the telephone booths against the rear wall. Thumbing a nickel into the slot he called a number. Some seconds later a cheap feminine voice asked him who he wanted. "Lemme speak to the Big Shot, sister. Yeah, Tony Scilli. And make it snappy. Never mind who I am."

There was another silence. Then a cold, flat voice came over the wire.

"Who is it?"

"Hello, Tony. This you? Yeah, Hardy. I want to see you tonight again. O.K. And tell them gorillas of yourn that you're expecting me. See you later."

Twenty minutes later Steve Hardy was in a private room with the stocky Italian gangster. "You know, Tony," he began, "we've been dickerin' for some time about pooling our interests against all the other mobs in town." Tony Scilli merely nodded his sleek black head. "Well," went on Hardy, "I talked this over with my boys and they are all for it—*all but one!*"

Tony viciously jabbed his cigaret into a tray. "Who's the punk?"

"Slim Withers," said Hardy with narrowed eyes. "That guy won't lissen to reason. He claims that you bumped off a buddy of his and swears he's gonna get hunk. See?"

The racketeer leaned still closer to Tony Scilli. "One of my boys said that he seen Slim take a car and a shotgun out tonight. And before the little runt drove off he said something about getting you at closing time tonight." Hardy tapped the gangster on the chest. "That's the kind of a pal I am, Tony."

The stocky Italian nodded slowly for some minutes. "I getcha, Steve. I'll take some Tommy men up to the corner and give this punk a swell welcome." Then Tony smiled crookedly at the Broadway racketeer. "You've done me a favor, Steve; now I'll do one for you. And she's some hot mama!"

"Yeah," smirked Hardy. "Blondes is my dish, Tony."

"There's a wow downstairs, a hoofer from the big time," Tony smiled inquiringly. "Want to meet the broad?"

Steve said that he did and about an hour later he was making fine progress in one of the private rooms in Tony's dance-hall dive. Steve was not a heavy drinker, but whatever his blonde companion poured out he swallowed.

Through a drifting cloud of blue-gray cigarette smoke Steve leered at his gay girl friend. Again he took in her fuzzy, bleached hair; the greasy mascara smeared around her starry eyes; the streaks of powder half-concealing the dissipated wrinkles of her cheeks; and the cherry-red lips that were boldly inviting.

"You know, big boy," she cooed, "I just adore handsome clever papas like you. And I—"

"That's me all over, kiddo," admitted Steve, lifting another glass. "You know, tonight I'm pullin' the damnedest, cleverest little job. Fact is, kiddo, I'm too clever for one man. Wait up! Pour me another.

"You see, blondie—"

"But," cut in the actress, "I don't think you're as clever as little Tony. I ain't heard so much about you." She had already made one bottle of gin look sick and started on another. "Tony has his picture in the paper every day," she pointed out between gulps of gin. "He's a Big Shot and—"

"Hell he is," blurted out Hardy nastily. "He's nothing but a cheap dago!"

"You big mutt," she flared up, "don't you dare call my little Tony a—"

"Aw, go to hell!" Steve pushed her in the face and she toppled off the chair to the floor. She started up, then sank back. The floor was nice and comfortable and she was full of gin. So Blondie didn't bother to get up. Steve struggled into his vest and coat. Then grabbing his hat slammed out of the room. In the hallway he stopped muttering to himself.

"So I ain't as clever as that little wop, ain't I?" He stopped suddenly at the door leading into the main dance floor. There, talking to Tony Scilli was Detective McCarthy. They seemed to be arguing. Suddenly Tony turned abruptly and walked off into his private office. Steve Hardy waited until McCarthy looked his way and then beckoned to the detective. McCarthy swaggered into the hallway with a surprised look on his face.

"Don't ask questions, Mac," snapped Hardy reeling slightly. "Listen to me. I'm gonna give you a great chance to get Tony red-handed so you can send him up the river to burn. That wop is as slow as hell with his payments to you. Now if I take over his territory, Mac, I'll make you a rich man. You know me, Mac. We get along swell."

"Sounds good, Hardy, but if you double cross me I'll—"

"Take it easy, Mac, it's on the up and up. Now listen. In about an hour Tony is gonna take some Tommy guns and get a guy in a blue sedan up at the next corner. Never mind who the punk is. Let him shoot the guy. Then you and the two carloads of dicks jump Tony. Easy, ain't it? You got the punk that was killed and the guy that did it. How's it sound, Mac?"

"It's a go, Hardy."

Then McCarthy saw the gangster coming out of his office, so he left Steve in the darkened hallway and went to meet Tony.

Hardy looked over his shoulder at the room where the actress was sprawled on the floor. "I ain't clever, eh?" he sneered. "Fact is, I'm too damn clever for this racket." He steadied himself against the wall. "Well, I'm sure doing things tonight. Saving my neck for killing that bull in Brooklyn, getting rid of that runt Withers, the only guy who knows about it, letting Tony do the dirty work and then sending Tony to the chair. Haw! Haw! And on all that I'm getting in solid with Mac and headquarters." Steve adjusted his tie and hat. "And that dumb broad said I wasn't as clever as Tony."

Hardy pulled himself together and walked out into the main room. Glancing at his watch he saw that it was five minutes of three. Just one more hour and Slim Withers would ride into his double-baited trap.

The racketeer chuckled to himself. It was pleasant to think that he would be master of gangland at four o'clock! Again he consulted his watch. Good time now to be getting out before the fireworks started.

At the cigar counter in front of the dance-hall, Hardy met the stocky Italian gangster. Grinning from ear to ear, Hardy slapped him on the back. "Swell broad, Tony. Me and her hit it up great. She's sleeping it off now. Don't bother her, will you." Then Hardy stepped closer to the mob leader. "Get your men out there, Tony, and burn up that mutt Withers. We'll make a great team, Tony. Both be in Florida in a few months. That's the kind of a pal I am. See?"

With that Hardy pushed through the door to the street. A short flight of stone steps and he was on the sidewalk. His own car with an armed chauffeur was a block and a half down the street. Walking to the curb he signalled to it.

He was so busy looking down the street that he did not see the stealthy approach of a blue sedan around the other corner. Did not see it slow down as it came even with him.

Then with a choked cry Hardy saw the sedan and the white face peering over the gaping muzzle of a double-barreled shotgun.

Crash!

The street rocked with the terrific roar of the double-charged shotgun.

When Tony Scilli and his mob of gunmen reached the street they saw a mangled form sprawled grotesquely over the curb. From nowhere at all Detective McCarthy popped into sight. He strode up to Tony, who was questioning the frightened chauffeur.

Then he looked down at the mangled body of Steve Hardy. Clasped in one outstretched hand was the gleaming face of a watch. It read two minutes past three. McCarthy muttered the time aloud.

Hardy's scared chauffeur looked up quickly at McCarthy as the officer spoke the time. His pinched face brightened. "Naw, Mac, yer just one hour behind the times. Cripes—didn't you see in the papers that daylight saving time begins tonight? Didn't you shove yer watch an hour ahead? Cripes, Mac, it's *four o'clock!*"

Gangster's Revenge

By JOE ARCHIBALD

A story of an underworld Czar's revenge on the one who dragged him from his throne—a tense, fighting, dramatic tale of gangland's most dangerous rods!

OUT OF THE WINDY DARKNESS of a side street a man emerged, hugging close to a building as he rounded the corner into the faint light cast by a gas lamp which leaned crookedly from the curb. Just above the collar of his overcoat, pulled well up over his face, high cheek bones protruded. A flat derby was pulled well down on his head but the shadow cast by the brim failed to hide the glittering whites beneath peculiar, elongated lids.

After a momentary pause and a furtive glance around, he plodded silently onward for another half block, and then melted into the darkness of a doorway.

The speakeasy was crowded. The man with the flat derby had a hasty drink at the bar and then crowded through the hard looking group and disappeared through a door to the rear. There were two men in the room and they glanced up expectantly as the newcomer entered. Preliminaries were dispensed with. The slant-eyed man got down to business immediately.

"Well, I've come for my cut. Have ya got it? I'm blowin' this burg tonight."

One of the men laughed crookedly and handed over a bulky envelope. "Sure. Three grand, Diamond. I'm glad it's you an' not me that's gettin' it. Foolin' with the Czar is—"

"Aw, go t'hell!" was the man's only comment as he hurried out of the room, pocketing the money.

Ten minutes later he alighted from a taxi two blocks from a suburban railroad station. It was after midnight and the streets were deserted. A chuckle escaped the man as he watched the little red tail light of the cab disappear into the gloom.

In the next second the laugh changed to a choking cry of fear. A big car with no lights and curtains drawn thundered out of a divergent street. The man started to run like a frightened rabbit. A long spurt of flame ripped apart the darkness and spat forth a message of vicious death. Another streak of flame. Another. Above the staccato report of the machine gun came a hoarse scream of terror.

A powerful beam flashed from the car and played full and brilliantly on the sagging figure on the sidewalk, following it as a spotlight follows an actor on a darkened stage. Another stabbing, intermittent blade of red flame and the man fell to the pavement, writhing and twisting from the force of the deadly stream of hot lead.

Then the spotlight disappeared. The savage snarl of the machine gun ceased. An engine raced and then the murder car was scurrying into the night, leaving a limp, torn, and broken thing on the pavement.

Czar Rohan had just been to a funeral. In fact he had personally arranged for the elaborate ceremony which was the last rite for Diamond Gavoni who, only a week before, had pillaged one of Czar Rohan's richest gasoline galleons of its amber liquid.

His venture had ended with a funeral cortege a mile long, a bronze casket that had set the Czar back five grand, and numerous floral wreaths from sympathetic henchmen. Behind the machine, carrying the remaining Gavonis, Czar Rohan had ridden alone, nodding complacently to the police along the way who were holding back other traffic to let the procession pass.

Now that it was over, Czar Rohan was speeding toward the outskirts of the city where he had recently built a spacious abode. "The House That Booze Built," it had been laughingly christened by the Czar's intimate friends who, by the way, amounted to scarcely enough to count off on his ten fingers. Those who were associated with him in his various activities were given their choice of being ruled or ruined. Diamond Gavoni had chosen the latter and had been speedily accommodated.

The Czar swung his big car from the boulevard into a side street. A hundred feet farther on he suddenly straightened in his seat, his hands jerking up convulsively from the steering wheel. The blood drained from his pain-distorted, unusually florid face, leaving it pasty white and the lips tinged blue.

As the Czar's body stiffened, his foot pressed on the brake with a loud retching sound that could be heard for blocks. The patrolman on the corner came running. He found Czar Rohan limp in the driver's seat, one hand clutching his left side. Huge globules of perspiration stood out on the gang leader's forehead. His breath came in gasps. Czar Rohan grinned painfully as he looked into the face of the policeman.

"Oh-h, h-hel-lo-o, Au-August," he mumbled weakly. "N-no, it w-w-wasn't a slug. G-guess I-I h-had t-too much g-grub. Be okay in a m-minute."

"Better not start right away, Mister Rohan," advised the patrolman anxiously. "Maybe now I'd better drive you 'round to the Doc. He'll give you a shot o' somethin' to fix you up."

By way of assent Czar Rohan moved weakly from behind the wheel. The policeman hopped into the driver's seat and swung the car around and back toward the boulevard.

"You wait out here, August," said the gang leader when the car pulled up to the curb in front of an apartment house. "I can get to the elevator all right. Somebody might steal the car. There's a lot o' crooks around here." And Czar Rohan grinned as he walked into the building.

When the gang leader came out some time later, the patrolman saw that he was still grinning, but there was a difference. The humor seemed to be forced. But the officer knew Czar Rohan well enough to refrain from asking any questions regarding his visit upstairs.

"Thanks, August," he said, "I'll be gettin' along now." And as he spoke he handed the patrolman a big cigar wrapped in a crisp green banknote.

"Thank you, Mr. Rohan. Thank you. You're sure you oughta—?"

"Hell's bells!" roared the gang leader, as he stepped into the car. "I don't need no nursemaid. Can't a guy get indigestion once in a while?"

The big car shot forward leaving the patrolman standing on the sidewalk, a quizzical expression on his face. Czar Rohan at the wheel was smiling no longer. Once on a straightaway, he stepped viciously on the gas and the powerful machine hummed over the concrete thoroughfare at terrific speed. Motor cops wasted but a glance. They liked Czar Rohan. He gave out expensive cigars wrapped in ten dollar bills.

There were no tender words, or anxious lips, waiting to greet the gang leader as he entered the door of his home. Czar Rohan had no use for women. Liquor and women softened a guy. You had to be hard to survive in this racket. He tossed his hat to a man servant and walked upstairs without a word. Entering his den, Czar Rohan slumped down in a big chair and confronted his problem. Mechanically he reached for a cigar but his hand was arrested by the recollection of the doctor's words.

Three months to live! His heart was rotten. By avoiding any excitement and abstaining from nicotine he might manage to stretch it out a little longer.

Czar Rohan swore and selected a long weed. He bit off the end viciously and rammed the cigar between his teeth. Three months to live! The words bit into his brain.

Not that Czar Rohan was afraid to die. He had laughed in the face of death a hundred times since ascending the throne as the high potentate of gangland. But he shuddered at the thought of dying in bed. There was Monk Drew who had died of pneumonia. The gang had shown their contempt by preparing Monk for the grave with little or no ceremony. He had had but two lines in the newspapers just above the classified section. A few lilies and a cheap box. That was Monk Drew's reward for dying in bed.

It would be easy for Czar Rohan to just take a walk into the lair of the enemy and get a burst of lead through his heart. But that would leave his realm wide open to Scar Ferrini, the one man whom he had sworn to get— "Ferrini the wop," who slowly but surely seemed to be undermining the Czar's throne.

When nineteen years of age, Czar Rohan, known then simply as "Red," had wrested the title of chieftain of all the apprentice gangsters of the west side from the grasp of "Little Mike" Zarotto. Following this bloody raid, Rohan had begun to rule. He had directed raids on warehouses, trucks, and merchants, planning the jobs with a skill that left nothing to chance.

He had had little to worry about from the law. Rohan knew all the cops throughout his domain personally, and they knew of him and his activities. They recognized his power and let him alone.

When the war broke out, Red Rohan lost little time in enlisting. He came back from France a top sergeant, with two wound stripes on his sleeve. He came back to find his kingdom under the rule of one Bouncer Carrigan. Three weeks later the body of Carrigan was found in a blind alley with enough lead in it to make a six-inch pipe. The police were at a loss to know how it got there, but nothing was done about it.

Red Rohan was back. He found that prohibition had assured unlimited prosperity to his profession and he made the most of it. He found the liquor traffic blocked to the north by a gang lord, self-styled "Butcher" Lewis. Rohan assembled his hosts and marched on Lewis' stronghold. The casualties proved heavy on both sides. Butcher Lewis was given an impressive funeral. Red Rohan called himself Czar and ruled the city.

On several occasions one or more of his lieutenants had sought to rebel. Their fate had been certain and swift. Outraged citizens demanded that the law do something about bringing their murderers to justice. The police had protested that no hint had been given as to the identity of the killers.

They were right. None had been given. But they knew. The press knew. The average man in the street could guess. But nothing was done. Czar Rohan's position grew more and more secure as time went on. He was to find, however, that there were other rulers as powerful in their own backyard as he was in his. One of these had extended his control throughout a whole section of the country. He was called Scar Ferrini.

The wop was ten years younger than Czar Rohan but he was a shrewd ruler, as ruthless as he was shrewd. For Ferrini, Czar Rohan had had respect. So long as the wop did not encroach on his territory there was no reason to declare war. Rohan was content with his own wealth and power.

However, Scar Ferrini was different. His lust for power was never satisfied. His mob moved into Rohan's town by ones and twos, under cover. It had taken two years and had been carefully figured out. It was the last big stronghold east of the Mississippi that Ferrini did not control. He had to have it.

When he thought his men firmly enough entrenched in Rohan's realm, Ferrini himself moved east and sent an emissary to the Czar himself. That incident had convinced Czar Rohan that Ferrini was yellow. He sent the emissary back in a box with a declaration of war. And it had been war, bloody and ruthless.

Diamond Gavoni had been the twelfth of Ferrini's men to die. The Czar had crossed nine guns off his payroll in accomplishing this slaughter. It had proven a bonanza era for undertakers. Ferrini, however, continued to wage a war of conquest. Other gangsters from his western strongholds trickled into town and filled the gaps in Ferrini's ranks.

Czar Rohan had challenged the wop to stand up and battle, the winner to take all, but Ferrini was yellow. He kept to the waterfront in a huge brick building with barred windows and steel doors. Armed guards protected both entrances day and night. When the wop did go out he was followed by a big gorilla with guns in holsters slung under each arm.

Czar Rohan began to realize that Ferrini's power was slowly but surely gobbling him up. His flow of liquor was tapped until the money that must be paid for protection began to loom up as an enormous sum. High police officials had been approached by Ferrini. His bids for the rights to liquor traffic were higher.

Czar Rohan was asked to ante accordingly. He found that there was no sentiment in business. He knew that these men higher up could have him snuffed out even quicker than his rival could. Czar Rohan paid, but he knew that his little empire was crumbling.

No, the Czar was not afraid to die. But he did not want Ferrini to live on and reap the fruits of his years of strife in his own town. He sat in his chair with his chin on his chest. His eyes were closed, deep ridges crossing his forehead. On the arms of his chair his hands were clenched in rigid, motionless fists. The Czar was no more than forty-five years old but as he sat there he seemed to age twenty years.

His mouth was a straight grim slash, his eyes sunk into dark caverns and, as he blinked the lids, blazed with unholy light. He was thinking fast. He knew that he could not get into Ferrini's lair without being spotted by the wop's henchmen. He would be filled with lead before he could get within a mile of Ferrini.

"God! I've got to do something!" Czar Rohan jumped up, cursing in desperation. "I've got to do something!" Time after time he paced up and down the room, hands gripped behind his back, muttering to himself. Three hours later he was still struggling with his problem. He was afraid to go to bed, haunted by the horrible thought that he might die in his sleep. It was nearly morning when he fell asleep in his chair, exhausted.

He was awakened at noon by one of his body guards. The man thrust a newspaper into his hands. Czar Rohan remembered the doctor's warning and remained relaxed in his chair. The expression on the gunman's face already had betrayed the fact that the news was bad.

"Chief! Fer God's sake, ain'tcha gonna—? Why don'tcha read it?"

"Keep your shirt on, Pigeon," answered Czar Rohan calmly. "I haven't woke up yet."

"Ferrini's—"

"Shut up! I'll read it for myself," snapped the gang leader, slowly raising the newspaper. The gunman watched him intently, waiting for the usual snarl of rage that promised swift and deadly reprisal. It did not come. Instead Czar Rohan let the paper fall back into his lap and looked up at the perplexed gunman, his expression unchanged.

"So they got Carmody, Pigeon," he said absently. "He must've got careless. Huh! Took him for a ride. Ferrini would do that. It's safer."

Czar Rohan's eyes blazed. The gunman's question froze on his lips.

"Sure! They'll pay, Pigeon! But you'll wait for orders like you've always done," the gang leader snapped. "I'm still runnin' this town."

"Okay, chief."

When the gunman had gone, Czar Rohan walked wearily to the window and stared out into the street. So they had got Carmody. Ferrini had not been slow to avenge Diamond Gavoni's death. Carmody! The best man left under the Rohan banner.

It was at Carmody's funeral that Czar Rohan and Scar Ferrini met each other for the first time. The friends of the deceased and their enemies had complied with the unwritten law of gangland and had attended the ceremony minus their rods. The wop, assured that his life was in no immediate danger, confronted the Czar.

"So you're Rohan!" he sneered. "The king of this burg. Well, you're dam' near through!"

"Yeah?" answered the Czar quietly. "Listen, Ferrini! You're a cheap yellow skunk. I hear you only dug down into your pocket for a little lousy wreath for Carmody." Czar Rohan was grinning now. "And after I set myself back ten grand for Diamond's funeral. Do you call that gratitude?"

Ferrini's dark eyes snapped. "Listen, Czar. There's only one funeral that I'm going to pay for. And that's yours. I'll let you name the kind o' flowers you like now. Never mind the expenses. Will you have a bronze kimona or a plush one?"

Czar Rohan laughed and turned to the group of gangsters. "You heard what the wop said, boys. In case I kick off sudden like, I'm dependin' on you birds to see that he keeps his word. His word's no good to me. I want plenty of roses, boys, and a bronze box. The bugs don't get you so quick."

Ferrini sneered. "Grandstand stuff, Czar, huh? It's goin' to be too bad that you won't be able to smell them pretty roses—"

"By the way, wop," interrupted Czar Rohan. "I was thinkin' that a double funeral would save the boys money. Name your posies, Ferrini."

The Italian laughed. "Get this, boys," he said. "If I get bumped off by Rohan, you can wrap me up in poison ivy. And if I was you," he snapped at the Czar, "I'd get out o' town tonight. I've got you licked, Rohan. My mob outnumbers yours two to one. If you're in this burg tomorrow night, the morgue will be packed next morning with some o' your best guns."

Czar Rohan laughed quietly and turned his back on the wop. It was time to help carry Carmody to the hearse outside for his last ride.

That night Czar Rohan summoned his lieutenants to his home. He told them that he was going away. It was the doctor's orders. That was all the explanation he cared to offer. He knew that they did not believe him. They had heard Ferrini order him to leave town. There were mutterings and veiled threats. Czar Rohan was conscious of quick movements. Then he stared into the muzzles of four automatics.

"Go ahead and shoot," he scoffed. "The wop'll pay you sweet dough!"

The guns dropped. There was an embarrassed shifting of feet. Czar Rohan smiled wanly.

"Listen, you guys," he said. "You know dam' well that Ferrini has got us licked. We're fightin' the whole dam' country. I'm tellin' you to take a sneak for yourselves. The cops from the big chief down are throwin' in with the wop. Our dough now is nothin' but chicken feed. I'm through. If you want to run things go ahead."

Czar Rohan went away.

With the last big city overcome, Scar Ferrini sat enthroned over an empire of crime that stretched from the Atlantic to the Pacific, from the Canadian border to the Gulf of Mexico. He was the law. The other law in the land was not for Ferrini. He gave it but a passing thought, lived outside of it, broke it openly.

The press clamored for his downfall and it became a joke to Ferrini. High police officials laughed with him—it was so amusing. Now and then to satisfy the newspapers, the King of Crime would arrange the demise of one of his notorious henchmen. There was nothing that Ferrini could not do.

But the one triumph over which the wop never ceased to gloat was the removal of Czar Rohan. Ferrini had been afraid of the Czar. Now he had scared him out of town. Czar Rohan was yellow. All gangland, with the exception of the handful who had known Rohan personally, shared his opinion. That handful had to be shown, but they kept discreetly silent. It would be like signing their own death warrant to still claim allegiance to the Czar.

Secrets travel with incredible swiftness through the labyrinth of crime known as the underworld. One of them, dropped casually from the lips of August Rhyne, patrolman, was snapped up and relayed to all corners of Ferrini's realm and finally reached the ears of the King himself. Czar Rohan's heart had gone back on him. He had nearly passed out on his way home from Diamond Gavoni's funeral.

Gangland looked upon the fallen Czar in a new light. Ferrini had toppled him from his throne, but in doing so the new leader had become the victim of a rare joke. The wop had pledged his word that he would give the Czar an elaborate funeral in case of the latter's sudden demise. All gangland appreciated the significance of the Czar's last gesture and laughed at Ferrini. Ferrini put a price of ten thousand dollars on Czar Rohan's head and broadcast it far and wide. Rohan was to be brought in alive. Those were the instructions.

Two months passed and no word regarding the Czar. Seemingly he had disappeared from the face of the continent. In fact that was just what had happened. Czar Rohan was far beyond his enemy's reach. While Ferrini's snarling voice was sending out gangsters to bring him in, Czar Rohan was sitting in a cafe in Buenos Aires. From there he sailed to Egypt. In the next month he was to know Singapore, Samoa, Rangoon.

He cut himself off from his own world, the hard, sordid, ugly labyrinth of crime, all with a definite purpose in view. The Czar wished to be forgotten. He would go back only when he was ready to die. Three months, the doctor had said, perhaps a little more if the Czar heeded his precautions as to the excessive use of tobacco and lived a life of peace and quiet. The erstwhile gang leader had followed this advice although it had made his existence nothing more than slow torture.

In the beginning of the third month gangland began to forget the Czar.

Ferrini had more important things to worry about. In various parts of the country his vassals began to revolt. Those districts needed his undivided attention if he wished to retain his vise-like grip on his kingdom of crime. A new menace threatened in the west. Wolfe La Motte, lord of the Pacific coast, taking advantage of internal strife in Ferrini's domain, began to throw off the shackles that had tied him to the wop. When the minor revolts were finally squelched, Scar Ferrini headed for the coast. It was necessary to draw from his forces on the eastern front.

During the bloody gang war that followed, Czar Rohan was completely forgotten. Gangland was satisfied that the deposed monarch's heart had failed him in some far away district where he was not known. The doctor had only given him ninety days. Czar Rohan had been away one hundred days. They offered a toast to his memory and put him out of their minds.

Ferrini came back from the coast, his head bloody but unbowed. The threat against his throne had been wiped out. There was nothing to worry him now. He moved from his steel-doored sanctuary on the waterfront into a fashionable hotel in an exclusive section of the town. He even approached the outer fringe of society. He gave his Packard to one of his lieutenants and bought a Rolls-Royce.

One night, feeling in a festive mood, Scar Ferrini motored to Bachman's, a cabaret catering to the heavy spenders on the north side. The Rolls carried the king, two painted women, and a body guard.

It was a rainy night and few revelers had ventured out. Bachman's was host to a thin crowd. The big car pulled up to the curb and a liveried chauffeur jumped from the driver's seat. He swung the car door open and Ferrini and his party stepped from the luxurious confines. As was the custom the king of the underworld instructed his chauffeur to take the car to a nearby garage where he would call for it when he was ready to leave.

A few minutes after Ferrini had walked through the pretentious entrance to Bachman's, a small sedan pulled up to the curb on the opposite side of the street. A man stepped out and lifted up the hood, evidently to examine a balky engine. Passersby favored him with but a perfunctory glance or a sympathetic comment. The rain beat down steadily but the man bending over the engine seemed oblivious to the drenching he was getting. He tinkered with the machine for a few minutes, then let the hood down, shook the water from his coat, and walked over to Bachman's.

The girl at the checkroom accepted the man's soaked overcoat with haughty disdain. The owner of the garment smiled and handed her a crisp banknote.

"Sorry, sister," he said, "but they won't poison you. Anyway, I didn't order the rain." Then throwing back his shoulders, he stalked into the dining room. The head waiter showed him to a table but it was not to his liking. He picked one to suit himself. There were no arguments. The head waiter had decided upon that when he had caught the steely glint in the newcomer's eyes.

The man gave his order and after a hasty glance around the dining room reached into his pocket for a pencil. He wrote swiftly on the back of the menu.

Ferrini, at a table directly across the room, was waxing merry with his fair companions. He had not seen the man enter, but gangster's intuition soon warned him that there was a sinister presence somewhere nearby. He put down his glass and swept the immediate vicinity with his little black eyes. They finally came to rest on the man sitting directly across the room.

Ferrini stared, his brows knitted in perplexity. The man was familiar. That mustache fascinated him. It seemed as if it should not be there. A hoarse cry fell from the Italian's lips as recognition flashed to his brain like a bolt of lightning. Desperately he strove to maintain his calm. The women looked at him curiously. One ventured a query but Ferrini at the moment was not interested in women.

He rose from his chair and walked to the table where his body guards were sitting. He whispered two words in their ears. The men straightened in their chairs and looked quickly in the direction designated by a swift movement of the wop's eyes.

Czar Rohan had come back!

Ferrini knew that Rohan had seen him, but the Czar's expression had not changed. The wop gloated. Perhaps the deposed gang leader felt secure in his disguise. His hair was uncut and he had acquired a mustache. He was much thinner and although browned by the sun had an unhealthy white line edging his lips. Yet, despite the change that a few months had wrought in him, there was no mistaking Czar Rohan.

The wop knew he was in no immediate danger. The two men a few feet away had never missed at that distance. Ferrini, however, had other plans. He waited until the Czar had finished his coffee and had called for his bill. Rohan ignored the tray of change that the waiter brought back to him and pushed back his chair. The wop waited until he was on his way to the checkroom before he barked his orders.

Czar Rohan was in no hurry. After retrieving his hat and coat he paused at the entrance to light a cigar. It was one of those little smokes one selects when there is a limited time in which to indulge one's desire for a puff. The first twin wisps of smoke had just emanated from his nostrils when he became aware of the presence of the two men who had stopped by him, one on either side. Hard, metallic objects pressed against his ribs.

"Let's go, Rohan. Outside!" The words were rasping. From behind Czar Rohan came a guttural laugh. The Czar knew that laugh. He walked steadily out of Bachman's. Ferrini spoke to the doorman and slipped him something.

Crossing the street, Czar Rohan spoke. "Well, boys, I suppose I'm goin' to take a little ride. You picked a helluva night!"

"You picked it, Rohan," snapped Scar Ferrini.

"Yeah! So I did. Well, a Rolls is nothin' to sneer at."

Ferrini laughed. "You don't think I'm goin' to get my car all messed up, do you, Czar? We're goin' to use yours."

"Still cheap, ain't you, wop?"

"The boys won't think so tomorrow when I order that bronze kimona for ya, Rohan," snapped Ferrini. "I told ya I'd get ya, Czar. You didn't think for a minute that that disguise of yours fooled me, did you, you dumb Irishman? I ain't been forgettin' you!"

"I coulda plugged you fulla holes while you was wipin' up your gravy but I wanted to go for a little spin in the country with you, Czar Rohan." The last two words were sneered.

"Yeah! I wasn't tryin' to fool anybody, wop. Didn't I clear out an' let you have all the rackets to yourself? I just come back to town to enjoy one more night among the bright lights. I was told that Bachman's was a swell joint. It's new since I went away, wop, an' I didn't want t' croak before I'd seen everything in my old burg."

Ferrini laughed. "Well, I'm going to enjoy shelling out for that little spread I promised you, Czar, now I've got you. I thought your dirty yellow heart would cheat me out of the pleasure of wiping you out."

"Yeah! You got me, wop."

Ferrini turned to one of his men. "You'll drive, Sam. I ain't takin' chances on gettin' drove into the side of a house. We'll put Rohan in the back seat. It's goin' to be a nice, snug little party."

Czar Rohan climbed into the sedan. Ferrini and one of his gunmen followed and sat on either side of him. The gangster who Ferrini had called Sam settled into the driver's seat.

"All set?" snapped Ferrini to the driver.

"Naw, git the key to this tin can. How in hell can I—?"

Rohan produced the key with difficulty. "It's cramped back here, ain't it, wop?" he grinned.

"You won't have to worry, Czar. It ain't gonna be cramped where you're goin'."

The men laughed. Sam's foot pressed on the starter.

The explosion had been terrific. The thick plate glass windows of Bachman's had cracked like eggshells. A flying headlight from the sedan had struck the doorman and bowled him over like a toy soldier. Bits of metal, wood, and rock had flown through the air like shrapnel from a high explosive shell. Pedestrians in the vicinity had been hurled to the pavements to lie there stunned. Windows of houses on the entire block had been shattered. The bomb that Czar Rohan had planted in the engine had been made by an expert.

When the riot squad arrived, they found a heap of splintered wood and twisted metal in place of Czar Rohan's car. Gruesome heaps of human wreckage spotted the scene of the holocaust and fouled the rain water in the gutter with a crimson tint. Thin curls of acrid smoke still floated lazily above the morbidly curious crowd which began to choke the street in spite of the long sticks that swung in the hands of a score of policemen.

Detective Sergeant O'Brien, after examining the gruesome objects strewn amid the wreckage, pushed his way through the crowd into Bachman's place. After a ten minute grilling, he had all the dead men identified but one. O'Brien called the head waiter and asked to be shown the table where the man with the mustache had been sitting. He had a strong hunch.

The table was just as it had been left by its recent diner. O'Brien picked the napkin up, shook it, and tossed it aside. He rummaged among the dishes, lifted up the table cloth, and looked under the table itself.

Then his eyes rested on the menu lying on the floor. He stooped for it quickly and turned it over in his hands. A low whistle of surprise escaped him and his eyebrows arched as he read the writing scrawled on the back of the card. O'Brien's mouth twisted into a mirthless grin as he turned to the policeman standing beside him.

"Huh! So they said Rohan was yellow, did they?" he rasped. "Listen!"

> Remember, boys—plenty of roses and a bronze box for yours truly. Poison ivy for Ferrini!
>
> Czar Rohan.

Rough on "Rats"

By ANATOLE FELDMAN

It wasn't the boodle that figured, and it wasn't the lead, and it wasn't fear—just the heartbreaking business of a filthy double-crossing trap that put too much lead into guts where it didn't belong. A Chink, a Jew, and an Irishman—plenty brains—but nobody spotted the rat anyway. Read this hair-raising novel of Underworld intrigue and the gun-moll who knew everybody's onions!

THE HANDS OF THE OPEN, BOLD FACED CLOCK in the tower of the Jefferson Market Court, pointed to three. Three in the morning of a raw, blustery day in early March. The streets were deserted of all save an occasional drunk sleeping off the effects of a bottle of potent "smoke," and a few stray felines, commonly referred to in the neighborhood as "Garbage Inspectors."

Then life and movement began to animate the scene. The heavy-timbered oak door of one of the many private houses silently opened into the night. A thin crack of light pierced the gloom in the street, then was snuffed out as a gusty gale of wind zoomed around the corner.

A squat, dark visaged man, with cap pulled low over his eyes, sidled down the short flight of stairs from the door onto the sidewalk. His movements were furtive, sly; as swift as any predatory creature of the night.

A brass-buttoned, blue-coated flatfoot pounded his heavy feet down the end of the street and the man in the cap flattened himself in the dark shadows against the house. He waited a moment, tense, until the copper had passed, then with an agile leap sped across the sidewalk to a waiting machine.

With one movement he was behind the wheel with his foot on the starter. A low rumble of power suddenly echoed in the quiet street as he jammed his foot on the gas pedal. Then he slipped into gear and took the next corner on high.

A scene, very similar to this, was transpiring at precisely the same time, at a point in the city some three miles north. And still a third individual, with slinking, furtive movements, surprisingly like those of the first gunman, started out in a speedy machine from a point five miles south.

A half hour later, within thirty seconds of each other, the three denizens of the night entered a shabby waterfront cafe on West Christopher Street.

The honky-tonk was foul with the stale odor of flat beer and the acrid fumes of bitter black tobacco.

This was Silent Joe's dump. Joe, its proprietor, was deaf and dumb. Anything and everything, murder, arson and rape, had been planned across the beery tables of Silent Joe's place and there were only five notches carved on the bar.

Notches, you ask? Yes; that was Silent Joe's idiosyncrasy. Every man, or woman for that matter, who was sent up to the hot seat from his dump, had his epitaph carved into Joe's bar with a notch.

The three late arrivals drifted to a dilapidated table in the far corner. Joe approached them; Joe of the sharp, unnaturally bright and ferret-like eyes. That was nature's compensation; hear and speak he could not, but he could read a letter out of the corner of his eye across the room.

One of the men at the table went into a graphic description of a bottle. Joe understood; he had received that order many times before. He turned to his bar and returned to the table a moment later with a bottle of whiskey. The drinks were poured.

"Salud!"

A grunt.

"Faugh!"

And thus the formalities were attended to. The formalities to the planning of—

Now New York is a town of a million rackets, gunmen, gangs and suckers. And over the flaming, vicious underworld of the city ruled three men. Three men as cold, relentless, brutal and yet as sentimental as ever killers were. One ruled the mob of two-gun gorillas that used the streets and alleys north of Tenth Street as their stamping ground. Another found a fortune in the crooked sinister alleys of Chinatown and the flaming east-side. And the third, like a blood-thirsty pirate of old, sucked wealth from the river on the west and the teeming warehouses that crowded its banks.

Shanty Hogan, quick thinking, witty, brilliant, ruled the North Siders, and such was his guile at playing crooked politics with even crookeder politicians of the city, that his activities in crime extended as far north as Columbus Circle.

Smooth, oily, affable China Cholly ruled his renegade tong with a honeyed tongue and the most subtle, treacherous poison known to the East. But be it said for China Cholly that he reserved this refinement in diabolical death only for a squealer—a rat! The entire underworld approved!

To make this curious triumvirate complete, there was in the west, Hymie Zeiss. Now when a Jew is tough and a bad egg—he's just that. Wicked. Hymie Zeiss, "Little Hymie," as he was affectionately referred to by his henchmen, was not a lovely thing to look at, as a man. He was short, flat-faced and wizened, but his eyes were the soft, mellow brown of the Semite. On more than one occasion, Hymie had plugged a man, plugged him dead, and a half hour later endowed the widow with an annuity for life.

Among these three mobs there was not open warfare. In fact, some sort of truce had been agreed on between them. But there was friction, jealousy, unrest. The seething dynamite of hell brewed beneath the surface, needing only the spark of one overt act to blow off the lid.

Among the three of them they had fairly well divided up lower Manhattan for criminal exploitation, but down the center of the island, between the domain ruled by China Cholly on the East Side and the haunts of Little Hymie on the west, was a narrow band of territory that all exploited equally. It was this neutral section of the city that was the chief bone of contention among the three gang chiefs. Each one suspected the other of reaching out greedy fingers for it; each one feared the aggression of the other.

And for the past six months now, the seething tempers and bitter hatreds so long kept below the surface, were gradually emerging toward an open break; towards open warfare. It started with minor violations of the truce among the three mobs and developed with one reprisal after another to a situation so desperate that Police Commissioner Mallen, down at Headquarters, neglected his duties as official welcomer of the city, and went into executive session with his lieutenants.

There was a certain three-story red brick house on West 10th Street, just off Seventh Avenue, that was used by Shanty Hogan as headquarters. The three upper stories were occupied by a crew of hungry, flea-bitten hack writers, but the low English basement, the pet graft of Shanty's, was the most notorious and thriving dispensary of booze in the district.

At eleven a.m. of the morning following the surreptitious meeting of the three mugs in Silent Joe's, Shanty stepped briskly into the private bar in the little room behind his public speakeasy.

From the outside, the place looked innocent and harmless enough but one glance around the inside revealed a veritable fortress and arsenal. Nothing short of a battery of six inch guns backed up by a company of Marines could have broken into Shanty's hideout—once the bars were down.

Two men were there before him, awaiting their chief's arrival. One was Smiling Jimmie Hart, the other, Groucho Griffo. They were Shanty's lieutenants, tried through a hundred gang fights and not found wanting.

Smiling Jim and Groucho were a living demonstration of the theory that opposites attract. Their names alone told the story, but either one, at an instant's call and without an instant's hesitation, would have laid down his life for the other.

Shanty tossed his soft grey felt onto a convenient hook and slouched into the chair at the head of the table. His two henchmen eyed him quizzically as he withdrew a hammered silver cigarette case, extracted a butt and lit it thoughtfully. Smiling Jimmie's freckled face broke into a broad grin. Groucho's dark one scowled still more.

"Boys," began Shanty at last, "I got a red hot tip-off."

"On what?" growled Groucho the practical.

"On a load of booze under bond coming in tonight."

Smiling Jimmie tilted back his chair, threw back his blond head and a thin piping whistle escaped his pursed lips.

"Can that! Can that!" snarled Groucho.

"Yeah. What's the idea, Jimmie?" asked Shanty jokingly. "Your Irish pan is ugly enough without screwing it up like that. Anyway, when you whistle you're thinking—and I don't like you to think. What's on your mind? Out with it."

Smiling Jimmie's chair came to the floor with a bang.

"You bet, Shanty, I'm thinking. And you, dumb guy," he added, turning to Groucho, "don't get sore at me if you ain't got no brains. It's this, Shanty. Don't it seem God damn queer to you there's been so many tip-offs lately? Funny, eh?"

"Jeez, Jimmie," replied Shanty consideringly, "now that you mention it, you're right."

"And all the tip-offs haven't been to us. China Cholly has had a lot of dirt spilled to him and the same goes for Little Hymie. Now tell me, who is so interested in our welfare that they're handing us fifty grand on a silver platter? And another thing that strikes me queer about these tip-offs is the way they have a habit of not coming off the way we expect; or if they do come off we get the double cross and the bulls is waiting for us."

"What you're trying to say," growled Groucho, "is that there's a rat some place. Is that it?"

"That's it, Groucho!"

"But why?" insisted Shanty. "Give me the gimmick. How does it work out? We get a tip-off, the office. China Cholly and Hymie Zeiss, the same. What's the dirt, the low down? Who's playing us for a sucker and why? Where's his percentage?"

"Don't know yet," replied Smiling Jimmie. "But we got to find out. And the best way is to go through with this hi-jacking expedition of ours tonight. Unless I miss my guess, hell will pop loose along the road and out of the hell we might get the galoot back of this double, double cross and figure his game."

"Figure his game, hell!" snarled Groucho. "Let me get a squint at the double crossing rat and I'll pump him full of lead."

"You would, dumb-bell!" smiled Smiling Jimmie. "You drill him before I get a chance to make him talk and you'll be giving birth to a load of lead yourself."

"Can that talk, boys," urged Shanty. "Let's work this thing out, first."

The three hitched up their chairs closer to the table and bowed their shaggy heads together in conference.

To look at his round, placid, moon-like face, one would never have suspected China Cholly of being a bad man—killer. Especially so on this same morning as he ambled serenely up the Bowery and turned into Pell Street. Cholly greeted all his countrymen with an expansive chatter of high-key Cantonese and balanced the rakish checkered hat over one ear.

China Cholly was in a very genial mood that morning and with good reason, too. For there had come to him, via the complicated underworld grapevine, word that a load of genuine booze under bond was coming into the city that night.

Three doors down on Pell Street, he stopped before a low, dilapidated wooden structure. On the window was painted in shaky English letters the legend—Hop Sing, Laundry. As if to make the statement good, a few fly-bespeckled collars and one solitary antiquated dress shirt huddled together in one corner of the window.

Cholly looked once up and down the street; snapped his cigarette butt out into the gutter with a deft flick of his wrist and then gently rapped on the door. It opened on silent, well-oiled hinges for him and closed on his retreating back as swiftly and secretively. Hop Sing's place, at one time in the distant past, might have served as a laundry, but that far off day had been forgotten even by China Cholly.

He passed swiftly through the main store, now heavy with flaky dust and tangled with spider webs. This outer sanctum was presided over by a sallow, pig-tailed Chinaman, who drowsed in a Buddhistic attitude at the door.

Cholly gently pulled aside the heavy curtains hanging at the rear of the room and slipped down a short damp hallway. He pulled up abruptly before a blank wall, while his agile fingers traced an intricate pattern across an inlaid panel. Under his manipulation a concealed door swung inward through which he swiftly disappeared.

No matter how tough a gang of Chinamen may be, they never look it. China Cholly's outfit of killers was as murderous as any that haunted the underworld of New York, but to look at their bland, smiling faces as their Chief entered, one would have suspected them of nothing more vicious than an occasional puff at the pipe.

"Monling, boys," sing-songed Cholly. "How's everything? Hokay?"

"Hokay," they answered in chorus.

China Cholly pulled up a chair, extracted a bag of Bull Durham and proceeded to roll a rice paper cigarette with yellow-stained fingers. He inhaled deeply for a minute. No one spoke, but six pairs of slant eyes followed his every movement. Cholly didn't encourage questions from his men. He ordered, and they obeyed.

"Have all boys here nine o'clock tonight," he jerked out in his sing-song voice. "I have tip-off."

"All light. Boys he be here," answered Soy Low, Cholly's deputy.

"We take booze come in under Government bond," continued Cholly. "You have all boys ready, Soy Low. By God, we make fifty grand tonight, maybe. Nine o'clock I be here. Have boys ready with guns."

"Hokay," replied the stolid Soy Low.

With the assurance that his brief orders would be carried out implicitly, Cholly reverted to his native tongue and gave vent to a long string of Chinese incantation. His followers beamed on him. China Cholly was a "funny fella," and fifty grand would buy many hours of bliss via the poppy route.

It seems that the tip off that both Shanty Hogan and China Cholly thought their own private property, had been broadcast, for still another underworld chief made plans that morning for the capture of the load of good booze coming into the city under bond. "Little Hymie" Zeiss, in his strong-hold back of an abandoned water front warehouse, also went into executive session with his mob of rods.

"Boys," said Little Hymie, "there's money to be picked up tonight. A big piece of change. I got the tip-off straight."

"Yeah?" growled Butch, his right hand man. "I remember the last time you got the office straight. We ran into a load of bulls and federals and damn near got shot all to hell!"

"I remember that too," answered Zeiss, "but this time we'll be ready for 'em if they come. Have the boys loaded down with artillery. If somebody gets funny along the way, blow 'em to hell and don't stop to argue or ask any questions. Read about it in the papers."

"The lay is queer, I tell you," insisted Butch.

"I got a hunch that way myself," agreed Little Hymie.

"Then why step into hell?"

"Because," answered Hymie, "it's time for a show-down. This might be a frame. Maybe this is Shanty Hogan's dirt or maybe the Chink's. Then again it might be somebody else trying to give the works to us. If my info is good and on the up and up—we get the booze. If somebody's put the screws to us, this is the way to find out."

"It's the screws, Hymie, it's the screws," complained Butch.

"Then what's eating you?" barked Little Hymie. "Don't we know what to do with stool pigeon punks? We'll give 'em the works and collect a bounty from Hogan and Cholly."

The bleak March day passed uneventfully. So stilled were the rumblings of the underworld that many knew it for the calm before the storm. The three gangs were busy with preparations for the night. Guns, revolvers, knives and automatics were brought out and oiled and polished; trigger fingers were limbered. A man's life depended that night on how fast and straight he could shoot.

But the underworld was not alone in making preparations. There was a great show of activity in an altogether different quarter of the city that day. Police Headquarters buzzed with more than the usual excitement. Something big was on foot.

The same held true for the Federal Building, a few blocks south on lower Broadway. Closeted in his office with five of his most dependable officers, sat Silas Yelton, the fanatical head of the Prohibition forces for New York. Yelton was mentally gloating over the massacre he was planning for that night. He expected to make a big name for himself, in a big, spectacular way. What matter if half a dozen men or so were lost? Hadn't he been appointed to uphold the sanctity of the Law?

"Men," he began, "I have again received information from that mysterious source that has tipped me off so well in the past."

"Then it's on the level," chortled Yancey, one of his deputies. "That guy who's squealing, who ever it is, is the inside. He's got the right dope. God help him if ever Little Hymie or Shanty Hogan or China Cholly spot him."

"That's not our worry," snapped Yelton. "He's informed me that all three, Hogan, Zeiss and the Chink, are going to make a try at hi-jacking that load of whiskey coming into New York tonight. That's our opportunity. This is the time to make a real clean up. Those outfits have caused us too much trouble all ready. They're a menace to the law.

"We'll let the three gangs converge on the booze truck, kill each other off and then we'll charge down and clean up the rest."

"But good Lord, Yelton, what about the driver of the truck. He'll be killed," complained. Yancey.

"That's not our concern."

"But unless you warn him, it's murder."

"We are only doing our duty; our duty as we see it. And it means promotion for us all."

At the word promotion, Yancey dissented no longer. Not that the promotion in itself meant anything, but the bigger the job, the bigger the graft.

Eight o'clock that night found Shanty Hogan at the bar of his speakeasy on Tenth Street. He was tense, on edge, and because of it he drank. Whiskey straight was Shanty's order.

He always felt that way an hour before setting out on one of his numerous ventures into crime. He wasn't yellow, he didn't have a case of nerves; Shanty was just pleasantly stimulated by the coming danger. It was all a game to him. A live and die existence.

Nothing sweeter than the acrid smell of burnt powder and the growl of gats.

After his third he entered his private back room strong-hold as cool and placid as a lilly on a mill pond. His mob was awaiting his arrival, a gay, carefree buccaneering crew headed by Smiling Jimmie and Groucho.

"Howdy, Boys," greeted Shanty with an inclusive wave of his hand. "All rarin' to go?"

"All set, Shanty," replied Smiling Jimmie. "Just waiting for the word from you."

"Artillery?" questioned the gang chief.

"Plenty," growled Groucho. "And I got a weird hunch we're going to eat smoke before we're tucked into bed again."

"Just so they don't tuck you into a wooden kimono," laughed Smiling Jimmie. "If they send you over the river tonight, buddy, I'll guarantee you plenty of company."

"Well, we've gabbed enough," grinned Shanty. "Let's go! The side door, boys. The cars are parked on Waverly Place. Groucho, you take the second car. Jimmie, you drive the first. I'll step with you."

At his words, Groucho opened a concealed door in the back wall and led the exit into a dark alley that ran the length of the house. The mob, pulling their caps still lower over glinting eyes and taking one last reassuring feel of their hips, followed him out into the night. Smiling Jimmie and Shanty brought up the rear.

Swiftly they piled into the cars and a moment later, with roaring exhausts, careened away from the curb. The staccato bellow of their pounding engines echoed thunderously through the canyoned streets, only to be carried away on the tearing blasts of wind that screamed around the corners of the tall buildings.

Little was said. There was no need for words. What lay before them was action; an argument to be settled with the whine of hot, searing lead and the ominous growl of revolvers.

The two black cars, with lights dimmed and license plates bespattered with mud, headed north and east, making a bee line for the tangled maze of streets that rotated from the hub of the bridge to Long Island at Fifty-ninth Street. The blobs of light from the street lamps flamed by with an ever increasing rhythmic regularity.

As they approached the shabby east-side section where they had decided to way-lay the truck-load of booze, an electric tension gripped the men.

Guns were smoothly pulled from hip holsters and carefully examined for the last time. Safeties were snapped back, and gnarled and grimy fingers crooked around a score of triggers.

If all went well as they had planned it, this was to be a quick raid, with or without blood-shed. They were to drill the driver of the truck if necessary, roll his limp body into the gutter and then make their get-away.

The expedition was dangerous in the extreme, right in the heart of the city, but fifty grand was worth plenty of risk.

There was no question but that Shanty Hogan and his mob expected trouble but little were they aware of the direction from which it would come. Two blocks away from the approach to the bridge, Shanty pulled the cars up to a halt in a dark, blind alley. It was a strategic point—for the booze truck, passing off the bridge, would have to pass within ten feet of his men. They waited; five, ten minutes. Time that seemed ages-long to their expectant nerves. Cigarettes were consumed at a furious rate and men on the ragged edge passed slurring remarks concerning the parentage of their companions. Remarks, which if passed under normal conditions, would have been answered by a flash of six inch steel or a hurtling hunk of lead.

Far down the deserted high-way a faint light twinkled. A moment later the hum and throb of a heavily loaded truck was carried on the chill night breeze to the waiting gangsters in the alley. Shanty made a last inspection of his men.

"Here she comes, boys," he said. "When the truck is abreast of us, let's go, and let the driver have it. Groucho, Jimmie and I are going to make for the wheel. You guys cover us in case he has a guard trailing him. Watch your fire. Don't shoot unless you have to. But when you do burn smoke, make it count!"

The men replied with grunts and low spoken profanity. It wasn't the first time they had hi-jacked a truck load of booze. Bring on that truck! Let 'em have it over with!

The Government man behind the wheel of the heavy, six-ton Mack, was congratulating himself upon an uneventful trip into the city, as he swung off the bridge onto the streets of Manhattan. If he was to have had trouble, it would have been on the dark, unfrequented roads of Long Island.

Here in the city, he had nothing to fear. His thoughts were of his home. His old woman and the kids would be waiting up for him.

In an excess of good spirits, he pursed his lips and piped out the chorus of the latest popular song.

Suddenly a whine past his ear; then a pang and the tinkle of glass. Simultaneously with the last, the man behind the wheel heard the growl of a revolver. Instinctively his foot jammed down on the gas and even as the heavily loaded Mack lurched forward with a roaring exhaust, a fusillade of shots broke out in the night. Spattering lead splintered his wind-shield. Vindictive bullets flattened themselves savagely against his instrument board. The broken tinkle of glass and the gurgle of flowing liquid told where an acid wasp had eaten into his precious cargo.

He crouched low behind his wheel, gave the bus all the sauce she had and drove straight ahead.

Shanty, at the head of his men, led the drive on the truck. He was three yards ahead of his mob, his gat flaming fire as fast as he could pull the trigger. But suddenly he staggered in his reckless charge, lurched forward and only by a tremendous effort of will saved himself from going down. A slug of burning lead ate its way into his shoulder and his automatic clattered to the asphalt from his nerveless fingers.

The shot that had drilled Shanty was evidently a signal, for a split second after it, a fusillade of shots rang out from the opposite side of the alley. The black night was pierced with stabbing flame.

The surprise attack took Hogan's mob completely unawares and at the first burst of raking fire two of his men fell prone into the foul gutter.

Shanty was quick to realize that he had fallen into a trap. The booze truck was speeding by; was even now out of danger. To hell with it now! His men came first! His right arm was paralyzed, dead. A growing pain lived in his breast. Shanty fell back a few feet and rallied his men.

On the other side of the street, Hymie Zeiss was taking full advantage of his surprise maneuver. With guttural profanity he urged his mob on, leading the charge with two barking, sinister guns in his hands. He well knew that it was Shanty Hogan's mob he ran into and now that the warfare had broken out between them—let it be finished. Gun Law would rule and Little Hymie had the most potent gang of killers in the city.

By his sheer guts under fire, Shanty saved his men from utter rout under that first withering burst of lead. He wrenched an automatic from the limp and bloody hand of one of his fallen henchmen and held his first line, insecurely fortified behind a galvanized garbage can.

The night awoke to vivid, hectic life with the ominous rattle and growl of guns. The black alley was punctured with livid stabs of flame from the automatics, and the weird bursts of light etched in a scene of carnage.

But Shanty Hogan and Hymie were not to have it out alone that night. Two minutes after the two rival gangs had taken up positions of vantage on either side of the street, China Cholly's horde of yellow gorillas swept down on the fray. The yellow men went into action with a reckless daring and spattered their foes, both Hogan's men and Zeiss' mob, with a deadly fire that took ghastly toll.

• • •

From then on it was every man for himself! It was hard to distinguish between friend and foe. The evil, dirty street was made heroic with the crash and thunder of glorious combat; the growl and bark of guns; the terrible blasphemous oaths of the fighters and the despairing death cries of the mortally wounded.

For a full ten minutes they carried on a miniature war. Neither side gave way, yielded; neither side gained despite the slaughter. The street became a shambles. Blood ran like water through the fetid gutters. The living stumbled over the dead, cursed them and kicked them out of the way. The three gangs would have fought it out there to the last man but—

Yelton, at the head of a squad of Federals, decided that the carnage had lasted long enough. In three high-powered cars they careened down the street, straight into the heart of the fray. Machine guns thrust their blunt, ominous nozzles from the windows of the cars and splattered a murderous rain of hail into the middle ranks of the gangsters. Friend and foe alike, Chink, Jew and Irish, fell like toy soldiers before that first, treacherous burst of lead. Confusion! Devastation! Pandemonium filled the street. The curses and death rattles of the dying rose on the howling wind above the roar of the guns.

In another few minutes Yelton would have carried out his intention of wiping out the three gangs. At this new, unexpected threat, the three mobs were utterly routed. All of the men were attacked from three sides at once and no one knew which fire to return first.

Half of the men had been mowed down in the first minute of bitter warfare before an answering round of singing death was spewed forth from their guns at the new foe. A foe more to be hated than any rival gang or gangster.

With a sick heart Shanty saw his men wither before the barrage of lead from the Federals. All the acid bitterness in his heart that a few moments before had been directed at Little Hymie and China Cholly, concentrated into one burning lust; a lust to kill Silas Yelton! But what was he to do? Retreat? The longer he held the few remnants of his mob there, the target for three fires, the less chance he would have of fulfilling his vengeance. For the first time in his long career as a gangster, panic seized his heart. Not that he was afraid to die—die with a hunk of lead in his guts. He had long realized that that was the way he would eventually go out. No! Shanty was filled with panic on realizing the terrific carnage amongst his men.

Common sense dictated retreat but never yet had he stooped to such an ignominious course. Then it was, when all seemed lost save honor, that inspiration came to Shanty Hogan. There came a momentary lull in the firing and in the brief silence he raised his voice and bellowed into the night.

"Hymie! Cholly!" he roared with all the power of his leather lungs. "It's

Yelton and the bulls. "Let's forget our battle and clean them out!"

Two answering incoherent bellows assured Shanty that his words had been understood and agreed upon. He breathed a half muttered prayer of relief. Quickly he rallied his men, encouraging them with bitter promises of vengeance. Revolvers and automatics were loaded again for the last time. Bleeding, stricken dying men rose to the last emergency like heroes.

"Now!" rang out Shanty's voice above the chaos and din of battle.

As one man the few remaining survivors of his once indomitable mob swept into the street and headed for Yelton's mob, still firing from the security of their machines. Hymie Zeiss at the head of his gang of gunmen joined them from the opposite side of the street. And on their flank, China Cholly, grinning devilishly, swept forward with his villainous crew of Chinks.

Involuntarily a blood curdling yell of triumph swelled from their lips, as with a united front they swept irresistibly forward. Nothing could stop them. They knew it. And Yelton and his men knew it too. At the sound of that savage, atavistic death cry from the mob of killers, panic and yellow crawling fear filled the heart of the Federals.

They returned an irresolute fire, but the underworld, united for once that night, was invincible.

The front of their ranks presented one continuous flame of fire as they advanced savagely up the street, guns and automatics belching death. When one man fell in the van, there was another from the rear, ready and eager to push up. Chink, Jew and Irishman battled shoulder to shoulder!

Slowly, at first, Yelton began to retreat. Then more swiftly. But ever that raking, deadly, unrelenting fire from the united mobs of the underworld, pressed on. The retreat became a route, a ghastly massacre. Men died, hurling terrible blasphemy on Yelton's head.

Of the forty deputies that he had marshalled to what he believed a killing, less than half returned. Twenty men out of forty and of course Yelton himself. He saw to that!

The complete panicky route of the Federal men brought a temporary lull among the foes of the three gangs. They needed the next few minutes for the bitter task of collecting their dead. With sorrow-laden hearts they went about the gruesome work. They picked up the riddled bodies of their followers and placed them in machines.

In the course of the heart-breaking task, Shanty, Cholly and Little Hymie came together, elbow to elbow.

"Got to thank you, Shanty," growled Little Hymie, "for comin' through against Yelton."

"Same goes here," chimed in China Cholly.

"Forget it, you mugs," snapped Shanty, slightly embarrassed. "This bloke yours?" And with the words he gently rolled over a stiffening corpse in the street.

Little Hymie claimed the dead man. There was a sob in his voice as he spoke.

"Louis, they got you too, did they? Don't worry, old pal, I'll get 'em."

"We better lay off each other tonight," continued Shanty. "Enough hell."

"Yeah," agreed Little Hymie. "We got plenty dead to bury."

"How in hell all this hell start?" queried China Cholly.

"You guys trying to shoulder in on my racket!" growled Shanty.

"Your racket?" snarled Little Hymie. "How ya get that way? Since when you got a monopoly on the booze peddling in this town?"

"Sure, no your racket, Shanty. Me got to live too," put in China Cholly. "No your racket Shanty any more Little Hymie's or mine."

"All right, all right! Forget it!" snapped Shanty. "All the stiffs taken care of?"

They looked around the street which at last had been cleared of its ghastly cargo. With a curt nod and a grunt to each other, the three gang chiefs turned on their heels and returned to their mobs. A minute later the blustery March wind had cleared away the acrid smoke of gun fire.

It was a weary, disillusioned remnant of his gang that Shanty Hogan led back to his retreat on Tenth Street. And it was with a stricken heart that Shanty counted the cost of the ill-fated expedition. And that was not alone in sorrowing his heart. The booze truck, the thing that had cost so much bloodshed, had escaped entirely.

Groucho had been right that morning when he had forewarned him of trouble. He too had suspected it, but the venture had turned out otherwise than he had planned. For the greater part of the time it had been out of his control. Only when the new menace of Yelton's men had crashed down on them had he risen to the situation.

Just what was the low-down on the ill-fated expedition? Was it just a quirk of fate that had brought Little Hymie and China Cholly there on the scene at the same time as himself?

Who had tipped off the Federals that the attack was to be made? There were many questions, bitter and brutal, that Shanty mulled over in his mind that night.

The heavy, rumbling voice of Groucho thrust itself in on his meditations.

"Well, Shanty," he began, "what did I tell you?"

"Don't rub it in," growled Shanty. "Hell! I feel lousy enough now."

"The whole damn lay is queer," put in Smiling Jimmie. "Something damned crooked some place. Jeez, with the three of us fighting it out and

Yelton piling down with the machine guns, I thought it was curtains for all of us. If you hadn't come through then, Shanty, Yelton would be collecting a bonus from the state on all our hides right now."

"Hell!" complained Shanty. "You're trying to let me down easy. I didn't do anything but get you all into a lot of lead and lose half our men."

There was a deep silence between the men for a few minutes. They sucked greedily at their cigarettes, each one preoccupied with the problem of the double-crossing rat in their midst.

"Say, listen Shanty," said Groucho at last. "I hate like hell to mention it but I have to."

"What?"

"Well," began Groucho slowly, feeling for the right words, "there's a leak somewhere. You know that. Has been for some time. This isn't the first little party of ours that's gone wrong. And always there's been the Jew and the Chink to screw up our plans. Now, I put it to you, what do you make of that?"

Shanty had a sneaking idea to what he was referring but for the sake of discipline he wasn't going to let him get away with it.

"What the hell you driving at?" he demanded. "Don't give me none of your riddles. Ain't in the humor for 'em. Speak out! If you have something to say, spill it."

"Now don't get sore, don't get sore," persisted Groucho. "It's this. You've been running around a lot with Sadie. Now I ain't saying that Sadie ain't on the level, but after all she's Little Hymie's sister. You couldn't blame her much if she—"

But Groucho never had a chance to finish his accusation. With a bellow like that of an infuriated bull, Shanty threw himself across the table and entwined his sinewy fingers around the throat of his lieutenant. The weight of his hurtling body crashed Groucho clear out of his chair onto the floor and as he fell, Shanty plunged down upon him. His hands tightened about the throat of his henchman until Groucho's eyes bulged.

Smiling Jimmie dove across the room and flung himself on his chief's back. It took all the strength of his hands to pry his fingers from Groucho's throat.

"Easy, Shanty, easy," he begged. "Now what do you want to do a thing like that for?"

Shamefacedly the Irishman released his lieutenant and then helped him to his feet.

"Sorry Groucho," he apologized. "My nerves are ragged. Forget it."

"Sure," growled Groucho, rubbing his swollen throat. "Sure. No hard feelings. I know how you feel."

"But Groucho is right," put in Smiling Jimmie. "Shanty, you got to look the facts in the face. You been running around with Sadie. Nice skirt and all that. That's okay. But maybe she is squealing to Little Hymie."

The first seeds of suspicion and doubt had been planted in Shanty Hogan's brain. His hands constricted into hard knots. His eyes narrowed and shot fire. His rugged jaw shot dangerously forward.

"By God!" he exclaimed. "If she is, she'll never squeal again."

"Now don't do nothing hasty," counselled Smiling Jimmie. "Maybe she's on the level. Figuring her crooked don't explain China Cholly. We have to go at this thing slow. We can't make any mistakes."

"We can't make any mistakes, all right," agreed Shanty, "but we can't go slow."

Shanty Hogan was not the only one who spent an anxious questioning time that night. Hymie Zeiss, too, put many unanswerable questions to himself as he stamped the length of his headquarters after the disastrous fiasco with the booze truck.

He did not know whom to curse first for the misadventure that had cut down so many of his best men.

Of course, there was Shanty Hogan, but then Shanty, by rallying the three gangs, had saved them all from destruction. And China Cholly had been there, too! There was no getting to the bottom of the thing. There had been a leak; a double cross—that alone was clear. Little Hymie concentrated all his mental powers on finding the rat.

For a half hour his yellow crooked teeth masticated the mangled end of a cigar. Then a cruel streak of suspicion entered his brain. His hairy nostrils dilated and his brown eyes narrowed down to dangerous pin points.

"Matz!" he bellowed to the outer room of his hangout.

The imperious summons was answered by a hatchet-faced, blue-bearded individual.

"Go out and get Sadie," snapped Little Hymie. "I want to see her at once. Here!"

Matz grunted his understanding and shuffled out of the room. Little Hymie continued his impatient pacing of the room. It was the bitterest blow of all to be compelled to doubt his sister, but he could see no other possible leak.

Ten minutes later Sadie entered. Little Hymie eyed her shrewdly in silence. Sadie was none abashed by his scowling glare and answered him eye for eye. She flippantly swished her abbreviated skirt aside and perched jauntily on the corner of the table, revealing a tantalizing length of silk clad calf. Her body was lithe and slender but plump enough to the touch.

"Sadie," began Little Hymie, "I got to speak to you."

"Shoot kid," replied Sadie. "I'm here. What's eating you?"

"Plenty, kid. I got a good idea to croak you!"

Sadie's slender leg was suddenly stilled. Her pretty, full mouth sagged open a moment in utter surprise.

"You're going to do what, Hymie?" she asked.

"Nothing!" he replied curtly. "Listen, you little tart. There's been a leak out of my place. Info is getting to Shanty Hogan. Somebody is squealing!"

"Why you dirty, low down crumb!" flared out Sadie. "Are you insinuating that I'm spilling any dirt to Shanty?"

"How does he get the dirt on every move I make?" insisted Shanty.

Sadie jumped off the table and like a flaming Amazon charged across the room at her brother. Her small, sleek head jutted out until it was within a foot of the gangster's distorted features.

"How the hell do I know how it leaked? But I'm not that kind of a rat— see? And anyway if I was, do you think Shanty would listen to me?"

Little Hymie by now was pretty convinced that Sadie was on the level but he could not back out of his accusation just then. He shifted his attack.

"You think that dumb Irishman is a pretty wise guy, don't you?" he scorned. "You know I've told you a hundred times to quit running around with him. Now I got enough. You got to make a choice. Either you quit Shanty Hogan or you quit me. Which is it?"

Sadie backed away a few feet from Little Hymie and surveyed him contemptuously with searing eyes.

"Well, if you want me to choose, I will. I'll take Shanty. You can go to hell!"

That was only the beginning of Sadie's "say" to her brother but he cut her taunting hot words short by slapping her viciously across the mouth with his open palm. This parting love token presented, the gang chief turned on his heels and stamped out of the room.

At one of the beer tables in the dark shadows of Silent Joe's place on Christopher Street a little celebration was on foot that night. A celebration of three; a Jew, a Chink and an Irish Harp. Hogan, Zeiss and China Cholly would have been mighty interested to have heard the words that passed between the men. Lots of things and incidents that were puzzling and mysterious would have been readily cleared up. And there would have been three more stark figures on the cold marble slabs in the morgue.

The three men were jubilant. They toasted each other's health many times in raw, stimulating whiskey and toasted the ultimate success of some secret venture among them. Tonight they had struck, craftily, wearily and it would not be many weeks more, they assured each other, until they would have in their hands alone the disposition of all the underworld rackets.

Things had gone even better than they had anticipated. As a result of their cunning and craft, the three rival gangs were on the point of entering a war of extermination. That was just what they wanted. Let Jew wipe out Chinaman, and Chink clean up Irish, and the Harps pulverize the Semites. Then these unholy double-crossing treacherous rats would step in and take command.

Sadie's loyal heart was filled with an all consuming rage after her scene with Little Hymie. That she of all people should be accused of being a rat! A double-crossing rat, squealing on her brother!

In the heat of the moment, as she stormed out of Little Hymie's headquarters, she planned and vowed a thousand fantastic vengeances. She would show Hymie, if he insisted on thinking her crooked, just how crooked she could be. The thing that hurt most of all was the implied reflection on her lover. Little Hymie had said what he had just because she was running around with Shanty. And she knew that Shanty Hogan would be the last person in the world to take double-crossing info from her.

But Hymie was right. Information was leaking somewhere. The thought sobered Sadie's flaming anger against her brother. She spent a bitter half hour in trying to locate the leak. Who was the rat? That he existed she felt sure. The only way she had of vindicating herself in Little Hymie's eyes, was to show him the real punk in the outfit. The more she mulled over the proposition, the more surely she came to the one conclusion. She would put the matter up to Shanty himself.

Late into the night, Shanty, Groucho and Smiling Jimmie brooded over a bottle. The room was heavy and bitter with the acrid smoke of many cigarettes. Their words were few and monosyllabic.

Then came a discreet rap at the door. At first they ignored it. The knock was repeated, this time more insistent. Shanty raised his bloodshot eyes from the table and turned his shaggy head toward the door.

"Well, what is it?" he snarled.

At his voice, the oaken panel slid open and the head of one of his henchmen thrust into the room.

"Sadie's outside," he said. "Wants to see you bad. Right away."

The men stiffened in their chairs. Smiling Jimmie and Groucho silently eyed their leader, wondering how he would meet the situation. A thousand doubts assailed Shanty. A thousand fears, loves, hates and lusts. Could it be that the girl he loved was playing him dirt; was playing him for a sucker?

His love and desire struggled with his hate. Should he see her? He was about to send out word for her to go to hell when a sudden thought stayed him. Just what was so important that Sadie had to see him at that hour of the night? Had little Hymie sent her to him to get his new plans of campaign?

"Send her in, Scraggy," he said at last. And his voice was cold, ominous, deadly.

Sadie swept confidently into the room, the swish of her skirts revealing her insinuating hips. Straight up to Shanty she marched, her hands reaching out for him.

Then she staggered back, for even before she could touch him, he sent her reeling across the room with a powerful right arm.

She recovered herself swiftly and was immediately on the defensive. She was not quite sure how to take this new attitude on the part of her lover.

"Say, you bum," she began, "is that your idea of a love tap. It don't fit in with mine."

"Love tap, hell!" answered Shanty. "It ain't. That mushy stuff is over between us, girl. What do you want here?"

Sadie was taken completely aback at this line of talk.

"Shanty—" she began pleadingly.

"Can it! Can it!" he growled. "That boloney don't go any more, see. You made a sucker out o' me long enough. What kind of a sap do you think I am. Dumb? By God, if I was only positive you're the one that's been double crossing me, I'd choke that neck of yours till your tongue dropped out."

At this new attack on her honor, Sadie was indeed stricken.

"You too, eh, Shanty?" she said sadly. "A hell of a lot you guys know about women. Hell. All men are lice, anyway." Then her pride and anger got the better of her.

"You're just as dumb as that dope brother of mine. First he kicks me out with a clout on the jaw for squealing to you and now you give me the works for squealing to him. It's a laugh, eh? A great big laugh! You're a lot of wise guys! Wise, hell! You're all hams, palookas. If I wanted to rat on you, don't you think I could have done it long ago. Put you on the spot dead? And the same goes for that flat-nosed Jew brother of mine. Men are all lice."

"Easy what you say," began Shanty threateningly, but Sadie's flow of angry words could not be stopped.

"To hell with you dumb mugs," she flung out and her lashing tongue stung the three men to silence. "Of course there's a leak somewhere—a blind man could see that. But I'm not the stool—see? Not for you, Shanty Hogan or for Little Hymie Zeiss. But I guess the only way I can make you believe that is to get the dirty rat myself. You guys are too dumb. All you do is sit on your cans and talk, talk, talk. Lice! All of you."

"Listen here, Sadie . . ."

"Aw, go to hell!" she flung back.

And with this defiance on her lips she stamped out of the room, complete master of the situation.

"Now I wonder," muttered Shanty, when the door had closed behind her. "I wonder. Sadie was a pretty swell kid."

Sadie didn't get to bed until five o'clock that morning. Tired as she was, aching in every limb, she did not sleep. Restlessly she tossed from side to side, thinking, thinking. There was some tiny germ of inspiration fermenting in the back of her mind. In vain she tried to bring it to light.

She began by marshalling all the facts of the three gangs before her. Then something very startling struck her.

Her brother, Little Hymie, thought that somebody was squealing to Shanty Hogan and the latter thought the same thing in reverse. And to make the situation still more complicated, China Cholly also got inside information on both the rival gangs.

What did that mean in the final analysis? Simply, there must be more than one squealer! Then inspiration!

The most obvious thing was that there were three rats, one in each gang. That would easily account for the double, double-cross. What their object could be she had not the slightest idea, but the more she considered the matter, the more surely she felt that she was right.

She knew that she would get no consideration from Little Hymie and pride forbade her from going to Shanty with her theory. Only one resource remained open for her. She would see China Cholly and put the matter up to the shrewd and wily Chink.

With this resolution in her mind and a faint smile of triumph on her lips, she at last found a deep and untroubled sleep.

With all the oily, subtle grace of his race, China Cholly extended the hospitality of his house to Sadie when she called on him the following afternoon. At a clap of his hands, tea and rice cakes were served to them by a mute Oriental who bowed deferentially to the white woman.

When they were alone China Cholly smiled enigmatically but said nothing. He waited for his visitor to begin. Sadie swallowed the last of her tea at a gulp and dove into the heart of the matter.

"Cholly," she began, "there's queer things going on."

"Velly queer, Sadie," agreed Cholly with a smile.

"Queerer things than you know, Cholly," continued Sadie. "Something's got to be done about it."

In a few brief words she told him of her break with her brother and Shanty, and of their suspicions. Cholly listened attentively to all she had to say, but offered no word in reply. Mentally he was analyzing her words; silently he was analyzing the girl before him. China Cholly put his keen subtle perceptions to work on the problem of whether Sadie's visit was on the level or merely one angle of some cunning plot to trap him.

Sadie went on, unaware of Cholly's thoughts and suspicions. But the more she talked the more she convinced the Chinaman of her sincerity.

"And what you want from me, Sadie?" he asked at last.

"Listen, Cholly," she replied. "Listen well. This is what I've figured out and I want you to help me. For your life and all your mob is at stake as well as Little Hymie's and Shanty Hogan's life."

"Go on. I listen. I am all ears," Cholly assured her.

"I figure it out that there are three rats," said Sadie. "One in each mob. Get me? One in your mob, one in Hymie's and one in Shanty's. They're playing a crooked game together. Why, I don't know. But their game is to make trouble, see? Trouble between the three outfits. One spills the dirt on the other. Maybe what they're trying to do is to have you and Shanty and Little Hymie kill each other off and then take over the works. I don't know. Maybe. But it's clear as hell they're working against the gangs."

A slow spreading smile of comprehension spread across Cholly's face. He nodded approval.

"Now, I can't get Hymie or Shanty to play with me," continued Sadie, "so I've come to you. Just give me the tip-off, a name, that's all I ask. You say nothing, Cholly. You know nothing and I know nothing. Okay?"

"Hokay," smiled China Cholly. "You velly smart girl, Sadie. Maybe you better watch Solly Gold. He velly funny man."

Sadie had gotten the office! So Solly Gold would be worth watching, eh? She was so impatient to be on the job that she utterly ignored all of Cholly's courtesies and rose abruptly. With a light hand on her arm the Chinaman escorted her to the door.

"You let me know what you find out, eh, Sadie?" he said. "I work with you on this."

"Okay, Cholly, thanks."

"Hokay," he sing-songed back to her.

Sadie wasn't slow to follow the tip given her by China Cholly. For two days she literally lived on the trail of Solly Gold. He led her a merry chase from bar to speakeasy to gambling dump but not one suspicious thing did she see. She even pondered the revolting project of playing up to Solly Gold. A girl of Sadie's calibre had lots of ways of making a sucker out of a guy. She vetoed the proposition, temporarily, however, deciding to save that line of attack for a last desperate endeavor.

By the end of the third day she was at her wits' end. She even began to doubt China Cholly's word. The situation, as far as she was concerned, demanded immediate action.

It was then she thought of Silent Joe's place. Mentally she cursed herself fluently for not having thought of it before. She killed the early evening until eleven o'clock over a greasy pack of cards, dealing out endless games of solitaire. When at last she "beat the Chink" she took it as a good omen, slipped into a silk-lined leather jacket, jammed a white beret over one saucy ear and sallied forth.

She hailed a passing cab and gave the driver the Christopher Street address. Twenty minutes later she called him to a halt a block away from Silent Joe's dump. She jammed her slim form close against the dark shadows that masked the dreary buildings that lined the shabby street and slowly began her approach on the dive.

Suddenly she flattened herself in a dark doorway as a car raced down the street and pulled up with screaming brakes before Joe's place. Sadie was all alert. Her nerves tensed and her sharp eyes pierced the gloom ahead.

A man jumped out of the machine and sped speedily across the sidewalk to the basement entrance of Silent Joe's. As the door opened for him she caught a fleeting glimpse of his silhouette in the doorway. She was not positive, but the man greatly resembled the squat, ugly Solly Gold.

Sadie was about to venture forth again when a second car pulled up to the curb ahead of her. She lost herself in the shadows again. This time she was sure the new arrival was a Chink.

Well, that accounted for two of the members of the conspiracy she had mentally pictured. She decided to wait to see if a third rat arrived, and she was not disappointed. Five minutes later a third car pulled up to Silent Joe's dump and a third man stealthily entered the place.

Sadie considered her position. What was she to do? Follow the traitors in or pass on the word to Little Hymie and Shanty?

"To hell with those mugs," she muttered to herself. "I'll run this thing to the ground myself. Anyway, I don't know anything definite yet."

With her hands in her pockets she boldly swaggered on down the street past the hangout. A few feet beyond was a dark, narrow alley. On a hunch, Sadie dodged down it and carefully felt her way along by the wall of the house. A thin beam of light at the rear, shining out into the murky night, caught her attention. Swiftly she approached it and with a beating heart saw that it came from a window that gave onto Silent Joe's dump.

Dropping on one knee she pressed her eye to one corner of the dirty glass and peered in. Directly opposite her at a corner table, sat three men. Her spirits soared and she could have sung for joy for her judgment had been vindicated. One of the three men was Solly Gold, another a Chink whom she recognized as a member of China Cholly's mob. And the third was Lefty Dugan, a tin-horn rod belonging to Shanty's outfit.

Sadie's elation suddenly changed to bitter fury. These were the three gorillas responsible for all the trouble and bad blood among the three gangs!

These were the three mugs responsible for her break with Little Hymie and Shanty. Her fingers itched and constricted around the butt of the .32 automatic in her pocket.

• • •

First she had to hear what they were saying. She waited a moment until a boisterous gust of wind rattled the window, then she gently pried it up an inch. To the opening she pressed her ear. Voices came to her, faint and indistinct but she caught a word here and there and her inflamed imagination filled in the gaps. She had been right. Shanty had to listen in on that conversation!

She slipped out of the dark alley again and sped down the street. On the corner was a dingy, greasy all-night Coffee Pot. Sadie darted inside and locked herself in the telephone booth. Not having a nickel in her purse, she dropped a quarter into the slot and breathed a number into the mouth piece. A breathless pause and then a brusque voice answered at the other end.

"Hello. What you want?"

"Listen, guy," said Sadie. "This is Sadie Zeiss. Put Shanty on."

"He ain't here!" came back the voice.

"Listen, bozo," snarled Sadie. "Don't hand me that line of manure. I know he's there. Tell him it's Sadie and I got to speak to him."

"All right. Wait a minute. I'll see if I can get him."

A moment later Shanty's irritated voice growled over the wire. Sadie cut his sarcastic profanity short with her hurried words.

"Listen, Shanty, I'm in the Coffee Pot on Christopher Street a block away from Silent Joe's. There's a little session going on down there that you got to listen in on. One of your men is there, one of Little Hymie's and one of the Chink's. If you want the low down on the double crossing business, now's the time to get it."

"Say," began Shanty with deep irony. "You think I'm dumb? What's this—a frame? You little bitch, you trying to put me on the spot?"

"Aw, for Gawd's sake, Shanty, don't be like that," pleaded Sadie. "What kind of a bum do you think I am, anyway? I wouldn't pull any dirt like that on you, and you know it. I'm giving this to you straight because you wouldn't believe me if I told you. You got to hear yourself."

"Where'd you say? Silent Joe's?" questioned Shanty.

"Yeah. Make it snappy. There's an alley running south of the dump. Go down there and you'll find me by a window looking in."

"Okay, kid, I'll be there, but if you—"

"Hell, no! Please Shanty, don't be like that!"

After he had agreed to keep the rendezvous with Sadie, Shanty was half sorry for his decision. The thing looked suspiciously like a trap, but still, deep down in his heart, he felt sure that Sadie would not put him on the spot. In view of the suspicions of Groucho and Smiling Jimmie, he did not tell them where he was to meet the girl.

"Where to?" asked Smiling Jimmie, as he retrieved his hat and slouched toward the door.

"Going to see Sadie," answered Shanty defiantly. "Any objections?"

"None here," answered Smiling Jimmie. "But just as a precaution, better see that the gat is loaded."

"Don't worry about me," answered Shanty. "I can take care of myself with that moll without a gun."

"Where you meeting her, just in case you don't?" shot out Groucho.

"None of your damn business," growled Shanty and with the words he slammed the door behind him.

After putting in her phone call to Shanty, Sadie beat it back to the black alley and her spy-hole by the window. Again she pressed her ear to the inch opening and listened. The three traitors were still speaking of their plans for disrupting their respective gangs. Their words came to her too indistinctly for her eager ears. She gambled on opening the window another inch and, swiftly following the attempt, came disaster.

The noise of the sash raising in the frame attracted Solly Gold's attention. His head shot up and he glanced swiftly across the room. Sadie had been quick but not quick enough. The eyes of the other men at the table followed the direction of Gold's gaze, just in time to see a disappearing head. Instantly the men were on their feet, guns drawn. Gold took swift charge of the situation.

"You stay Lefty," he barked. "If he shows himself again, plug him. The same if he tries to get in the window. Come on, Chink. We'll head him off down the alley."

Without waiting for more the two men barged out of the room onto the street. They charged down the sidewalk and at top speed turned the corner into the alley. There was a sickening collision as they hurtled pell-mell into Sadie facing down from the opposite direction. The shock of their contact threw them apart for a moment, stunned, and Sadie's automatic was wrenched from her hand to go sailing off into the night in a wide parabola.

In an instant Gold had recovered and was on her. He threw one rough arm around her head in a hammer lock, at the same time clapping his foul hand over her mouth. Sadie struggled violently, viciously, with tooth, nail and hoof, but to no avail.

The Chink came to Gold's aid and between the two of them they managed to drag the twisting, squirming, struggling girl out of the alley onto the sidewalk.

Sadie knew their intention with her. If they once got her away from that place in a car—it was curtains. She fought like a mad woman with all the desperate abandon of an Amazon. But their combined weight was too much against her. Struggle as she might in their grip they slowly bore her to the curb and a waiting machine. Lefty came out to join them. He cursed bitterly at the sounds of struggle. Doubling up his fist, he pulled back and crashed a stiff-armed right flush to Sadie's jaw. She went limp with a little panting sigh, and then was still.

Like a heavy sack of wet wash they threw her into the machine.

At the height of the struggle before Joe's place, Shanty in his roadster turned into Christopher Street. He saw the swaying forms on the sidewalk and his first impulse was to charge down and investigate. Then his old gang sense asserted itself. That was an old gag—the street corner fight. The chances were that if he barged in on it, he would receive a load of lead poisoning for his trouble.

He slowed down and approached cautiously. Dimly he made out the swaying figures of three men and a girl—and that girl was Sadie. His heart constricted. Trap or no trap, he was going to investigate. With one movement he jammed his foot on the gas and whipped out his blue steel Smith and Wesson .38 special. But even as his car gained momentum he saw that he was too late. He saw with an agonized heart the slugging blow that felled Sadie; saw her tossed like a limp rag into the waiting machine; saw the three men pile in after her and roar away.

Shanty's gun growled once and he took up the chase. A fusillade of shots answered him from the speeding car ahead. Then the two drivers, Shanty and Solly Gold, got down to the fine points of piloting careening machines at sixty miles per hour through the narrow back alleys of New York.

They saved their lead for more sure shots, or until it was a question of fighting it out with death. Now that the other car was trying to escape, Shanty was convinced that the fight on the street was on the up-and-up and that Sadie had been on the level with him concerning the tip off.

A great sigh of relief welled to his lips. Sadie, what a damn swell kid she was! He had known all along that she wouldn't play him dirt. And now she was being taken for a ride, for his sake; because he had tried to thrust onto her shoulders the responsibility for all his dumb mistakes. Well, he would make it up to her!

He nursed his throttle and spark and coaxed a few more revolutions out of his already straining engine. But ever the car ahead crept away from him. Corners were taken on two wheels with a skidding rush and a tear. Early morning milk-wagons were somehow miraculously missed. L pillars were skimmed by inches.

Shanty cursed bitterly, futilely. The car ahead was out-distancing him; was now a full block away. His bus was traveling with all the sauce she had. The needle on the speedometer trembled around the seventy mark but no matter how he nursed the gas, he could not get it above that mark.

Suddenly the car ahead took the next corner on two wheels and disappeared. Ten seconds later Shanty made the same turn. A burst of lead greeted his skidding advent and spattered with a spray of flying glass through his wind shield. The escaping machine had tricked him and instead of continuing the flight had pulled up to the curb to finish him off as he passed.

A stabbing, searing pain ate into Shanty's breast. The car swerved crazily and it was only by a tremendous effort of will that he straightened it out and saved it from tangling disastrously around a lamp-post. His eyes became blood filmed. Shanty knew he was going out. Instinctively, before utter blackness fell over him, he shut off his gas and threw his gear shift into neutral.

A half hour later Shanty slowly climbed back to consciousness out of a deep well of blackness. His head throbbed abominably and a searing pain shot through his breast. He tried to sit up and found it impossible. He closed his eyes again and slowly strength ebbed back into his racked body. A moment later he stirred again to discover that he was bound, hand and foot. His mind was blank and empty. His brow wrinkled as he concentrated his hazy brain on the events of the evening. Then slowly it came back to him. The phone call from Sadie; the fight on the street; the chase and the trap.

Then a low, strange, unfamiliar sound attracted his attention. Shanty recognized it at last as the sound of weeping. A girl was crying softly by his side. He stirred.

"Shanty! Shanty! Tell me they didn't get you. Tell me you'll pull through," pleaded Sadie's tearful voice.

With a great effort Shanty slowly moved his lips and spoke.

"Sure, kid, I'll pull through," he muttered weakly.

The crying ceased. Sadie snuggled her young warm body up to the stricken gang chief.

"I'm sorry, Shanty, sorry I got you into this," she whispered. "But anyway, it'll show you I didn't rat on you."

"I never really thought you did," answered Shanty. "It's okay, kid, we'll pull out of this."

Their whispered conversation was abruptly cut short by the opening of a door. Solly Gold entered, holding a lamp before him, followed by Lefty and the Chink. The three traitors stood above the prostrate figures and gloated. To show his contempt, Lefty savagely kicked Shanty in the ribs with a heavy boot.

"So you've come to, have you?" he growled.

"Yes, I'm okay, you rat," answered Shanty. "What the hell's the big idea?"

"You'll find out soon enough," answered Gold. "Your days as a tough guy are over, Hogan."

"Let me up out of here, and I'll damn soon show you different."

"The only way you'll go out of this room is in a wooden box," laughed Gold. "Now just keep your mouth shut and nobody'll step in it. We got you where we want you. The next guy we're after is Little Hymie."

"Hymie is too slick a guy for you to get the way you got me," scorned Shanty.

"Well, if he's slick, we got a slick trick he'll fall for."

Without more ado, he bent down, grabbed the hem of Sadie's skirt and yanked. The flimsy material was rent in two, revealing a dainty array of silken underthings. The three mugs guffawed uproariously at Sadie's futile efforts to conceal her shapely limbs.

"Never mind that stuff, Sadie," laughed Lefty. "It all won't matter in a little while."

"What are you going to do with that skirt?" she demanded.

"Send it to Little Hymie. Even if he is on the outs with you, that Jew brother of yours will come looking for you hot foot if he thinks you're in trouble."

"So you're the three punks who've been playing the double-crossing act?" snarled Shanty.

"Punks, hell!" laughed Gold. "We got brains. After tonight we'll have the three gangs and all the gravy."

"Don't bank too much on that," warned Shanty. "The night ain't over and I ain't croaked yet. You might get a nice quiet funeral instead."

Ten o'clock next night found Little Hymie snozzling beer with his henchmen in his headquarters, back of the water front warehouse. A game of poker was suggested and in a few minutes the men were busily engaged in cheating each other out of huge sums of money which they in turn had fleeced from some one else.

A half hour after the game had been in progress, there came an interruption. The guard at the door ushered into the inner sanctum a little gutter-snipe with sniveling nose.

"There he is, kid," said the guard pointing out Little Hymie.

The street brat approached Zeiss with awe in his eye.

"Say, mister, are you the guy they call Little Hymie?"

"Yep, that's me, son. What are you doin' here?"

"A broad give me this to give you," said the urchin and with the words he reached inside his greasy blouse and extracted the tattered remnant of Sadie's skirt.

Little Hymie took it from him and turned it slowly over in his hand a moment before he recognized it. Then he flushed and if his swarthy complexion would have permitted it, he would have paled a moment later. His arm shot out and grabbed the urchin with a vise-like grip.

"Where'd you get this, kid?" he demanded.

"Don't hurt me, mister. I'll tell you."

"Well?"

"A lady give it to me. Shoved it out of a crack in a window. Told me to give it to you and to take you there. Said you'd give me a saw-buck, mister!"

"Anything you want, kid, if you can take me there."

"Sure. Come on. But do I get the ten spot?"

Little Hymie crushed a crisp bill into his hand, considerably larger than the requested saw-buck. Then, literally picking the boy from the floor, he strode towards the door.

"Need any help?" flung out Butch after him.

"No. I'll handle this alone," answered Little Hymie.

The brat led Little Hymie down many dark alleys and around many twisting corners. So sure was the gang chief that Sadie was in trouble, that he never once thought that he was being put on the spot. At last the urchin stopped before a dreary, three story red brick building on Mulberry Street. The place had every appearance of desertion and decay.

"That's the place, mister," said the boy, pointing with his finger.

"All right, kid. Thanks. Now beat it!" growled Little Hymie.

The youngster took him at his word, turned and scampered down the street, clutching the fifty dollar bill tightly in his fist.

Hymie eased the gun in his hip pocket and stealthily mounted the steps to the front door of the house. Slowly his hand went out to the knob. He tried it and to his surprise it turned. Gently he eased the door open a foot and then squeezed his massive bulk through the opening. Then as carefully, he closed the door behind him.

A faint rustling came from the dark shadows in his rear. Little Hymie spun around with lightning precision, but just too late. He felt the breeze fan his face before the blow struck. Then something murderously heavy sloughed down on his skull. He threw his hands up instinctively but the blow crushed home. He was conscious of a blazing flash of heliotrope made jagged with vivid streaks of red. The smoky taste of sulphur was in his mouth. Then utter blackness.

Little Hymie's knees sagged. Unconscious, out on his feet, he staggered forward for two steps, then crashed headlong to the floor. Where he lay, a thick pool of blood collected around his head.

The three traitors to the gangs found China Cholly not so easy to deal with. One ruse after another failed to entrap him and as a last resort the rats had to carry out a daring piece of kidnapping right off the crowded pavements of the Bowery. True, they got China Cholly in an off moment and before he had a chance to make a draw, two blunt nosed automatics were grinding away at his guts.

It would have been asking for death then and there, to have refused the invitation to go for a ride. Silently China Cholly obeyed. He stepped into the car and crushed himself on the seat beside Lefty, closely followed by Solly Gold. The Chink took the wheel of the machine and frisked them away to the sinister house on Mulberry Street.

When the thick skull of Little Hymie finally threw off the stunning effects of the blow he had received, he came to, to find himself amongst friends, as it were. At least, he had a very intimate knowledge of all those present in the room. Propped up against the wall on either side of him were his two underworld rivals, Shanty Hogan and China Cholly, and a little further on he saw with relief his sister, Sadie.

Facing them, leering, triumphant, sneering, were the three rats, automatics held suggestively in their hands. Little Hymie took in the motley gathering with a wry smile. Then he bravely essayed a grin.

"Jeez," he said, "I've been trying to get together with you mugs for a long time. And I'll be damned if I didn't have to be shanghaied to do it."

"And before the night's over you'll be dead!" croaked Solly Gold.

"Well," answered Little Hymie, "worse things than that have happened. But I ain't dead yet, see. I ain't dead till you plug me in the heart with a load of lead. And you, you crawling scum, you ain't got the guts."

"I ain't, ain't I?" flared out Gold. "Well, God damn you, I'll show you."

He raised his automatic, drew bead and would have fired point blank if Lefty hadn't knocked his gun down.

"Cut it out, you sap!" he growled. "We don't want to croak 'em yet. They all got nice little bank balances we can collect in the morning. No use lettin' it go to the state."

"So," continued Little Hymie tauntingly, "you're the yellow, crawling vermin that's been doing all the double crossing around these parts. Faugh!" With the words, he spat viciously at the three men standing over him.

Solly Gold suddenly flicked his wrist and brought the barrel of his gun in a tearing slash across Little Hymie's face. The gangster took it without moving, without a mutter. His silence above the tap-tap of his blood dropping to the floor, was more deadly than a thousand words.

A long pause. Then:

"I'm telling you now, Solly Gold, you better plug me! If you don't, I'll tear out your heart!"

"Horse collar!" snarled Gold.

Then Little Hymie turned to the other captives.

"Fellas, I'm sorry for gettin' you wrong. I apologize."

Lefty had heard enough. He swaggered across the floor to the prostrate

Jew and spat into his face.

"Well, Hymie," he began after this insult, "now that you've made your little speech, I'm going to give you the low down. Seeing what we intend to do with all of you, it's only fair. We're going out and start your three gangs off on the war path. When they've about cleaned each other out, then, we'll step in, take over the works and consolidate. See? The Chink, Solly and me are going to be the big works. Get me? We're going to run the underworld. We're going to run the rackets. We're going to get the gravy."

"And what about us, you double crossing, yellow livered pimps?" sneered Little Hymie. "You think we'll lay down and take it?"

"You'll have to, Hymie. You'll lay down and take it in a coffin. You'll be dead, see? Come on boys, let's go!"

With evil, triumphant smiles on their lips, the three rats inspected once again the bonds on their prisoners and then left the room. A moment later the outer door was heard to close behind them.

No sooner were they alone in the house than there was a concerted move on the part of the four prisoners to free themselves from their bonds. But they were well and cunningly tied. They squirmed and twisted and turned but their bonds held. In vain one tried to free another. The air was livid with profanity as they struggled with the ropes that bound them but what they needed then, rather than sharp tongues, were sharp knives.

But at all costs they must succeed in freeing themselves. If not, it was very possible that the three rats would succeed in carrying out their threat of annihilation. They feared, not alone for themselves, but for their men, who even at that moment were being led into useless slaughter.

When the three rats left the house and their prisoners on Mulberry Street, they immediately separated, each going off in a different direction. Lefty made tracks for Shanty's headquarters on Tenth Street; Solly Gold made for Little Hymie's warehouse on the west side; and the Chink soon lost himself in the tangled streets of Chinatown.

A half hour later the three traitors had the three mobs worked up to the murder point. Men saw red and at the same time their chance of vengeance; a vengeance they had been seeking for months now. Brisk sharp orders were given and executed even before the words died out.

To the usual assortment of sawed off shot guns, revolvers and automatics, blunt, savage sub-machine guns were added and China Cholly's tong pulled off the racks their heaviest hatchets. This was to be a war of extermination. Within minutes of each other the three mobs left their respective headquarters and piled eagerly into their waiting cars. The advance was begun. All speed laws were broken that night, as the machines loaded with death and destruction, hurtled through the night streets of the city toward one another.

. . .

A half hour later, the prisoners on Mulberry Street were desperate. Despite their most strenuous efforts to free themselves, they were in exactly the same position as when their captors left them.

It was then, when all else had failed them, that Shanty Hogan had inspiration; inspiration of a very desperate sort, it is true.

"Listen you guys," he said, "I got an idea if you want to gamble on it."

"Shoot," said Little Hymie, "we can't be any worse off than we are now."

"Those wise guys left the lamp here," continued Shanty. "There's oil in it. We can set the damn joint on fire and let the fire department yank us out—if they get here in time."

For a moment they considered the proposition. Sadie was the first to break the silence.

"My vote goes in yes," she said.

"Me, too," assented China Cholly.

"We'll gamble the roll," put in Little Hymie.

"Good!" grunted Shanty. "Now you guys and Sadie back into the other room. That'll give us a few minutes leeway, anyway."

They rolled, hobbled and lurched across the uneven floor and passed into the next room. Shanty was left alone. The oil lamp, burning brightly, was perched on a box in the center of the room. He scanned the dark corners of the place for a last time, judged the distance back of him to the door and then fell heavily into the box.

The lamp went down with a crash and a trail of flaming oil darted across the dusty floor. The old and moldy wood took fire at once. In a moment the spongy walls took flame. Shanty waited to see no more. He rolled himself across the floor, away from the fire, towards the door, squeezed through and slammed it shut behind him.

Breathlessly the captives waited behind the slender barrier. Had they made a mistake? Had they been foolhardy? Was their end to be the fearful one of dread by fire? A thin wisp of smoke curled under the door jamb; then a flickering light lapped through.

A moment later they heard the ominous roar and crackle of flames in the next room. The air became uncomfortably warm, then stifling hot as the acrid smoke still continued to seep in to them. Sweat poured off them in streams. They gasped for air. They choked and their lungs were a living hell.

The roar of the consuming flames sounded like an orchestra of hell. The heat became terrific and the door that sheltered them from the raging inferno inside warped and bent. Well, anyway, they were going out in a blaze of glory.

Then above the seething hiss of the flames a shout sounded in the street outside. The alarm was given!

The four prisoners suffered all the agonies of hell for what seemed an eternity before the air was pierced by the screaming wail of a siren and the clang of engines. They willed to live through that bath of flame.

The clang and roar of heavy trucks and the swelling throaty cry of the gathering crowd in the street filled the room. A moment later dark forms appeared at the window. The panes of glass were shattered and three helmeted firemen clambered over the sill. At first they thought the prisoners there quite dead but a string of hurried orders and instructions from Shanty convinced them otherwise. In a thrice their bonds were cut and they were carried to the waiting ladders.

The fresh clean air revived them. Greedily they sucked it in in hungry mouthfuls and by the time they had reached the ground they were ready to carry on.

Four streams of water were now playing on the blazing structure. The street was a bedlam of noise, cries and pounding engines. Under cover of the confusion, Shanty herded his three companions together and streaked them outside the police ring.

The red painted body of a police car caught his eye.

"This way, this way!" he urged and elbowed his way to the curb. "Jump in, you guys. This is our best bet!"

Hymie, Cholly and Sadie were quick to obey and before the sweating policemen knew what had happened, the commandeered car was careening down the street in high. Shanty gripped the wheel in two strong hands while Little Hymie ground the siren to a high moaning wail.

Traffic officers cleared the streets for them for blocks ahead. Like a red juggernaut of doom the gangsters sped through the streets, their course of destruction speeded on by the hand of the Law. Sadie alone appreciated the humor of the situation and could not resist the temptation to thumb her nose at each flatfoot they passed.

The three rats, each one with the particular mob he had betrayed, did their work well. So well, in fact, that when the gangs converged from three points of the compass, in the neutral strip of territory between the East and West sides, flaming hell broke out with a cataclysmic roar. The heavy artillery went into immediate action and the sinister growl and rattle of sub-machine guns sounded like a skeleton's dance.

The gangs tore right up to each other and went into a desperate hand to hand conflict. No time this for seeking refuge down dark alleys; no time this for spotting off a bloke from the security of a roof top. There was bitter hatred between the men; hatred that could only be purged by personal contact.

A savage horde of madmen, a raging mob of insane demons, the gangs milled about the street, bleeding, sweating, cursing. Sawed off shot guns were jammed into enemy guts and emptied of their leaden poison; the asphalt became slimy with the tangled bowels of fallen men.

Ever and anon a pineapple would be dropped in the midst of half a dozen struggling gorillas, with the result that friend and foe alike were rent asunder by the flying shell.

The struggle was elemental, colossal! Here were bitter foes, struggling with brute force, face to face. There was no subtlety of brain in play here. There was no master mind strategy or ingenuity. Lust was given full play. Kill, kill, kill or be killed! That was the Law!

The massacre could not have lasted for long. There was only one inevitable outcome to it. Another half hour more and all there would have found a blessed annihilation in gory death.

Suddenly, however, there darted straight into the swirling haze of gun smoke, a streaking red car. With a scream of brakes it pulled up directly in the center of the fire. The advent of the hurtling machine was so sudden and unexpected that for a moment there was a lull in the bitter warfare.

The three gang chiefs were quick to take advantage of the brief respite. As one man they stood up in the captured police car, waved their arms violently and shouted hurried words. A terrible silence filled the air. The gang chiefs rejoined the torn and battered remnants of their once powerful organizations. Sobs of sorrow and hate struggled for dominance in their throats, as they surveyed the shambles.

And for this massacre three double crossing rats were responsible. God help them!

So great was their grief that they were momentarily stunned into inactivity. It was quick-thinking Sadie alone who saved them from another disastrous blunder. Her eye caught a furtive movement among the mob of restless gangsters, where the three rats edged their way to one of the parked cars.

Swiftly she wrenched a heavy colt .45 from a limp wrist and confronted the three traitors. A savage feline ferocity marked her face with terrible doom. Her lips curled evilly into a cruel smile revealing two rows of sharp white teeth. Teeth she would have been glad to sink into the traitors' throats.

The rats fell back before her, more in fear of her passion-distorted face than of the threatening gun in her hand with which she covered them with a slow fan-like movement.

"Shanty!" she called. "The rats! Watch them or they'll make a get-away."

At her words the three chiefs started towards her.

The traitors saw their plot go sky-high on Sadie's words. Death was all about them. They made a break and on the instant Sadie's gun barked three times. The three explosions came so close together that they sounded like one and the three rats tumbled simultaneously to the gutter.

Little Hymie rushed to his sister.

"What'd you do, kid," he asked hurriedly. "Kill 'em dead?"

"Hell, no," replied Sadie. "Just drilled 'em to keep 'em quiet. I'm saving them for the boys to finish off proper. They deserve it."

A half hour later a weird and terrible scene was being enacted in a dirty, musty room of Little Hymie's warehouse. The three rats had been strung up by their wrists to a raftered beam in the ceiling and their ankles manacled together. Then the terrible revenge of the underworld began!

Each of the survivors of the now united mobs, all armed with evil, glinting knives, marched by the dangling figures and slashed. It was a slow death! A torturous, horrible death. The blows were struck cunningly with hateful lust, just deep enough to torture, not deep enough to kill at once. For a half hour the gruesome retribution lasted, then silently the three chiefs and Sadie, followed by their henchmen, left the scene of horror.

The three, dangling, disfigured corpses bore mute testimony to the terrible revenge the underworld wreaks on a traitor—a rat!

"Drinks, men, the best in the house for all of us," said Little Hymie when the mob had left the death chamber. "From now on the three gangs are one."

"And Sadie here," said Shanty, putting one arm affectionately around her, "has agreed to become Mrs. Shanty Hogan. It's this kid here, boys, that saved us all from being sent to hell by those stiffs inside."

Bottles of good rye! Lifted glasses! A toast!

"Death to all traitors. Long life and prosperity to the new mob. A mob of Chink, Jew and Irish! Skoal!"

One Hour Before Dawn

By WILLIAM McNEIL

The moll belonged to Big Jim Regan, and the mob thought she belonged to Italian Joe, and maybe Eddie the Dope knew where she DID belong, but—

FLOSS O'CONNOR WAS BIG RED REGAN'S MOLL. The fact that Red was doing a stretch up in the Big House that would take five long years out of his life, and hers, hadn't seemed to change her a bit at the start. Even the tabloids had spoken of her as a loyal, courageous girl.

That is why the river mob were struck dumb when she took up with Italian Joe Mercurio. The wise ones shook their heads knowingly. One or two felt sorry for Red, but then, that was something for Italian Joe and Big Red to settle between themselves—someday.

There were those who hinted that Italian Joe had framed Big Red Regan. The olive-skinned, oily haired wop and Big Regan had clashed on several occasions. But the big, good natured Irishman, secure in his control of the river mob had laughed it off. Only once had he given a display of the killer that he was. He had openly slapped the Italian across the face.

"Some day, Joe," he snarled, "I'm gonna burn you down."

Italian Joe's face on that occasion had displayed no greater emotion than it had on that later day when he stood staring at the door through which they had taken Big Red. He was one of the last to leave the crowded courtroom when the session was over.

At first Floss O'Connor had fought tooth and nail to aid her man. She knew that the jury wouldn't give Red half a chance. His reputation had been against him from the start. In her futile rage she threatened to 'get' Phil Moran, the detective who brought Red in. She had argued it out with Moran later on the street.

"You cheap flatty!" She twisted her full lips into a snarl as she spoke. "Red Regan was planted an' you know it!"

Moran laughed. He admired this cheaply gaudy, painted girl of Regan's for her nerve and the fight that was in her. He could have told her much that she didn't know about the crooked deal they had handed Big Red. Maybe he would—someday.

"Listen, Floss," he grinned, "I'm admittin' we couldn't prove all the stuff we checked up against Red right now. If we could only get you to talk—the way he did—"

"What do you mean?"

The detective's face became serious.

"Double-crossin' you like he did. Why the very night we picked him up in the Princess Hotel, do yuh know who he was with? That dame from Torreli's place."

Floss O'Connor's small white face was within an inch of his own. Gone now was the happy, careless girl that had been Big Red Regan's moll. In her powdered face her eyes were dark as the night. Her nervous, highly polished fingers twitched. But her voice was low and well under control.

"Phil Moran," she said, "you're a liar! There never was a squarer shooter in this world than Big Red, an' you know it. He'd have gone to hell for any one of his friends. You know that too. An' I'm tellin' you right now that I'm out to get the man that double-crossed him. I know more than you think I do. I'm out to get the man who—"

"Who is he?" grinned Moran. "Do I know him?"

Floss O'Connor's painted young mouth twisted into a bitter laugh.

"You know him, Mister Moran—an' so do I."

But before the first year of Big Red's sentence had passed, Floss seemed to have forgotten her promise. She never spoke of Red any more.

She didn't even seem to avoid Italian Joe Mercurio, although it was common knowledge now that the wop had used Red as bait for the law. She seemed gay and happy although something hard had come into her face.

But it wasn't until after the Jersey payroll robbery that she actually seemed to yield to Italian Joe.

The wop had drawn on Eddie the Dope for a remark passed about Big Red being double-crossed by her. Everyone knew that the success of that bold daylight holdup had hinged upon the expert timing worked out by Big Red Regan months before.

The Italian had simply made use of Big Red's carefully worked out plans. Since Regan couldn't possibly be imagined disclosing these plans to anyone, with the exception of Floss O'Connor, the wise ones again nodded their heads knowingly.

No one else said anything. Eddie the Dope was fool enough to talk, that's all.

From that time on the entire river mob knew that Floss was Italian Joe Mercurio's girl. Some of them felt sorry for Big Red. Eddie the Dope, slinking down side streets to avoid the Italian, kept his mouth shut now, but his scheming brain was ever on the alert.

Alone, or in dark corners, he would heap vile curses on the head of the man who had not only made himself head of the river mob, but had stolen Big Red Regan's moll as well.

"Wise guy!" he spat venomously. "I'm a dope, am I? Well, snake, before I'm t'roo wit' you, I'll show yuh which one of us is the dope, you or me!"

The curious thing was that Floss O'Connor, the cause of the bad blood between Eddie the Dope and Italian Joe, had taken sides with the cokey.

"Leave 'im alone, Joe," she screamed, fighting mad at sight of the Italian's automatic. "You're not going to burn him down while I'm here. Get behind me, Ed!"

Then, more softly she added, "What do you want to let your wop blood run away with you for? I don't want to lose you, yet!"

The smooth, oily haired Italian eyed her with the look of a hungry animal. Then a satisfied grin crossed his heavy lips.

"Don't you worry about losin' me, kid," he smirked.

Floss O'Connor shivered a little, but her painted lips curved in a smile. Eddie the Dope's lifeless eyes wandered from the girl's face to Italian Joe.

Then with a vile curse he turned his back on them. But anyone who by chance had met the cokey later that night, slinking along back streets, would have noticed first of all the shrill little laugh almost of triumph that broke from his lips from time to time.

Eddie the Dope had planned his revenge well.

Up in that grim hell, the Big House, the fading daylight filtered in upon Big Red Regan. Clutched in his fingers was the dirty scrap of paper that the guard had just passed to him. Scarcely moving his lips the big Irishman crumpled the paper in his powerful fist and shot a question at the slouchy uniformed man who stood watching him.

"You got this note from Eddie the Dope himself, or did he send someone?"

"From Ed—he's been down in the village since last night," the guard whispered hoarsely.

"Has he got any of the mob with him?"

"Listen here, Red," countered the guard, "when do I get them five grand for fixin' this getaway for you?"

"Just as soon as I'm on the outside, Doyle," replied Big Red. "You know me an' you know that I never went back on my word in my life. All that I want to do is to get out for twenty-four hours."

"If I c'n get you out at all yuh might as well stay for the rest of your life, or until they pick you up again," growled Doyle. "I'm takin' a hell of a chance, Red. I wouldn't do it for any guy but you—"

"An' what about Ed?"

"He's alone. Got a stolen car with stolen license plates. He's fixed it so there'll be a second car, about eight miles. From there on a milk truck'll carry yuh through. You'll be in N'Yawk about an hour before dawn."

"An hour before dawn," breathed Big Red Regan, his lips setting grimly. "Thanks, Doyle. Don't be surprised if you find the hot seat waitin' for me by the time I come back."

"Gawd, the chair!" gasped the guard. "Listen Red, there ain't no dame in the world worth goin' to the chair for."

Then he shivered with the fear that gnawed at his soul. "What'll happen to me if they find out how you made your getaway?"

Big Red Regan laughed grimly.

"No one will ever find that out, Doyle. No one knows that Eddie the Dope is your brother so even if we're stopped there'll be nothing to connect you with the break. When I'm once clear of the gates I'll go to hell before I'll let any guy stop me until my job is done. After that I don't give a damn. There'll be an investigation with the usual hokum—a gun smuggled in to me somehow— You'll say that you were beaten unconscious an' your keys stolen."

The guard interrupted him nervously.

"I—I guess that for five grand, Red, you c'n make a real job outa that beaten *unconscious*. I got it all fixed for Smolsky an' the gate to let yuh through. But yuh need clothes, an—"

Big Red Regan's grim smile widened at the guard's words. Turning his back to Doyle, Big Red bent forward. A second later he swung around to face him again and the guard's face paled with fear. Over Red Regan's arm hung a folded suit of clothes while his right hand gripped the ugly, cold steel of a Smith and Wesson Special.

"Gawd!" gasped the guard. "Where an' when in hell did yuh get them?"

Red Regan's only answer was a hoarse chuckle at the fear that lined the guard's face. Then his eyes clouded with the determination of the killer who felt his lean fingers closing upon his victim's throat.

"I've still got some—friends, Doyle," he whispered.

But the guard only shook his head. It was more than he could understand, why a man should be willing to go to the chair on account of a woman. His brother, Eddie the Dope, had told him all about Floss and Italian Joe, but even Eddie hadn't known about the clothing and the gun that had been smuggled in to Big Red. If such a thing had been done right under his nose and the noses of the other guards, then—

"Gawd!" he muttered again. "An' a big time guy like that is willin' to risk his neck on account of a moll. Ain't life one hell of a riddle?"

In a large rear room, directly over Torreli's place on Eleventh Avenue, Floss O'Connor and Italian Joe Mercurio sat face to face over a table on which, exposed to the feeble light from above, lay over two hundred thousand dollars in money and stolen jewelry.

The look of anxiety that filled Joe's eyes faded as he admired the richly loaded table. All of this represented the work of only a few months. The sight of it all filled him with pride. But again the film of anxiety flooded his eyes.

"I was a sucker to show you where I had all this stuff hidden," he whined, the beads of moisture dripping from his swarthy face. "Supposin' the cops should come bustin' in? Where t'hell would I be then?"

"Aw, Joe," Floss O'Connor cried, "ain't part of that stuff mine? Ain't I been in on every deal with you? An' ain't I your girl? I just wanted to look it over again, that's all."

"But yuh didn't know where I had it hidden, an' now—"

Floss O'Connor's painted lips broke into a smile.

"You wasn't going to double-cross me, Joe, was you?"

"I don't trust any skirt," Joe growled.

The sound of footsteps passing in the hall outside brought a little cry to Joe's lips. Bending forward he tried to cover the gems and money while his strained eyes watched the door, and the beads of perspiration stood out on his forehead. The footsteps passed his door and continued on down the hallway. Italian Joe breathed a sigh of relief.

Floss O'Connor watched the Italian's face closely. Then her eyes returned again to the shimmering silver and platinum; the pearls and other precious stones, and the crisp bills, counted out into neat little piles of various denominations.

Italian Joe wet his lips. Ever since he had hung around with the river mob he had envied Big Red Regan's split on the various rackets put over by the gang.

Now that big split was his. He was sitting pretty and with almost four long years to go before Big Red could ever bother him again.

He had certainly made a clever move the day that he had planted the big Irishman for that cheap little Long Island job and then fixed it so that Phil Moran, the flatty, would pick him up.

Big Red had been the most surprised man in the world when they had fished the three rings and the platinum bar pin out of his pockets. Italian Joe laughed as the scene flashed before his eyes again.

Suddenly Floss O'Connor bent forward, listening. A clock was striking somewhere. Three times it struck. Italian Joe reached forward to gather in the jewels that lay before him on the table. Floss O'Connor smiled and touched Joe's hand.

"Joe," she whispered. "Let's go away tonight, just you an' me!"

The Italian eyed Floss with the look of a man who is about to realize the one thing that life had cheated him out of. He had stepped into Big Red's shoes as far as power and money were concerned.

His had been a rule of blood clouded by the smoke of his automatic. But as yet he had failed to gain control over this active, fighting moll of Regan's. True the river mob recognized her as his property—his girl. She herself at times, as tonight, admitted the claim.

And yet, at other times, she ignored him and almost jeered openly at him. And now, at sight of the riches that lay scattered about the table, she had come to a final surrender.

Italian Joe Mercurio smiled complacently.

"Joe," Floss breathed again, "let's pack this stuff in a bag an' head for Canada. You've got your car outside. None of the mob will get wise to where we're going. And tomorrow we'll be in Canada, just you an' me. What d'yuh say, Joe?"

Italian Joe put his fleshy fingers over her own. This was his moment of final triumph over Big Red Regan. And yet his avaricious mind clung to the power and wealth that might be his if he stuck on here with almost four long years ahead of him. He could even have Big Red taken for a ride when the Irishman finally was released from stir. And yet—

There was a new light in Floss O'Connor's velvet eyes as the hardness died out of them. Again she reached forward and touched his hand.

Her touch was magnetic. The hot Italian blood stirred in his veins as he eyed her bare throat and rounded breasts. He leaned forward, his lips seeking hers. For a brief second a flare of hatred flashed into the girl's eyes. Her slim body trembled and her small hands gripped the table's edge. Then her red lips curved into a smile of triumph. She knew that she had won.

Carrying the heavy black bag that contained the money and gems, Italian Joe Mercurio led the way down the narrow stairs that brought him to the street. Close at his heels came Floss O'Connor. Eleventh Avenue was deserted, although the lights in Torreli's place were still going strong. Quickly Joe crossed the sidewalk to where his trim little roadster was parked. Without a word he threw the bag into the car and climbed in behind the wheel. Floss followed him, throwing an outer garment over the bag that rested on the floor between her feet.

At the same moment the huge bulk of a man slipped out of the shadows of the doorway that adjoined Torreli's. The light fell full on his face as he approached the car. It was Phil Moran, the flatty.

Italian Joe eyed the detective suspiciously as he rested one huge hand on the car, leaning forward with a grin on his heavy lips.

"Off on a little trip, just the two of you, eh?" chuckled the detective. "What t'hell's the rush? Checkin' out at three o'clock in the mornin'?"

"What is it to you?" asked Floss bluntly.

Italian Joe squirmed uneasily in his seat. But the flatty retained his good-natured grin. He acted like a man who had valuable information to give—if he cared to. Joe's uneasy fingers played with the wheel.

"Got a little news that might interest you, Floss," Moran added with a throaty laugh. "Your old sweety, Big Red, was all set for a break tonight. My idea is that he was comin' down here to 'talk' things over with you. Well, at any rate, Eddie the Dope was to pick him up outside an' rush him in a stolen car down to where nothin' could keep him from droppin' in on you. Big Red, as you probably know, is all hell let loose when his temper's up. But"—again he laughed—"somebody filled Eddie the Dope full of snow again an' he got to shootin' his mouth off. Told the whole works—"

Floss O'Connor's face was white and drawn. A sob burst from her painted lips. The next second she had leaned forward and struck the detective full in the face, her tiny fist drawing a trickle of blood from his lower lip.

Phil Moran caught the girl's two hands and forced her back into her seat. He admired this fighting moll. With the back of one huge hand he wiped the trickle of blood from his lip. Again he grinned.

"I've got a damn good mind to keep you here in N'Yawk where yuh belong, Floss—with me," he said.

"I told yuh once before that there are many things I could tell yuh—about Red goin' up to the Big House, f'r instance—that yuh might wanta know. Yuh told me once that yuh was gonna 'get' the guy that double-crossed Big Red, an'—"

Italian Joe Mercurio's face was gray-white in the light reflected from Torreli's windows.

"Come on, Floss," he cried sharply, "let's get goin'!"

"You'll get goin' when I'm damn good an' ready," snarled the detective suddenly, "an' that'll be when I get a look at what yuh've got in that black bag, Joe!"

As if ashamed of his weakness of a moment before, the detective suddenly pushed Floss O'Connor aside roughly and reached for the bag. Italian Joe Mercurio's nerve failed him. With a sullen whine he gave up.

"How much?" he asked weakly.

He was satisfied to get away without exposing the contents of the bag to Phil Moran's greedy eyes. Floss O'Connor eyed the Italian's trembling fingers with a sneer. And this yellow rat was the man who thought he had won her.

The detective slipped the money into his pocket—two grand wasn't bad for a night's work. His hoarse words reached Floss O'Connor's ears as the trim little roadster pulled away from the curb.

"I coulda told you a lot if I'd wanted to, Floss. You coulda been my girl if you'd played on the level with me. I could even ha' tipped you off about Eddie the Dope shootin' off his damn mouth an' the law stepping in just at the minute that Big Red Regan was makin' his break for liberty!"

Through the silent towns that bordered the Hudson River, Italian Joe's trim roadster tore on. Off in the distance a sleepy clock chimed the hour. Four o'clock! She had timed the distance from Yonkers well.

Italian Joe, bent over the wheel, kept his eyes on the winding road, leaving Floss to her own thoughts. And with the passing of each mile her heart grew lighter. The happy, careless girl of old seemed to come to life again within her.

Town after silent town was left behind them. As they neared the village of Ossining, Joe's nervousness seemed to increase. Big Red's threatened break put the fear of God in him. It was lucky for him that he had been tipped off about Eddie the Dope in time. His fingers clutched the wheel grimly as he tore through the town. Then he breathed a sigh of relief. The Big House—and Red Regan—lay behind him. Ahead was Canada and safety.

His nerve returned to him again by degrees. Why should he let the spectre of Big Red Regan haunt him? He had played a desperate game and won. The old arrogant, complacent smile returned to his lips.

And then, suddenly, he saw the black hulk of the car that blocked the road ahead of him.

There was no room for him to pass it. To think of turning around was both foolish and futile. Besides—the Big House lay back there—and Red Regan— With a grinding of brakes he stopped short, and then he laughed, nervously. The black hulk had turned out to be nothing more threatening than a milk truck.

But a shiver of fear went through him as he watched the truck's driver, apparently attempting to turn on the narrow road.

But God in Heaven, what was this? The man who had been seated beside the driver had jumped out and was slowly approaching the roadster. And then Italian Joe Mercurio cried out in fear as he caught sight of the man's face in the faint light of approaching dawn. It was Big Red Regan!

The driver was Eddie the Dope, the cokey that Phil Moran said had talked too much and consequently spoiled Big Red's break for liberty. Italian Joe's face was the color of putty as he turned to Floss O'Connor.

"We're trapped, Floss!" he screamed. "Gawd! Big Red's got us!"

To his great amazement the girl only leaned back in her seat and laughed.

"Here he is, Red! Just as I swore to you I would, I have delivered him right into your hands!"

Then turning to Italian Joe she went on, "I swore to God I'd get the man who double-crossed Big Red. Well, here you are, you rat! Get out an' take what's comin' to you!"

Big Red Regan, wearing the clothes that his moll had smuggled in to him under the very eyes of the guards, reached one powerful hand forward. A second later Italian Joe Mercurio was standing out in the road facing him and almost slavering with fear. His rat eyes wandered about hopelessly in search of a means of escape. Eddie the Dope jumped forward, insane rage firing his muddled brain.

With a quick jerk of his right wrist he swung an ugly looking automatic into view. Before Big Red or Floss could make a move to stop him the automatic went into action. The crashing slug tore straight into the Italian's head. The wop went down. Eddie the Dope did a dance of rage, pumping slug after slug into the body at his feet.

And they left him there, beside the road, his body riddled with bullets. They stopped only long enough to give Eddie time to ditch the truck, then, with Big Red Regan at the wheel of the wop's roadster, the two gunmen and Big Red's moll tore on into the night.

In the Grand Hotel in Montreal, Big Red Regan opened the black bag and spread money and jewels out on the bed. At sight of the fortune before him Eddie the Dope gave vent to a shrill whistle and hurried to the door to assure himself again that they were locked in safely. The big good natured Irishman counted out the money.

"You better take yours in cash, Eddie," he laughed. "I don't want you to get all snowed up an' go peddling any of these things around up here. There's no sense in inviting the bulls to jump on our trail."

Eddie the Dope looked hurt, but his eyes brightened at sight of the pile of dollars that came his way. As far as he was concerned, the hell with Canada! He would be off for New York again before the night was over. When he had left them alone together, Big Red Regan grinned.

"We'll disappear for a while, Floss," he said. "After all, as Doyle said, I might as well stay away for the rest of my life, or until they pick me up again anyway." He laughed. "Five grand of this goes to him, Floss. Then it'll be me an' you for England an' the continent for a while. I've got a hunch that we'd both like to live on easy street for a few years. What d'yuh say?"

Floss O'Connor's eyes were soft as the night again, and her round white breasts quivered under his hand.

"I'll go any where you say, Red. Ain't I your girl?"

Rod Rule

By CYRIL
PLUNKETT

*Who won the upper hand: gangland's
most powerful leader, with his mob of
hi-jackers, racketeers and coldblooded
killers—or his gun-flashing henchman
who played a lone game?*

"Count" Corrigan slammed the door leading from the blind stairway to
the card room above Rigo's and sauntered up the aisle to the front of the
confectionery store. His tall, thin body was faultlessly attired in a dark suit.
The Count sometimes affected a monocle which, however, was not to be
smiled at. It was thus he had gained the name "Count." Rigo grinned at him
from behind the soda fountain.

"You lost, eh?" he asked.

The Count laughed. One could never tell from his expression just what
the Count was thinking. His half smiling mouth, showing even, white teeth,
gave him a cynical, amused air.

"Does this look like it?"

Rigo's eyes bulged. The Count had pulled out a roll as big as his fist.

"Fix me up a drink, Rigo," Corrigan continued. "Something cold . . . and
no liquor! Get it?"

"You keep da head clear," Rigo grinned knowingly

"Right!" Corrigan answered. Facing the street he swung the glass to his
lips. It remained there, poised, while his body seemed suddenly to freeze.

On the street two distinct things had caught his eye. He was conscious of
them both as of the opening and closing of a camera's shutter. The first was
a girl, face white as chalk, black eyes terrified, imploring. She waved her

hand, her mouth forming the single word "down," her eyes staring straight into his as she slipped from his vision.

The second was a large black touring car which had drawn up to the curb. In its back seat were two swarthy men. Over the side, protruded the muzzle of a machine gun.

The Count dropped to the floor. There was a harsh report, the splintering of glass. From the street came the roar of the car's motor—within the store the sharper crack of a forty-five. The Count's arm jerked with its recoil. He sent five bullets into the tonneau of the fleeing car.

"Hit?" cried Rigo from behind the counter.

"No," muttered the Count. "Tell the bulls it was a customer you didn't know."

Crouching, he ran to the back of the store, flung open the door to the card room and its three white-faced inhabitants, shut the door from the inside and locked it.

"Frankie Meser," he snapped. "Fade before the bulls come." He strode to the window, opened it and ran lightly down the steel firesteps to the alley below.

Far downtown, in his luxurious suite in the Carlton, Benito Moreno surveyed himself in the mirror. Three months earlier he had nearly met death from the gun of one of his men. From that time Moreno had conducted his operations at the Carlton.

Rigo's was an excellent place, but dangerous. Moreno could not entirely escape the feeling that now one of his men had shot it out with him, others would nurse a desire to do the same even though that man, one Serbny, had been killed.

Across his sleek, smug face ran a frown. The long jagged scar over the temple was a source of anger to him always. Serbny's bullet. He looked down at his left arm, stiff, impossible to raise above his chest. But the right arm remained flexible.

A light buzzing from the corner interrupted his thoughts. He crossed the room, touched a framed picture which opened like a door and took out a phone. It was the private line to Rigo's.

"Hello," he muttered. He was silent a moment, his eyes narrowing. "Frankie Meser, eh? Good work, Rigo. You say he didn't get the Count? Okay. What? A girl? You noticed her, eh? Bette Murchinson, Frankie's moll? Okay, Rigo. Send Pesquina and Carillo up to me at six."

He hung up and cursed softly. So Frankie had tried to get the Count. And the Count Moreno's right hand man! That was close. If they got the Count he would be next. Well, Frankie had signed his death warrant.

The house phone rang. Moreno listened.

"Send him up," he ordered.

He poured himself a drink and lighted a cigarette. He could move about here in the Carlton with perfect safety. The floor clerk was his own man. The stairs were likewise under gimlet eyes. As Moreno sank to a chair the door opened and Corrigan entered.

"Hello, Ben," he said.

Moreno eyed him without answering.

"Is that a hole I see in your hat?" he asked at length.

The Count laughed.

"You didn't miss it. I hope this doesn't keep up or I'll go broke buying hats." He flung the hat across the room. I suppose Rigo reported?" Moreno nodded.

"Frankie's going on the spot, Count." Corrigan's eyes flashed but he said nothing. "Yep, Frankie's done. Almost got you, didn't he?"

"Close," Corrigan admitted.

"Who was the girl?" Moreno asked suddenly.

"Girl?" the Count frowned.

"You heard me."

"I can't say that I know what you're talking about," Corrigan answered slowly.

Moreno's eyes glittered.

"Do you know Frankie's gang?" he asked purringly.

Corrigan nodded.

"All of them?" Moreno continued.

Again Corrigan nodded.

"Do you know Bette Murchinson?" Moreno shot at him.

Corrigan's mouth quirked at the corners. Moreno, watching the smiling mouth, did not notice the eyes.

"Yes, I know Bette Murchinson, Moreno—when I see her."

"Oh," Moreno nodded, "when you see her. See her today, Count?"

"No," Corrigan replied sharply.

Moreno sucked at his cigarette and poured another drink. As he looked back to the Count his eyes narrowed, his voice came softly, smoothly.

"Corrigan, you've been with me three months. A damn short time to be my lieutenant, but you've produced. You got more brains than all the rest of my men together. But there's just two things I'd like to know. One of them is, *where did you come from?*"

Corrigan smiled.

"Now Moreno, I'm going to tell you something. When we first got together you were in a bad way. You'd damn near cashed in from Serbny's bullets. And get this, Ben—you were afraid to go back! You wanted to run out only you didn't want to leave your graft. I came at the right time. You needed me. Now listen, Moreno. You're afraid of me and I'm *not* afraid of you. Get the difference? So where I came from is none of your business."

"Suppose I make it my business?" Moreno purred.

"You're at liberty to try," Corrigan replied.

"All right," Moreno sighed, "we'll let it slide. But I'm boss, don't forget that! Now, the second question." He leaned forward. "Why do you deny you saw Bette Murchinson today?"

"I did not see Bette Murchinson today," the Count replied evenly.

The two men stared at each other, their eyes flashing. Moreno squirmed in his chair.

"Corrigan," he cried, "damn you, there's things about you I don't like. You've increased my graft, doubled my alki trade and my power, but the three stickups you engineered went flat, caught cold, the men in stir and not a chance to blow them. I'd blow you to hell if I thought—"

"I was double-crossing you," Corrigan finished. "You'd never live to get that gun out, Moreno. Forget it, forget the girl, and slip me your orders."

Moreno's face became crafty again.

Frankie's going on the spot . . . and so is Bette Murchinson!"

"Bette? Why Bette?"

"Because I said so. And listen, Corrigan, you're going to put her there!"

Corrigan was about to answer when the phone rang again. Moreno looked at his watch. Six o'clock. He listened for a moment, smiled slightly and picked up the receiver. "Send 'em up," he ordered. He turned to Corrigan again.

"Nothing doing," Corrigan snapped.

"Do you take my orders or not?"

"I do, but not that order."

The door opened and Pesquina and Carillo slouched in. Moreno sat up straighter, felt suddenly more powerful. He looked at the two: young, well dressed, but sallow, hard.

"Got a job for you two boys," he said and reached into his pocket. He drew forth a roll and peeled off ten one hundred dollar bills. "A grand now and another when it's done."

Pesquina reached out a stubby hand.

"Okay, boss. What's de dope?"

"Frankie Meser. Take him for a ride. He hangs out at the Purple Parrot. I've had him checked this long time. He comes about eleven. His moll Murchinson will be with him. The Count here will finish the plans, work things out for you and he'll ride with you boys tonight. *Get that*?"

He grinned evilly at Corrigan.

"Take 'em both. And if you three slip—if you *three* slip," he repeated, "it'll be just too bad."

Corrigan sat tight lipped. His eyes seemed to burn into Moreno's.

"You got my orders?" Moreno asked sharply.

Corrigan stood up, shrugged his shoulders.

"Yes, I got your orders, but some day—"

"Some day what?" Moreno blustered.

"Never mind," the Count said.

As the Count, in company with Pesquina and Carillo, shot down the elevator, his usually smiling mouth was drawn tightly together. He cursed Moreno softly. He had played directly into Moreno's hands. Moreno long had feared him. Were he to hold a murder over his head he could easily crush him. And so Moreno had calmly planned that murder.

That it was a girl mattered little except that the killing of a woman would cause twice the publicity and, in so doing, subjugate the Count to him even to a greater degree.

But Bette Murchinson was not to be put on the spot. Not if the Count could do anything about it. For Bette had saved him that very afternoon. Why, he did not know. The Count was not the man to think things out in the face of action. Reasons could wait until later. But she had saved him and he would not repay her favor with a bullet. There were ways open to the Count of which Moreno did not dream.

His lips quirked up slightly, but his eyes remained hard. Once on the street he hailed a taxi. The three crawled within. Pesquina sat stolid and silent, gazing straight ahead of him. Carillo's hands and mouth twitched, his eyes shifted.

Carillo was a hop-head. He needed a shot and then, primed, he would go savagely about his death-dealing task. But that task was to be vastly different than either of the two imagined. The Count grinned to himself.

He ordered the cab to Rigo's, got out and went inside, followed by his two henchmen. Once in the upper back room he sat down at the table and faced them.

"Listen," he said softly. "Moreno gave you orders, but I'm changing them. We take two cars. Tony drives you two. You sit in the back with a Tommy gun. Mike and Sloppy will go in the second car with Causto at the wheel. Here's the idea . . . Bette Murchinson is not going for a ride!"

His blue eyes bored into those of the other two. Pesquina's mouth opened, but he did not speak. Carillo's hands jerked.

"You ride with me or you don't! Speak fast, with your guns or any other way!"

Carillo looked away. Pesquina spoke slowly.

"We ride with you, chief."

Corrigan smiled.

"Causto is to follow me, stick tight to me wherever I go. Tony drives you to within a block of Frankie's hangout. When he comes out get him. If you miss there get him at eleven at the Parrot. That's all. Round up the bunch and tell Causto I'll be ready for him at seven-thirty."

At seven-thirty the Count climbed into a taxi. One of his men sat at the wheels The cab nosed out into the street and was followed by a large black sedan which hung a hundred yards in its rear. For nearly a half hour the taxi rolled swiftly onward.

It stopped before a flashy apartment house in the West End. Corrigan got out, told his driver to wait, and walked toward the entrance. From the corner of his eye he saw the sedan pull up farther down the street. Its lights went out. Corrigan entered the doors.

He stopped at the telephone desk.

"Tell her it is very important," he finished to the operator.

"Your name?" the girl asked.

"No name," Corrigan answered.

"You may go up," the operator said a moment later.

He knocked at the door, heard a gasp and hurried steps within. The door opened. Outlined, the light of the room playing on her hair, stood Bette Murchinson. Her low cut gown revealed the beauty of her throat and arms. The Count caught his breath at her loveliness.

"You!" she gasped.

"Me," he smiled. He pushed aside the door and entered the room.

"You know me?" he asked.

"Yes," she answered, "you are Count Corrigan."

"I came to thank you for this afternoon," he said then. "Why did you save me?"

"Oh," she cried, "I—I don't know. You'd better go."

"Frankie? Don't worry about him. I'm not. Listen, Bette, you're through with Frankie."

Her eyes were wide.

"Through with him?" she echoed. "What do you mean?"

"Frankie's going on the spot to-night."

"You or Moreno?" she asked dully.

"Moreno. I wouldn't stop it if I could, not after this afternoon. But you're coming with me. If you don't—well—" He did not finish.

She sank into a chair, her eyes fastened on him.

"Is there no chance for Frankie?" she whispered.

"Not a chance. You did me a good turn this afternoon. I'm doing you one now. With me you're safe. So, in the future you're the Count's girl or not. Take your choice."

"I'm the Count's girl," she said tonelessly.

"Good!" he grinned. "Come on."

"My wraps?"

"Grab a coat. You need some new things anyway."

"All right," she said. She whirled suddenly and faced the door. It opened with a crash and Frankie Meser stood there, his lips drawn back into a sneer.

Corrigan hunched forward his shoulders, his arms crooked, fingers spread, clawlike. His eyes were narrowed to mere slits. Frankie stepped within the room and kicked shut the door.

"Well, I caught you both. Figured something like this would happen after she put you wise this afternoon."

Bette backed away to the wall, stood there, her arms outstretched, seemingly impaled.

"Takes a woman to play a guy dirty," Frankie continued.

"She didn't play you dirty," the Count interrupted. "I came up here to get her. She didn't have anything to say about it."

Where had he slipped up? the Count wondered. Pesquina had missed Frankie. That was evident. But what of Causto and his men? Or had Frankie slipped in from the side or behind? How had he known? Did he have his men with him? His coming in without a gun in hand argued that he did. Still Frankie believed himself the slickest man on the draw in the city.

"You're dumb, Corrigan," Frankie sneered, "to come here. I got this place watched. You weren't inside the door before I knew. And now you can't get out!" He breathed the last, his teeth showing. His words continued snarlingly. "I'm going to kill you, Corrigan. I can do it and get away with it. And you know it!"

Corrigan's mouth twitched slightly. Frankie's hand suddenly flew to his coat. There was a sharp report, but it came from Corrigan's pocket. A look of utter bewilderment flashed over Frankie's face as he sank to the floor.

"Never try to beat a man at his own game," he grinned. "Come on, Bette, we gotta go. Self defense, kid. I had to shoot him and I'll alibi you up tight. I can fix anything."

As they ran for the steps they heard a cry behind them. The shot had been heard. They ran on. In the lobby Corrigan slowed. Bette had not said a word. He looked out the door. His taxi waited at the nearest curb. Across the street stood a long black touring car. He looked down the street but could see nothing of Causto. He turned to Bette.

"Frankie's men. I'm going to have to shoot it out, I guess. You walk to the taxi. Not looking for you, they might not notice. Leave the door open. Then I'll come out. If there's any shooting slam the door and beat it to Rigo's."

Tight lipped, she obeyed him without a word. He watched her enter the cab. Hand in pocket tightly clutching the gun, the Count opened the door. Five feet, ten feet. Fifty more to the cab. Across the street a man got out of the touring car, walked toward him. Twenty feet to go. Would Bette stick it out if there was shooting?

Suddenly the man stopped, his hand flew to his side. There was a spurt of flame. But the Count was shooting also, shooting as he ran. He tumbled into the cab. Bette crouched on the floor. The cab shot forward. The other man lay crumpled in the street. But the black car had leaped out after them. The Count raised his head and ducked immediately. Bullets rained around the cab. Machine gun!

No chance. Corrigan looked at Bette. Poor kid. He hadn't wanted her. But he had taken her to save her and now—this. The taxi rounded a corner and Corrigan gasped. Out of the side street reared a black sedan. Hunched over the wheel was Causto, tightlipped and white.

The nose of the Tommy gun peeked out the back. The sedan careened past the Meser car. There was a fusillade of shots and the touring car slithered to the curb. Causto turned down an alley. The taxi continued on.

Bette smiled up at the Count.

"Is that the end of Frankie's gang?" she asked.

He nodded.

"And the beginning of Corrigan's." He leaned forward and prodded the driver. "Good work, Joe," he said. "I'm going to need men like you. And by the way, Joe, stop at the next drug store."

He looked down at the girl by his side. How beautiful she was. He wished she had not belonged to somebody else. Still . . . The car stopped.

"Back in a minute," he said. "I gotta phone."

A minute later:

"Moreno? This is the Count. Frankie took a ride and so did a few of his men. The moll? She's feeling fine. She belongs to the Count now, Moreno. Get that?"

The count grinned. Moreno got it.

The Highway to Hell

By WILLIAM H. STUEBER

Sputtering machine guns, high-powered death cars, double-crossing gangsters . . . racing down the Highway to Hell!

A SUDDEN, KEEN FEAR smote the three hard-boiled men in the powerful automobile tearing along the broad concrete road just south of the Canadian border.

The chauffeur, a bundle of nerves perilously close to snapping, clung to the steering wheel, kept his hard, narrow eyes glued to the roadway. Silently, he cursed the torrent of rain that was making the fifty-five mile an hour pace doubly dangerous; cursed the spasmodic flashes of blinding, zigzagging lightning and the ominous peals of thunder.

"What the hell do yuh mean—step on it?" he growled aloud. "I'm givin' her all she's got!"

"Yeah? Then it's curtains fer us!" "Mad" Reddel snapped as his fearful eyes continued to stare through the rear window of the sedan. "Yuh ain't losin' that other car unless this old wagon comes to life. Why, damn it all, she used to do sixty-five without half trying. Cripes! They're comin' fast! We've got to do somethin', and do it quick! I think—"

"Don't!" the fidgeting hulk on the rear seat beside him roared. "You'll get brain fever! What a fine kettle of fish you made out of this trip. Why in hell didn't you let Mike stop when they hailed him?"

In a less tense situation, Reddel's retort to the insult might have been a bullet. He was too busy mapping a course through which to escape the pursuing car to pay the slightest attention to his henchman's thrust. Escape he would! Ten to fifteen years in the penitentiary, loss of twenty thousand dollars in contraband would be the price of capture. He was frantic, insane with rage.

"Slow down easy, Mike. Get that shot gun ready. Ace, you handle the machine gun—I'll do my share with this brace of automatics. Hole everything 'till they're abreast of us. Don't stop altogether, Mike—don't take her out of high! Be ready to give her the gun as soon as I yell."

Hopefully, quickly, Mike obeyed the commands that spelled certain death for the pursuers. He threw out the clutch, gently applied the foot-brake. When a comparatively safe speed warranted it, he dropped his huge left hand from the wheel. In less than a minute he clutched a sawed-off shot gun, cradled the business end in the crook of his other arm. A nervous finger of his left hand was on the trigger, his right hand guiding the car.

Ace Christy fondled the portable machine gun, its death dealing nozzle resting on the sill of the open left window. The overwrought Reddel had lowered the rear window. The tips of both his automatics were trained on the car now rapidly approaching.

"Easy, Mike—and ready. A hundred yards to come. Steady now," Reddel cautioned in a death-like whisper.

The hundred yards dwindled to fifty—to ten. The radiator of the pursuing car was even with the rear wheels of the gun car. A guttural growl, like that of a tiger preparing for the killing leap, escaped Reddel's twisted lips. He saw two regulation State Troopers' caps, the shoulder belts of two natty uniforms.

"Pull over there!" one of the officers commanded acidly. "Be quick about—"

"Let 'em have it!" Reddel yelled.

The command was given at the precise moment when the two victims were directly under Mike's shot gun. Two blasts, two flashes seemed to come from Mike's elbow. As the victims dropped back a trifle, Ace raked them with the machine gun.

"Step on it, Mike!" Reddel bellowed through the staccato of shots.

The car shot forward, not a second too soon to escape being rammed by the victim's wildly careening car. Absolutely certain that both had died instantly, Reddel nevertheless emptied both his guns at the slumped figures in the front seat, distance making all save his first shots useless. With the last of his split-second shot, he squealed with fiendish delight as he watched the progress of the driverless car.

"They're off the road. Bang! In the ditch and up against a tree! They'll never butt into *private business* again!"

"For cryin' out loud, Mike, get that accelerator down to the floor and keep it there!" Ace Christy implored fervently as chills chased each other up and down his spine and beads of clammy perspiration rolled from his forehead. "If I get out of this jam, yuh can bet your last buck I'll never get mixed up in snow-running again!"

Hot automatics reloaded and crammed into his coat pocket, Reddel laughed raucously. "Won't you? That listens sweet, comin' from a guy that's had me bulled into believin' he was real hard. And you, Mike? You gettin' soft too?"

"Hell no! I've bumped 'em off before. Why worry? It's over now. It was them or us. The best men always win!" Mike answered with far more relief than he felt.

"Win?" Ace ejaculated. "Yuh talk as if we were out in the clear—safe already!"

"It'll be daylight before some hick finds the bodies," Reddel reassuringly prophesied, "and by that time we'll be so far away we *will* be safe."

Ace found little comfort in the words, the confidence of his allies.

"Fools have too much luck," he moaned. "Somebody's liable to find 'em in half an hour. And suppose they ain't dead? The cops and the troopers will burn up the telephone wires. Cripes! We ain't got a chance!"

Reddel's anger got beyond control. His bony fingers closed about Ace's throat like a suddenly sprung steel trap. He blazed with venom. "You yellow-livered mutt! Another groan out of you, and you'll be joinin' them dead troopers!"

"Hey! Lay off him, Reddel," Mike yelled over his shoulder. "Get out of one jam 'fore yuh lay pipes for another!"

"Aw, he gives me the willies!" Reddel exploded and released the cowering, sniveling Ace. "Burnin' up the telephone wires—with what kind of information? *If* they do talk, I doubt like hell they will, all they can say is that it was a Glen-dann sedan. I had brains enough to smear the license plates with mud. Why damn it, they didn't even know how many of us was in here!"

Neither Mike nor Ace replied. For the best part of an hour, Mike kept the sedan hurtling through the pouring rain. Suddenly he swerved the car to the white concrete guard posts at the right and halted abruptly. Beyond the ghost-like posts with the two strands of heavy cable was a stretch of thick woodland. Mike turned the spotlight affixed to the windshield toward it. He glanced back at Reddel.

"I ain't worryin'. But just the same, we'd better unload the artillery. Ace might be right about burnin' up telephone wires, and havin' the guns in the car certainly ain't goin' to help us wiggle loose if we are stopped."

Raging inwardly, Reddel was mute. For the first time in his miserable life he wished he could drive a car. Instead of unloading artillery, he would have unloaded two corpses!

"Well?" Mike thundered. "Do we or don't we? If we don't, Ace and me will be leavin' you *here* and *now!*"

With an empty chuckle supposed to be a laugh, Reddel flung open the car door, stepped out into the downpour. The small machine gun was cradled in his arm, the two automatics in his pocket.

"O.K. with me," he said with perfectly feigned amiability. "But if we bump into more trouble where artillery would help us more than chin waggin', don't blame me."

"We won't—"

"One thing more, just so we understand each other. Every dollar I've got in the world is tied up in this load of coke. We're goin' to get it through to Fu Wang—get it through *somehow*. Understand? If we don't—well, the less said about that, the better."

"Meanin'?" Ace inquired meekly, his voice surcharged with mixed fear and curiosity.

"Aw, nothin' much—only that you two came along fer a share of the profits, and by God yuh'll get a share of the *profits* of killin' those two troopers if we're nabbed. They can only burn you once—they burn you just as crisp fer two murders as they do for six! If we ditch the artillery and get stopped, we're S.O.L.—if we keep it, we can shoot our way clear."

"Tell yuh what," Ace said slowly, carefully. "Let's keep the automatics. They ain't hard to hide. Just ditch the shot gun and the machiner."

Reddel laughed. He yanked the two automatics from his pocket, flung them on the seat beside Ace. "Thought yuh'd see the light. When we get back to New York, yuh'll see other lights, too!"

Ace winced under the veiled threat. Mike thrust the shot gun toward the boss of the expedition with a terse, "make it snappy. I craves distance!"

Reddel snatched the weapon, walked swiftly to the road guard. He was over the cable, trudging down the slight slope of ankle deep mud. Just as he reached the first of the gigantic oaks, the sharp bark of an automatic roared above the sound of rain pelting upon trees.

A gargling noise escaped Reddel's agonized lips. Death cut short his incoherent plea for mercy. He staggered a few feet as though badly intoxicated. He dropped the cumbersome weapons of death. At the base of an oak he pitched heavily to the soft blanket of dead leaves.

"I guess we won't see those other lights he was chinnin' about, hey Mike?" Ace barked.

"No. We won't—if you go and make sure he ain't goin' to recover."

"Sure I'll go. I'll take both the automatics with me! I ain't the wise guy Reddel always claimed to be—but I've got some common sense. And I know that twenty grands' of coke might make yuh try ter slip me the same dose Reddel got!"

"I won't. I'll play square with you as long's you do the same with me."

Ace took the automatics with him nevertheless. It was a useless precaution. Reddel was as dead as the leaves. Ace was back in the car again in a moment, slamming the door.

"The steadier that speedometer sticks around sixty, the better I'll like it," he said.

That delightful ecstasy of a man who suddenly, unexpectedly finds himself the possessor of a tidy sum, warmed Mike. He settled down to the business of lessening the miles that lay between their location and the almond-eyed, parchment-skinned power of the underworld who would eventually exchange crisp greenbacks for the cocaine. Mike was effervescent with good cheer.

"How's it feel to be rich?" he laughed over his shoulder.

"I ain't thinkin' about that!" Ace grumbled, a tremor in his voice. "I never count my eggs 'till I've got chickens to lay 'em. I'd give a lot to be in Fu Wang's den right now. I've got a hunch we're headin' fer the cemetery. Wish I'd have steered clear of this whole damned business."

The words inspired Mike. Twenty thousand dollars' worth of the insidious drug would, profit considered, soon be converted into twenty-five thousand dollars in cold, easy-to-spend cash. Twenty-five thousand divided between two. Humph. Not so bad—and yet, *why* divide it? If he could have it *all* . . . he would! The resolution came as sharply, as suddenly as the terrible flash of lightning that seemed to strike close at hand. Mike glanced at the miniature watch upon the dash.

"I'll make Albany by three o'clock," he remarked with extraordinary friendliness. "You'll just be in time to grab a ticket and swing on to the New York bound Montreal Limited. If your knees are rattlin' that bad, yuh can go—"

"And leave all the snow with you?" Ace snapped belligerently.

"Cripes! I've heard about guys wantin' doughnuts with a dime plate of soup—you tie 'em! You'd get a kick out of me takin' all the chances and handin' yuh half the pickin's on a silver platter, hey?"

A brief struggle between lure of cash and fear locked Ace's lips. Eventually he hurled defiantly, "I'll stick! I've gone through half of it—I won't leave all the cake fer you!"

Mike scowled blackly. A blaze of hatred and greed seered him.

"Stick then, but quit groanin'. And if there's another shindy, don't forget to do your bit! You can start now by takin' this wheel fer a while."

The switching of places was an ill-destined move. Ace had barely settled down behind the wheel when an illuminated sign at the roadside brought a screeching of brakes.

"Construction work ahead. Proceed with caution and at your own risk," Mike read aloud with drooping spirits.

The overwrought Ace cursed a blue streak and started the car again. A stiff grade, deep holes and treacherous mud made difficult going for some minutes. At last they reached the summit of the tortuous stretch, rounded the last bend and were face to face with a steep descent.

"Long Valley," Mike informed, as through the gloom the blinking cluster of lights far below met his eyes.

"Looks like we were on the top of a mountain—as if that was hell way down there," Ace groaned and hesitated about beginning the perilous dip.

"Sit here and wait!" Mike barked. "Maybe an angel will carry us down."

"I'd better go down in—God! What's that?"

The three words were brimful of agony. Half way down the rutted, sharp decline, a tiny white light was bobbing up and down. Mike's eyes were wide with wonder; Ace's with fear. Simultaneously their minds reverted to earlier events of the dismal, fatal night. They were experiencing again that spasm of fear, that need of a quick decision that faced them when two troopers had signalled them to stop; signalled them in this very positive manner.

For a few seconds they were mute with terror, both their minds blazing with possibilities. Had Ace's prophesies of burning telephone wires come true? The car started backward with a jerk.

"You damned fool, you can't turn around here!" Mike snarled. "There isn't room enough—they'd be here before you got half way 'round! Go ahead! There's no two ways about it—yuh've got to go down. Here! Take one of these gats—let them do any talkin' that's necessary. Step on it! Damn the springs—let 'em break!"

Teeth chattering, hands trembling, Ace shot the car forward. The hill, the heavy foot upon the accelerator, soon resulted in a forty-five mile clip. The sedan bobbed around like a cork in an angry sea. Closer came that waving, sinister light; tenser became Ace's and Mike's fears for tires, springs, mechanical failings.

With an agonized cry, a realization that death was probably a matter of scant minutes, the pair discerned a light car diagonally across the torn road. There was no room for them pass; neither to the left nor right. In the glare of their own headlights they saw the tell-tale shining belt of a trooper's uniform.

"The left!" Mike screamed frantically. "Your only chance! Ram it—ram it hard! That light boiler will swing around!"

Mechanically Ace obeyed. Things happened with Gatling gun rapidity. A blue uniformed figure hurled grotesquely through the rain. Steel crashed into steel. Mike's automatic barked three times. Then a terrible scream—a woman's scream—rang out.

A sickening sensation turned Ace's stomach as he realized that the other car was fast entangled with their own. In spite of his best efforts, the motor of the sedan labored—stalled. A frightful oath came from between his clenched teeth. He was out of the car like a shot. Quick as he was, Mike was quicker. They saw the sturdy steel bumper of the other car between the spokes of their rear wheels.

The superhuman strength of madmen was behind each tug at that cold, twisted bit of steel. With the help of the slippery clay, they did succeed in dragging the front of the lighter car aside sufficiently to free their own. They then turned their excited attention to their front left mudguard which the impact had forced down upon the tire. Together they grunted and groaned as they remedied that condition. Meanwhile the rain had abruptly ceased.

Ace was behind the wheel again with the agility of a trained acrobat. He cursed the leisurely moving Mike who was coming around the front of the car.

Mike suddenly froze in his tracks. A queer sound came from his mouth as he swooped upon something laying in the sticky clay of the road; something that Ace could not see.

"Holy mackerel! What a streak of dumb luck that I stepped on this," Mike laughed and held their front license plate for Ace's inspection. "Our goose would be well-cooked if we left this here!"

"Put it on! Stop chinnin'! Come on!" Ace commanded with the anxiety of a man eager to be moving from a ghastly scene.

"Hold your horses—I'm goin' to see if they're both dead—"

"Then by God yuh'll stay here alone!" Ace fired with white hot heat, immediately pressing the accelerator.

With a catlike leap, Mike reached safety, swung to the running board. Momentum fairly hurled him into the seat. If Ace had been low in Mike's regard before, he was at sea-bottom level now. Mike was burning with rage, thoroughly disgusted with his confederate. Yet he eased the pressure on the trigger of the automatic in his right hand. It would not do to kill Ace while the car was traveling at 35 miles an hour over the bumpy road—time enough for that minor detail later.

"Later" arrived when they were again on the smooth concrete, and Ace stopped the car with a whimpering, "You take it—I'm half blind."

"With fright," Mike exclaimed emphatically and stepped out gingerly.

Ace squirmed past the gear shifting lever into the seat Mike had vacated. Even before he could voice a protest against the just accusation, there came the terrifying realization that the business end of the automatic in Mike's steady hand was aimed at his heart. Ace saw the flash, felt the cruel stabbing pain of death.

The sole survivor of the crimson expedition leaped to the car door. A few minutes sufficed to unload the remains of the last barrier between him and the twenty-five thousand dollars. With a fiendish chuckle, Mike carried the inert form to a nearby clump of underbrush, unceremoniously dumped it from his shoulder. He dashed for the car. In a twinkling he was on his way again.

"Twenty-five thousand! Twenty-five thousand!" he gloated with unadulterated joy. "A good night's work—damned if it ain't! And to think how it would have all been spoiled if I hadn't stepped on that damned license plate!"

He was in an entirely too jovial mood to give even a moment's serious thought to his chances of getting through to Fu Wang; entirely too busy, erecting rosy air castles of the future, to think that perhaps somewhere on this road of death was the slight accusing thread that often winds about the necks of his kind and draws them relentlessly toward the chair.

It was evening of the following day when Mike sought a conference with the wily, hard-bargaining Fu Wang. With light footsteps, highest hopes, he followed the sandaled yellow servant into the gorgeously furnished room where Wang usually discussed important business.

The Oriental master bowed low, his face as blank as a poker player's.

"That stuff you wanted 'Mad' Reddel to get for yuh from Canadian friends is in town," Mike fired straight from the shoulder.

"And my friend Reddel?"

"Is gone on a long journey! That shouldn't cut any ice—"

"None—except perhaps that he would not take unkindly to this humble person's regretful saying that the need for the stuff has passed," the clever Wang drawled as he read the meaning of long journey; knew that here was a splendid opportunity for securing contraband at a great bargain. "You see, my friend, the police have grown weary of watching my other sources of supply—I have plenty on hand. However, since you have no doubt risked life and liberty in my humble behalf, I will—"

"Take the stuff off my hands for about half what it's worth, hey?" Mike rasped. "Well, the price stands at what you offered Reddel—take it for that, and take it quick or the market's going up! Twenty-five thousand in cash. If that hurts your ears, Soy Ling will be glad to see me."

Mere mention of his most formidable competitor in narcotics gave Wang a tremor. An offer rose to his tongue. He gulped it as Mike already turned toward the door.

"Never be it said that this humble party retracted an offer—I pay you the set price, pay you gladly—when you deliver the goods here!"

"Nix! You come with me to where the goods are; you give me the cash and bring the men to lug the stuff away!"

Wang shrugged his stooped shoulders. "It is well. I most humbly agree. The address?"

"Oh, no you don't, Wang! You pulled that stunt on Jenks—got the address and hijacked him out of the stuff. Fer this deal you pay cash and then carry. And until you're safely on your way, just about a dozen gats will be ready to spit lead at the first sign of a double-cross."

"We will go—"

"Now!" Mike ejaculated decisively.

"My friend does not reckon with the hour—nor my own caution. Banks are closed and I do not have twenty-five thousand dollars at my unworthy fingertips."

"Then at nine thirty in the morning—"

"Be of good cheer, my friend, the drug it does not require great haste. It does not evaporate. In the morning I am busy. I will await your pleasure after the hour of four tomorrow afternoon," Wang declared with convincing finality.

"No—aw, all right then. Four o'clock and with twenty-five thousand in your jeans—and no schemes in your nut, either! Get me?"

Mike was bowed out as elegantly as he had entered.

Leaving the wily Fu Wang, he hastened to his rooms. Through his dirt-streaked window that opened on a filthy court, he could see the long row of tin garages, one of which housed the car and the dope. He turned to the paper he had snatched on his way from Wang's. Its glaring headlines brought a chuckle to his lips—a chuckle and a greater sense of security. He plunged into the fine type, the story of the mysterious slaying of two State Troopers by assailants who left not a single clue.

Further down the page, in a tiny footnote, he read of the finding of the body of one readily identified via the Rogues Gallery as "Mad" Reddel. Ace Christy's passing merited an even smaller notice, and on the next page the mysterious death of State Trooper Neldan and his fiancé were amusingly recorded as a lover's quarrel that ended in suicide and murder.

Mike flung the paper from him, chest puffed with conceit. "If I ever get so dumb that I can't make a living otherwise, I'll join the police force. Of all the fatheads in the world, they're the cream! Imagine not being able to hook those three things together," he soliloquized while a broad smile swept his face.

Fully clothed he flung himself upon the filthy bed and thought of the morrow and the twenty-five thousand dollars that would be his. How long he lay there, he did not know. Suddenly the creak of a rusty hinge brought him to his feet like a released jack-in-the-box.

Frantically he dashed to the window. Three figures were idly trudging through the two rows of garages. They did not hesitate. They were soon lost in the shadows. With tremendous relief, and a deep sigh, Mike slumped into a chair. He could see the lock on his own garage shining in the moonlight. The men had evidently been in one of the other garages—perhaps that creaking hinge had been mere imagination.

In spite of his own repeatedly mouthed assurances that all was well, Mike found sleep an utter impossibility. All night he sat at that window telling himself that he had nothing to fear; but finding a denial in the very air.

At dawn he was haggard and drawn. By three o'clock he was on the verge of insanity from the rigid suspense. With a prayer of thanks that at last the hour had arrived, he made ready for his trip to Wang's, made ready by cramming an automatic in each hip pocket and making dire predictions against the health of the yellow man, at the first false move. He went down the dark hall cautiously; down the rickety stairs two by two.

His eyes narrowed, his heart seemed to stop as he opened the vestibule door and looked across the street. A man bearing all the tell-tale marks of a detective was intently studying the front of the tenement house. Their eyes met.

Mike knew retreat would arouse suspicion. Boldly, with a nonchalant whistle and a weak mental reassurance, Mike stepped to the street. As he walked hurriedly, fearfully, he watched the other out of the corner of his eye as long as possible.

"Imagination." Mike mumbled to himself as he walked another block and was not followed. He quickened his steps toward Wang's, feeling more secure with each step.

His happiness died a sudden, violent death as he laid his hand on the doorknob of Wang's and saw what appeared to be that same detective on the next corner. There was no choice. He had to go in!

"To Hell with your damned tea!" he growled at Wang's proffered hospitality. "Dimes to apple pie I'm being trailed!"

He dashed to the window opening on the street, turned wild eyes toward the corner. He laughed uproariously as a second man approached the first and wrung his hand. Arm in arm the pair trudged off.

"My mistake, Wang!" Mike said apologetically. "He wasn't a gumshoe artist after all—just waitin' fer another bozo. I will take a cup of that tea—stronger than tea if you have it!"

Wang yanked a heavy silk cord hanging near the door. Within a minute he hoisted his glass, clinked it against Mike's.

"To our mutual success and the damnation of the police!"

"To the police! Our jails would be full if they was smarter!"

Mike, Wang and two stolid Chinamen went out through the back door, down a rank smelling alley; hurriedly entered a waiting car. Mike's hands were on the butts of his guns even while he directed the chauffeur. Not until the last minute did that solemn-faced individual know his ultimate destination.

"We're here, Wang. And don't forget what I told you about gats waiting fer the first crooked move," Mike lied perfectly with a purposeful glance at the windows of the tenements.

Wang bowed regally. "It is said that only a fool tempts fate."

Quickly Mike unlocked the garage door. The four entered; the door was then closed and latched on the inside. "Under the rear seat you'll find the stuff. Let's feel the cash!"

The servants dove for the seat while Wang surrendered a pile of greenbacks. Mike snatched them like a starved man snatches food. Then suddenly came an ominous pounding on the door.

A gun flew from Mike's pocket; his face was twisted with rage. "You lousy yellow dog! You may gyp me after all—but by God you'll pay for it with your life!"

Wang cowered before that wavering gun. Fear of death was in his eyes; his knees trembled. "May all my honorable ancestors be eternally damned if I have done anything wrong!"

The patter of many feet drifted through the door—the crunch of a heavy object smiting the flimsy wood. The shining edge of an ax came flashing through at the second stroke. Mike jerked the trigger of the automatic in his hand; jerked it as rapidly as nerves could be commanded. Gun emptied, he flung it aside; drew its mate from his pocket, emptied that.

A stifled scream from the outside. A harshly barked, "trade lead with 'em, if that's what they want!"

The rat-a-tat-tat of a machine gun, the splintering of wood, the whine of lead followed hard on each other. Bullets chewed a circle of wood from the door, then came streaming in without restraint. The two yellow servants were first to feel the bite of lead, Wang next.

Even before the agonized scream of Wang had died out, Mike felt three terrible hot stabs of pain about his neck and chest. The whole world seemed to tremble, to whirl, to turn black. He felt himself falling, felt the additional torture of his head heavily striking the stone floor.

• • •

Slowly, painfully, Mike opened his eyes. Sight of a blue uniform, brass buttons shining beneath the glare of electric lights, stabbed him worse than his bodily pain. Through the haze came the realization that he was in a hospital ward. He smiled inanely, tugged at the blue on the right side of his cot. "Hey—what happened?"

"You got in the way of lead and—"

"Cripes, you're as thick as the rest of 'em. I know that! I mean what wised you guys up to me?"

"Nothing. You'd better lay back there and try to sleep now. . . ."

"Hey! Don't try ter pull the wool over my eyes—I—I know I'm going. I'd go laughin' if I knew how—"

"Then I'll tell you. You led us a great chase. You would have gotten away with this, all of it, if only that license plate hadn't come off your car when you crashed into the trooper's—who by the way told us before he died that his car was disabled and he signalled you merely to ask for a tow."

"But—I found—it—we didn't leave the license plate—behind—"

"No, you didn't. But somebody stepped on it and the letter C and the first three numbers on it were imprinted into the clay of the road. Too bad it didn't rain more and wash that trade mark away. It didn't! Then all we had to do was check up on all cars with plates beginning with C 3-5-9.

"Last night we found Reddel's name in the license bureau. What a fool he was to register his car in his correct name and address! We turned up his garage, found the car smashed, learned from nosey neighbors that you brought it in last! We got a duplicate key from the owner of that row of garages and found the drug under the rear seat."

"Wise guys, hey? Decided—to—wipe out Fu Wang at the—same time, hey? And that stuff in the newspapers—that was bunk?"

"Yes. Bunk! It's always our motto to get two birds with one stone."

"Yeah—but you can't convict me—you can't convince a jury that I killed anybody—you can't—"

"No, we can't. Your case is in a judge's hands who doesn't have a jury in the court room."

A spasm of agony gripped Mike. Through clenched teeth he laughed; groaned, "Twenty-five thousand bucks! Twenty-five-thousand—"

He sank back upon the white pillow. A shudder passed through him, shook him like a gale shakes a sapling. His wide eyes lost the sparkle of life. He was on the main highway to Hell.

Gangster Stories, February 1930

Editorial by the Publisher

LIFE IS LIKE A GREAT CANVAS, framed by Birth and Death, on which each writer portrays his vision of "things as they are." We judge his stories by his nearness to truth. If they are unreal, and their characters merely stuffed images that move automatically against false backgrounds, then we know them to be useless extravagances of the mind. But if they are stories written out of the raw of experience, so to speak, with human people in accurate surroundings, our conclusion is that such stories are worth while. And not only worth while because they are entertaining to read, but because they convey life as it is, and contain deep object lessons of true experience. Seeing how others have suffered; how the "other half lives"; how complex are the dangers that beset our journeys day by day, we gain a vicarious experience of our own that aids us in fighting the great battle.

Stories of the West and cowboys would indeed be tame and without value were they not written by those who know the frontier. Stories of the air and the birdmen would be dull and uninstructive if they were written by those ignorant of the science of aviation. The same holds true with detective and gangster stories.

In the pages of this magazine you meet a cruel race of humans; people who move through the dark alleys of crime and terror. They are but the creations of the writers' minds, however, and are only reflections of actuality. One has but to pick up any newspaper in order to read the actual accounts of gangsters and racketeers. This magazine would indeed be of little worth were it to portray the racketeer as "he isn't." We must show him in his true colors, in his real environment. We must go to the depths of his twisted heart and soul. Yet, in spite of all this, these pages are but figments of the imagination. They are only true in their balance of actuality and fancy. The characters you meet are only a continuation of the imaginative line of literature produced by such masters of underworld life as Balzac and Charles Dickens.

You can gain much from these pages in truth; you can guard your own hearthstone from these modern brigands by understanding them and their ways. Knowledge is power, power is truth, and the truth will set you free. Knowing of these crooked byways of crime, and the people who walk there in darkness, you will be forearmed and forewarned about the pitfalls that are on all sides. But look only upon these pages as stories—the creations of our writers' fancies—and if you gain valuable knowledge through entertaining reading, then indeed we have fulfilled a real purpose in publishing this periodical.

Racketeer Stories, February 1930

A Page from the Publisher's Notebook

THE STORY IS THE THING.

Yet we must not forget, that no matter how real it seems, it is, after all, only the weaving of a writer's imagination. The characters are also only figments of the mind. The exciting situations are merely the creations of brilliant authors.

Keep these things before you as you read the amazing collection of yarns we have gathered together in the first issue of RACKETEER STORIES. They are—every one of them—only stories. They are intended for your entertainment—an escape from the routine of dull, daily life.

Many of the characters seem to triumph in crime, but if we could go on with them beyond the ends of these stories, we would read of their eventual downfall. Glittering as they seem crime can never pay, in the long run.

Crime is the product of weakness. And weakness is a disease of the mind and body. Therefore, in reading of the underworld, one must remember always that these pitiful children of evil are only red shadows in the shadowy realm of unreality. Let us read of them, but believe in them—no!

Rather let us gain a lesson from their ragged existence—a lesson in terror and pity that should help us to watch our own steps and beware of stupid temptations and idle pleasures gained at the price of our souls.

In these pages, you find the dregs of existence—moving paragraphs of horror, drama and even humor—and these pages are but loose leaves from the book of an imaginary life created for your entertainment and also your guidance.

Faithfully yours,
HAROLD HERSEY

Triple Cross

By JACK COMPTON

Honesty among gangsters—that was what the new Commissioner thought. But the tough old police captain had different ideas.

THE NEW POLICE COMMISSIONER HAD SOME DEFINITE IDEAS.

"There's only one way to handle these gangsters and racketeers," he pompously told the grizzled old detective captain. "And that's to be their pals. Give them an even break. They'll meet you half way."

"Bunk!" grunted the captain. "The only way to handle them birds is to kill 'em off—the faster the better. I've been on the force twenty-five years and I know."

"Twenty-five years," repeated the commissioner meaningly, "and you only a captain. Now take my—"

"I never did get a break on political graft," cut in the captain, studiously flicking an imaginary speck from his uniform.

"Sir!"

"No offense," the veteran officer replied simply. "I was just telling the truth—and you know it." The captain rose from his chair and grinned at the over-dressed commissioner. "When you get near enough to them racketeers to give 'em an even break, I'd like to be around." He moved the door.

The commissioner stopped in the act of taking a cigar from his desk humidor. "If you would like to be on hand, Captain, just remain in my office here for five minutes."

Like a man who suspects his hearing of playing tricks on him, the grizzled old detective turned around. "Huh?" he inquired.

"I said," explained the commissioner, as he adjusted a tiny flower in his button hole, "that if you remain here for five minutes you will see my theory become a fact. You will see me put an end to all gang war in this city." The Police Department head coughed importantly and said, "The three biggest racketeers of the underworld are coming here at my invitation."

"Suffering cats!"

The commissioner ignored the captain's outburst and lit a fragrant Havana. "Of course, Captain, you've heard of Tony Sarotto?"

"The blackest murderer unhung!" snapped the detective.

"And of Mike Morgan?"

"Sure," replied the captain sourly. "Mike's checks will bounce him into the stir some day."

"And of Big Sam Stevens?"

"Ugh! He'd drop his phoney money into a blind man's cup."

At that moment a pasty-faced clerk stepped into the commissioner's office. "Mr. Sarotto, Mr. Morgan and Mr. Stevens to see you, sir. Shall I show the gentlemen in?"

"*Gentlemen!*" snorted the veteran officer.

The commissioner looked annoyed but did not reply to the detective's sarcasm. He turned a stern face to his nervous clerk. "Show them in."

And in came the racketeers three. First was the swarthy-faced Tony Sarotto. The short, stocky gangster crossed the floor quickly. His right hand was deep in his coat pocket as he glanced from side to side as if suspecting a trap. He nodded curtly to the commissioner's cordial greeting and slipped into an indicated chair. A taunting smirk creased his dark features when he saw the detective chief.

But the veteran officer paid him no heed. He was thinking what an ass the new commissioner was about to make of himself. Second of the trio was the red-nosed Mike Morgan. The cocky Irishman swaggered into the room with a big grin for everybody. He dropped into the chair next to the captain and bummed a cigar.

Last was Big Sam Stevens. He tapped his ill-fitting derby in mock salute to the commissioner. Taking a celluloid tooth pick from his vest pocket he went vigorously to work while waiting for the commissioner to begin.

"Gentlemen," smiled the new Department head to the assembled mob leaders, "I have called you here today so we can get together and put an end to this murderous gang war. I'm not a bad fellow to do business with. In fact, I'm going to offer a proposition to you that will double your income and save funeral expenses."

Quickly following up his lead with a dollar cigar to each of the racketeers, the eager commissioner went on. "I have divided the three biggest rackets in this city into equal parts." He turned to the lynx-faced Italian. "To you, Sarotto, will go all the rum business. No one else is to sell or truck it."

Tony grinned as if to say, "Not a bad break." The other two looked suspiciously at both the gangster and the commissioner.

"To you, Morgan," the Police head continued, "will go all the bad paper. And anybody giving you the slightest competition in rubber checks will meet the severest penalty of the law."

It was Mike Morgan's turn to look pleased. And he did. Big Sam Stevens's face twisted in a scowl and his hand edged toward the bulge at his hip. Where did he come off in this million dollar deal?

But the dapper commissioner was speaking to the big, raw-boned Swede. "To you, Stevens, will go the entire counterfeit money and slot machine rackets. And anyone else putting out a label or slug will get a life sentence."

Three happy racketeers marched arm in arm from the commissioner's office. No one would think that just an hour before they were planning to chop each other down with machine guns.

When they had left, the commissioner patted his pomaded hair and smiled triumphantly at the detective chief. "Well, I did it!"

"Baloney!" retorted the captain disgustedly. "Them gorillas will be throwing pineapples at each other in twenty-four hours. They couldn't keep from fighting if they wanted to."

"I'll bet a brand new hat that my scheme works," cut in the cock-sure commissioner.

"O.K.," grinned the captain. "I need a new hat."

When the three mob leaders reached the street, they each in turn dismissed their waiting armored cars and grim-faced henchmen. Then all three piled into a taxi bound for Mike Morgan's apartment to celebrate.

Half an hour later they were comfortably seated in Mike's luxuriant apartment. A score of whiskey and gin bottles covered every available table space and the room reeked with cigar and cigaret smoke.

It must have been about five o'clock that afternoon that the party was interrupted by a letter arriving by the elevator boy. Mike Morgan shifted his big cigar to the left side of his mouth and opened the envelope. With a booming laugh he turned to Tony Sarotto who was busily nursing a quart of gin.

"Here's business for you, Tony." The Irishman explained. "My brother-in-law who lives just across the state line wants ten barrels of rye before midnight. Will you sell them to me?"

"If I sell 'em to you," the gangster pointed out shrewdly, "what's to keep you from selling 'em again to the night clubs?"

"You can truck 'em across the state line yourself," smiled Mike. "It's on the level. See? And here's my brother-in-law's check to close the deal."

The Italian gangster jabbed a cigaret into his mouth and fired it. "Deal's O.K., Mike, but how do I know that check is?"

"Don't have to take it," snapped Mike, his grinning mouth straightening into a taut line. "I'll write one myself," he added.

"Geese, do you take me for a sap?" Tony wanted to know. "Cripes! your checks are too damn gummy to suit me. Wait up! No hard feelings, bozo. This is business!"

Big Sam Stevens who had been taking it all in, leaped to his feet with alacrity. He grabbed Mike's arm playfully. "What's the sense in you two punks fighting just as we're about to crash the big dough. Ain't you got no brains at all?" The big Swede reached for his well-stuffed wallet. "Tell you what, fellas, I'll give Tony cash for that rum shipment. And you, Mike, give me your personal check to cover it." The Swede raised a protesting hand as Mike started to speak. "No," he firmly told the Irishman, "don't say a word. I know that you wouldn't stick a pal with bad paper. Neither would I set-up Tony with phoney money. Would I, Tony?" Tony rose to his feet "Let's see it."

Big Sam pushed a handful of crisp bills into the gangster's hands, and jabbered like an insurance salesman. "Phoney money? Hey, guy, just look at these bills. Handle 'em. If they're phoney, I'll eat 'em!"

Taking the yellow-backs, Tony walked to the window and gave each a thorough examination. "Look O.K. to me, Sam. I'll get over to the warehouse and load the trucks."

Mike Morgan sat down at his writing desk and scratched off a check to Sam Stevens. "Of course, Sam, I wouldn't throw you bad paper."

Pocketing the check, the big Swede reached for his hat. "I'll be running along with you, Tony," he told the gangster. "Got to get home and slick up. Taking a swell skirt to a whoopee brawl."

"Come around again, boys," invited Mike as he took his new found friends to the door. They patted him on the back and said that they would.

Tony Sarotto's black-curtained death car drew up before a gloomy, brick warehouse. Quickly stepping from the machine he walked up to a barred door under the weather-beaten shingle that read OFFICE. In a few minute's time the heavy curtain behind the glass was slowly pulled aside and a grim face looked out. Then the door creaked open on rusty hinges. Tony snapped a few words in Italian to the man and led the way back into the interior of the warehouse.

Weaving in and out between barrels, cases and kegs, the gangster stopped before a group of men in sweaty under-shirts. He nodded for them to go on with what they were doing. Tony then sat on an upturned keg and struck up a cigaret.

"Geese," he muttered to himself, "I'd be a sap to ship good rye to that dumb mick's brother-in-law. He won't know the difference anyway. Cripes! It would be a cinch to water the barrels."

"Hey, Angelo," he called to one of the workmen, "fix up ten *special* barrels of rye right away." Tony then hailed another dark-skinned man. "Cappo, get out your fastest truck for a run across the state line. Take three men with you—and Tommy guns. Maybe that mick will try to hi-jack the stuff." The gangster's swarthy face split in a wide grin. "It'll be damn funny if he does."

Angelo trundled out an empty barrel and held a grimy rubber hose over the brim. He twisted a spigot in the wall and water splashed into the barrel— nothing but water. When it was almost full Angelo fitted a small open-topped can into the water and adjusted it to the sides of the barrel. This he filled with his best rye. With a grin Angelo pressed the barrel top into place.

Tony got down from his perch and thrust a liquor gun into the opening barrel top. He drew a good shot of pure rye from the can. That's exactly what Mike Morgan's brother-in-law would do. But the other three quarters of the barrel would be water.

With ten barrels faked, the gangster ordered the men to the truck. One climbed to the top with his Tommy gun and two squeezed into the bullet-proof cab with Cappo. A harsh grating of gears and the truck lumbered off into the night.

Big Sam Stevens was having one whoopee time with his swell skirt. From her frizzed red hair to her stilt-like French heels she was "there." A lot of other guys thought so too and Big Sam had his hands full for a while. To this point he had broken two heads and sent one fresh wop for a ride. Then he and his redheaded lady friend settled down to emptying whiskey bottles.

It was well past midnight when he was showing her the fine points in the difference between real currency and the kind that he made. He bragged, "Not even that little dago Sarotto could tell the difference. It was easy fooling that mutt. Why, I stuffed a whole wad down his throat and they was phoney—phoney as hell!"

To Mike Morgan it seemed that he had just got into bed when his telephone jangled. Mike hurled several hot suggestions at it and rolled over with his pillow wrapped around his ears. But the instrument rang loud and stubbornly. Finally the Irishman slid his feet into bedroom slippers and knuckled the sleep out of his eyes. Reaching for the telephone he bawled:

"Who is it?" When the voice at the other end identified itself, Mike cooled down. "Oh, it's you, Joe. Get the rye all right? Fine; but why the hell get me outa bed at this hour to tell me?—WHAT?—Them barrels *was watered!*—The old can trick, eh?—Huh? You're gonna stop payment on that check?—It's my tough luck, is it?—You dirty low-down—"

A click on the wire told Mike that his brother-in-law had hung up. The racketeer sat fuming and spluttering for the best part of a half hour. "Hell!" he growled. "I expected to make a neat little haul on this job—because that check I gave to Big Sam was a rubber. Now I'm sunk!" He leaped to his feet with clenched fists. "And it's that damn little dago's fault. I'll fix him! He double-crossed me. Hell, you can't trust nobody any more."

The new Police Commissioner selected a fragrant Havana from his humidor and glanced at the dainty clock on his glass-topped desk. It registered fifteen minutes past ten. He looked out of his window at the serene fall morning.

"There's only one way to handle gangsters and racketeers," he told himself, "and I know—"

At that moment the grizzled old detective captain burst into the private office with a handful of precinct reports. He tossed them under the commissioner's nose. "I know what's on 'em," he snapped, "so I'll tell you and save time."

The dollar cigar dropped from the commissioner's gaping mouth. That flinty gleam in the captain's eyes told him that something—everything was wrong.

With a grim smile, the detective chief started off. "Sarotto's warehouse has just been bombed. Two of the wop's death cars are smashed up in front of Big Sam Stevens' printing plant. A dozen pineapples were tossed at the plant and it looked like the Frisco 'quake had parked there all night. Five of the Swede's best rods are stiff in the street in front of Mike Morgan's hang-out which looks like all the bullets in the world had struck it. And a couple of Morgan's high-speed armored cars are decorating lamp-posts in the wop district."

The commissioner slumped in his chair and groaned.

"Yep," said the captain as he moved toward the door, "the only way to handle them mutts is to kill 'em off. And I'm taking out a dozen riot squads right now to do just that little thing." With his hand on the door knob, the veteran detective flung over his shoulder, "When I get back we're going out and buy me that new hat!"

Kid Dropper Plays It Alone

By CLEMENT WOOD

The job seemed as sure as The Dropper was safe from bullets that he could play it alone—but he forgot one thing—he was butter in the hand of a skirt!

IT WAS SAFE TO VISIT THE PLACE IN THE DAYTIME, that he knew. But, safe or not, Kid Dropper would have gone ahead.

Nothing had ever stopped him yet: nothing ever would, the whole Suffolk Street gang knew. If he was safe at black midnight in the thick of East Side gunmen and cops, what should he fear when bright noon sparkled over these April Westchester woodlands?

The car rattled across the bridge over the tracks just above Garrison, and took the uphill road. For a mile, the way was flanked by the evergreened borders of two great estates. Then they turned up a steeper, wilder road to the right, and were at once in the midst of the untouched forest.

The car groaned in zig-zag fashion up the narrow rocky road, high above a noisy torrent in the hill pocket, just below them; so they made for the top.

Here the Dropper had the car parked in an unkempt grassy opening. "Come on, Abe," he called to the chauffeur. The two of them set out on foot for their goal—the lofty outside of the house called Aiken's Folly.

You must have seen the place, if you ever rode down the Hudson past Garrison, or stopped at West Point or Highland Falls to stare across the swirling river. Aiken's Folly is the tall shell of a house, four stories high, smack on the top of a great cliff. It has always been a shell. Some say that a Wall Street plunger gave his wife exactly a million to build it; and, when this sum was sunk in the concrete base and the cavernous structural steel framework, refused her another cent to complete it.

Native guides point to the deep concrete pits in front, and tell of interrupted German plans to place guns here, during the World War, that would have blown West Point to bits. All these may be only myths: but there the high hollow shell of a house stands, in the eyes of the curious tourist world good for nothing, and used for nothing.

Kid Dropper knew otherwise. He had stumbled by accident upon the secret; he was quick to make use of it. That was why he was closing quietly in on the place, an early April morning, at an hour when he knew it should be empty. But he took no foolhardy risks; empty or not, all the way his hand was on his gun.

Eyes peering intently, he reached hemlock. Nothing stirring yet . . .

"Keep yer iron handy," he cautioned Abe Beck, the close-mouthed chauffeur.

Like two velvet-footed shadows, the two men sped across the open space to the shelter of the building. Like human flies, the Dropper in the lead, they scuttled noiselessly along the concrete wall, to the first opening.

The Kid swung himself recklessly up to the floor level, disdaining the exposed plank trodden by most of the few curious visitors. Beck was at his side at once. The two men, dwarfed into insignificance by the immensity of the high-ceilinged shell on whose rim they stood, stared suspiciously into the interior.

"It's clear," said the Dropper casually. "Come on."

The flooring was of iron, and clanged hollowly at their softest step.

"Speed it," the Kid ordered sharply, and hurried ahead across great vault-like rooms, till he came to the only enclosed space in the building. He knelt here on the floor, pointing to a huge padlocked trap-door to the basement.

"That's where they keep the stuff, when any's here," he muttered cryptically. "I dunno—other way's sure, anyhow. Yeah, it's gotter be the other way. Come on—hurry; if them guys turned up—"

Back to the main hall he hurried, leaving Abe Beck to wonder who the "other guys" might be. But he said not a word: in good time he would know. When they reached this place, the interior of the house rose, without intervening floors, four stories high.

Up the center zig-zagged an iron stairway; for this the leader made. They went clear to the top landing, and so out upon the highest balcony leaning on the sky.

The view of river and hill from here was magnificent. But not to the Dropper: his eyes measured only the hill road they had come, and the far ribbon of brown below that was the Post Road back to New York. Suddenly his eyes grew tense: there was a city taxi coming, where no city taxi should be.

"Speed it," he hissed suddenly, taking the way down in great flying leaps, that set the echoes leaping and shrieking metallically all around them. Disdaining cover this time, they made for the red and black taxi that had brought them, and piled in. "Give her everything," he ordered fiercely.

The car slid and slithered down the rocky hill road. At the bottom, the leader ordered Beck to slow up, to turn right instead of left, to drive across the shallow ditch at the right of the road, and to hide the car behind glossy-leaved rhododendron and mountain laurel clustered conveniently at the corner.

Not a moment too soon—the city taxi groaned up the easier hill, and turned up the way they had gone, hardly three minutes afterwards. Abe Beck's eyes widened in amazement as he saw who was in the car. He could not keep silent this time: "It's Little Goldie," he marvelled, "an' 'Get 'Em' Engel—most of Allen Street, Kid!"

"Yeah. An' Suffolk Street don't love any of 'em too much."

Beck chuckled grimly. The rivalry between the two gangs had cost more than a dozen lives in the last six months.

"What's the game, Kid?"

The Dropper explained to Beck as much as it was good for him to know. "It's rum-runnin', Abe. Them wise guys horned in on the swell boot-leggin' game. The border runners bring the stuff this far down from Canada, an' hide it under that old tin loft. Then Little Goldie's gang picks it up, in milk trucks—whaddya know about that! Big money, boy. So tomorrer night—that's when they run it in, Choosdays an' Fridays—that's when we come in."

"The gang?"

"I'm playin' this all alone—me an' you, Abe. I got my own little debt to pay. It's all worked out. To make it look nice, you see, for the cops, they ain't even got a guard ridin' in—only that Mike Spadoni chauffin' the 'Meadow Dairy' truck. Then I hi-jack 'em, see? It's stewed rhubarb, this job is."

"Tomorrer night, eh?"

"We'll beat it out of Noo Yawk about midnight, an' get to Peekskill before three. The truck leaves up here just at three. Come on, we can get started now."

Abe backed the car savagely back to the road. "That lob ain't got a chanct in the worl'!"

Moe Korn, known all over lower Manhattan as Kid Dropper, was, in the eyes of the police department, the toughest gunman on the East Side. Not a gang murder for four years, the knowing ones said, but he had had his hand in it some way. Yet, before any living witnesses arrived, like a shadow he had dissolved away.

Barring one jail sentence for being seen throwing away a gun, his record was clear; even that case, he claimed, had been framed up against him. Nobody knew a thing against his record: just as nobody was fooled as to what he really was. In the eyes of reformers, he was an utterly vicious killer, with not a good word to be said for him.

In the eyes of the Suffolk Street gang, that he ruled with a grip of steel, he was the ideal man, with only one fault. That fault was women. If it wasn't Bessie Laut, it was Mamie Kaplan; if it wasn't Mamie, it was Yetta Wolff; if it wasn't Yetta, it was that uptown blonde of Saul Cohen's, or some other soft-eyed skirt.

Heretofore, the Dropper had changed his girls as easily as he changed his necktie or his name. But Yetta Wolff was different.

There was something hard about her eyes much of the time—something hard and fine. She saw the Kid's easy smile answer the open invitation on the admiring face of Saul Cohen's uptown girl, and her eyes grew hard and beautiful.

"Look yere, Kid," she crooned to him, voice still gentle, "lay off that uptown cheese. She's nothin' to you—an' you've got me—ain't it honey?"

"You got a nerve," he said. "You ain't got no mortgage on me."

Her eyes flashed hard and dangerous fire. "I'm straight with you, Kid; you play straight with me."

"Aw, I wouldn't lift my little finger to save that skirt's life, if she was drownin' in apple sauce," he assured her easily.

"Don't let me catch you playin' around with her, just the same."

"Whaddya think I am, anyhow? Aw, be reasonable, baby. My mind ain't on no uptown jizzies. I got a big job on, Yetta—real pile for me an' you, an' no dividin'!"

"Come on, tell me!"

"Aw, I couldn't yet—"

But no fly in the web of a spider was more hopeless than Kid Dropper in the hands of a woman. Yetta kept at it, and out it all came—the whole plan to get hold of the priceless week's truck-load of contraband rum from the Allen Street gang.

"You'll be spendin' every cent of that wad, baby. Think I'd bother about another dame?"

"Don't let me catch you doin' it, that's all."

She had to be content with this; but she kept her eyes open. This had been several days before; and she knew the Kid, and his weakness for ladies. It wasn't hard to pump Meyer Korn, the Dropper's brother who was studying law in his vacations from gunplay. Meyer never guessed what she was driving at: his mind was whirling with torts and arsons and law quizzes. But he leaked enough to send her flying, the very night that the Kid returned from his jaunt into Westchester, over to the dance at the Labor Temple.

She didn't see him at first; she almost hoped Meyer had been wrong. No, there he was, he and that uptown blonde, clinched as tight as a large family in the subway at rush hour, while the band jazzed out some seductive Blues. This was enough.

Yetta started to slip away, eyes blinded by a sudden sting. The Kid saw her just at this moment, and waved a worried hand at her.

When he came across to see her, as the dance ended, she was gone.

He threw it off lightly; a synthetic pearl choker, a little soft talk, would make it right. He forgot entirely that Sollie Fein, who was right in the heart of the Allen Street gang, was Yetta's cousin. And, before her anger had time to cool, she had found Sollie, and had poured out the story of her abandonment in his receptive ears.

Sollie kept on his pinochle face. "Yeah, he's a bad egg, the Dropper is. Ain't much of a real man—"

"Little you know!"

"Ahhh! he always skips when his gang's in trouble—wouldn't dare do a thing by himself—"

Her breast rose furiously. "Why, right now, Sollie, he's goin' to stick up a bootleg truck tomorrer night, an' hi-jack the whole load, all by himself!"

A sudden suspicion formed in the gangster's agile mind. "He wouldn't dare fool around our truck—"

"Oh, wouldn't he!" She had already said more than she intended; she ended by saying more still.

"He's lyin' to you, Yetta," Fein taunted. "He'll be playin' around with that blondie again."

Out it all came now; the very thought of that other woman drove all caution out of her mind.

Sollie's face threw off its mask. "I'll fix him!" with gritting teeth.

"Don't hurt the boy," suddenly contrite. "He's my man, if he'd only play straight—"

"We'll just scare him off," he lied easily.

Within half an hour, the willing ear of Little Goldie itself had the whole thing. The brains of the Allen Street mob were gotten together. Kid Dropper—and alone! This was the chance they had always waited for.

They argued long and hard over the plans, and at last worked out what ought to settle the Dropper's hash completely.

At three a.m. the next morning the milk truck started, loaded to its roof, except down the center, from Aiken's Folly. But it was not Mike Spadoni who drove down alone. Hunched beside him on the driver's seat sat Max Engel, "Get 'Em" Engel, the crack shot of the whole gang; inside the truck crouched Sollie Fein and Morris, his brother; and, starting out three minutes behind, Little Goldie himself followed with a carload of his mate's, all with guns out. There would be no slipup on this trick!

As they started from the hill above Garrison, the Dropper and his taciturn chauffeur reached Peekskill. They drew up the car before a drowsing all night lunch, its nose pointed toward New York. They sat waiting quietly. It was still night, but something in the air said that day was near.

"He's startin' now," Kid muttered smilelessly. "We'll tail in behind him, an' when he reaches the first likely space on the road—"

"Yeah," Abe Beck nodded in grim joy. "That lob won't have a chanct in the worl'!"

A solitary policeman owled out of the Peekskill dimness, took one look at the peaceful pair parked before the restaurant, then thumped hollowly away into the dimness. No one else was in sight; there was no traffic stirring on the Post Road. The last night revellers had started homeward, the morning traffic had not commenced.

The Dropper carefully went over the plans again, in a low voice.

"There!" he suddenly interrupted himself, holding up a warning finger.

Abe heard it now, a low heavy rumble from the distance far behind him. It might be anything heavy—furniture moving down the Hudson, farm produce from upstate trucking down, a legitimate milk load, or the "Meadow Dairy" truck from Aiken's' Folly.

They leaned out in stiff expectancy.

Louder and louder, in the crisp air, the noise grew.

Abe set the engine going. The Kid stood at ease in the shadows behind the car, to make sure that he read the name right.

• • •

The flicker of lights at the turn three blocks away, and the heavy truck swung into sight, coasting with easy power. The Dropper tensed himself, although it was not yet necessary. He felt the presence of an enemy, even before the truck came close enough for him to spell out its name.

A block away—half a block—

"Watch it, Abe!"

The truck slithered swiftly by.

" 'Meadow Dairy—Best Milk'!"

"That's her," he whispered savagely to the driver, as he swung himself noiselessly into the back seat. "Drive like all everything, Abe—keep her in sight!"

'Round great curves the truck swept ahead of them, the car hugging the trail of its small red light a block and a half behind.

As they thundered through the hush of sleeping Oscawanna, the Dropper had his car begin to cut down the distance. After the pale lights of Tumble Inn had slashed into the gray murk and faded behind them, he told Abe to put on more juice.

The truck shot swiftly down the reversed curve of Soap Hill, and through the echoing stillness of Croton. The car gained constantly, until at the bottom of the rise to Harmon it was within a hundred feet of the flying goal.

"Now," ordered the Kid with terrible intentness.

On this hill, the loaded truck faltered a trifle. The pursuer took it on high, and at the crest, was side by side with the other vehicle.

"Get your nose in front," whispered the Kid harshly.

The car slid smoothly ahead; and side by side, the taxi's nose ahead of the truck's snub front, they raced along. The truck might have thought that the car was merely trying to pass.

The Dropper's pistol was out; he hung over the car door, his gun trained on the driver of the truck. His voice boomed startlingly above the mechanical purr of the two powerful motors. "Stop her—an' stick 'em up!"

Spadoni, who had been expecting this, slowed down at once. "Don't shoot, mister," he whined, as if frightened.

Before the truck had stopped the Dropper was aboard it, crowding over the two men on the driver's bench, as he held two guns boring upon their chests.

"Drive on—an' do jus' what I say; get me? Or I'll pump you so full of lead you'll bust the truck springs!" he gloated in savage warning.

Across the level height of Harmon, down toward the crossing that led to Ossining, the captured truck continued. The game was in his hands, the Dropper thought exultantly. The two men beside him, the two gangsters crouching out of sight in the truck's hidden interior just at his back, thought otherwise.

Abe Beck, as directed, took it easy about a block behind.

Suddenly the Kid stiffened, as he heard a sound behind him.

It was not the sound he should have heard—the sound of the two Fein boys aiming their guns through the two holes bored in the truck, which opened directly just where the Dropper's heart was bound to be, with three men crowded on the front seat. . . . Oh, Little Goldie had it all planned out.

It wasn't this the Kid heard—it was a sound from farther behind, like a tire blowing out, or the engine missing fire. . . . A single hollow pop borne faintly to him by the rushing wind—one, and then another.

Oh, well, Abe could look out for himself. Everything was swimming in gravy.

Behind him, if he could have seen, a car still followed the truck. But the car held Little Goldie and his gang. The taxi the Dropper had come in, at this very moment was plunging and veering wildly down the steep hill fields, with a dead man at the wheel. The car was not found until two days later, lying overturned in a black arm of the brackish swamp, where Croton River emptied its delta into the Hudson. The man beneath it was not found until the car was pulled off him.

The Kid guessed none of this. But he lifted his head suspiciously, as he felt, somehow, danger in the lightening air. A minute later, and he would have stopped the truck to investigate. It was thundering now across the new bridge over the Croton River. As soon as they crossed it, he decided, he would stop her and investigate—

"Now," whispered Sollie Fern, a tense, terrible whisper in the hidden darkness just behind the Dropper. Out of the two holes in the truck right behind his back there was a double spurt of flame, the sudden thunder of two shots together, the acrid spread of smoke.

After a moment's silence, Mike Spadoni stopped his engine. The brakes ground to a standstill. Engel, crouched between the chauffeur and the enemy gang leader, slid his hand down toward his gun.

The truck stopped entirely. Only then they dared look at the still, white face of the gangster beside them. It stared sightlessly ahead. With a strange, convulsive movement, the Dropper's body tumbled over the running board, upon the roadway beneath.

"Got him!" breathed Engel unbelievingly. "Bumped the lob off!"

The two Fein boys were crawling toward the back of the truck, over the boxes of contraband. Sollie reached the back door and clawed for the catch. "Get 'Em" Engel swung himself out on the river side, Spadoni following close after him. As they reached the ground they looked down for the dead body of the gangster.

It was not there!

Unbelievingly they stared at each other. The Dropper had gone, after all—nobody would drop him! Hard common sense swung back—of course the truck had moved forward a trifle, and the body had rolled back. They fell on their knees, peering toward the rear.

The car following them knew differently. Goldie, eyes tense on the slowing truck ahead, was the first who had seen the figure that rolled out from under its wheels thirty seconds later, and started running uncertainly toward the base of the hill. The first gray of dawn was triumphant in the sky now: the man was plainly visible, running more confidently with every step.

"Hey, cut round him, Angie," he ordered fiercely.

At this place, as Goldie remembered, there was a wide, flat, grassy circle, the beginning of an intended park. Round this the car shot, and, having gotten the man between it and the truck, swung skillfully toward the west again, catching him in the full glare of its headlights, which died away beyond him against the milk truck and the distant river mists.

"Abe," called out the Dropper exultantly, "we'll shoot 'em up yet—"

"It's the Kid himself!" marveled Little Goldie.

Before the Dropper had time to take a second step toward the car, two spurts of flame, and two more. He stopped dead still in his tracks.

It wasn't Abe at all! Something had gone wrong again.

The men in the car saw him take one sweeping glance around, and make for the only shelter at hand—a stone monument to the dead in the World War, hardly ten steps to the side. He threw himself leaping toward this.

"Missed him," groaned Goldie.

Angelo, the chauffeur of the car, turned it slightly sideways, so that the lights washed the big hollow boulder that was the base of the monument. There was the Kid, disappearing behind the shelter.

Panting rackingly, he crumpled to the ground, his two guns out. Only one thing, he realized, had saved his life—the one thing that Allen Streeters had not counted on. There had been that unexplained murder of a policeman less than a month before—nothing to connect it with the Dropper or his gang; and the officer, as the whole department knew, had been wearing one of the new bullet-proof vests. The papers had been full of pictures of Officer Reilly wearing the armored garment, while pistols were shot off harmlessly close to his body: so the Dropper had shrewdly sent his bullet through the officer's brain. One fumbling minute after the Kid's delightful discovery of the garment, it had disappeared down the street with the shadowy gang leader. Since then he had had it on except when sleeping. It was absolute protection against a body shot.

The two bullets from the interior of the truck had stunned him momentarily, but that was all. As long as the Allen Streeters did not guess this he was almost safe against gun or knife.

It was growing brighter by the moment, as the dawn gray spread farther and farther up the east. He took one quick look at the truck—a shot was his reward. Well, with Abe Beck gone, there was only one thing to do—to get back away from this open space, and that at once.

He rose to his full height in the shelter of the rock, prepared to run for it. Meanwhile the Allen Streeters had piled out of their two vehicles and were calling to each other plans for a concerted rush against the one desperate foeman.

All the time that this battle had been waging two other cars had been burning up the road between Manhattan and Ossining, in the endeavor to be in at the finish. For this night, starting even before the Kid's car had left the city limits, had marked another of the periodical round-ups of the East Side gangsters. This time the department was after information concerning that very policeman whose bullet-proof vest the Kid was wearing.

They found out nothing about that policeman's death. But the astute officers had rounded up not only all the gangsters available, but their girls as well. And Yetta Wolff, of course, had been one who had fallen into the net.

She had lied desperately at first; she knew nothing about anything. But somehow they had tripped up her tangling story, and by a lucky guess had played on her jealousy of the Kid and other women. She was so angry still, that she could not hold it in. So out came at last the story of what he had planned for this night, and the fact that the Allen Streeters had been tipped off.

At once two carloads of officers were started, desperately driving north, to take control of the hi-jacking game, and net all of these trouble-makers of both parties at the same time.

As the Kid, erect, started his spring toward freedom out of the grassy park circle toward the temporary safety of the pumping station a hundred feet away, the two powerful police cars swung around the curve a hundred yards off.

He sensed the coming of the cars at once. Well, friend or foe, they could not be worse to face than what lay behind him. Out of the rain of shots that whistled harmlessly around him, he ran straight for the headlights, calling aloud for help. Even ordinary travelers might protect him for a moment's breathing space against the enemy behind—and then—

Too late he noticed what new enemies were these. At that, he thought with painful rapidity, the cops had nothing on him. Still, better make a break, anyhow. He leaped from his indecision for one more try at freedom.

He had delayed too long. Two muscular officers caught him before he had taken two steps, and flung him to the ground. Before he could rise to his feet they had the bracelets on him. He found his guns wrenched violently out of his hands. He was yanked and bundled into the back car, under the guard of the police chauffeur.

The two officers joined the others, who had gone after the truck and Little Goldie's car.

The gangsters realized that this game had reached its end. Here they were, in territory alien to the rat holes and basements they were familiar with. There, too, was the truck load of rum, and no way to get it out of sight.

Morosely Goldie gave the order not to shoot. They were outnumbered; it would mean only a fight to the death. The penalty for rum-running, anyhow, was nothing compared to penalties they were always running the risk of. Hands above their heads, the four from the truck and four of the men who had been in the car came forward into the light.

At least, it had taken eleven policemen to net the nine—no, the eight of them, Little Goldie was glad to notice. Eight—he ran his eyes over them again. Who was missing? Ah, where was Harry Weiss, who had sat right behind him in the car?

Dirty little yellow squirt! Always ducking out when there was trouble. The others had warned him not to trust Harry—he only hit from behind. Where had the squirt gone, anyhow?

"We ain't doin' nothin—" Goldie began, sparring for time, as the irons were slipped over his wrists.

A powerful blow against the mouth stopped his words at once. "Shut your trap, till you're spoken to," ordered an officer, one of the unsleeping Strong-Arm Squad, bred in the gutters of the East Side, and by police wisdom matched against its lawlessness, as the only force that could end it. "If you don't dry up, I'll—"

"Aw, I wasn't sayin' nothin," muttered Goldie.

One of the officers meanwhile had brought up the car of the gangsters. The nine captives, including the Dropper, were divided, three to a car, with an adequate guard over each. Two officers were detailed to bring the truck of contraband rum down to the city.

"Got you this time, Goldie," said the sergeant in command, with a complacent sneer.

"Fer what?"

"Rum runnin'—I don't know what else."

"I ain't with that gang," said the Dropper, master of himself at last. "You know me—"

"On suspicion—Officer Reilly's death," the sergeant gloated.

"I got a alibi—wasn't in Noo Yawk a-tall when they bumped him off. You ain't got nothin' against me—you know that, Sarge. Better turn me loose."

"I ain't got no evidence, no," worried the officer aloud. "You're a bad guy, Moe Korn—I got just one thing to say to you: Noo Yark ain't big enough to hold you an' the police department. We gotter git out, or you have. You get me? You gotter get out, an' stay out. I'd turn you loose now, if you'd give me your word—"

"I ain't with this gang," he temporized. "Wouldn't be caught dead workin' with 'em. They wuz stickin' me up!—you seen 'em. You seen me comin' for help, ain't you? I'm Suffolk Street—"

"I know." The officer considered carefully. "If you don't stay out of Noo Yark, Moe Korn, you'll get it, an' good—lemme warn you—"

"Lemme go now," said the Dropper, a crafty look veiled in his eyes. He could see Abe Beck, and then—"Turn me loose here, Sarge. You know I ain't runnin' with them toughs."

"Take 'em off," ordered the sergeant curtly, after a long stare at the gangster. "These other boys is who we want. But don't lemme catch you in the city again—"

As his hands clicked free, the officer relieved him of a third pistol, swinging from a hidden holster at his side.

The Dropper trembled, for fear the police would discover the bullet-proof vest. That would be something to connect him with Officer Reilly's death. But the cop, after making sure that there were no more weapons, did not investigate any further.

"You get—an' stay got," he ordered shortly.

"This way," said a sudden tense voice from the side of the car just beside them.

Little Goldie thrilled suddenly, as he recognized the unexpected voice. It was Harry Weiss, the little squirt!

Before another word could be said the anemic little gangster rose to his runty height on the running board, his face working palely. Before any one could guess his intention, he had placed a pistol against the Dropper's chest and had pulled the trigger.

There was a roar and a flash almost at the same instant.

A brawny police arm knocked the man spinning across the road. Two officers were on him before he could rise. His face was all blood as they brought him back to the car.

The Dropper stared at him, shaken but uninjured. "Not that way," he smiled stiffly. "The man ain't livin' can poke me off— So long, Sarge." His mind was already working furiously. There was something still to be done at the vast shell of a house called Aiken's Folly. So he disappeared into the murk of the dawn.

Gangster Stories, March 1930

A Page from the Publisher's Notebook

THE GLITTERING PEOPLE ABOUT WHOM YOU READ in these rapid-action stories are a weird lot. Many of them might have easily stepped out of the pages of Charles Dickens.

A forlorn yet fantastic army of the underworld!

To believe in their reality would be stupid. After all, they are creatures of our writers' imagination and nothing else. The test of a writer lies in his ability to make them seem real, but for us to believe all we see or even half of what we hear, would be permitting ourselves of but a fractional part of the brains given us by a wise Deity.

If we are shrewd we can read a great lesson from these pages, as well as be entertained by the machine-gun plots, the hair-trigger situations.

These characters are along the fringe of things. They live in shining splendor for a short time. They appear healthy. However behind them always are shadows sinister and weird: Death, Disease and Retribution!

Sooner or later, mostly sooner, their fantastic hours are over. They go forth to rot in prison cells. They are shot down by their enemies, their bodies left in alleyways and open lots. Their wealth is lost by gambling and reckless living. The haunts they once knew, no longer know them—in fact they are completely forgotten.

They pay dearly for their moments of high speed. Let us read of them but bear in mind that this army of the underworld is only a shell that glitters under the spotlight, but which is being crushed like a giant worm as it winds through the spotted darkness.

Faithfully yours,
HAROLD HERSEY

Racketeer Stories, March 1930

Paragraphs from the Publisher's Notebook

TINSEL CHILDREN OF THE DARKNESS are the characters in these stories—wayward children—yet spawn of the Devil himself!

They dance—marionettes in dazzling finery—in the white spotlight our authors throw upon them. They dance the dance of death. Their thin faces smile, but it is only a set grin of pain when you examine them closely.

Their finery is as gay as their laughter sounds, yet we see that there are patches; their jewels only paste. Their lives are rapidly being snuffed out; they soon pay their debts to nature and to Humanity in full.

Read of them, yes! But follow them—no! They teach us to beware of the clammy touch of temptation and sin.

These stories are entertaining—smashingly so—but they are also object lessons to help us in life. For knowledge is power. If we know, then we are not apt to run innocently into trouble.

HAROLD HERSEY,
Publisher

A Regular Moll

By LLOYD ERIC REEVE

Scar wouldn't keep a skirt what wouldn't blot anybody they caught giving him the double-cross! Scar's skirt was regular!

CROUCHED BENEATH THAT DUSTY HALL STAIRWAY, "Scar" Ladrone, gangster, was out to get the low-down on Fannie Duffin.

Fan was Scar's regular moll, had been for two years; he'd taken her out of "Pipe" Hendrix's "race-track" dance hall, fitted her up with a slick joint of her own, put her in the pink right. Then, only this morning, he got word that she was handing him the double-cross.

Money was Fan's soft spot; she craved the stuff like a dope did his needle. That fat dick, Garlan, had promised her a roll—so the office stool had tipped Scar, and she came across.

Now, Scar wanted to wise up the details. Garlan would never take him in alive. Scar had too many friends at the office; besides, there was the opposing liquor gang, rival racketeers, who had greased Garlan's palm.

Not alive; no, Garlan would bait a trap. Scar would walk into it, and before he could even touch his rod, their scatterguns would riddle him.

Then Garlan would make his smudgy report: "resisted arrest; officers fired in self defense." All jake; Scar Ladrone would never hi-jack another booze truck; while Garlan—Garlan could retire on easy street. Soft, eh? Scar's hand nervously twitched at his bright red necktie.

The hall door swung wide. With a wintry blast of snow and city coal smoke, two figures dodged in, Fan and the beefy, heavy-jowled Garlan.

Three feet from Scar, they whispered; Scar could pipe every word they uttered.

Finally, Garlan growled. "It seems jake. But there's big money in this—two grand for you. You're sure Ladrone'll come?"

Fan laughed a metallic laugh. "Damn' tootin' he'll come. I'm his regular tart, see? Re-al soft on me, Scar is; just can't resist my lures!" She made a swaggering movement of her hips. "I'll raise an' lower th' window shade twict, see? That's y'u're low-down. Less'n five minutes, he walks out the door. Y'u fellers can't miss; he won't never have a chanct. Now how about that pin money y'u promised?"

"You get the jack," Garlan rumbled, "when Scar Ladrone has cashed his checks—for resistin' arrest, see?—an' not before! All right; now watch your step; we'll play our part." He turned ponderously, and lumbered out the door.

Repeating that low, metallic laugh, Fan murmured, "Two grand! My God, think of it!" She climbed the creaking stairs, above Scar's crouched body.

Listening, the gangster's hand had closed on a hard object in his pocket. But Scar didn't draw; instead, a sliver of a smile settled on his thin lips.

That evening, slouched at a table in Pipe Hendrix's speakeasy, Scar awaited a telephone call. His hand twiddled constantly at his red necktie, a sure sign that he had something big on.

Finally, the telephone jingled. Pipe, himself, answered, talked a moment, then sidled up to Scar.

"Fan wants y'u come right over, Scar. Says real important." The words seemed to dribble from a corner of his weasel face.

"Uh-huh," Scar nodded, "expectin' 'er to call."

Pipe asked curiously, "Got a job on?"

"Big one," admitted Scar. "Fan, she's gonna get a damn' double-crosser tonight—for me, see? Just like a regular moll." He bit off a short laugh.

"Huh?" Pipe was puzzled.

But Scar buttoned his thin mouth; taking his long overcoat and hat, he left the saloon by a rear door.

To-night, Fan was real soft with Scar, even though she did wheedle him out of the money he carried. Scar thought grimly, "Anyway, she's givin' me a swell send-off!"

He leaned toward her quickly. "I hate a squealer!"

She jumped. "What made y'u say that, Scar?"

"Nothin'—only I'm being double-crossed. Double-crossers are rats. Sometime I'm gonna have you get that damn' double-crosser for me. Y'u can."

She stared at him, uncertain, puzzled.

"Fan, I've done plenty for y'u. Y'u'll do that job for me? Like a regular moll?"

"Of course. Sure—but what—"

"Never mind; tell y'u some other time—only, I wouldn't keep a skirt what wouldn't blot anybody they caught double-crossin' me. I got to know y'u're regular, don't I?"

When he was ready to leave, she idled to the window, spun up the shade, and glanced out. "Still snowin'," she observed.

Scar studied her, his lips a curved slit. She pulled the shade; then again, carelessly ran it up and down.

"Hell, Fan, y'u're hand shakes!"

She whirled, her eyes narrowing. But Scar was picking up his long overcoat and plug hat; apparently his words were a casual remark.

"I've got to go," he said slowly, "but y'u come with me—to the door."

She drew back. Two spots of rouge leaped out against her whitening cheeks.

"What's th' matter? Don't y'u wanna go to th' door with me?"

She tried to brazen it out. "Sure, Scar, I'll go to the door with y'u. Why not?"

"Why not?" he repeated softly; and put his arm around her, and they went down the creaking stairs to the hall door.

He leaned toward her. She kissed him quickly. Then, as his hand closed about the door knob, she dodged to one side.

Scar laughed. He caught her by the shoulders, whirling her around, facing him.

"Scared now?"

Suddenly hysterical, she blurted: "I didn't double-cross you, Scar! I didn't!" She opened her mouth to scream, but he clapped his hand over her lips.

"Y'u didn't double-cross me?"

She shook her head frantically, gurgled in her throat.

"That's jake!" He suddenly swept his coat around her shoulders, jammed his plug hat on her head, and swung wide the door. With a hard shove, he sent her stumbling into the snowstorm. "Now, prove y'u didn't double-cross me!"

The words were still leaving his lips, when that cordon of sawed-off shot guns bellowed.

Swiftly Scar whirled, dodged down the hall, and slipped into the rear alley. "Sure," he muttered, nervously adjusting his red necktie, "Fan got the double-crosser for me—just like a regular moll!"

Hair-Trigger

By William E. Poindexter

Benny was leader—and now he was out—croaked by one of his own mob! But. Benny never needed to hire a rod to protect himself! Even in death, Benny would get the rat that got him!

BENNY APPCO, YOUTHFUL GANG LEADER, lay dead in the front room of his home. Suffocating masses of flowers, tribute not only of gangland, but of many within the law, were piled high about him, filling the room and overflowing into the other parts of the house, accentuating the air of death that pervaded the place.

Stella Maud sat by her bedroom window, staring somberly down into the street which was still crowded by the morbidly curious, tears in her heart but not in her eyes.

Stella Maud was an anomaly of the underworld. She was a one-man woman. Since that time almost six years before, when the young Italian had swept her off her feet and carried her triumphantly from under the very guns of "Red" Vernon and his North Side gang, she had been loyal to him.

Stella Maud rose and paced the floor, lighting a cigarette only to crush it under her heel the next minute. The yellow morning sunlight streaming in upon her picked out hard lines in her face that had not been there yesterday. The word had gone out that Red Vernon had put Benny on the spot, but she didn't believe it. It had none of the earmarks of Vernon's work. She knew. With a quick, terrible exclamation deep in her throat, she threw open her door.

"Are you there, Steve?" she called huskily.

Steve Maris was there, small, quiet, insignificant-looking. As far as appearances went he might have been an elderly ribbon clerk on his day off. His eyes were those of the killer. Deadly eyes. Chilled steel.

"Steve, now that Benny's gone, you're the only one of the mob I can trust. This thing looks queer to me—damn queer. Has Rat Martin been around lately?"

Steve looked at her without apparent emotion, and shook his head slowly. "You don't think he—"

She hesitated a moment in indecision. "No, I don't," she said at last with a gesture of contempt. "The rat wouldn't have the nerve to do it himself. But he might know who did do it. He knows everything."

Steve's eyes grew a shade paler, a degree more deadly. "I'll make him talk," he said laconically.

"No, Steve, you're a good egg, but let me handle this. Do you know where I can locate the Rat?"

He gave her a number. "It's early, probably won't be up yet," he said with an economy of words.

She nodded, flung on her hat and coat, saw that the efficient little automatic in her handbag was ready for business. She went out, avoiding the room where Benny lay, and stepped into her low-slung Cadillac sedan with its cleverly armored body and bullet-proof glass. Twenty minutes later she stood before a door in a cheap rooming house. She tried the knob, found the door unlocked, and without hesitation pushed it open.

As she stepped in, the man on the bed turned in one swift movement, covering her with an automatic. She made a gesture of disdain.

"Put it up," she said contemptuously. "Getting careless, leaving the door unlocked, ain't you?"

"Guess I was drunk last night," he admitted a bit sheepishly. "What you doing here, Stell?" He sat up, running his fingers through his tousled hair, his narrow, red-rimmed little eyes regarding her shrewdly.

"Listen Rat, who croaked Benny?"

"How do I know? Probably Red—"

"Hell!" she spat at him. "It wasn't Red's work and you damn well know it. You know who done it—you know everything."

He chuckled, then his eyes grew hard. "You're right," he said slowly, "I know who done it an' I'm going to tell you. I've got a good reason for lettin' you know. It was Slink Douglas who put Benny on the spot."

A slight swaying of her body was the only sign that the news was a terrific shock to her. Slink Douglas, Benny's most trusted friend, with the exception of Steve Maris. Sudden divination came to the girl.

She nodded without apparent emotion. "But I'll guarantee that you had your finger in it, too," she said, and forced her mouth into a smile.

The Rat grinned back. "Maybe," he admitted complacently, "but it was Slink who put the lead in 'im. Now listen here, Stell, you know yourself that the gang's been ready for a new leader for a long time, an' Slink fancies himself for the job. That suited me all right, I never had any love for Benny, anyway. So I did what I could to help him. But I didn't know till afterwards that Slink not only wanted Benny's mob, but he wanted Benny's moll as well!"

"He did, huh? Well, what's that got to do with you?"

"It's got everything to do with me. Think I'd spill this if it didn't? As long as Slink only wanted to be leader of the gang, I was for him. But now that I know he wants you, I'm against him.

"Stell, Benny must have at least a hundred grand soaked away, maybe two hundred. You an' me are goin' to take that coin, baby, an' beat it to New York. From there we'll go to Paris, we'll see the world. To hell with the gang—an' with Slink Douglas, too!"

Stella Maud opened her hand-bag, took out a powder puff and patted her nose with it. When she replaced it she neglected to close the bag.

The Rat rambled on. "I've always known you was crazy about me, Stell," he stated with noticeable lack of modesty, "only you didn't dare cross Benny. Now that he's out of the way, you're gonna be my girl, an' we'll take a long trip—"

Her hand stole again to the handbag. "You mean you're going to take a long trip, Rat." Her voice broke, rose in a shrill falsetto of passionate, ungovernable hate. "A trip to hell, damn your dirty soul, a trip to hell!" The automatic gleamed evilly in her hand.

"Listen Stell, for God's sake put that thing down! Stell! Don't be a damned fool!"

His face livid with fear, he flung himself at her and she pressed the trigger twice. His body fell against her, almost knocking her from her feet, and there were twin holes in the center of his forehead.

She dropped the pistol back in her bag and deliberately placed her foot upon his still writhing mouth, ground down upon it with a cruel heel, elemental hate and fury in the action. Almost instantly she regained her composure and stepped hastily to the window.

A policeman walking his beat had heard the shots and was running towards the building. Without an instant's hesitation she jammed her hat lower over her face, pulled up the fur collar of her coat and flung up the window.

"Help! Police!" she screamed at the top of her voice. The cop saw her, increased his pace and clattered up the stairs. She met him in the dimly lighted hall.

"Oh, my God!" she moaned, apparently half-fainting. "They got him, they got him!"

"Pull yourself together, miss," the policeman cried hoarsely, catching her not ungently by the arm. "What's the trouble? Who got who?"

"Oh, quick, quick!" she screamed. "They'll get away—down the back stairs!" She leaned weakly against the wall, and the cop dashed away, revolver in hand.

As soon as he was out of sight she walked down the steps, turned the corner without haste, entered the Cadillac and a few minutes later was back in her room.

"The Rat talked," she told Steve with a grim little laugh. Then as an afterthought: "But he won't talk again."

The gunman shot a quick glance at her but said nothing. She walked the floor with quick, nervous strides, her graceful body swaying with unconscious seduction. Her keen mind was working in swift flashes, forming plans, revising them, rejecting them. Gradually a light dawned in her eyes, a triumphant light. She turned to Steve.

"Listen, Steve, I croaked the Rat. He had it coming to him, but he was only a tool in the hands of the one who got Benny from spot." She paused, her body strangely tense.

"Steve, you know how Benny always was. When anybody did him dirt, he didn't hire a gun to even things for him. No, he always settled his scores in person. Steve, let the word go out that before Benny is put underground, he'll get the one who killed him!"

"Stell, stop that!" Steve's voice was sharp. "Don't let this thing get you. You talk like that an' you'll land in the bughouse. Benny's dead, Stell."

"You do as I tell you, Steve," she insisted. "I know it sounds crazy, but if you want to help me, do as I say. Pass the word around that Benny's not through yet. Tell 'em Benny'll get the rat who croaked him!"

Steve looked at her thoughtfully. "Why not let me know who killed him, Stell. I'll get him for you. You know you can depend on me."

"I know, Steve, but think how it would please Benny to know that he'd steeled this affair himself." She choked suddenly, then straightened defiantly, forcing back her emotion. "I've got a better way, Steve. Please do as I say."

Again he looked at her with that curiously appraising stare that seemed to bore straight into her innermost thoughts.

"Oke, Stell," he said at last.

"And Steve—be sure the mob is at the funeral this afternoon; all of 'em."

He nodded. "They'll be here," he said briefly, and turned silently away.

A few minutes later Slink Douglas entered and leaned in the doorway, his eyes flaming as they devoured her lithe body.

"Rotten luck, Stell, Benny gettin' it like that. But it's how he'd like to pass out—with a bullet in 'im. The boys are givin' him a great shove-off, too. Benny was a grand little guy."

For an instant she bit her lips savagely, fighting desperately for self-control. Her hands twitched at her breast and she lowered her eyes so that he could not see what was in them.

"Yeh," she said at last, "and it's the grand little guys who always get bumped off—shot in the back—by their friends. Friends!" She fairly spat the word.

"Aw, Stell," Slink remonstrated, "you shouldn't ought to say that when nobody knows who croaked him. But, whoever done it, I'll find him, kid—I'll get him for Benny—an' for you."

"Lookit, Slink!" Stella Maud whirled on him so passionately that his beady black eyes narrowed swiftly. "Lookit, Slink. Benny never needed nobody to get a guy for him—an' never will. He never asked nobody to do what he could do himself, and do better."

"Sure, Stell, sure, but you gotta remember that Benny's gun finger is stiff now!"

Stella Maud reached into the front of her black dress and brought forth a small revolver which was constructed with the care and delicacy of a high-priced watch. Slink straightened up and eyed her calculatingly.

"That's Benny's rod," said Stella Maud, fondling it, caressing it, "and I'm going to plant it with him. He'll need it maybe where he's goin'. He didn't think no more of it than he did of the hand he used it with. See, it's got a hair-trigger, Slink. If you breath hard it says 'hello' and 'goodby' at the same time. Slink, Benny knows who got him, and as sure as hell, Slink, he'll get the yella, lousy rat that croaked him before they put him under the dirt!"

Slink Douglas shifted his feet uneasily and fumbled for a cigarette.

"All right, Stell," he soothed, "this thing's gettin' on your nerves. Now listen, baby, I don't want to rush matters, but Benny's as dead right now as he'll ever be. The boys all know me an' they'll take orders from me. I'm ready to carry on where Benny left off. Stell, you know I've always been crazy about you—"

"Too crazy, maybe," she said evenly.

His eyelids flickered rapidly. "What do you mean by that?" he snapped. "What do you mean by it?"

She shrugged her shoulders. A little smile came to her lips as she raised her eyes slowly to his. There was seduction in her eyes, a promise in her smile. His heart leaped as he stepped towards her.

"I always loved you, kid," he said softly, "an' now that Benny's gone, you could do a lot worse than play along with me. Gee, kid, what do you suppose I've hung around all these years for? Just waitin', Stell, for the time when I could have you!"

His face flushed, he reached out his arms for her. For an instant she hesitated, filled with a terrible nausea. In her green eyes were little flecks of red light. She swayed forward, allowed her slender body to mold itself against his.

Black thoughts were racing through her mind. "I could put an ounce of lead in his guts right now," was the thought that burned through her. "The dirty, lousy rat, I could send him to hell so quick he'd be there before he knew it. No, no, I mustn't do it that way!"

Her full mouth was against his, her hands were running through his hair caressingly. He was mumbling incoherent things into her ear that she did not hear.

"Benny," she whispered deep down within her, "you understand, don't you, honey? It's for you, Benny. We'll send him to hell, Benny, you and me."

She pushed Slink away at last and sat down suddenly as her knees gave out from under her.

"You was Benny's friend, wasn't you, Slink?" she asked at last, her hands clenched close to her sides. "You was his pal, the one man he could depend on, wasn't you, Slink?"

"Sure, I was Benny's pal," he replied quickly. "An' as long as Benny was alive I never tried to get his moll away from him, even when I loved her. That's how square I was kid."

"Because you was yellow, you rat!" said Stella Maud, but she said it to herself. Then aloud: "Benny always trusted you, Slink. Why he used to say to me often, 'Slink is the only guy in the whole damn mob that I'd trust to the limit.' Only last night, not an hour before he was croaked he said to me, 'Slink's one white guy. I'd trust him with my life, my moll or my money.' He sure thought the world of you, Slink."

Douglas bit his lips and writhed nervously. She watched him, taking a fiendish delight in twisting the knife in him. He changed the subject.

"That's over with, Stell. Let's forget it. I'm chief of the best gang of guns in the country now, an' as soon as I get things lined up, we'll make more money than we ever did before. This is the time I've waited for, lived for. It's been hell, kid, to love you as I do, an' see you with another man. That's over with. Gee, Stell—"

He reached for her again. She shrank back, almost at the end of her endurance, but he caught her fiercely by the shoulders, drew her from the chair and caught her to him. His lips bruised her mouth, his possessive hands ravaged her body.

"Don't," she half-sobbed, "don't!"

There was a faint scraping sound at the doorway, and Slink turned sharply, his face paling and his hand reaching towards his hip. Steve Maris stood there, his face as emotionless as ever, his eyes seeming almost white, a heavy black automatic held close to his side.

"Let her go, Slink," he said, his voice a low, even monotone. "Stand back from him, Stell. He's lived long enough."

Slink's face turned a sickly yellow. "You keep out of this Steve," he snarled. "What business you got buttin' in on me an' Stell? You sweet on her yourself?"

"Stand away from him, Stell." There was no change in the killer's voice. "I promised Benny years ago that I'd look after you if anything happened to him. Stand away from him."

Stella Maud suddenly threw herself back into Slick's embrace. "No, no!" she cried fiercely, "stay out of this, Steve. It's all right, I tell you. You leave him alone."

"She loves me," boasted Slink. "Don't you baby?"

"I—I—yes, I love him, Steve," she answered, not meeting his accusing eyes.

The gunman stared at her, one corner of his mouth drawing down in a grimace of contempt. "All right," he said at last, "I guess Benny and I was both wrong. You ain't worth protectin'. Benny would be proud of you, Stell—in another man's arms before he's cold yet."

"Steve—don't!" The word was a sharp cry of pain. "You remember what I told you this morning, Steve—leave this thing to me."

Again he subjected her to that searching stare that seemed to penetrate her most secret thoughts, and what he saw caused him to put the gun back in his pocket with a quick jerk of his arm.

"Oke, Stell," he said laconically, and backed silently from the room.

"What's the matter with the fool?" snarled Slink, brushing the perspiration from his face with a shaking hand. No one knew better than he how near death he had been.

She shrugged her shoulders. "He's always been sort of a watch dog where I'm concerned," she said, forcing a laugh. "Forget him. I'm going to ask you now, Slink. You'll be here at two o'clock for the funeral, sure?"

"I'll be here, kid," he promised her. "And tonight, tonight you'll be mine, won't you baby?"

"I'll be yours tonight—if you still want me then, Slink," she said steadily. "But don't forget, Benny's going to get the skunk that croaked him. Funny how I know, ain't it, Slink?"

"Cut out that crazy talk, kid," he said roughly. "You better lay down and rest till the funeral. I'll be back later."

As soon as he was gone, she stepped quickly to the other room where Steve paced idly about. "Steve," she said, "I want to be alone with Benny for awhile. Don't let anyone come in. And whatever you do, Steve, leave Slink alone. Get me?"

He nodded without speaking, and she went into the room where the body of the gang chief lay, closed and locked the door. Once he heard something like a tearing, strangled sob from her, but when she came out a half hour later, her face wore a strange look of peace and exultation.

It was two o'clock in the afternoon, the room had been crowded and for an hour a long line of people had filed past the casket where the young king of gangland lay. Stella Maud stood aloof, watching, her eyes dry and bright. When Slink Douglas edged slowly up to pay his last respects to his chief, he found Stella Maud by his side.

"Benny was a grand little guy," he whispered, his hand on her arm.

She nodded. "And he'll get the man who croaked him, Slink," she whispered. "Look at him. He knows who croaked him, and he'll get him, sure as hell!"

Douglas shivered slightly and would have passed on, but she held him back.

"Benny always said you was his best friend. Don't leave him like this. Shake hands with a grand little guy for the last time!"

"You're batty," he muttered uneasily, but she caught him frantically by the arm.

"If you love me, Slink!" she whispered tensely. "You'll do it for me if you love me like you said. Here—stand—here!"

The gang chief's body, in the open casket, was covered with flowers, leaving only the wax-like face and one hand exposed. There was no way for Douglas to avoid it. With a noticeable shudder he reached down and took the cold fingers gingerly. There was a muffled report and he fell to the floor, writhing, hands clutching at his stomach, his face twisted in pain and horror.

Before anyone could move, Stella Maud bent swiftly over him, her eyes flaming into his dying ones.

"Do you still want me now, Slink?" she mocked in a whisper of fierce hate and triumph. "I told you Benny would get the rat who croaked him, and he did! May your black soul rot in hell forever!"

Slink knew and understood, but before he could speak, the life-blood dyed his lips.

The police never discovered who killed Slink Douglas, for they never thought of accusing the dead man. Only Stella Maud knew that in Benny's hand, concealed by the flowers, was a small revolver. A thread was attached to the hair-trigger so that a touch on the other hand fired the weapon.

Racketeer Revenge

By HOWARD BEAUFORT

Dirk Petroni, the leader, was dead, burned down by Pete Robinson and his gang. An eye for an eye—that's the law, so Dirk's mob was out to end Robinson. Only, if you're making any plans, leave the women out!

Two MINUTES BEFORE HE DIED, Dirk Petroni was basking in the sun on the steps of the Mansion House, drawing appreciatively on his after-breakfast fragrant Havana. His bodyguard, Joe Scalisi, stepped through the swinging doors into the lobby of the Mansion House to buy a pack of cigarettes. Undoubtedly the few steps were worth the effort they cost—for they saved his life!

For at that very moment a long, ominously black car which had been roaring down the side street, skewered about at the corner, and then stopped with a strident shriek of brakes, abreast of the Mansion House entrance. And simultaneously, there flashed in the dazzling sun, the barrels of a Thompson machine gun, grimly held by one of the scowling, tight-lipped men who occupied the car's rear seat. Like hail stones, furiously driven onto a tin roof, the machine spelt out its message of sudden death. Dirk, caught unawares, made a desperate effort to get behind the broad colonial pillar that flanked the steps, but he fell gasping, one hand clutching at his side, and a trickle of blood weirdly distorting his agonized face.

The buzz of restrained power that betokened the car's great speed increased to an avalanche of energy, and just as a few cautious heads, aroused by the rapid shooting, were being thrust out of the windows, the death car swept down the street rapidly gaining in speed. And thus, Dirk Petroni, ruler of the beer running and racketeer trust of Laster County, passed the way of all flesh in the seventh month of his reign.

That night his henchman, lieutenants and subordinates met in the council room of the gang, a concrete walled chamber in the basement of the Mansion House, to discuss the ways and means of avenging the insults and ignominy that had been heaped on the Laster Gang through the death of their chief.

"I told Dirk to stay clear of Buck County," Bad Ross, a newcomer to the Lasters growled. "What in hell did we want to hi-jack Robinson's trucks for anyway? He stayed out o' Laster County." He looked around the room for support, but at every turn he met a hostile glance.

"Well we did it, didn't we?" Red Connors snarled at him. "Dirk was the boss, an' he knew damned well what he was doing. You took your share of the split! Robinson, the lousy son of a hound pulled this deal . . . well, fellows, what do you say?"

Red leaned forward tense, with the look of a killer glinting in his steel blue eyes. "Do we bump off Robinson, or do we listen to this rat's yapping?" With a wave of his hand he scornfully indicated Bad Ross, who sat with a baleful look on his face seething with anger.

At those last words, Ross, who was Connor's rival for the throne which Dirk had so suddenly vacated, sprang to his feet with a muttered curse.

In a flash a grim, blunt nosed automatic appeared in his hands. There was a terrific roar; another, coming so suddenly on the first it seemed but an echo, two piercing flashes of orange flame, and then the acrid smell of burnt powder.

Gingerly, Red arose from the floor where he had hurled himself at the first threat from Ross, and approached the dead man. He looked thoughtfully for a moment at the remains of the man who would be king, and then calmly surveyed the onlookers who were silent. There was a questioning look in his eyes that evoked an answer from Joe Scalisi.

"O.K., Red. You're giving the orders. Whaddye say?"

The other men slowly nodded approval. Red was liked, and he was unafraid. In the eyes of the mob he had just won his right to leadership.

"Well, get this. We don't want no trouble with the Buck County mob. There's plenty of jack in Laster County for us. But—they've killed our leader, and you know the rule. Fellows, ye're goin' to get Robinson!"

There were murmurs of approval that were silenced by a brisk tapping on the door. The men looked at each other, and a few hands dropped into capacious pockets to clutch at steely, hard objects.

Red nodded to Joe and he opened the door cautiously. On the threshold stood a tall, beautifully dressed woman. She was clad in a tight fitting red velvet dress, that creased in soft folds as she entered the room. Marie was Dirk's moll, his tiger moll as she was known, for she was tall and sinuous. Her walk was the cat-like gliding step of the denizen of the jungle. And she was like her ferocious namesake. She had a great love for her man, and an implacable hatred for her enemies.

She had just heard of Petroni's death, but for her there was no time to weep. Now, like her tiger name sake, she must strike back! Grief could enter later.

"We're all damn sorry about this, Marie. Of course you know the bunch will take care of you. . . ."

"Me! What about the dirty lousy crook who killed Dirk? What about him? Who'll take care of him, the dirty dog!" She stopped short, gasping from the terrific emotional strain she was under. Joe sat her down in a chair as tenderly as if she had been a child.

"We were talking about that when you came in, Marie. Don't you worry, Robinson will get his."

"How? Are you goin' to talk, or act?" She was hard. Once more she had regained her self control, and now she concentrated on the deadly purpose that had become her aim in life.

Red came quickly to the point. They were going to act but they needed to get Robinson alone away from his gang. They would kill him and spare the rest.

"Say," Tony Picarelli broke in, "here's the dope. Robinson used to be damn sweet on Marie here, before she met Dirk. Supposin' she traps him?"

A curious light crept into the dark, murky eyes of Marie, and the wisp of a smile hovered in the corner of her mouth.

"That's fine! Are you game to pull a plant on him?" Red demanded of Marie.

"Me?" Marie seemed to be thinking deeply. "Sure. What's the lay?"

They were in a quiet conference. Marie was to do this and that. Joe understood his part? Joe understood. Tony and Mike were to stay down by

Foster's new barn, right at the turn of the road. Good.

"Go on, kid, give him a buzz." Joe held out the phone to her.

"Wait! I've got a better plan. What in hell's the use of risking Marie," cut in Red. "Here's the idea. Robinson's got a storehouse of his own private goods over on Morgan Pike. Even his own gang isn't on to it, see. An' the only guard he's got is Al White. Well, his name might be white but he's got a yellow streak runnin' down his back. All we got to do is get the jump on White and make him phone for Robinson to come over. Tell him the Prohibition guys came around and want to be squared. That's simple. Then when Robinson comes . . ."

And Connors with a half grin shrugged his shoulders.

"Whew, that's a slick one." Joe whistled at its ease and simplicity. "O.K., fellows, eh?"

"We'll take care of this without you Marie, don't worry."

"You gotta swell nerve. Worry? Gawd! I ain't scared to do my share. All I want to do is see that guy croak!"

"Go on home. We have to be gettin' busy. Here, Mike"—he turned to the little runty Sicilian, whose scarred face bore witness to innumerable lusty combats in the past—"take care of Ross." Red indicated the body of the dead man which had been piled into the corner and lay neglected there after Marie's entrance. "Now go beat it, Marie. Get a good night's rest and maybe we'll go down to Atlantic City tomorrow."

Marie turned and departed with a sour look on her face. As she drove home to her hotel where she had been luxuriously kept by Dirk, she smiled grimly to herself in the darkness, and patches of white showed above her knuckles from the intensity with which she gripped the wheel of her car.

Under Red's direction he and four other men trooped out to a speedy Duesenberg touring car, that had conveyed the lookout and guard for many a truckload of illicit beer. They carried a small arsenal with them. A sub machine gun, a similar to the one that had cut short Dirk's career, two sawed-off shot guns, viciously loaded with eight-gauge slugs. There were automatics all around, and in addition, Joe carried three eggs, hand grenades, that were intended to spell finis to the night's operations.

Red was at the wheel, driving fast. The moon was full, and the road lighted by its reflection flashed by swiftly. There was little talk in the car. Each man concentrated grimly on their single motive. Revenge. And at the same moment, revenge in another form was complicating their carefully laid plans.

Dirk's tiger moll was at the telephone.

"Hello, lemme speak to Pete Robinson.

"Never mind who I am, I want Pete.

"Hello. Pete? Listen, this is Marie. I know damn well it was you, but Dirk's dead now an' he's outa the picture. If a message comes tellin' you to hop down to the Morgan Pike hideaway you keep, remember, it's a frame-up. Never mind how I know, but I'm warnin' you, and say, Pete, maybe we can get together again." Her voice sounded seductively soft over the phone, and her gracefully molded body arched towards the phone, as she purred into the mouthpiece. Then abruptly she hung up! There was an enigmatic glint in her eyes that had turned hard and treacherous. But Pete Robinson was not there to see her. For him was the memory of her warm tones and sensuous appeal.

Scarcely twenty minutes later, Red's car slowed down from its mad pace and turned off the Morgan Pike. He drove up a dirt path for twenty yards or so, then turned the car around and backed half-way into the nearby underbrush. There it was hidden from casual sight and ready for instant flight should the need arise.

"Where's the lay?" Mike whispered.

"About thirty yards through these trees. It's a small bungalow. You and Joe sneak up the back and Tony and Jack come with me." The men nodded. Silently they filed through the woods till the bungalow confronted them. Then Joe and Mike departed to get around to the back of the house to cut off any escape. Only a dim light showed through one of the side windows and not a sound was to be heard. Even the night breeze seemed muffled as it moaned through the trees, and for a few moments a drifting cloud obscured the moon.

Red motioned to his two accomplices to stand alongside the door, then, with his left hand in his pocket and his hat pulled down over his eyes, he rapped on the door. Silence, for another moment. Then the sound of shuffling feet, and a man's cautious voice.

"Who's there? What do you want this time o' the night?"

"Is Pete Robinson in?" Red spoke in a low voice.

"Pete who? Don't know the guy. You got the wrong address."

"Yeh. Well, we're Prohibition agents, see? And we've a warrant to search this dump. So open up."

"I'm not opening up for anyone. What are you goin' to do about it?" There was a false bravado in the man's tone.

"Let's crash the door in," Jack whispered. "We can blow the lock off."

Red hesitated. It was lonely there, but still, he wasn't ready to disturb any sleeping neighbors and have the bulls break up the reception he was going to hold for Robinson.

"Give you ten to open up, then we blow the lock off!" He spoke sharply.

There was no answer.

"One—Two—Three . . ."

While he was counting there was noise of a scuffle at the back of the house. Then a muffled curse and a deep grunt. Joe sang out.

"O.K., Red. He tried to get away back here. I slapped him stiff with me black jack. He'll come to in a minute."

Red chuckled. His ruse had worked and they had made no noise at their entry. "Bring him inside," he called, "and let us in."

A bucket of water doused over White's head brought him to. Then a long draught of Robinson's best three-star sufficiently revived him so that he was able to sit up weakly and glare at his captives. They hadn't bothered to bind him, for it was known that he had a chicken heart. Red nudged him with his boot. There was a command in his voice when he spoke that the palsied gangster was quick to note.

"Get to the phone and do what I tell you to do. No stallin' or"—and he shoved an automatic into the man's ribs.

White clambered to his feet and took the phone in his hands.

"Now, you lousy hound, call up your boss, I mean Pete Robinson, and tell him this place is raided.

"Tell him the bulls landed here and we want to be squared aplenty if he's to get off. And have him hurry right down here, alone. See? One bad word from you and you won't live to say another. Get busy!"

Al White delivered his message. And for it he was rewarded by as hot, as furious and as elegant a burst of long-distance profanity as it had ever been his fortune to hear. But there was one sentence he could repeat and did repeat to Red. It was to "tell them blankety-blank crawling worms that I'm comin' to pay them in full!"

At Red's directions, Joe and Tony left the house and took up a strong position on either side of the entrance. They were hidden back of fallen logs, and each had a sawed-off shotgun and his automatic; those precautions, in case Pete came with his mob. But they didn't think it likely.

Jack stayed at the back window with his automatic and a hand-grenade. Mike and Red were at the front, with their Thompson submachine gun, their eggs and automatics ready to receive their visitors. Poor Al White lay trussed on the floor in the inner room.

In a very few minutes they heard a car roar up to the path that led to the front door and stop. Its lights were out, but evidently the driver was well acquainted with the topography of the place. For about twenty seconds absolute silence prevailed. Then a cautious voice called out:

"Come on out if you want to see me." There was a sound of shuffling. Evidently the car was being vacated. Then a heavy, powerful light that stood by the front running-board nearest the house was played full onto the scene.

Behind, the car was in absolute darkness. "Come on out! What in hell are you afraid of, you lousy bulls!"

The door of the bungalow, in the white glare of the light opened, and a nervous figure, blinded by the dazzling light, shuffled into the open. Then came the deluge! Spatatatat! It was a hidden gun playing its deathly tune. The advancing man staggered for a moment, curiously like a trussed fowl with its head chopped off, and then fell prone.

Before the occupants of the car, startled by the unexpectedness of the killing they had done, could recover from their surprise, a hail of hot lead poured out on them from three sides. They were taken by surprise. They had no target for their machine gun and could only play it wildly onto the bungalow that was spraying their car with lead. One by one, the occupants of the car either fell groaning, or ducked for cover and raced back into the darkness. From the woods came a vicious sweep of tearing lead. Crash! A grenade had been skillfully tossed with experience born of trench service at the Meuse, and the car was literally transformed into a twisted carnage.

There was the sound of a car that had come up the road being stopped. Then swiftly turned around. Red instantly guessed that their quarry was escaping. He had been too canny to fall into the trap and had sent his cohorts ahead to a terrible death. Of the machine's occupants, three lay dead, and two possibly, no more, had escaped, wounded or otherwise.

"Quick!" he shouted. "After that car!" But they were too late, for the car, gathering speed, had disappeared into the darkness. With barely a glance at the prostrate form of Al White who had walked with his hands bound behind him, and gagged, a victim to the sacrifice, Red gathered his men together and made for their car. They could never catch up to the speeding Robinson, but they were not to be denied their revenge.

"We'll get that hell-born cur yet!" he swore as they drove back from the scene of destruction. Marie will have to go through with her share. We'll carry out the original plot. Joe was cursing softly at their failure. Tony clapped him on the back and laughed.

"What the hell! Counting Al we got three of them, didn't we?"

"To hell with them! We gotta get Robinson!" Joe snarled back at him. The others were grim and silent. At the Mansion House they piled out of their car. All save Red. He was driving the machine home to the luxurious house he had fitted up for his moll out at Beau Lake.

"You guys be here tomorrow at two p.m. sure. Then we'll fix him. Watch out you ain't ambushed on your way home. And go well heeled. Keep away from the booze, too."

The men nodded, and he whisked off.

The next day they were in deep consultation with Marie. She appeared willing, even eager to go through with her original plot.

"Remember, I'll drive down toward Danbury sometime between midnight and two a.m. I'll be drivin', and I'll wear my red hat and scarf. You can't miss me. Then, right near Foster's barn you can pull the job." She was breathing hard, and there was a tense, eager light in her eyes that stirred Red. Poor kid, she seemed to be taking Dirk's death bad. They'd settle with Pete for that.

Marie stepped out to a corner drugstore to phone Robinson. For as she told them she didn't want her call to be traced.

"Hello, Pete. This is Marie." She spoke softly, eagerly, into the mouthpiece.

"Well, what do you want?"

"Didn't you follow my instructions? I meant well. Honestly, I did." She seemed very humble, begging his pardon for the catastrophe of the night before.

"I fell into their trap last night. I was a fool not to listen to you and I damn near got bumped off for it. Three of my boys got theirs." He was silent for a moment, then suspiciously, "Why the hell did you give me the tip-off?"

"Can't you guess, Pete? Now that Dirk's dead you're the only one that matters to me." There still remained that soft tone to her voice, but a curious grim smile was on her lips. "Can't I come to see you? I'm leaving this gang."

Pete softened under her melting warmth. "What's the idea?"

"I'm yours, Pete, if you'll have me." Marie choked a bit on the last. Pete's heart leaped within him. Marie in love with him! She was always his woman, even if he had married that jane, Bess. Perhaps that was why he had bumped off Dirk. Jealous.

"Do you mean that, Marie, dear? But hell, I'm married!"

"I know Pete. But I've got to go away. Come with me, just for a while. Then I can take an apartment in Danbury and you can visit me."

Pete thought for a moment. The thoughts of her tantalizing warm, slim body, her rich lips, and thrilling caresses, stirred him!"

"C'mon over baby. We'll blow outa here tonight. But watch out you're not being tailed."

Again that curious lopsided smile spread over the warm beautiful mouth of Dirk's moll, and again her murky eyes glistened for the moment as she thought of her tryst of the night. She went back to report to Red, and then she went home to rest.

She felt curiously light-hearted, but terribly weak. Before her shut eyes flashed Dirk's picture. Strong-faced, heavily muscled paws, dark hair and dark eyes. A nose that was a bit too broad, but a man of action and a man of love.

And then Dirk as he lay in death. A curious pallor over his features. Gone was his striped suit and ornate silk shirt. In their stead were quiet, rich garments, worthy of a gang chief's shroud.

Then came Red's face. Boyish at times. Quick tempered, with the fiery impulses of his Celtic race. Red hair. No, copper-colored hair, and eyes the color of hard turquoise stones. She would have liked to run her hands through his heavy copper-colored hair. But, then Red had his moll. And there had always been Dirk.

And before Dirk . . . Pete Robinson. Tall, handsome, suave Pete. Immaculately neat and quiet. But he was cruel, his mouth was heartless, and thus she had left him for the rising young Italian gangster, Dirk Petroni. And now, that evening, she was to meet Pete once more. Would she still feel her heart bound at the sight of him? Would he still stir as he used to? She missed his cold, cruel love-making. Why had she saved him on the preceding night? Would she wreck Red's plans and flee with him tonight. Or . . .

At eleven-thirty p.m. that night she stepped from her roadster and strolled haughtily into the speakeasy that provided the Buck County gang with their headquarters. There was disguised amazement on the faces of the persons there who recognized her as she asked for Pete. But they had their instructions and she was shown into a back-room, where Pete, all alone was awaiting her. At her entrance he arose and held out his arms for her.

She went to him, and slowly he pushed her head back and planted a passionate caress on her full ripe lips. For a suffocating moment she was under his spell, but then arose a picture of Dirk.

Slowly she pushed him away and released herself from his embrace. Scarcely restraining a shudder, she smiled at him, and said:

"Later, Pete. Not now. Hadn't we better go before someone phones your wife?"

"You're right, kid. Still usin' the old bean. Just a couple of shots and we're off." He filled two glasses from a bottle that stood on the table, and handed one to her.

"To the end," she held out her glass and looked warmly at him.

"To the end," he repeated and they touched glasses, then tossed their drinks off.

They had another, and then another. Marie glanced at her watch. It was getting late and the gang would be waiting. She took her victim by his coat lapel and snuggled her head into his shoulder.

"We must go now, dear." They departed. Marie was wearing her heavy fur coat, and on her head was the crimson hat she had spoken of. It was matched by her scarf. She led the way to her car. Now they were driving down towards the Danbury road.

Where are we going, baby?" He was slightly under the influence of liquor, and it made him at once, more romantic and a trifle suspicious.

"Let's spend the night in Danbury."

He agreed. It was another perfect night. Drink was burning her brain. Supposing they turned the car about and went off together? She glanced behind her. Would they be happy? Could she forget Dirk to live with his murderer? Then she noticed that she was being tailed. A car filled with Red's men was quietly following her. To protect her! She sneered. Pete noticed her looking back. He looked and saw the car, and suddenly he grabbed the wheel from her hands.

"What the hell's this? We're being followed. You damned hell cat. If you've tricked me . . ." He left the rest to a menacing silence.

"Here, stop this car. If you've pulled a phoney it's going to cost you your life." He stripped off his coat and hat and thrust them at the girl. You wear these. Now gimme yours, and I'll drive. If we're ambushed it's you that'll get caught. Not me."

Dumbly, the girl obeyed. She would have her revenge. The man drove on in silence. Foster's Barn, Marie knew, was but a few miles distant. At the speed they were making they would soon be there. She would be revenged for Dirk's death.

"Pete," she spoke pleadingly, "you don't think I'd frame you, do you? You're the only one who gives a damn about me. Pete!"

Pete made no answer, but drove along grimly silent. If they got out of the hole they were in then he could love this moll. Right then . . . It would never do to increase the speed of their car. The car behind was swifter than theirs. That would bring matters to a head. Best to keep the pace. Hope to make Danbury, or slip off onto some quiet road if they had the chance.

Marie was silent. She was brooding deeply on her past. A thought occurred to her and she chuckled slightly at the humor of it. She decided to come clean.

"Pete," she said. "Do you want to hear the straight lay of it."

"Well, what is it all about."

"Do you want to know why I tipped you off last night to the raid?"

"Why?"

"I didn't want them to kill you, Pete. You see, you killed my man, the only man I ever loved. You killed Dirk, and"—she paused then finished a trifle breathlessly. "I want to be the one to lead you to your death." Her nerves cracked under the strain. "You dirty, thievin' murderer, now you'll get what you . . ."

Pete stopped her with a curse and slapped a broad hand heavily across her face. She was flung back into the corner of the car by the blow and her hands, caught in the pockets of Robinson's great coat, could not ward off the next punch. They came in contact with something hard. Pete's revolver! Then the car that had been following them shot alongside crowding them towards the ditch. Pete cursed wildly, grotesquely in his girl's attire. But he was unheard. The attention of Red's gunmen was concentrated on the man's figure sitting alongside of him, crouched, as though with fear, into the corner of the seat. A terrific crash of shots rang out and the roadster, as though freed of control left the road and went into the ditch.

Joe stopped his car and Red and Mike ran out with guns drawn. The other car had not overturned, but all was quiet. And when they looked they received a tremendous shock. The driver of the car, in the girl's coat and hat, at whom they had not aimed was Pete Robinson. He was stone dead, with a bullet hole in his right temple. An impossible wound for them to have delivered. Alongside of him, and wearing his coat and hat was Dirk's moll, Marie. Her face, what remained of it, was terribly battered. She had been instantly killed by the fuselage fired by Red's men. In her right hand she held Pete's .38, which cleared up the mystery of Robinson's death. Her left hand was fingering Dirk's picture, which hung framed about her neck. And over her ghost of a mouth, even in disfigured death, there still played that queer, twisted, enigmatic smile.

Gangster Stories, Racketeer Stories, April 1930

A Page from the Publisher's Notebook

THE CRIMINAL MUST BE CURBED. He is running rampant over the country.

Not a day passes but that the daily newspapers feature on their front pages the intimate details of some exploit of an underworld character. It is obvious that the public is sincerely interested in these accounts; otherwise the daily press would not be so intent upon the giving over of its columns to crime and criminals.

The stories in this magazine are superbly done, but they are not the real thing as published in the newspapers. They are but dreams and figments of our writers' imaginations. Yet, in spite of this, they are moving lessons that should help us guard our homes and our dear ones from these modern desperadoes.

The restless army of the underworld waves its tattered banners in a wind of newspaper words. The world stands aghast as this terrible cavalcade goes by our front doors. What can be done about it?

The police and the secret service are working day and night to protect our fireside from these beasts of a jungle that come to our very hearthstones—a jungle where the cries of the lost are like the drone of a myriad tropical insects humming through the menace of a fungus darkness.

In the pages of this magazine the criminal cannot win, any more than he can in real life. Death, or Fate or Justice overcomes him in the end. There is no escaping the net of human law and order that is spread for the criminal.

Truth is power, whether in story or in fact. Here, in these pages, the underworld excites like a fairy-tale spun for grown-up entertainment—a glittering series of yarns selected each issue with infinite care on the part of our editors.

We aim to please you, but at the same time we are glad to serve as a guide to warn you against hidden pitfalls that are on every side.

Faithfully yours,
HAROLD HERSEY

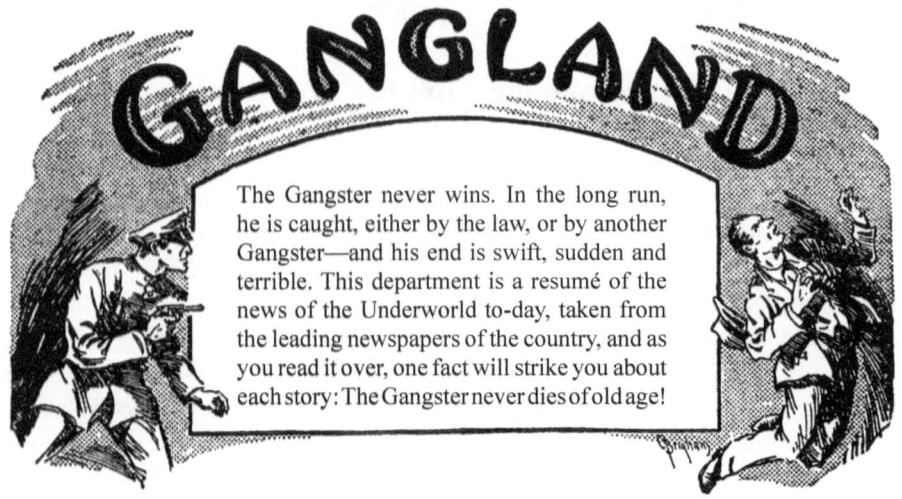

GANGLAND

The Gangster never wins. In the long run, he is caught, either by the law, or by another Gangster—and his end is swift, sudden and terrible. This department is a resumé of the news of the Underworld to-day, taken from the leading newspapers of the country, and as you read it over, one fact will strike you about each story: The Gangster never dies of old age!

A Department Gathered from the News

The Leader of the Dock Gang

The fight for the leader's seat over the Dock Gang, in the Red Hook district of Brooklyn, has long been a much coveted position, although a dangerous one. The fight for the control of dock loading privileges has cost many a man his life. Among the ranks was the famous old racketeer Wild Bill Lovett, who was the first leader.

Red Donnelly was an old hand in the game. He was fifty years old, which is pretty old for a gangster, and he had old-fashioned ways, which didn't please some of the new members of his gang. They wanted him to go in for liquor and dope running—a much better paying racket.

But Red refused. He was satisfied with the stevedore racket, and he could control it entirely, so why butt in on booze and junk peddling, when he would have to share with every other gang leader in Brooklyn?

Red began to hear rumors floating around with the wash of the water against the slimy piles that unless he got a bit more modern, his gang wanted a new boss. And everyone knows what happens to the old boss when a new one steps in! But that didn't bother Donnelly. He just laughed; a short contemptuous laugh. He was used to this sort of thing. Held five times for murder, and he laughed himself out of the court house.

Things were quiet for a while after that, with only one or two minor shootings along the waterfront. But then one night, while Red was watching the stevedore at work, a man came up to him and said:

"You're wanted down on the pier, in the checker's booth."

With a gruff "Okey," Red walked down the pier towards the booth.

The workers, who were left on the dock, saw him enter the booth; almost at once they heard two shots.

Quickly dropping their work, they ran toward the booth, grabbing anything they could use for weapons. When they got to the booth, they found Red sprawled across the sill, with his head sprayed full of lead. Blood was slowly seeping into his hair, turning the grey back to the flaming red color it once used to be.

That left the gang without a leader. Naturally, there were plenty who wanted the seat, but there's a difference between wanting it, and getting it. Who was going to get it?

Jimmy Murray, old timer, and former lieutenant of Wild Bill Lovett, finished a ten year rap the other day. He was a high man in the gang when it first started, and there was never a doubt in his mind that he would be the leader now that Red was out. So he stepped in.

This didn't please the gang any too much, because Murray, like Red Donnelly, refused to peddle dope and booze. And he had another quarrel with the gang; they had neglected to keep him supplied with his cigarette and chewing gum money while he was in stir.

They were all sitting together in the Dock Loaders Rest Room. Murray got up to lay out the plans for the gang in the future. He said he would not only take over his old leadership in the Smoky Hollow district, which is the waterfront extending from Joralemon Street south to the Erie Basin, but also would step into Red's place as controller of the dock area from Joralemon Street north to Dock Street.

Six shots cracked out, glass was broken, chairs and tables were overturned, and about a dozen men dashed into the street and scattered in various directions.

When the bulls arrived, the Dock Loaders Rest Room was in darkness, the windows shattered, as a cold wind sweeping through the room. One of the flatties put on his flash, and lying on the floor, mixed up with chairs and overturned tables, was Jimmy Murray, shot through the head, but still alive. The radio was still playing. One of the cops turned it off, and began to question Murray, trying to find out who shot him. But Jimmy just shook his head.

Later on, a priest was called in to give Murray the last rites. The priest tried as hard as he could to get Murray to say something about his killers, but Jimmy only shook his head.

Later on, the police rounded up nine men of the gang, some of whom had been held in the Red Donnelly murder.

• • •

THE JERSEY KID SNEERS AT THE JUDGE

"Can't you make it sooner, Judge?" sneered the Jersey Kid, with a hard laugh.

There had been a long silence after the jury had risen and given the verdict of "Guilty."

The Kid's three pals took their death notice without a word.

Then the quiet was broken by the screams of the women relatives and the friends of the condemned men. Order was finally restored, and the judge, pale with suppressed rage immediately denied the customary plea for a new trial.

The jury had deliberated for six hours before finding the four men guilty of first degree murder. The men had held up a motor bus garage on October 1928, and killed the cashier. The men, admitting they were guilty, pled that they had not intended to kill the cashier, but that the gun had gone off accidentally. Then they said that before leaving the garage, they telephoned for an ambulance for the wounded man, thus showing that they had not intended to harm him.

BEGINNER'S LUCK

The other day, over in East Orange, a kid, dressed up to the hilt with derby, spats, and a carefully folded muffler, sauntered into a filling station, and calmly lit a cigarette. He sure was a cool customer! That is, he looked cool enough, but his voice shook like the base of a Tommy when he spoke.

"High as they'll go!" he ordered.

A grin spread over his face when he saw how easy it was. The proprietor offered neither fight nor chin music. He simply stepped to the nearest exit, hands higher than he ever thought he could lift them and stood there.

The kid walked over to the cash register, and removed some twenty iron men with a deft scoop.

At that moment a car drove up to the filling station, and a woman blew her horn. The kid looked out, and grinned when he saw who it was.

"Only a broad." Then he turned, to face Patrolman Thomas Carrigan who had just sauntered in. The kid backed and filled for a moment, but the cop was just as surprised as the kid was, as he had just come in for a chat with his friend the proprietor. He wasn't used to seeing his friend scratching the ceiling, but then, in these days of fads, you never can tell from one hour to another what the latest wrinkle in reducing will be. He was just about to ask what it was all about when the kid said:

"You play that game, too!"

Then the kid ran out, tipped his derby to the lady, and got into her car.

"Sorry to put you out like this, madam, but I must ask you to start the car at once!"

The woman gave him one look, and let out a scream. Then she bolted.

The kid moved over to the driver's seat, and started the car, but before it moved two feet, Patrolman Walter Laird, who was on duty on the corner, ran up and smashed his fist into the window of the car, breaking the glass. He saw the youngster tugging for his gat, his derby slightly askew, his face dead white over his natty muffler. Before the kid could draw, Laird fired six shots. The kid slumped over the wheel, blood pouring over his muffler, his derby falling back on his shoulders.

As far as the police could learn, it was the kid's, Lawrence Russel by name, first job. He had done two jobs in one: his first and his last.

PLAIA AND SCALFONI BITTER ENEMIES AS THEY WAITED FOR DEATH

"Put those two men in the same cell for five minutes and the state would only have one man to kill to-night," said a keeper the day before they were executed. The two men were consumed by a deadly hatred for each other— more deadly than their fear of the chair. For weeks they had blamed each other for the murder of Sorro Graziano and his wife—the crime for which they both died.

Plaia was the first to go to death. He swaggered to the chair, and died smiling, his cigarette still smoking on the floor beside him.

Scalfoni was the next. As he walked over to the chair he asked for a towel.

"The least you could do would be to give me a clean chair!"

To the amazement of the witnesses, he began to dust off the death-chair with a look of disgust on his face, as if the idea of sitting on a chair that Plaia had sat on nauseated him.

"Pardon me." He swept the room with his eyes, pointing at each of the witnesses; then slowly shook his head.

IN THE GRIP OF THE WHITE DEATH

The Grey Ghost, the fastest rum runner between Canada and Cleveland, which streaked back and forth across Lake Erie, carrying fortunes for her owners in expensive liquor, was caught at last.

But it wasn't the law this time.

Gripped fast in a tortuous ice jam off Pelee Island lies the low, streamlined craft, with a dead man sitting stiff and straight at her wheel, staring ahead into the whirling snow.

ON THE SPOT

Paddy King was a king all right. He was boss of a large mob, who played as many games as the weeks had days, and then some. Booze and dope peddler, burglar, gambler and hold-up man were some of his pastimes. But he laughed his scornful laugh once too often.

On December third he was found in a dusty dismantled gambling house on the second floor of a building which recently housed the Club Royale.

The plaster of the walls was spattered with holes from bullets. Empty shells were strewn on the floor, and Paddy's revolver lay by his clenched hand, two chambers empty.

The tailor's mark on his coat first balked identification. Then the police learned that he was Paddy King, a name that had marked up the police blotters many a time. He was the brother-in-law of Frank and Peter Gusenberg, two brothers murdered with five others of the Bugs Moran push in the gang massacre last February. Paddy was wearing Peter's coat.

Paddy himself was held at the time of the St. Valentine's day shoot-up but he was released. Also he had been held for a series of theater holdups, but in each case was released.

A KILLING A DAY

"A killing a day" is the motto of the Chicago Underworld. If a day should pass without a killing they would feel that their manhood was at stake; that the rest of the underworld, from Frisco to Hell's Kitchen would think of them as milch cows.

On February second Joseph Cada, a twenty-nine year old racketeer, was taken for a ride. Cada was shot to death at the wheel of his high powered sedan by two companions, who then stopped the car, got out, dusted themselves off, and ambled leisurely away, chatting.

Early Thursday morning Barney J. Mitchell, treasurer of the Checker Cab Company, and his driver, were shot to death not many blocks from where Cada met his death.

On Saturday, a stool pigeon, named Julius Rosenheim, was shot and killed because someone knew that he knew something about someone. And a lot less than that is needed for a man to die in the underworld.

BLACK TONY THE DOPE KING

Black Tony lived at a fashionable uptown hotel in San Francisco. He dressed about as well as a man can be dressed; he went from party to party, and had about as good a time as a man could have.

But Tony, whose real name is Antonio Parmagini, did a great deal of telephoning, and the telephone company notified the police that in the course of two months, three hundred and sixty seven calls were made to the same address—and the company seemed to know a great deal about that particular address.

And dope had been coming in as easily as it ever did. This is the way it works. Practically all the opium that comes into the country, enters along the Pacific coast. It comes in mainly at the ports of Los Angeles and San Francisco, and it is sent from Macao, a Portuguese possession near Hong Kong.

Through agents, the big dealer (in this case Black Tony) sells the dope to inland towns in California. The consignments are shipped up and down the San Joaquin and Sacramento valleys before they reach San Francisco again for distribution.

Black Tony has the control of all the coast, except for the section around Los Angeles and Hollywood. This is held by a man named Murphy.

Well, there were many men who wanted Tony's job. Naturally it paid good money. But there were few who had the nerve to try for it, much less work it when they got it.

However, there was one man who did try. He thought up scheme after scheme, but Tony was with him every trick, and one ahead at that. And he didn't even have this man put on the spot, such was his feeling for the feeble gestures the man was making for Tony's throne. He just laughed.

When the man finally saw that it was hopeless, he gave up. But he hadn't been planning against Tony without picking up one or two little things—and these items he took to the police.

This information, coupled with Tony's telephone bill and a slick Eastern dick soon had Tony in the clutches of the law.

Since Tony's incarceration, there has been what amounts to a dope famine in California, and as one tenth of the dope users in the United States are Californians, this is quite a step in the progress of dope elimination.

WIN FIVE DOLLARS

Five dollars will be paid for the best newspaper account of a gangster killing, either by law or by another gangster, sent to the Editor of GANGSTER STORIES *before April 15. Any others used in this department will be paid for at regular rates. Send your clippings to* GANGSTER STORIES, *25 W. 43 St. New York City.*

City of Bullets

By JOHN GERARD

*The biggest racketeer in the city was Mike Regan—yet he is
threatened by a blood-lusting gangster from Chicago
without a brain in his fat skull. Mike was
stumped . . . and all his plans to
outwit Killer Joe failed,
all except one . . .*

THE RAW CHILL WIND WHISTLED AROUND CORNERS and up the street, chasing little
flurries of dirty snow into the night air. From a basement in one of the dark,
squalid buildings, two men emerged and paused a moment to turn up their
coat collars against the biting cold.

"Good-night, Bill."

"Good-night."

At that instant a car skidded around the corner behind them. Before the
pair could turn, a stream of fire had belched from the ugly muzzle of a sub-
machine gun that protruded from the car's curtained window. Bullets riddled
the bodies of the two with their merciless impact.

A menacing, hollow peal of laughter resounded from the interior of the
car, mingling in ghostly mockery with the howling wind after the roar of the
gun. Then the car shot forward in high, leaving two motionless corpses on

the sidewalk.

Not a sound came from any of the buildings in the long street. No one left his house to rush to the assistance of the two huddled bodies sprawled on the wet pavement to see if a spark of life yet remained in them. The fear of Killer Joe Catanesi, overlord of the gang that was terrorizing the city, the knowledge that his work of destruction would be all too thorough, hung like a pall over men's hearts, paralyzed them with fear.

And the raw gusts of wind piled up the snow in drifts against the corpses of the murdered men whose ebbing life blood transformed it from a dirty white into a dark, ominous crimson.

The next morning the newspapers ran the story which had by now become monotonous, of another killing in the gang war which had earned for the city the unenviable nickname, the "City of Bullets."

In the dining room of a large house overlooking the river a man and a woman were just finishing breakfast. A tense silence had fallen between them. The man's eyes gazed in furious concentration at the paper before him.

"There's nothing more to be found out from that rag," said the girl crisply. "What's needed here, Mike, is action and plenty of it!"

"I know it, Billie," replied the man, pushing back his chair and walking over to the window from which he could look down on the endless, moving panorama of the river. "Bill Gehagan and Frank Schwenke, my two right-hand men, bumped off by this lousy wop from Chicago!"

"I know how you feel, Mike." Billie came over to him and put her hand on his shoulder. "You've always been on the level, Mike. You've never pulled the rough, crooked stuff this swine Catanesi hands out all the time. Pull yourself together!"

Her eyes looked up into his, almost challenging him to act. "Show this dirty crook you're not licked yet!"

"That's very easy to say, Billie," answered the man. "But he's managed to slip out of every single trap I've laid for him so far."

It had been by ruthless disregard for the ethics of racketeers that Joe Catanesi, one of the most notorious characters of Chicago's south side, had succeeded in gaining almost undisputed control over the city's underworld. One after the other, the gang leaders and racketeers who had peaceably divided the city before the Killer's advent, had been put out of business. Mike Regan alone still held out.

And Catanesi had thrown a large sized wrench into Regan's skillfully organized gang. Desertions had taken place almost every day, with the Irishman's inability to get the better of his enemy.

The man's eyes glinted angrily. "I was the biggest racketeer in this city until Catanesi came along."

"Yes, and you thought nothing could touch you. Well, now you've lost two of your best men, and Catanesi's put it over on you every time." She paused a moment, as if making up her mind to a desperate course. "Look here, Mike, will you let me handle this situation? The Killer has no brain, but he can act!"

Billie Ross was right. Catanesi's success had been due to one factor alone; the lightning-like rapidity with which he struck. He had very little brain, only a devouring lust for slaughter and a certain cunning which prevented his attacking an adversary until he was sure of victory. Regan had underestimated his enemy; the Killer had carved a blundering way out of the traps Regan had set for him. And now he was actually threatening the power of the Irishman, the biggest and cleverest racketeer in the entire city.

Regan looked at the exquisitely groomed woman before him, at the curve of her white throat, at the rich cloth-of-gold negligee that set off the beauty of her black hair and dark, fiery eyes.

"I don't see what you can do, Billie," he said slowly. "It's a long time since either you or I had to pull any rough stuff."

"We've been the brains of the outfit a long time, Mike," acknowledged the girl, "but I don't think either of us has forgotten how to fight."

"I've tried to put Catanesi out of business, and I've failed," replied Regan. "But you're right, Billie. The situation calls for action, prompt action and plenty of it. So go ahead."

"The plan I have in mind will put the heart back into our men and dispose of the Killer at the same time. Tonight's Friday, isn't it? Remember how the night shift at the steel factory on Cranford Avenue gets paid off every Friday night?"

"That's out," replied the man abruptly, "where I'm concerned. The directors of that factory are personal friends of mine. Besides, there are plenty of easier ways of making money if you use your brains. We got through with that sort of stuff a long time ago. And—"

"We've discussed all this before," interrupted Billie decisively, "and I'm with you. Well, my idea is to give Catanesi the dope about the pay-roll truck. He'll try this particular game just as soon as he finds out about it, anyway. So why shouldn't we gain by it? We'll have our men there to hi-jack the Killer. In the meantime I'll take care of the boss himself."

"There's a lot in what you say, Billie," admitted Regan, "but I don't like the idea of your going to Catanesi. You'd be running a terrible risk. Suppose he suspects you?"

"I'm going upstairs," replied the girl, ignoring the man's last remarks. "When I come back, I want a detailed lay-out of tonight's plans that I can take along with me."

"But how'll I know that you've put it over on the Killer?" said Regan, allowing himself to be persuaded by the girl's determined manner.

"You'll know all right," Billie told him. "You'll get a signal from me that you can't mistake. And I won't tell you what it is. She turned and ran up the stairs while the racketeer crossed over to a concealed safe in the wall to get her the information she had requested.

A little later a completely transformed Billie entered the room. A bright red tam o'shanter was pulled rakishly down over one ear above a mass of flaming red hair. A black and white checked jacket covered her blue sweater, while a tight skirt of the same material revealed a pair of perfect legs which terminated in black shoes with high scarlet heels. The exquisite girl Mike Regan knew had been changed into a tough, hard-boiled gangster's moll.

Regan stared hard. "What a makeup!" he exclaimed admiringly. "It's just what'll appeal to that tough wop from Chicago."

"There'll be plenty of lead flying around tonight, or I miss my guess," remarked Billie with affected toughness as she knotted a bright blue and red silk scarf around her neck. "So long, Mike. I'll kid that low-life wop into thinking he's the only guy on earth. I'll tell him this hold-up's a pipe and that he and his new moll between 'em will finish up Mike Regan's outfit."

"I'll tell Red Conners to get the gang together in our hide-out near the river front. That's where I'll expect your signal."

"Listen, Mike," said Billie, leaning against the door. "You see how I look, now. And remember how you used to look—feel . . . hunted! All this"—she pointed to her make-up—"is behind us. Our life has been so peaceful until lately—"

Mike was puzzled. "What do you mean, Billie? You want to—"

"Yes, Mike." She looked at him steadily.

Mike frowned thoughtfully.

"The idea isn't exactly a surprise, Billie. I've suspected you wanted to—to—"

"Quit—go straight!" She shot out the words defiantly. "I'm no coward, you know that, Mike. For that reason I insist on getting rid of Catanesi! But after that—"

Mike drew her to him.

The long, passionate kiss of farewell between the two showed their understanding.

Regan looked at the closed door, listened for a moment to the rapid footsteps dying away down the corridor. Then, instantly, he became all action. Here was the dearest thing in the world to him, gambling her life on a desperate venture. And no one knew better than she how desperate that venture was.

• • •

Meanwhile Billie Ross was being whirled rapidly in a taxi to the Killer's headquarters at the other end of the city. At the door of the big house where Catanesi lived in almost royal state, she stepped out, slim, provocative and alluring.

Four burly gunmen accosted her in the hall, demanded to know her business while their expert hands patted her clothing for a hidden rod. But she had anticipated this and had come unarmed.

"I want to see Joe Catanesi," she told the men coolly. "And you'll get one hell of a bawling out if you don't take me up to him right away."

Her words had their effect. Two more men, lounging in the spacious hallway, came up to inspect the newcomer. In one of them she recognized a deserter from Regan's gang, one of the few who had known her in the early days. Since their rise to fortune she never saw any of the gang except the most important of Regan's lieutenants. Here was luck! "Tell these guys who I am, Charlie."

The man looked at her in amazement. "If it isn't Billie Ross!" he said, staring at her. "You haven't changed much. Why, it must be years, since—" He broke off to eye her doubtfully. "But what about Mike Regan?"

The girl extended her hand, thumb downward in a significant gesture. The Killer's rods looked at each other. So Regan's moll was giving him the gate!

Without more delay the girl was rapidly escorted up a broad winding staircase and along a lofty corridor. Before a massive, oaken door her guard halted and knocked.

"Come in," growled a hoarse voice. The door was flung open and Billie found herself in an enormous room whose walls were lined with books from floor to ceiling. Her feet sank into the thick luxurious carpet, making no sound.

"So you're Mike Regan's moll, huh?" A massive bullet head in which two small, blood-shot eyes glinted evilly under black, bushy eyebrows, raised itself slowly at her entrance from the papers on the carved walnut desk at the far end of the room. The thick, cruel lips parted to reveal irregular yellow fangs in a smile which was plainly intended to be one of welcome.

The girl could scarcely repress a shudder. Here before her, if she had ever set eyes on them, were lust, treachery and brutality. But she summoned an easy smile to her lips, ripped off her tam, gave her head an impertinent toss and crossed over to the table.

"I *was* Regan's moll," she corrected him, seating herself on the edge of the table and swinging one slender, silk-clad leg provocatively. "But I ditched him. The big mick hasn't got the guts of a louse in all that big body of his. I like a man!" she went on, letting her gaze travel admiringly over the burly hulk of the man before her.

The girl's trim figure and alluring beauty plainly had their effect on the Killer. Her instinct told her that she had been right to disguise herself. Her toughness and her appearance would have a far more telling effect than if she had come in her ordinary clothes.

Catanesi grinned and shifted a little in his chair to obtain a better view. "How do I know Regan ain't sent you here himself?" he asked, suspicion lowering in his small eyes. He reached for the house phone on his desk while Billie continued to smile at him with calm insolence. "Send Charlie up here," he ordered.

"I haven't come empty handed, Joe," she retorted meaningly, drawing a slip of paper from her pocket and handing it over to the Killer. "Regan's desperately hard up and he's planning to hold up this pay-roll truck tomorrow night."

The wop's big head nodded slowly as he took in the rough sketch on the paper, noted the minute description of the truck and the accuracy with which its progress from the bank to the factory had been timed.

"You're new to this town, Joe," Billie told him, "and with me to tip you off on stunts like this, you ought to clean up!"

The Killer grinned and, with a clumsy effort at gallantry, stretched out one hairy paw to the gay silk scarf encircling the girl's white throat.

"Red for blood and blue for hope," she said with a laugh, letting him pull it off. She could tell that he still mistrusted her, but she must play a bold game. Leaning forward, so that the seductive perfume of her body enveloped his senses like wine, she said with flaming eyes: "I thought you had guts, Joe! Haven't you got this town where you want it? Why is it called the city of bullets?"

"I guess that's my work, Billie," answered the Killer, proudly puffing out his chest. "You're right! This town's mine!" He clenched his fists until the knuckles showed white under the swarthy skin. "I'll shoot up that truck tonight—"

The bright scarf slipped to the floor. Catanesi half rose in his chair, his great arms out-spread to encircle the girl.

At that moment the door opened to admit Charlie, the former member of Regan's outfit. He lounged confidently in, making no excuse for his delay in answering his leader's summons. The Killer, plainly annoyed by not being able to show the girl the iron discipline which he had instilled into his gang, turned angrily to face him.

"What's the big idea, of keepin' me waitin'?" he snapped.

"I didn't know you was in a hurry, boss," replied the man, although his swaggering began to be a little uneasy. "I was just finishin' a game—"

"You lazy scum," barked the Killer, his eyes two smoldering pin points of savage fire. "Things are gettin' too damned easy around here. It's about time I showed some of you wise guys who runs this outfit." The shiny blue steel barrel of a Smith and Wesson .38 came slowly up from behind the table.

Charlie's eyes bulged in terror from their sockets. Like a flash his hand darted to his arm-pit. The gun in the Killer's hand roared once. The man slumped forward, pitching headlong to the floor where his fingers beat a horrible, soundless tattoo on the heavy carpet.

The girl looked at him coldly. He was a rat and deserved what he got. With a convulsive twitch the corpse lay still, while an ever widening pool of blood stained the carpet with its sullen crimson.

"The poor sap!" exclaimed Catanesi scornfully. "I was only going to nick him in the arm to show him I won't be monkeyed with, but he asked for it." He pushed a button on the table, then rose and walked over to one of the richly gleaming shelves that lined the wall.

The girl's mind was working like a steel trap. Obviously, the Killer was suspicious of her; even if she had him believe she was double-crossing Regan it would be difficult for her to send Mike the signal she had promised, unless—

She slipped off the table and picked up the square of silk all wet and discolored by the murdered man's blood. Her back was between Catanesi and the corpse. Instinctively she secured Charlie's automatic, slipping it into the pocket of her jacket.

"Hey, Joe!" she called, holding out her dripping scarf. Here was her signal ready to hand. It would whip Mike Regan into action like nothing else she could possibly think of. Besides that, she knew that the Killer's vindictiveness would make him send it. "How about sending this to Mike?" she went on. "I know where he'll be just before the hold-up. It ought to jar him plenty!"

"Say, that's great!" declared the Killer. "An' I'll make sure it gets to him. It'll get Regan so wild, maybe he'll hot-foot it over here, then I'll have him where I want him." His powerful hairy hands clenched and unclenched spasmodically. "Regan'll go out slow, but before I drill him I'll show him the moll who ditched him, ditched him for me, Killer Joe Catanesi!"

The man had fallen for it, hook, bait, line and sinker. But it would be Regan's moll who'd do the showing! The gangster moved toward her and she saw that one entire section of book-shelves had swung outward to reveal a small, but very well stocked bar. "I'll have a straight Scotch," she said with a laugh.

"And I'll take a kiss," said Catanesi, his breath hot and inflamed on the girl's throat.

"I'll be damned if you will!" Billie Ross jumped back from the encircling arms that were about to grasp her. "You've got to show me first, Joe, that you're the man you say you are. You wipe Regan off the map. Then—" Her eyes promised everything.

In vain the Italian pleaded and argued. The girl was adamant and something about her seemed to warn the burly gangster that it would be dangerous to lay hands on her.

"Cut it, Joe," she said at last, wearied by his demands. "What in hell's the matter with you? Tonight's only a few hours off. I'll be your moll, then—get me? Or are you scared you can't pull it off?"

Catanesi scowled furiously and poured her the drink she asked for. "I'm going to send my best man, Karl Mischek, on this job. We'll have a little supper served right here, and Karl can come back and tell us all about it." He looked at her inquiringly from under his bushy eyebrows.

"Then I'll keep my end of the bargain," the girl promised.

The door closed behind the Killer as he went out to make the necessary arrangements with his gang. Two men came in to remove the slowly stiffening body and clean up the blood-stained carpet. Billie Ross was alone. If her daring plan succeeded, they had the Killer licked. But luck and perfect timing were essential. She paced nervously up and down the room, longing for the hours to pass. She knew the man she loved well enough to be certain how he would act when he received her signal. As for the rest—

The big Irishman, all unconscious of the trick that was about to be played on him, was waiting with his gang in their hide-out on the river front. With the skill of a born general he had prepared for every possibility that might occur that night.

Everything was in readiness. The short day was closing in and it only remained to kill the few minutes before the start of the expedition.

Men sprawled in all attitudes around the long, squalid room; some cleaned and oiled their rods, others conversed in low, spasmodic voices, others again gnawed their nails and stared moodily at the cob-webbed rafters. Over all there brooded an atmosphere of tense expectancy.

There was a sharp, sudden creak on the rickety landing outside. Instantly all eyes turned towards the door which opened to admit the dilapidated figure of old Moe, a drunken wharf-rat.

"Moe says he's got somethin' fer ya personal, boss," said the sentry whose fingers were twined in the old man's collar. "So I brought him up."

"All right, Mac, you can go back to your post," Regan told him, advancing toward the limp scarecrow who was swaying unsteadily now that he was no longer supported by the guard's grasp. "What is it, Moe?"

"De guy as gave me dis," the old man fumbled in his pocket, "says to me ya'd maybe gimme de price o' a coupla drinks," he whined, succeeding at last in extracting Billie's bloodstained scarf which he waved feebly.

There was a sharp intake of breath, then, "Give me that scarf, you—" Mike Regan roared in a flaming burst of rage. Taking the silk square into his hands, he buried his face in it. "My poor darling, poor little kid, poor Billie," he moaned over and over again.

"Steady, Mike, steady!" Conners had sprung to his side and gripped him firmly by the arm.

Like a maddened bull, the big Irishman threw off the consoling hand of his lieutenant. "By God! I'll make that yellow punk sweat for this! He'll wish he'd never seen the light of day when I get through with him!" Knocking over the uncertain figure of Moe, Regan paused in the doorway, his eyes blazing. "You handle this job tonight, Red, and no quarter! I'm going on a still hunt for the Killer and I'm going to cut his heart out!"

Before Conners could reply, his leader was in the street. Remorse over Billie's sacrifice had kindled his temper to a white heat. One thought only was uppermost in his mind: to stand face to face with the Killer, to pound the yellow wop to a bleeding pulp with his own hands!

He ran wildly down the street, swung himself onto the footboard of a cruising taxi and bellowed hoarse directions to the driver. Regan was too blind with fury to see a furtive form that had been skulking in a doorway dart out and run to the nearest cigar store.

Catanesi had anticipated Regan's moves. When the cab skidded to a halt and Regan leapt out in front of the Killer's imposing residence, he found the massive front door closed against him. Whipping out his guns, he pounded furiously on the panels. The door opened and the racketeer stepped into the darkness of the hall, peering intently about him.

Too late the Irishman whirled about, sensing the presence of the men cowering in the gloom behind him. A black-jack descended with stunning force on his skull.

The Killer was in his study, enjoying an intimate dinner with Billie Ross when the house phone rang. Catanesi listened with evident satisfaction. "Bring him right up," he ordered.

Anxiously, the girl looked at the limp body of the man she loved, brought in on the burly shoulders of a Hungarian. Regan was unconscious and breathing heavily. The Hungarian let his burden slip to the ground, then propped the racketeer's body against a chair.

Catanesi misinterpreted the girl's glance. "I told the boys to be careful not to croak him," he said with a triumphant sneer. "He'll come 'round soon, an' then we'll see some fun!" He motioned the Hungarian to get out.

When the door had closed, Catanesi strode over to his concealed cellar. "I'm going to wake that big mick up so he can see his moll has given him the gate for a better man," he told Billie. "Here, stick this glass of Scotch down his throat yourself."

"You bet your sweet life I will," returned the girl, playing her part of the tough moll to the hilt, "and I'll give him a swift kick in the pants, too, for old times' sake. Pour a couple more for us, Joe."

Billie's eyes had discerned a slight movement in the huddled mass on the floor. While Catanesi's back was turned, she crossed swiftly over to Regan and stooped over him. Forcing the glass between his lips, she rapidly shoved the dead Charlie's automatic into the limp hand of the Irishman, noted how his fingers closed over it with the return of consciousness. Then, to disarm the Killer, she stood up and kicked the prostrate man in the ribs.

"Don't like him much, do you kid?" commented the wop with a satisfied sneer as he watched her small shoe dig repeatedly into the side of the defenseless man. "Come over here to me, Billie, and we'll drink to the swine when he comes to."

"You bet we will," the girl assured him with a parting kick at Regan. "Wake up, you big Irish stiff," she taunted him, "and see what a man I've picked for myself!"

Catanesi's chest swelled with pride. He strutted over to the table, put down the two glasses and came towards the girl, breathing heavily.

Mike Regan was struggling grimly up through a haze of pain to regain full control over himself. His head felt as if it were ten times its ordinary size, his whole body throbbed and pulsated.

But the liquor, and still more the knowledge that Billie, the girl he loved more than anything in the world, was alive gave him added strength. He fought hard to focus on the figures that danced crazily before him through a blood-red mist while his fingers tightened instinctively on the small gun the girl had slipped into his hand.

The mist cleared a little, and Regan ground his teeth with rage at the sight of the huge, awkward body of the Killer enfolding Billie's clean, slender beauty in its horrible embrace. Again a feeling of nausea swept over him, the figures grew indistinct.

"Your moll's left you for a better guy, a stronger guy, Micky Regan!" The taunting words burnt like fire into the Irishman's brain. But he must keep calm until he could see more clearly, until his strength came back to him.

Again the Killer kissed the girl. Then, giving her one of the glasses, he raised his own mockingly.

"You're going to give us a lot of fun in the next hour or two, Mr. Regan," he said ironically. "Yeah, Billie and me, we're going to hit it off swell, ain't we, sweetheart?"

"Sure we are, Joe," assented the girl with a laugh, longing for the moment when her man would rise to cram the cur's words down his throat. Why hadn't she taken her chance and shot him in the back? But that was not in her code. Even a swine like Catanesi couldn't be shot from behind in cold blood!

"I'm going to pin your hands to the floor with a couple of knives," remarked the Killer with anticipatory relish. "Then the fun'll start!"

Regan's eyes were closed; he gave no sign of the intense struggle he was putting up. If Catanesi came over to him, he'd discover the gun. Then the game would be up—for both him and Billie! For her sake he fought desperately to clear his fuddled, aching head of the mist that weighed on it.

"Another round of drinks, Joe," suggested Billie to gain time. "Give Regan another glass, too, Joe. He'll enjoy the fun all the more!"

Together, Billie and the Killer stood over Regan while the girl forced the glass between his lips. Then Joe went over to the concealed bar. Out of a drawer he took two knives. "These'll make him sit up and take notice," he said grimly.

At all costs, Billie realized that she must stall for time. That was the one element which would insure the success of her plan, time for Regan to recover, time for Red Conners to play his part. Quickly she poured another glass of Scotch and touched it to her lips; then she offered it to the Killer.

Out on Cranford Avenue the wintry wind howled a desolate song as it swept on through the scraggly brush and skeleton trees over the flats to the river. In the distance the sound of an approaching track could be heard. Men lurking in hedges, waiting tensely in cars hidden in a rutted lane, other men lying in readiness at an intersection, looked at their watches. The moment for action had come!

Suddenly, a wildly driven touring car came flashing around the bend of the road in front of the truck, forcing it to come to an abrupt halt. Instantly, the deadly rattle of a sub-machine gun tore through the night. The driver of the truck and his companion slumped sideways in their seats.

Men leapt from the tonneau of the touring car and hauled the two bodies from the truck, onto the side of the road. "Beat it, you two!" came a hoarse whisper. "All hell's goin' to be poppin' here!" Regan had taken care to warn his friends at the factory; the men had played their parts to perfection.

A man swung himself into the driver's seat of the truck and backed it across the road. Before it could turn, a venomous hail of bullets belched from rods concealed in the hedges. But the men in the touring car were prepared. A hot fire from two Thompsons projecting from each side of the car, ripped viciously into the enemy. The night air was alive with leaping, crackling, flashes of fire.

All at once there was a hoarse yell. Catanesi's men jumped from their cover and ran toward the car, firing as they ran to surround it. Regan's man in the truck had been put out of action long before.

Another moment, and the desperately fighting occupants of the touring-car would have been submerged by the wave of charging gangsters. But Red Conners picked that moment to swing into action.

Down the road three big cars roared toward the fight, cut-outs open, guns spewing lead from every window. Before the Chicago gang knew what had hit them, Conners' men had left a trail of dead and dying men in the road.

"It's a plant!" shrieked Mischek, the Killer's lieutenant. "Beat it, boys, beat—" His warning died away into a choked cry, as a bullet from Conners' grind-organ caught him full in the throat. A torrent of blood gushed onto the asphalt. The Hungarian's hands clawed wildly at his neck, and he pitched forward onto the road.

Devotion to Regan, vengeance for the imagined murder of Billie Ross, filled Conners and his men with murderous blood-lust. Recklessly they chopped Catanesi's men, careless of their own safety as long as they could kill an enemy. Regan's orders of 'no quarter' were obeyed to the letter.

But the Hungarian's dying words of warning had not gone unheeded. Catanesi's men broke and fled for their cars, keeping up a frantic fusillade on their pursuers. No time to save a wounded pal! Leaving the last car to block Conners, the survivors piled rapidly into the three ahead of it.

Running the gauntlet of fire from the enemy, as their cars started down the lane, a man jumped onto the car that blocked the pursuit and backed it out into the road. Instantly Conners' three cars turned into the narrow lane, rocking and bumping over the uneven ground in their mad haste to catch up with the battered remnants of the Killer's gang.

Soon the lane joined the highway again. Throttles full open, the pursuing cars shot down the broad road like streaks of lightning toward the glow of red tail-lights that marked their prey. Through the outskirts of the town thundered the six cars, their occupants keeping up a running fire.

Gradually the pursuit began to gain. Regan's drivers knew the town like the palm of their hand, and Red Conners had been a racing driver. Ceaselessly, the man beside him on the front seat pressed the trigger of his sub-machine gun.

The rearmost of Catanesi's fleet skidded wildly across a street to pile up in a plate-glass show window. As the pursuing cars flashed by, they hosed the wreckage with a hurricane of lead. Ahead of them the almost deserted streets emptied as if by magic.

All at once the two cars ahead parted company. Conners hurtled after the leader while his two other cars tore after the second, forcing it closer and closer to the side of the street. A last well directed volley made the driver swerve desperately. His right front wheel crashed into a fire-hydrant. The car swung around, hung poised for a second, then crumpled with a rending smash on its side.

Red Conners was pressing his foot almost through the floor in his effort to catch up with what was now the one remaining car. But its engine was more powerful than the one he was urging to give him its last ounce of speed. And they were nearing the Killer's house. Conners swore grimly to send that car to hell before they reached it.

Down a hill plunged the two cars, and up a steep road toward an embankment that overhung the river. For a fraction of a second Conners drew closer as the front car slowed up to hit the grade. The man beside him took his chance.

A jet of flame spurted through the air, and a hunk of lead buried itself in the head of the driver of the leading car. Up the hill it roared, veering wildly onto the embankment while its occupants struggled frantically to gain control of the wheel. Too late! The car crashed through the posts on the embankment, careened down the slope to be swallowed up in the black waters below.

Conners slackened speed for an instant to allow his two machines in the rear to catch up with him. Then the trio of cars swept on.

But the Killer, sprawled lazily in a chair in his luxurious room, was still insolently confident of victory. Billie Ross, perched on the arm of his chair, was still plying him with liquor in her desperate effort to gain time.

The sound of cars roaring down the street with cut-outs open came in faintly through the closed windows. Pushing the girl aside, Catanesi stood up.

"Must be the boys comin' back," he said, picking up his two gleaming knives and advancing toward the prostrate man. "I'll spread eagle the big mick to put on a show for 'em. The rod who bumped off the most men in Mike Regan's gang can have the first crack at the leader."

The girl shuddered at his inhuman cruelty, straining her ears for the sound of approaching footsteps. A swift glance showed her that Mike Regan had come to. Though he was as motionless as before, the knuckles of the hand that gripped his automatic were white.

Catanesi, the two knives held carelessly in his left hand, came toward his prisoner.

"Reach for the ceiling or I'll drill you!" barked Regan. The knives clattered from the Killer's nerveless hand to the floor. His jaw fell open, then he looked helplessly around him like a cornered rat.

"You needn't expect any help from me, Joe," said Billie with a cold laugh as she came up to remove the Killer's armament. "You promised me today that Regan and I would hear your lieutenant tell us all about it. Well, I think you're going to listen to a different story."

Muffled reports, a single sharp cry, and shouts of men fighting in the house reached the three participants in the grim drama. Each interpreted the noise in his own way. Billie Ross seated herself calmly on the table, a strange smile of triumph on her face. Regan, frowning anxiously, let his eyes wander for an instant. Seizing his chance, the Killer rushed for the door. Like a flash, the Irishman grasped a knife and hurled it. Catanesi howled with pain as the glittering blade ripped through his outstretched hand, pinning it to the panel.

"There must be some way we can get out of here, Billie," muttered Regan, jumping to his feet. "For God's sake don't make a noise! Do you know the back way?"

"We're going down the front way," replied the girl, calmly lighting a cigarette. "And you can put your gun away, Mike."

But Regan spun around, leveling his rod as the door was flung open and a group of men, headed by Red Conners, poured into the room.

"This is the story I wanted you to hear, Killer Joe Catanesi," shouted Billie Ross triumphantly to the impaled and writhing gangster.

A look of incredulous surprise was on Red Conners' face, as he saw that the two for whom he had exacted such terrible vengeance were alive and unharmed.

"I swore I'd make 'em pay and I did!" There was a ring of victory in his voice. "I busted that Chicago gang so wide open they'll never be heard of again!"

But the Killer was game to the last. In the bitterest moment of his life he had seen victory turn suddenly into humiliating defeat. At least he could kill off the author of it!

With his free hand he struggled to loose the knife which had pierced his wrist. Like a cat he turned to aim the dripping blade at the girl's heart. But the glint of the knife caught Regan's eye. His gun barked once, and the Killer crumpled slowly to the floor, a bullet in his brain.

Regan's thirsty henchmen made for the Killer's bar. As the drinks were passed around, comprehension of Billie's daring strategy slowly dawned in Mike Regan's brain. She had made him fight and conquer Catanesi with his own weapons. Lifting his glass, he toasted her.

"To Billie Ross, who's made this man's town really deserve the name of 'The City of Bullets' and to our last drink with you boys!"

They stared at him open-mouthed.

Gangster Stories, May 1930

A Page from the Publisher's Notebook

IN THE *NEW YORK TIMES* of February 26, a headline said: "Murder rate in States with the death penalty found more than double that in those without." This is the result of a statistical analysis by the League to Abolish Capital Punishment.

What are we to gather from this report? Is capital punishment a failure? Is crime on the increase? Certainly the latter is true if we are to make our test by the amount of space given to crime news by the most conservative daily papers.

It is well nigh impossible to find a newspaper without gory details of some crime featured on its front page. Is all this an aid or a hindrance?

We believe that the criminal must go. He is usually a cowardly fighter, shooting down his enemies from ambush; protected by shrewd lawyers; endeavoring to outwit the police; and banded together for further protection. He is a sort of fighting minority.

The majority of peace-loving citizens are seemingly at loss as to how to cope with these desperadoes.

The situation is alarming. We need knowledge of the facts involved, and we need steady concerted action.

This magazine welcomes opinions from its readers. The best letters will be printed from time to time. Who knows but that we might discover some simple method to tackle crime and criminals that would be of great assistance to the authorities?

Even though the stories we publish are only intended for your entertainment, and are of course but the creations of our writers from pure fancy, still there is no reason why we should not do our bit to protect the home from this army of the underworld.

Sit down and write us today. Give us your opinion, and any suggestion you may have toward the betterment of conditions.

Faithfully yours,
HAROLD HERSEY

Racketeer Stories, May 1930

A Page from the Publisher's Notebook

The Army of the Underworld Is Legionate

THEY MARCH THROUGH THE PAGES of the biggest and the smallest newspapers, their frayed banners waving in a wind of words. Their pitiful faces, warped with disease, would strike pity in our hearts were it not for the terror they arouse in the innocent by-stander.

Editorial writers, throughout the United States, fulminate against this army of the underworld. The police of a thousand cities work day and night to capture them and to guard our homes and property.

Many of the secret service lay down their lives. Reporters risk everything to get to the end of the trouble, so that we may know of the disease that is eating civilization and, through true knowledge, hope to eliminate them. For knowledge is power. It is only by knowing the truth that we can face the truth. Ignorance is weakness.

That is why a great good comes from the screaming headlines and detailed reports of the underworld that come to us daily in newspapers.

But these swarming masses of evil that twist and warp the crust of society are destined to an end so terrible that their very souls are shriveled by the death they know will overtake and snatch them suddenly.

Asleep, awake, walking the streets or conducting their so-called business—sooner or later it will reach out its bony hand and snatch them. In every breath, in every word, the gangster utters a moan of terror that must needs wring an involuntary cry of pity from our hearts.

For the gangster cannot win.

Gangland Stories, June-July 1930

A Page from the Publisher's Notebook

THE CROOK IS A MENACE TO SOCIETY. He is running amuck. He has become an octopus, whose tentacles are reaching over the country, drawing within its slimy folds our people—our very families, smothering them within his death-clasp.

Day by day he grows bigger and bigger. His huge form is towering over us, shutting out even the light and warmth of the sun. The menace of his toils is surrounding us, cutting off our very lives.

He is a gigantic parasite, feeding on the life blood of our society.

Every day the newspapers are full of accounts of his doings. Every day some innocent citizen is deprived of his right to make an honest living or even of his right to live! For the criminal is ruthless in his desires. He kills— and kills without thought or pity for his victim, to gain his own ends. And the small shop keeper, the independent manufacturer, is wiped out so that an individual can add one more notch to his boot-leg gun.

Many of our stories are written about the criminal. But they are merely for your entertainment, and in no way attempt to depict the criminal as he really is. In escaping from the humdrum reality of everyday life, you read these stories written by men whose one idea is to entertain you, to excite your imagination.

They are but incidents in the life of the criminal. We do not show you his menace. We do not show you his inevitable end.

But death is leering over the shoulder of the crook. Every breath he draws may be his last.

And he knows it.

Gangster Stories, June-July 1930

A Page from the Publisher's Notebook

WORD COMES TO ME that some editorial writer in a distant state, has referred to GANGSTER STORIES as the house organ of the gangster industry, or some such sarcastic phrase.

Although I did not read this editorial in a great newspaper, I am willing to bet that the writer failed to realize one thing. Did he take note of the moral value of this magazine? Surely he would admit that knowledge is power. And knowledge of the dangers that beset our paths in life can do no harm. Particularly is this so when we know and realize that these stories and the characters therein are but figments of the imagination.

It is true that even the front page of the stately *New York Times* is often filled with gangster news: deaths on the spot; trials with lurid details; executions, and jailbreaks. But these are only snatches out of the whole system of gangland. Whereas in this magazine we tell the stories of gangsters for your entertainment in complete form. We follow them from their beginnings to their crimson deaths. We know that what we read is not true, but we know it teaches us as well as entertains.

Knowledge is power—the power to give us strength to combat these forces of evil.

Faithfully yours,
HAROLD HERSEY

Racketeer Stories, June-July 1930

A Page from the Publisher's Notebook

THIS IS THE DAY OF PROGRESS. Progress in all ways, not the least of which is the ease of living. The small details that at one time kept us busy the better part of the day, can now be finished in a few minutes.

No more do we spend hours going about the house cleaning and filling oil lamps. No more do we take a whole day every week to drive Dobbin to the market to get the supplies for the week.

One might go on indefinitely, enumerating examples of the changes that have made the business of living a simple one.

But, unfortunately, the honest citizen, the man who represents the American public all over our country is not the only one who benefits by the great strides we have taken in science and invention.

The criminal has been turned from a large, beery, rough-neck, throwing bricks around aimlessly, breaking store windows and occasionally black-jacking some dandy behind the ear and removing his portables, into a menace that looms over our civilization like a cloud of doom. Machine guns, pineapples, poison gas, high powered cars, and all the newest chemicals have enabled the criminal to wipe out hundreds of not only his kind, but innocent people as well, and then vanish—so quickly that he eludes even the most cunning minds of the police.

Progress is for the greater comfort, the greater safety, the greater well-being of nations. Not for their destruction.

Let us see that the criminal, rather than using progress for his own diabolical ends, is eventually obliterated by it.

Faithfully yours,
HAROLD HERSEY

Blood Thirst

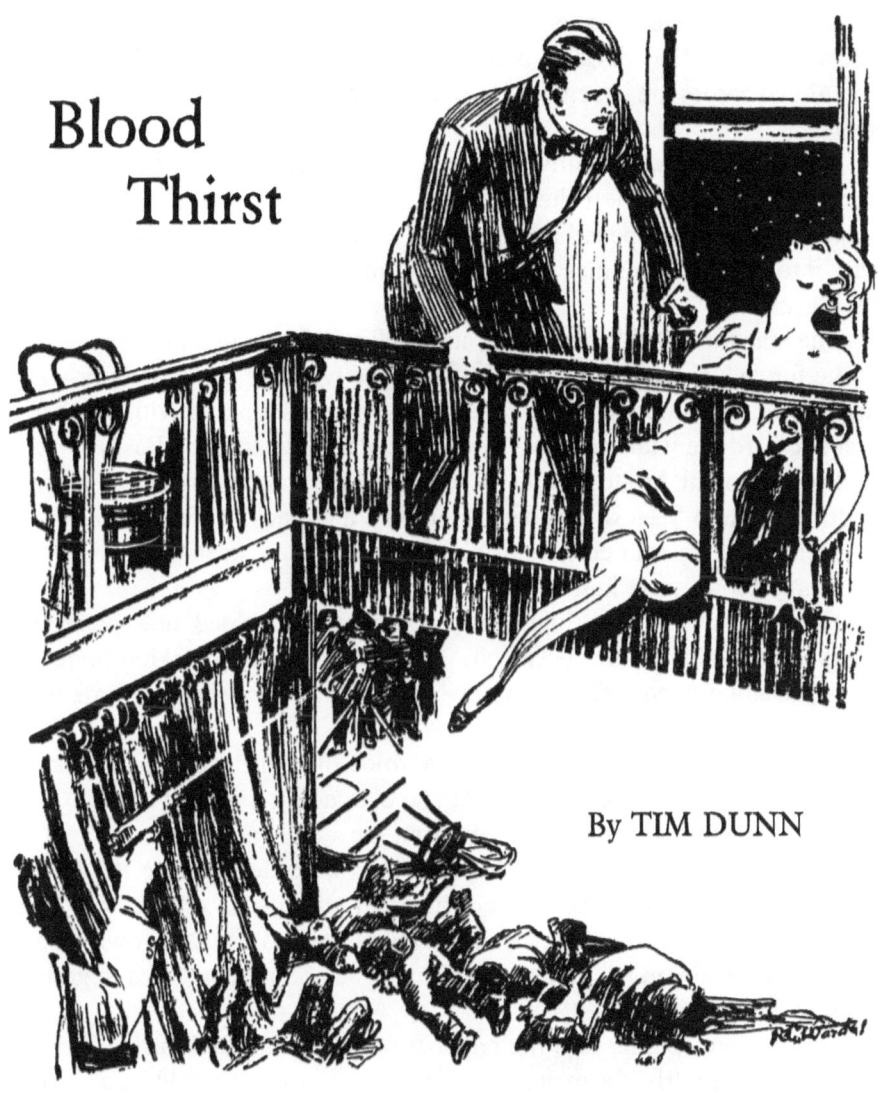

By TIM DUNN

*Kate wanted the stench of blood and the reek of death . . . and she got
what she wanted—in a way that she didn't expect!*

A LONG, LOW-HUNG MOTOR, MAROON COLOR, drew up to the subdued entrance
lights of an exclusive Sutton Place apartment. A man in livery hurried out
under the pavement awning, and opened the gold monogrammed door of
the car. The broad shoulders of a gentleman in evening dress appeared. J.F.
McCann stepped out of his Pierce Arrow, nodded to the obsequious attendant,
and crooked his elbow invitingly to the woman within the car.

A diamond buckled slipper was placed daintily on the running board, followed by a perfect leg, covered by a web of gossamer silk, and the lady known as Mrs. J.F. McCann laid a sparkling hand on the preferred elbow and glided across the pavement in an aura of rare perfume, jewels and costly sables.

The pair stepped silently over the deep rugs and into the automatic elevator, and silently left the elevator high above the street. No word was spoken as the man opened a heavy door and stood aside for the woman to pass into the huge entrance hall, where a fire flamed under the high, carved fireplace.

The man threw aside his top hat and stick and turned to relieve the woman of the furs which swathed her. The sable cape was a heap on the floor where the woman had stood and the woman herself was swinging with pantherish grace toward the wide windows which faced the lights of the East River.

For a moment, he stood, quietly regarding the shadowy ripple of muscles under the white flesh of her bare shoulders and back. There was a hint of amusement at the firm corners of his thin lips, but the keen gray eyes under the heavy brows were humorless.

He sank into a low chair, and picked up the folded newspaper laid ready on the small table beside it. The printed sheets crackled under his long, muscular hands. The woman whirled as though a shot had broken the stillness of the room.

"Damn you, Mack!" she cried in a voice that shrilled high against the rafters of the two storied room, "Are you ever going to open your trap?"

J.F. McCann glanced up casually from the stock quotations.

"I have already opened my trap, as you so politely phrase it," he said calmly. "As far as I am concerned, the deal was closed on the way home from the theatre. You are sick of this 'lousy life,' to use your own elegant expression. And you are damn sick of me. You are perfectly free to go back where you belong."

The woman sprang, tore the paper from his hands, and hurled it on the blazing logs. Swiftly, the man got to his feet and gripped her white arms with fingers that dug deep into the flesh. His steady gaze met her dark, blazing eyes indifferently.

"I dislike scenes, Kate," he said quietly. "I know what you'd like to say. You've said it. You are tired of the silks I've given you to cover your white hide. You're tired of the diamonds I've given you to play with. You're tired of luxury. You're tired of security. You're tired of me. You want something more. I'm not giving it to you. All right, go out and get it!"

He thrust her aside roughly. She stumbled and fell sprawling across the polished table. Her flung hand came in contact with a heavy bronze vase. Her white fingers curled around it, tensed for a moment, then relaxed. She crept to him and circled the broad shoulders with arms that already showed faint purple marks where his fingers had gripped them.

"Mack," she pleaded, "I don't want to leave you. I don't want to leave you! I want you to go with me. The damn play got me going tonight. You and me, Mack, dressed up like a couple of dummies in a show window, sitting in a box, watching a lot of ham actors pretend to be gangsters!"

She threw back her dark head and laughed mockingly. He stood immovable, watching the pulsations of her full throat under the circle of diamonds. The laugh died abruptly on the brink of hysteria. Quietly, he lifted her jeweled hands from his shoulders, and turned toward the stairs to the gallery above.

"You know where you can find the real thing, Kate," he said pleasantly. "Any number of them, ready to welcome you back, and all of them real, red-blooded, fast-shooting gangsters."

"Gangsters!" she shrieked after him as he ascended the stairs. "Gangsters! You know damn well you're a damn gangster yourself!"

A door slammed above, but she raised her voice still higher.

"Yes, damn it to hell, nothing but a gangster, even if you do use a fountain pen now instead of a rod!"

She flung herself on the velvet cushions of a davenport before the fireplace, and lay staring into the flames.

"I'd sell my soul to hell," she muttered, "to see some real gun play again." And she ran her tongue over her painted lips.

A moment later, her jeweled heels were clicking swiftly up the gallery steps. At the top, she paused. The rigidity of her taut body dissolved into languorous grace, and voluptuous curves. The red lips that had so lately called for blood were sensuously moist as she swayed across the soft carpet to the closed door.

Two days later, J.F. McCann unlocked the door to his private office at the unheard of hour of eleven in the morning. "J.F.," who always made a point of promptness, was late. He strode into the silent, spacious room, shrugged out of his overcoat, and settled at the huge, carved desk. There were six telephones on that desk, each one enameled a different color. J.F. bent over the pile of letters and documents waiting his attention. Swiftly, he ran through them, his thick brows knit in concentration. When he had finished, they were separated in neat piles on the polished surface of the desk.

He leaned back in his chair, and drew a small, white leather jewel from his pocket. He snapped open the lid. A ruby, like a huge drop of blood, gleamed on the satin lining of the box. J.F. reached for the telephone painted white.

A shrill jangle broke the intense quiet of the room. His hand moved to the instrument painted red.

"Yes?" he said, impatiently.

"Mike speaking," said a huge voice which seeped out of the receiver McCann held to his ear. "I've been tryin' to get you for hours, Mack. Trouble."

"Turn the switchboard over to Joe, and come up by the private elevator," said McCann, and hung up. He thrust the small white box back into his pocket, and whirled his chair to face the panelled side wall of the room. Presently, one of the heavy oak sections slid back, and a man stepped out of a small elevator and across the soft carpet.

"Sit down, Mike," said McCann. "Have a cigar? What's the trouble? Some of the clerks downstairs gone on a strike?"

Mike grunted and bit off the end of a cigar ferociously.

"You know damn well I wouldn't bother you with that, Mack," he replied. "I said trouble."

McCann leaned back in his chair and studied the heavy figure of the man whose striped suit and yellow shoes made a glaring note in the subdued richness of the room.

"Mike," said McCann casually, "will you ever learn how to dress for business? That flaming tie doesn't set well on you at all, especially when your face is as red as it is now."

Mike ignored the remark.

"Mack," he said, leaning far over the desk, "there's trouble brewin'. Hogan refuses to deliver. He says you'll have to fight for it!"

McCann transferred his narrowed eyes from Mike's loud shoes to the ceiling.

"Fight for it!" he said, quietly. "I don't fight. I take. Cross Hogan's off the list."

"I've done that, Mack," said Mike. "But that won't settle it. Our man in Hogan's mob says the Tenth Avenue bunch is backing Hogan. If he gets away with it with you, the Tenth Avenue push will pull the same trick. It means trouble, I tell you, Mack, and if . . ."

"It means more to you, Mike, than to me," returned McCann. "Naturally, you're a bit upset. Your cut-in on the booze racket is threatened. You see a nice, juicy ten-per cent fading out of your big fingers, eh? I don't blame you. But, to me, Hogan and the Tenth Avenue mob and all the rest of the miserable little booze runners don't mean that!" And he snapped his long fingers contemptuously.

"Yeah, maybe," drawled Mike. "But you ain't goin' to let 'em get away with it, just the same, are you, Mack?"

McCann's firm lips twisted in a smile.

"How much does Hogan think he's going to get away with?" he asked.

"Two truckloads, scheduled to come in tonight. Our man says . . ."

"Who is our man in Hogan's gang? Never mind. I remember. Little fellow—limps—black eyes—name of Bergen. Right?"

Mike's red face relaxed into a broad grin.

"Beats me, Mack, how you can remember! Yeah, that's the guy, all right, and he says . . ."

"Get him here," interrupted McCann, and started to finger the papers on his desk. Mike rose. "You mean here?" he asked.

McCann frowned, but did not look up from the map he was studying.

"You're getting slow on the draw, Mike. You know damn well no gangster steps foot in this office, or the one downstairs, either. Get Bergen on a wire somewhere, so I can talk to him," and he nodded a curt dismissal.

The panelled wall slid closed on Mike again, and J.F. McCann reached for the white telephone.

"Kate," he said softly, when the number was through, "I've got it—the ruby pendant you wanted."

"I usually do manage to get what I want, Mack," said the woman at the other end of the wire, and laughed softly.

The man's lips tightened a little. "Yes, when you want the things I'm willing to get for you, Kate," he said. "I'm glad you came back to your senses, old girl. I didn't want to lose you."

"You're not going to lose me, Mack, not yet. . . ."

McCann's long fingers tightened around the telephone till the knuckles gleamed white.

"What do you mean—yet?" he began, and turned his head at a slight sound from the wall.

"Oh, just a little joke," said the woman's voice in his ear, but he did not reply. His eyes were fixed on the slowly opening panel of the wall. A man stepped jauntily from the elevator behind the wall, and removed a tilted derby from his slick black head. McCann's hand flashed inside his coat. The man patted a bulge in the pocket of his checked overcoat, and smiled suggestively.

McCann drew forth a thick gold fountain pen, laid it carelessly on the polished top of his desk, and turned to the telephone.

"A little matter of business has come up," he said quietly. "I'll talk with you later."

He hung up, and faced the man who still stood with his back to the wall, one hand in the bulging pocket, the other, gloved in bright yellow chamois, holding the black derby against his chest in a gesture of mock humility.

McCann fingered his gold fountain pen.

"Well, Derby Dan, it's a long time since we met. What can I do for you?"

he said, casually.

Derby Dan's spatted feet took a stride forward.

"And how the hell did you get here?" continued McCann in an icy voice.

"Rode up in the classy lift," returned Derby Dan, in a high nasal voice, and slid into the chair lately vacated by Mike.

"No," he protested, as McCann reached for one of the 'phones. "Don't bawl 'em out downstairs. Ain't their fault. Only, you shouldn't hire good lookin' girls down there, Mack. They're liable to let things slip by into the elevator, when the things is as nifty lookin' as Derby Dan."

"That's enough," snapped McCann. "You're here, what do you want? Remember the last time we met, and make it snappy."

"Yeah, I ain't forgettin'," said Derby Dan. "The last time we met, you near choked the heart out o' me, McCann, because you thought I wanted that damn skirt of yours, the lousy . . ."

"Cut that," said McCann, leaning far over the desk. "She happens to still be my skirt, understand?"

"Yeah, and maybe she won't be when I get through talkin', Mack," said Derby Dan, with a yellow-toothed smile.

McCann made a move to spring from his chair. Derby Dan went on grinning.

"I'm here to talk, Mack, and I'm goin' to talk, if I have to plug you first and talk to a stiff after. I'm here to do you a favor, see? And what's more, I'm keepin' you damn well covered while I do it."

McCann raised the gold fountain pen an inch or two above the desk.

"You're damn well covered yourself, Derby Dan," he said quietly. "And have been ever since you pushed yourself into my private office. You can talk, but first, you can discard that sawed-off you've got in your coat. Put it in the center of the desk."

Derby Dan stared at the point of the gold fountain pen. It was trained directly at his heart, and the manicured fingers of J.F. McCann were holding it steadily at just that point.

"It's a .38, Derby Dan," said McCann.

Derby Dan placed the sinister sawed-off in the exact center of the polished table.

"Now," said McCann, "talk."

"It's about Kate," began Derby Dan sullenly.

"Of course," said McCann casually. "You think you've got something on her. You've been out to get something on her ever since she turned you down for me. Let's have your little rat tale. I don't want to seem impolite to an acquaintance of the old days, but the perfume you slather on yourself is abominable."

McCann leaned carelessly back in his chair, with his steady gaze on the beady eyes of the man before him, and the fountain pen poised for instant action.

"A helluva way to treat a guy . . ." began Derby Dan.

"Talk," said McCann, and raised the pen an inch higher.

"Kate's been seen in Hogan's speakeasy," said Derby Dan, and waited for an explosion. None came.

"What of it?" said McCann. "I can't keep a wealthy woman with lots of time from doing a little slumming."

"Slumming, hell!" yelled Derby Dan, then suddenly lowered his voice. "That damn skirt was mighty thick with Hogan, Mack. She thought nobody seen her, hidin' away with him, talkin' low, in a booth."

"What of it?" asked McCann. "Hogan's a friend of mine."

"The hell he is," exclaimed Derby Dan, his voice rising to a whine. "Say, you ain't so dumb you ain't heard . . ."

Derby Dan abruptly relaxed in his chair. His eyes darted about the room, everywhere but at the intent face of the man behind the desk.

"So," said McCann slowly, "you're in on that little business dispute between Hogan and me, too, eh?"

He reached into a drawer with one hand and placed a large, leather bound book on his desk. Still with one hand, he turned the indexed pages to "H," and ran down a list of names.

"I don't see you here, Derby Dan," he said. "Have you joined up with Hogan recently?"

"No, I ain't."

McCann transferred the sinister pen to his left hand, and picked up a pencil. The man at the side of the desk watched him trace the name, "Derby Dan," under the long list of Hogan's men, and started forward as the pencil wrote the word "rat" after that name.

"You got me wrong, Mack," he whined. "I ain't workin' for Hogan!"

"No, you're ratting on him," replied McCann. "Because you can't forget that a woman once turned you down for a man."

Derby Dan fumbled with his hat.

"Have it your way, Mack. What the hell? I'm here to tell you there's been a lot of talk goin' around about what Hogan's goin' to do to you, a lot of it, since last night, and it was last night that hell cat of yours was conflabbin' with Hogan."

McCann closed the book with a snap and rose to his feet.

"Well, Derby Dan, if you have nothing more interesting to report than a conversation which you didn't hear, I'll have to ask you to go. Use the public way this time."

"I heard enough of the conversation," muttered Derby Dan. "And what's more, I seen enough. She wasn't so careful when she got tanked up later on in the evenin' and spent an hour in Hogan's shootin' alley, flourishin' a gat, and braggin' about the blood she could draw."

"I trust she wasn't wearing her diamonds?" said McCann, with the first show of interest since the conversation began. "They're too valuable to flaunt around in a place like Hogan's speakeasy, when one considers the type that frequent the place."

"Cut the wise cracks, Mack," returned Derby Dan. "I ain't the type that lifts sparklers, if that's what you mean. She had 'em on, though, strung around her neck, and I'd like to have choked the breath out of her double crossin' heart with 'em. I hate her guts!"

"Good-day," said McCann, quietly opening the outer door. "You might take your gun with you."

Derby Dan picked up the sawed-off, eyed the point of the steady gold pen for a moment, and slunk toward the door.

"A helluva way to treat a guy," he said through his nose, as McCann politely bowed him out, and locked the door after him.

McCann crossed quickly to one of the windows and flung it wide. There were bitter lines about his mouth as he snapped the small white box open, and dangled the sparkling gem on its thin platinum chain over the sidewalk twenty stories below. For a long moment, the ruby hung there, gripped in his strong fingers, then he laughed a low, grim laugh, withdrew his arm, placed the pendant in its satin resting place, and turned to the desk. His hand hovered over the white telephone, then switched to the red. As he drew it toward him, another one of the six instruments buzzed.

"Limpy Bergen," boomed a voice, as McCann answered.

"Put him on," said McCann quickly. "That you, Bergen? Where is Hogan planning to store the two truckloads due to-day?"

McCann smiled as he heard the answer.

"Good," he said finally. "How do you get into this place? . . . Good. That's all I want. Except this. You're going to have an accident sometime today, Limpy, lose your arm, or leg or something."

Shocked protests from the other end of the wire.

"No, nobody's going to take you for a ride, Limpy. You're too good a man. On second thoughts, maybe a headache would serve as well. Anything that lays you off your job with Hogan for tonight, unless you want to mix in a fight, understand?"

He hung up, and wrenched the receiver of the red telephone from its hook.

"Send Mike up here immediately," he barked into the mouthpiece without waiting for an answer.

Presently, the wall panel slid open again, and Mike lumbered into the room, his beefy face two shades darker with excitement.

"What's wrong, Mack?" he spluttered. "Joe said you was fightin' mad."

"I dislike that expression, Mike," said McCann. "Sit down. Derby Dan has just paid me a call."

"Derby Dan! How in hell did he get in here?"

"That's what I'd like to know," drawled McCann.

Mike's jowls shook. "Cripes, Mack," he exclaimed loudly, "I swear to hell it ain't my fault. . . ."

"Never mind, Mike. As it happens, Derby Dan furnished me with some interesting information—very interesting. But don't let it happen again. Now, about this little matter of Hogan . . ."

J.F. McCann, the perfectly dressed, suave man of business, and Mike, his loud mouthed, cursing assistant, went into conference. When it was over, Mike's huge face was beaded with the sweat of excitement, and J.F. McCann stood ready for the street, one gloved hand on the door, the other twirling a malaca stick.

"Till to-night then, Mike," he said, and stepped out into the hall.

"Cripes, he's a cool 'un!" said Mike, and wiped his brow with the sleeve of his jazzy suit.

J.F. McCann stepped quietly into the huge entrance hall of his Sutton Place apartment, and handed his things to a trim maid.

"I hope Mrs. McCann is at home?" he asked.

"Yes, sir. Shall I . . .?"

"No, there she is now. That is all, thank you."

Kate, in a crimson negligee, was leaning over the railing of the gallery.

"You're home early, Mack," she called, stifling a yawn.

"I couldn't wait to bring you what you wanted, Kate," he said. "Come down and get it."

The white leather box was in his hand as she approached him. He held it away from her, and lifted her chin, critically.

"You look tired! I hope you didn't sit up late last night waiting for me?"

"No," said Kate, her eyes avid on the box in his hand. "Don't keep me waiting, Mack, let me have it!"

"Don't be in such a hurry, Kate," he said, as her eager hands clutched for the box. "I've something much better in store for you tonight—something you want much more."

She lifted her eyes from the ruby, wonderingly.

"Put it on," he urged. "You must wear it tonight. It's the color of blood."

He gripped her suddenly by the shoulders which the flaming negligee left bare.

"And tonight, my girl, you're going to see what you long to see—gunplay, good, old-fashioned, blazing gunplay."

Her eyes did not meet his. They fastened on the glowing ruby in her hands, but her body tensed under his gripping fingers.

"Where?" she breathed.

"A little affair at Hogan's speakeasy. Won't amount to much, I'm afraid. Hogan refuses to deliver two truckloads that belong to me. I know it's stored in his cellar and I'm sending four or five picked men over there to load it out. It'll be over in a few minutes. Hogan won't be prepared. And he won't suspect anything when he sees us strolling in. He always was a good friend of yours, eh, Kate? We'll take a grandstand seat on the balcony over the dance floor. It won't be the same as engineering a rumpus yourself, Kate, but maybe it will amuse you."

He dropped his hands and turned from her. She stood, hesitating a moment, then made for the stairs.

"I must dress," she said, and there was an undercurrent of excitement in her voice.

"Plenty of time, Kate," said McCann softly. "Come and talk to me a while."

"I really must," she insisted. "I'm—I'm going out for a moment."

McCann picked up a book.

"Run along," he said, carelessly, leafing over the pages. "I know you must have preparations to make for this little affair tonight. You're the sort of woman who'd wear her best gown to a murder, Kate."

"Yes," she said, nervously. "I really must get my hair done, Mack." And she darted up the stairs.

A door slammed above. McCann picked up the 'phone, and gave a number in guarded tones.

"Mike?" he said, his lips close to the mouthpiece. "Double the order for tonight. Understand? The customer is going to be warned." And he hung up quietly and took the book from the table again.

He had not turned a page before Kate was down the stairs in street clothes and swiftly circling the room toward the door. He intercepted her, and seized her in a steel embrace.

"Mack!" she cried. "Why are you looking at me like that?"

His long, muscular fingers crept to her white throat and circled it. For a long moment, he held her so, his gray eyes blazing into hers, his teeth bared in a slow smile.

Then he bent, pressed his mouth brutally to the red lips, and let her go.

"Just a little joke, Kate—gang stuff. Go out now and do what you have to do."

• • •

At ten o'clock that night, the maroon Pierce Arrow with the gold monogram drew up to the dirty doorway of Hogan's speakeasy. J.F. McCann handed out the woman known in Sutton Place as Mrs. McCann, and familiar to the underworld as Kate. He whispered a few words to the liveried chauffeur, and the car drew silently away from the curb.

There was real color surging under the rouge on Kate's cheeks as the pair passed through the dingy hall and signaled on the heavy door at the end for admittance. She entered the noisy, smoky room beyond, with the grace of a stalking panther, the rounded limbs slow and sure under the deep red satin that clung to them, the dark head high, the nostrils dilated. Her eyes were on fire. Her lips, moist and full.

Hogan himself came forward to greet them, rubbing his pudgy hands together, the fleshy folds of his face creased in a set smile. He did not look at Kate.

McCann bowed slightly to the huge bulk that was Hogan.

"Evening, Hogan," said J.F. McCann. "You know Kate, don't you?"

Hogan turned his pig eyes to the resplendent figure beside McCann, but his gaze went no farther than the blood red ruby on her breast.

"Sure," he chuckled, "it's a long time, Kate. . . ."

"Kate's homesick for old times, Hogan," said McCann casually. "How about a seat on the balcony?"

"Sure, sure," said Hogan. "Walk right up."

Kate swept through the room to the stairs at the back without a glance. The man at her side seemed absorbed in her, but his keen gray eyes were busy with the curtains of the booths which bulged and swayed suspiciously, and the figures lolling at the small tables through which they threaded their way—men, all of them—not a woman in the place.

"Let's sit here," she whispered eagerly, as they reached the top of the stairs. "We can see your men come in the front from here."

"No," said McCann in a low tone, and his hand was urgent on her elbow as he guided her down the dim, narrow back of the balcony and around to one of the little tables at the side. "This is the best place, and much safer."

"Safer!" muttered Kate. "What the hell do I care about that? You can't see a damn thing but the booths downstairs from here."

"Well," said McCann, pulling out one of the wrought iron chairs for her. "They might be interesting, too. Look! Hogan seems terribly excited about something. He's waddling in and out of those booths like a fat hen. Stay here and watch him. I've something to attend to."

He turned, and stepped toward the window which faced the dim section of the balcony on which they stood.

She was beside him in an instant, her hands clawing at his shoulders.

He faced her. There was a gold fountain pen in his hands. He turned it over casually.

"Nice little trinket, this, Kate," he said quietly. "It shoots a .38 bullet. Go back to your table."

Her dark eyes were fixed on his in the half light. The end of the fountain pen pressed under her breast, gently. Understanding dawned whitely on her face, as she saw him unfasten the window beside him with his left hand, and saw the lower pane yield, slowly, noiselessly, to the upward pressure of his long, sinewy fingers. Still she stood, motionless, till the night air from the open window blew full upon them. He jerked the spangled white scarf from about her shoulders, and waved it out of the window three times, then quietly motioned her to her seat. He slid the window down silently before he followed her.

The gold fountain pen rested under his hand on the small table between them, as a waiter hurried to them.

McCann ordered a bottle of the best. The waiter disappeared. Presently, another waiter appeared, and hovered about, busily dusting the vacant tables near them. McCann leaned over the railing of the balcony.

"Not very complimentary, Hogan," he murmured. "Only one man to take care of J.F. McCann, and a waiter, at that!"

He turned to the woman who sat silent, with her dark eyes fastened on the scene below. She started as a draft of cold air struck her bare shoulders. A muffled thud sounded behind her. Her lips opened.

"Quiet!" said McCann, tensely, and lifted his hand with the venomous gold thing from the table. "Everything depends on quiet—for you, Kate! Nothing's happened yet, except our extra waiter has disappeared."

As he spoke, two silent figures edged through the window he had left unfastened, and crept along the wall of the balcony, toward the rear. They were carrying something heavy between them.

McCann went on talking.

"Just a few extra men of mine, Kate," he said, smiling. "You see, I decided to make this a real gun fight, after you went out this afternoon. A little surprise for you, eh? Here comes two more of my men. The thing they're carrying is a machine gun, Kate. There ought to be plenty of blood down there, when the fight's over."

The woman's livid face twitched. Her throat worked spasmodically.

"Take it calmly, Kate," continued McCann. "After all, it's just a gun fight, and that's what you craved. I'm staging it for your benefit, Kate. The two truckloads of liquor are a side-issue. They're already loaded out of the second hand shop Hogan had them stored in this afternoon. They're probably in one of my warehouses, now. This is just a little play I'm putting on for your amusement. We might call it 'The Fate of a Double Crosser.' Smile, Kate. Hogan's looking up at you."

Kate's ghastly face peered over the edge of the balcony at the red, upturned moon of Hogan. Mechanically, she smiled. McCann called down in an annoyed tone.

"I wish you'd hurry up the service a little, Hogan. Things are getting a bit dull up here."

As he uttered his complaint, two more silent figures inched along the dark wall behind, carrying a heavy load. And at the window, and on the fire escape outside the window, a dark mass of men waited, with glinting gats ready in their hands.

Suddenly, from below, came the sound of a heavy door slammed back on its hinges. Kate leaned far over the rail. McCann made a motion above his head to someone on the balcony behind. The lolling men at the tables below were on their feet, their necks thrust forward toward the entrance, their hands bristling with guns.

"At 'em, boys!" yelled Kate, but her voice was lost in the volley of shots that came from the doorway. Instantly, the room below was a hell of shattering sound. Kate swung her body far out over the railing, striving to peer through the curling smoke of guns that cut the blue haze of tobacco.

"They've dropped," she screamed, "four of 'em, at the door! At 'em, boys!" She was shrieking now, heedless of the man beside her, heedless of everything but the smell and sound of battle, and the men below, creeping now toward the four prone figures at the door. Her form swung perilously over the frail wooden railing. She slipped, almost lost her balance, but a firm hand pulled her back.

"Don't throw yourself over yet, Kate," said a quiet voice in her ear. "There's more to come."

She turned on him. Her face was burning with mounting blood, her painted lips loose, her white bosom heaving.

"To hell with you! Bring on your battle, if there's more to come. . . ."

The ominous clatter of machine guns cut her short. It came from the rear of the balcony. Three deadly black nozzles were slowly swinging over the railing at the back, slowing swinging death down into the scurrying men below.

Miraculously, the four prone figures at the door below raised the sinister noses of sawed-offs and blazed fire into the men who sought escape that way. The floor was a milling mass of humanity, fighting for cover, stumbling over fallen bodies, slipping in spilled blood.

The bulging curtains of the booths below parted and disclosed men with rods belching burning lead toward the balcony above. But the slow swing of the meat choppers went endlessly on, spraying a thousand deaths a minute toward the trapped crowd beneath them. Sub-machines pushed their black noses through the side railings of the balcony and picked off those who were out of the radius of the machine guns. Eternity passed in those few minutes of clattering death.

Then, silence—sudden, intense. Not a movement, except the slow, curling smoke over the still bodies below.

Kate tore her eyes, mad with the lust of battle, from the bloody floor, and whirled on the man beside her. Her voice shrilled through the deadly, waiting silence.

"A damn good fight, McCann, while it lasted!"

The curtain of a booth below stirred. Another voice broke the silence—a high pitched, nasal whine. "There's the damn hell cat that double crossed us, Hogan!" It screeched. A yellow gloved hand thrust itself through the curtain. Red flame spurted swiftly toward the crimson figure at the railing above.

A dozen shrieking bullets from the balcony pierced the curtain through which the chamois glove had appeared, but Kate was not there to savor the stench of their burning powder, or hear the single nasal whine of agony that came from the booth. For Kate was a grotesque heap on the floor of the balcony.

The man she had double crossed bent over to lift her from the pool of blood in which she lay.

Death spewed into what was left of Hogan's mob. More bodies joined the gory spectacle which J.F. McCann had staged for the woman who wanted blood. And J.F. McCann lay gasping beside that woman, with a gold fountain pen clutched in his chilled fingers and a bullet under his heart.

"You got what you wanted, Kate," he breathed into the dead woman's ear, and spoke no more.

A Long Chance

By BILL BEYER

Her name was Take-It-Easy-Sal, and there wasn't a twist or a rod in gangland who didn't call her "Jonah" Sal! But this was one job she couldn't muff! What is better protection than a snapshot, a long evening, and the U.S. Mail?

"AND REMEMBER, AL, IT'S A FIFTY-FIFTY SPLIT," and the girl eyed the man opposite her at the little wooden table coldly.

"How come?" The man's eyes shifted under her gaze. "If I pull the job alone, the haul don't split that way, Sal."

"Whatda you mean, it don't?" The girl's temper was roused. "If I out the lay and cinch it for you, I git half. If you'd tackled it alone without my info, where'd you be? I'm tryin' to put you in on big business, right. And ain't I gonna be hanging around in a car to help with the getaway? There's gonna be five single grand notes at the place tomorrow and I want half of 'em. See!" Sal banged her fist down on the table with a vicious thud.

Shifty Al looked back at her with a sheepish grin. He could hold his own against a skirt's temper, better than face that cold hard stare from her eyes. He looked her over slowly and critically. The emerald green dress she was wearing was a little shabby. But she had told him she had been against her luck lately. The dress didn't matter anyway. Sal was about his speed—small, well-rounded, seductive. Devastating might have been the word used to describe her, but that word was not in Shifty's vocabulary. He leaned closer to her across the table.

"Maybe, Sal, we won't need to split. Whatda you say?"

The girl's eyes were narrowed as she too leaned closer, but the eyes were smiling beneath the heavy lids. She cupped her chin in her hand as her face almost touched his. He could feel the warmth of it.

"Maybe, Al," she spoke slowly and did not move her face away, "maybe that'll be O.K. with me. But I just gotta be sure of the business details in case it ain't. I haven't worked with you before. This is your try-out."

"Oh, this racket's gonna come through O.K., baby. You trust me for that, and afterwards—"

"Afterwards you come straight down the drive to the gate and turn to the left on the same side of the street. I'll be waitin' with a car I'm gonna hire, about a block down."

"That ain't what I meant, Sal."

"Well, that's what I meant. I want to be sure you got the lay of the getaway straight. After that—" She left the rest of the idea to be carried by a flash of her dark eyes. Al could understand that as he wanted to.

She rose from the table, flung on her coat and started for the door. Al was beside her.

"I'm takin' yuh home, baby."

"Not till you pull the job, you ain't." And she walked on through the dismal room that was the main portion of the dive, and was out through the door, leaving him where he was standing.

Another twist passed Shifty Al. She stopped and looked him over.

"Ain't gettin' mixed up with Jonah Sal, are you?" she asked.

"I sure am." Al was ready to defend his new partner. "What's wrong with her?"

"Wrong? Say, kid, she's always gettin' a new pal and every damn job they tackle goes wrong. Can't yuh see from her duds that she ain't pulled a job since the new styles have been in. That's some time to be without cash."

"I don't care about her rags, sister. She's class just the same. And this is one job she's not gonna be Jonah Sal on. It's a great streak o' luck she hitched up with me."

By this time Sal was speeding away in a taxi. Farther uptown she stopped at a hotel and when she came out half an hour later to hail another taxi, she was dressed in a chic evening gown of iridescents. Just now it was covered with a fur coat in the latest mode. She looked about her guardedly, then gave an address to the chauffeur.

At 138th Street she alighted and hurried into one of the smaller negro cabarets on the block, the Silver Slipper. She glanced around the interior, then walked swiftly over to a table where a man was sitting. This man was apparently waiting for her.

"All set, Sal?" was his greeting.

"And how, Jim! We've got it cinched. In that dive in Bleecker Street, they've never heard of Take-It-Easy-Sal. I'm still the Jonah."

"And you sure you picked a guy that works alone? I ain't going to have you mixed up with no mob, kid, and have you bumped off. Everything's fair, takin' swag from a crook. But it ain't safe it he's got a push in back of him."

"This bird I've landed, Jim, is just another o' them dumb yeggs. Never could handle a big job unless somebody like me stepped in and helped him. So he ain't missin' nothin' when you relieve him of it. He's fell for me hard, too. Thinks I'm the goods."

"And he ain't wise to what he's in for?"

"Say, Jim, I put it over great. Why, I could get a job on the stage if this racket fell through, I'm so good at it. I handed him a hot argument about a fifty-fifty split. He never thought for a minute I expected to get it all. Didn't even tumble to the racket when I outlined the getaway for him. He just thought I was so crazy about him that I wanted to be sure he'd come through safe. But say, what did you want to meet me up here for instead of the usual hangout?"

"It's gettin' a little risky at Joe's. Some of 'em know us a little too well and we don't want to be seen together too much. It might queer the act and, what I'm thinkin' of most, it might get you in trouble."

"But why did you pick this dump?"

"Well, here it's a cinch to spot the whites and give 'em the once over to see if they're somebody we pulled the trick on before."

"You got brains, Jim."

"I just want to look after you, Sal, so you don't get plugged with a hunk o' lead. You know I'm keen about you."

There was no need for Jim and Take-It-Easy-Sal to discuss further the job for the next night. It was set. Some dumb crook was lined up to take the chances and get the cash. All they had to do was to be ready to take the swag away from him as soon as he got it.

The two spent the rest of the evening dancing. When they left, they went in separate taxis. The next night they would have money and plenty of it.

• • •

Late the following night, Sal drove Shifty Al in her smart roadster to a Long Island suburb. A block from the Bernstein residence she brought the bus to a stop to allow Al to alight. He was to proceed on to the house, and she was to keep the car running at this safe distance for the getaway.

But Sal knew that somewhere between the Bernstein house and where she was waiting in the roadster, somewhere in the shrubbery, Jim was hidden. And before Shifty Al ever traversed that distance on his way back, he would be minus the swag.

She watched Al walk up the street and disappear. Then with the motor still running she leaned back in the seat to wait. But before long she was tensely at attention. A man passed and looked at her closely. He had not gone far when he turned and was coming back. When he was opposite her, he paused and lifted his hat. Oh, so that's what he was. It was not so bad as she had first thought.

But she did not want this interfering man around anyway. Al would be coming out soon and there would be a slight display on the street. The strange man's hat was back on his head and he had passed on.

Sal turned to see if he was moving away, but as soon as she had done it, she realized what a fool she had been. He was looking back, and he nodded again. He felt that he was getting some encouragement. He turned and approached her.

"Swell night for a ride, ain't it?"

"Lay off that stuff," and Sal's eyes blazed at him. "And I guess you'd better beat it or I'll get the police."

But the man only leaned closer across the window of the car and spoke. "Lady, that's O.K. with me, because I am the police." He flapped open his coat to expose a shining badge.

Sal looked furtively down the road and back to the man beside her. It certainly looked as though she was going to live up to the name of Jonah Sal. Jim might pull the job at any minute, and this dick would see him when he came from the shrubbery for the attack.

"I'm waiting for a friend," she told the man who was half leaning into the car, "so don't you think you'd better be moving on?"

But she had not handed him the ice pitcher soon enough. Shifty Al had appeared. He was coming from the gate farther down the street. Jim was almost certain to be unaware of what was going on back at the roadster.

Jim let Al pass, then quietly pushed his way through the shrubs that boarded the sidewalk. He raised a black jack over Al's head and Al sank to the ground with scarcely a sound at Jim's feet. Then with deft fingers, the swag was lifted from the inside pocket of the prostrate man.

Sal had caught the beginning of the scene and suddenly adopted her most telling manner for the benefit of the strange man still on the job of picking her up. Anything to divert his attention. She was all charm and seduction. But it was too late.

The man had followed her eyes and was watching the by-play down the street. Quick and sure as Jim's maneuvers had been, they were not quick enough. While he was still leaning over the prone body of Shifty, the dick was down the street and almost on him, gat out and leveled.

"Stick 'em up and don't waste any time about it," he yelled.

Back in the car Sal cursed her luck that there was no gat in her bag. She and Jim always travelled without them. It was safer, and they had no need for them when the job was fixed. It looked like Jim's finish and not a chance for her to get him out of the mess. She saw the dick grab something from Jim's hand. Gun still raised, he was looking it over. Five single grands there should be, and the dick had them. Had them! He was shoving them into his own pocket. He would have the cuffs on Jim in a minute.

No. Jim was turning and walking quietly in the opposite direction. So that was the game. The plainclothesman wanted to keep the coin himself instead of handing it over at Headquarters. Well, Sal wanted it too, and there was still a chance.

Jim was almost out of sight. He was safe anyway. The dick was coming back down the street. When he was alongside the car in which the girl sat, she took a glance at her watch, ignoring the fact that the man had stopped again. She made a pretense of releasing the emergency.

"Ain't gonna leave, are you, girlie?" the dick asked her.

"Yeh. I guess this is one time I been stood up. My hard luck. But I've decided not to waste any more time waiting around."

"Well, you don't want to spend a lonely evening just because some dumb guy didn't know enough to show up, do you?"

Sal's momentary assumption of hauteur was decidedly chilling. Then she slowly looked over the man on the sidewalk, and flashed a smile.

"Well, get in, cutie, since you're so persistent. I'll drop you wherever you're going. Where's it to be?"

He did not answer the question.

"Might as well get acquainted, girlie. My name's Benson, Oscar Benson." He flung his arm over the back of the seat.

"Mine is Sally—Donovan." And she decided she might as well get chummy. She snuggled into the arm that was held around her. "I kind of expected to spend a pleasant evening at one of the night clubs in the city. But I guess it's off. Where you want me to drop you, cutie?"

"You ain't gonna drop me. I'm the guy that's gonna show you that pleasant evening."

The girl looked at him through wide, smiling eyes.

"You know any night clubs, Ike?"

"Me! Say, girlie, I own 'em." He flashed his badge again.

She laughed, and he took the opportunity of drawing his arm closer about her.

When they reached the city and were threading their way up the Broadway traffic, Benson directed her to steer into a side street in the Forties and draw up to the curb.

Out of the car, he ushered her into a doorway and up the stairs. His presence worked like magic on the hostess who greeted the two at the door. They were shown a table in a secluded corner, and a waiter hurried around with drinks.

Sal did not know what her method of procedure was to be. She had seen Benson plunge the five grand into an inside pocket when he had gotten hold of it back on the street. But a carefully worked out technic had convinced her never to attempt anything crude. You always got caught if you did. She had seen it work out that way too many times.

A waiter came to take the order.

"Anything you want, kid, it's on the house," said Benson.

"Generous, aren't you, Ike?"

Sal ordered light on the food, but suggested that a bottle of something might cheer her up. They both drank and were cheered. Subsequently they ordered more.

Sal waited as patiently as she could for the drinks to show effect. She became rather discouraged when she saw that it was going to take a good many before Benson slopped over. Drinks were free for him, and he had accustomed himself to plenty of them. She was feeling just a trifle unsteady herself.

But she was going to get the coin in the dick's inside pocket. That steadied her. He was getting mushy and confidential. And above all she found that he liked to talk about himself. That she could work on, if only she didn't get too dizzy.

Benson was around on her side of the table by this time. He was even showing pictures of himself. He must be fairly well lit to get as friendly as all that, unless he was just naturally a bore. Sal patiently looked at snapshots of him in and out of uniform, when he had been just a flat-foot, and pictures cut from the tabloids showing him with famous criminals. Sal was not getting very far, and the supply of photos in Benson's wallet seemed endless.

"And here's one," he leaned closer over her shoulder, "here's one of the boy himself at the beach."

"Say, kid, that's great." Sal looked at it a long time admiringly. "You wasn't on the force then, was you?"

"Sure. That was just on a vacation."

"Well, Ike, I'd swear you was holdin' down a job as one o' them swell life-savers when this picture was taken." Sal held it up again, and gazed at it long, with gleaming eyes. Benson was smiling a pleased, self-conscious smile.

A half-drunken giggle from Sal. Then she turned to her companion with a serious expression on her face.

"You wouldn't let me keep this picture, would you, Ike?"

"Why, sure. Keep it if you want to," and he made a big-hearted gesture.

"Thanks a lot, kid. I know a girl friend that knows a life-saver down at Asbury. A little wizened-up guy, too. When I show her this it'll knock her cold."

Sal's flattery was working. Benson was leaning back, his thumbs pompously placed in his upper vest pockets. Sal laughed another silly laugh and then seemed to get a brilliant idea.

"Say, Ike, I can't wait. What you say I mail the snapshot to the girl friend right now. I can tell her I'm out dining with the picture himself in person."

Benson seemed to think it was a great idea, too. He called over the waiter and instructed him to bring an envelope and the other necessary equipment. When it was before them a few moments later, Benson leaned back to laugh again. Sal slipped the snapshot in the envelope and began to address it.

Benson was apparently feeling happy as he tilted back in his chair, waiting till Sal should finish. Sal felt that his attitude was most fortunate for her. He was not watching what she scrawled on the letter. In a moment she passed it over to the waiter to mail.

"And mail it right away," ordered Benson, authoritatively. "Then bring us another round of drinks."

"Thanks so much for your assistance," said Sal. There was a smile of sardonic pleasure on her lips, but she was certain that the dick failed to read its meaning.

With another round of drinks Benson's amorous attentions increased. But Sal's attitude had undergone a sudden change. She could not even trouble herself to be coldly polite.

"I'm leaving now," she said, as she rose abruptly from the table.

"Sure, we're both going." There was a fatuous grin on the detective's face. "You just come along with me," he continued in a confidential whisper. "I'll take care of you. And listen! That ain't all." It was impossible to let this opportunity to boast slip by. "I got cash with me, girlie, and lots of it."

He was reaching into an inside pocket.

"Never mind, Ike, I—" the girl began hurriedly.

• • •

But it was too late. Benson had drawn out his hand and there was a blank expression on his face. Sal scarcely glanced at him. She started to reel drunkenly in the direction of the exit. But Benson had suddenly grabbed her by the shoulders and turned her around.

"Where's the money that was in my pocket?" he demanded.

"What money, Ike?" She looked at him with wide eyes.

"That dough I got from the crook? It didn't take me long to get it, and send the yegg on his way. I guess you saw the scene all right!"

Sal started on again, down between the row of tables.

"You stay right here where you are." His firm grip stopped her progress.

"Now let's see. That crook had got hold of five thousand." Benson was thinking it out slowly. "And you was waitin' on the corner for somebody that didn't show up. No guy would throw you over if there wasn't some reason. I guess maybe the kid you was waitin' for was the one I sent on his way." He looked narrowly at the girl.

"I guess," he continued, "I'll just be takin' you over to the night court instead of seein' you home."

Sal was suddenly more sober. She faced the dick with a smile that was very like a sneer.

"What you goin' to tell the judge at the night court, Ike?"

"Well—I—" and Benson began to flounder. What was he going to tell the judge?

Sal helped him out.

"You're goin' to tell him that you caught a crook with the goods. And his next annoying question might be, 'Where is the goods?' Then what do you suppose you'll say?"

"Well, I—can—" Benson started again.

"Yeh, that's just about what you'll say, and some judges can be pretty funny. He might inquire as to when you developed defective speech."

"Aw, shut up," growled Benson, struck with a sudden idea. "I'm goin' to show him the goods."

"Hadn't you better make certain of that?"

"I sure will. Right now."

But a search of Sal's clothing revealed nothing. He seemed to grow more drunkenly furious at the way he had been trapped. He made a more thorough search, and all but tore the clothing from the girl's back. The only outcome was that he had to be convinced that the swag was not on Sal.

"All right," he said, and he reeled drunkenly in his rage. "I'll take you without it." He grabbed her arm and began to march her towards the door. "I'll fix up some story. The real crook got away. But you were his accomplice, waiting in a car to make good his getaway."

Sal looked at him quietly as she walked along.

"That's fine. You got a swell set o' brains, Ike. Of course, you kinda forgot that I'll be allowed to bring in witnesses. I don't think your story will look quite so good when I bring in the waiter there to prove that you been dining and wining with the lady accomplice for the last two hours. The judge might make some funny remarks. And when you stagger quite as much as you're doin' now, Ike, he might even suggest that you leave your nice shiny badge at Headquarters. So let's go ahead and see the judge. I'm curious to know if my guess isn't about right."

Benson halted suddenly, and his hold on the girl relaxed.

"Think you're a clever twist, don't you, puttin' it over on a plainclothes-man."

Sal shook her head decidedly in the negative.

"Say, you don't give me a chance to show how bright I really am. All dicks are so damn dumb."

"Yeh? Is that so?"

"Sure, it's so," laughed the girl. "If you weren't so weak on the head-work, you'd have thought of looking around where I was sittin' with you, when you didn't find the swag on me."

Sal saw that she had headed him the right way. Benson made a dive back for the table they had recently left. While he sprawled there on the floor, rummaging about, Take-It-Easy-Sal slipped out of the door and made her getaway without being followed.

Back at the hotel she expected to find Jim. But it was not till the next morning that he showed up.

"Well, we sure ran into hard luck that time, Sal," he said. "If that guy hadn't happened to be a crooked dick, I sure would have done a stretch. I didn't come around last night because I figured the dick might be wise that you was waitin' for me, and follow you, only to find me here. Then you'd have been in the mess to."

"Well, that wasn't quite the game. I followed the dick instead. And, Jim, the swag is ours."

Jim only stared at her. Then, "You got it here, now?"

"Not quite yet, Jim, but Uncle Sam is bringing it to me just as fast as he can."

She glided quickly over to the telephone and picked it up.

"Hello. This the hotel desk? Will you send one of the bell-boys up with the mail? O.K."

While they waited, Sal leaned back on the divan, lit a cigarette and recounted to her partner the events of the previous night. A few minutes later a letter was handed in at the door. Sal glanced casually down at the handwriting, saw that it was her own, and passed the envelope over to Jim.

"And the coin is in here?" he said with a pleased smile.

"Together with a picture of my latest boy friend," added the girl as she sank down on the divan again.

"Well, we can sure use the cash, Sal, but what the hell do you want to do with the photograph?"

"I don't know, Jim," said Sal, as she watched the blue smoke coiling to the ceiling. "Frame it, maybe."

"You already have, baby."

Jim's laugh was suddenly cut short by a sharp voice from the other end of the room.

"Stick 'em up, and be quick about it."

Jim whirled to the sound. Sal sprang like a tigress from the couch on which she had been reclining. The door had opened quietly and the open space framed Ike Benson.

Quietly he came into the room, a thirty-eight held steadily in front of him. Behind him came a man in uniform. Benson passed the automatic carefully to the copper.

"Keep 'em covered, Reilly," he instructed, as he approached the man and woman across the room.

From Jim's raised hand he snatched the long envelope, and was about to tear it open when something happened. The girl, regardless of the gat that was leveled in her direction, leaped suddenly forward and grabbed the letter. Immediately she flung her arms above her head again, but there was a sneer of enjoyment on her lips.

"I've still got you beaten, Ike," she said in a hard voice. "This is my mail, and I guess you ain't got no right to open it! Now if you still feel that you want to take me down to court, O.K. with me. But this letter gets there unopened."

"O.K. with me, too," said Benson, quietly, as he drew a gat from Jim's shoulder holster and snapped a bracelet over his wrist.

"You better hold off on the cuffs a minute, Ike," said the girl, "till you hear what I have to say. I told you if Jim and me go, we go with the letter unopened. But I've a hunch that we're not going, because I don't think you'd care much about listenin' to the judge's loud laugh when he opens the envelope and finds—what? See the point, cutie? A picture of one of our best plainclothesmen in a bathing suit in the same envelope with the stolen money. And the judge might not be so keen about the photo as you had an idea little Sal was last night."

"Headquarters knows all about that little play," said Benson, and there was a broad grin on his lips. "And I don't mind tellin' you that I got hell for it, too. The chief said something kind o' sarcastic about a bird in the hand.

But I took a long chance. I knew right away when I caught this bird with the dough"—indicating Jim—"that you were in on it, too, lady. I knew then who you were waitin' for in the roadster. And I guess the chief will change his tune when I walk in with the haul this morning."

Benson reached up and carelessly snapped the other bracelet around the girl's wrist.

"And you said something last night, lady," continued the detective, "that just about fits this case. Maybe I don't remember your exact words, but what I mean is, 'All crooks are so damn dumb.'"

The Author & Journalist, July 1930

How to Write a Detective Story
The Gangster Story
(Part 8 of a 13-part series)

By Edwin Baird
Editor of *Real Detective Tales*

WHEN IS A DETECTIVE STORY NOT A DETECTIVE STORY?

When, of course, it is something else again. As, for example, a mystery story, or an adventure story, or a horror story, or a ghost or weird story, or—special emphasis on this, if you please—*a gangster story*.

The gangster story, more than any other, is now masquerading as a detective story. As a matter of fact, it is nothing of the sort; but, so closely are the two related, it is sometimes difficult to tell one from the other.

Of late there has been a big boom in this type of story. They are appearing with increasing frequency in my manuscript mail. Magazines which ostensibly are devoted to detective fiction and nothing else are featuring them more and more. Other magazines are publishing them exclusively. Even the slick-paper periodicals and the book publishers are flirting with them coyly.

Whether this popularity is due to the nationwide fame of our jolly gangsters, or to editorial demand, or to a mistaken idea that such stories are detective fiction, is beside the point. The point is that the stories are being written by writers everywhere, and hence deserve our attention.

Because of this—and also because Mr. Hawkins suggested it—I am going to address myself in this chapter to an examination of the gangster story.

I believe I have read as many gangster stories, good and bad, as the next man. Every day I am deluged with them. I have bought what I considered the best of the lot (and at this moment am overstocked) and sent the rest back.

And those that went back outnumbered the others in the ratio of 200 to one.

Why do gangster stories go back home? For the same reasons, precisely, that earn a round-trip ticket for detective stories. In the first place, the writers obviously have no story to tell. A score of typewritten sheets, filled with what purports to be the argot of the underworld and a half-dozen assorted killings, do not make a story. Yet that is the substance of these manuscripts.

The gangster story, like its cousin, the detective story, must have a plot if it's to see the light of printer's ink; and the plot should be worked out just as carefully. Merely to describe how the gangs of "Scar" Rongetti and

"Hophead" Zookus settled their feud amid the blazing of automatics and machine guns, and how the police rushed in, when the fireworks were over, and sent the wounded to the hospital, the dead to the morgue, and the living to the station, isn't going to persuade an editor to order a check. Before you write your story, make sure that you have a story to write. Analyze its plot, if any. If the plot doesn't stand up, throw it away and try another.

While you're at it, see if you can give it an original twist. These gangster stories, though something new in literature, have already become terribly standardized, just as have the detective stories—and, for that matter, everything else, from automobiles to radio sets.

So remarkably alike are most gangster stories that if you read, at random, a dozen or so in my manuscript mail you would think that one person wrote them all. All have the same lack of plot, the same impossible slang, the same style and action, and the same beginning and end.

This applies, of course, to those stories that are palpably hopeless, that are rejected after a cursory reading. But the same thing is true, in a lesser degree, of those that get into print. Here, too, we find standardization—stories cut from the same pattern and built from a common formula.

For some inexplicable reason, the writers seem afraid to strike out in a new direction and explore fresh fields. And it seems to me they are overlooking an opportunity of tremendous importance. They concern themselves only with the superficial and refuse to look deeper.

Gang murder—putting men on the spot and bumping them off—is not the really significant thing. The significant thing is this: A handful of illiterate hoodlums, who can scarcely speak the language of our country, have obtained a stranglehold on our great cities, have accumulated vast fortunes, have shown open contempt for both federal and state laws, and have been quite unmolested, while doing so, by any of the constituted authorities.

They have nothing to fear, apparently, from state or federal government. They fear only each other. The so-called "big shots," such as Al Capone, may (and do) commit any crime, from murder down, knowing very well that nothing will be done to them, unless it's done by some rival gangster. Their bootlegging activities involve contraband liquor by the trainload and their income runs into millions—and not one of them, so far as I've observed, has ever served an hour in jail for it. (But try to peddle a pint of gin, and see how far you will get!)

Here, then, is the magnificent spectacle of a group of half-breed gorillas bulldozing the most powerful government on earth—and getting away with it. And our writers, industriously turning out gang stories, ignore that picture completely and display interest only in the incidental extermination of the vermin.

The truly great gang story—and one will be written before long, I think—

will not deal with the fighting among these underworld lice, but with their relation to men in public office. That they are closely allied, in a business way, with the very officials who are paid to prosecute them is too evident for argument.

Chicago has long had the reputation of being the fountainhead of this national evil, and it is accepted as a commonplace that Chicago is the world headquarters for gangsters of every stripe. But these honors, statistics show, really belong to New York City. Chicago's reputation is due less to its gang activities than to its vigorous press-agenting. The Chicago gangsters are more spectacular, and therefore make better publicity.

New York's gang killings, however, outnumber those in Chicago. In the first 135 days of this year 153 deaths were recorded with the New York police, or an average of more than one murder a day. As for other crimes of major proportion, such as highway robbery, burglary and the like, 135 or more are reported every week.

Grover Whalen, who resigned last month as Police Commissioner of New York, is authority for the statement that his city has more than 50,000 gangsters and racketeers. Their net income is in excess of three hundred million dollars a year. This doesn't include one hundred millions paid out in graft. The New York police know of 996 gang hangouts in their city.

And so, you see, when choosing a locale for your gangster story you needn't necessarily choose Chicago.

America's gangdom is the most conspicuous blot on its civilization. As such, it is worthy the attention of your best writers. And it is reasonable to assume that the gang story—now reaching a point where it is second in popularity only to the detective story—may soon occupy a place in Literature With a Purpose.

Meanwhile, however, my readers are probably more interested in hitting the magazines than in producing social documents, and would rather hear something on How to Write a Gang Story.

In the main, the same technique applies here that is requisite for the successful detective story. There must be a well-constructed plot, an element of suspense and mystery, and a dramatic climax; and the best way to attain these is to have a complete working synopsis of your story before you start writing it.

Also, it is best not to make your story a too faithful transcript of actual life. Better describe your bootlegger or hijacker—or whatever his racket is—as the average person pictures him. Only take care not to glorify him. There is nothing heroic about these hoodlums.

Have a care, too, about your slang. Gangsters, of course, use a language all their own, and while some of their words are clear to everybody, others are quite unintelligible. Before putting a slang word in the mouth of one of your characters, ask yourself if that word is generally understood. If it isn't, omit it. Many of the manuscripts dealing with gangdom are a hodgepodge of weird expressions that are as foreign to most readers as ancient Chinese.

When gangsters themselves try to write—as occasionally one of them does—they are almost incoherent. An eloquent illustration of their muddled talk may be found in Danny Ahearn's late book, *How to Commit a Murder*, published by Ives Washburn. This book, according to the foreword, was dictated to a stenographer by Ahearn, who is a notorious gangster and old-time racketeer, and is published verbatim. Consider the following gem, plucked at random from Danny's book:

> The best way to kill a man is not to confide in anybody. Keep it just between yourself—you can't trust everybody. He might have somebody in my own gang giving him information that I'm looking to clip him. I would look to see where he lives, or if he had an automobile I would put a piece of dynamite in his starter and blow him up in his car; or try to blow up his house. I would scheme another way, how to get a girl. I would get a broad to make him and give him a steer for me. I would take him that way, or else scheme him through her to give him a walk, and when he walks with her pick him up and throw him into a car. Take him and torture him. Find out who is steaming him on me. When he gives that information, kill him. . . . The real point, how to commit a murder, is always use your heart and scheme a man out. Have a little patience, and you can get him in a right spot.

You get the idea, I trust. If you permit the gangsters in your story to talk as gangsters actually talk, you're going to have a muddled jargon that will make your story seem ridiculous. Best play safe in writing your dialogue by striking a happy medium between the way gangsters *really* talk and the way they're *supposed* to talk. Thus you get realism.

And realism, other things being equal, has sold many a story to the magazines.

Gangster Stories, August 1930

A Page from the Publisher's Notebook

OUR FOUR GANG STORY MAGAZINES: GANGSTER STORIES, RACKETEER STORIES, MOBS, and GANGLAND STORIES—all with the world-famous *Blue Band* on the covers—both entertain and teach us to watch out for the dangerous glitter of the underworld.

In the pages of these periodicals, stark Tragedy lifts her arms up through the night; Terror and Death, her close attendants. The staccato whine of the machine gun bullet is like the drone of insects in a great jungle. The screech of the police whistle breaks through that droning darkness. The cries of the lost fill our ears with a music more like madness than anything else.

But, from these thrilling paragraphs, bristling with gun action, comes moving truths. We learn as we are being entertained. We see how the gangster inevitably comes to ruin, though his brief career is one of false glamor and excitement.

Read the moral if you will.

Faithfully yours,
HAROLD HERSEY

Racketeer Stories, August 1930

A Page from the Publisher's Notebook

BEGINNING WITH THE NEXT, or October issue, RACKETEER STORIES will be increased to 192 pages and sell for 25¢ a copy. This means another fifty-one thousand words for only 5¢ more per copy. It makes this periodical the same size and thickness as the other *Blue Band Magazines*: GANGSTER STORIES, MOBS and GANGLAND.

Fifty one thousand words, plus the sixty-five you are now getting for 20¢, in a great, bulky magazine of 192 full pages! And only 5¢ more!

More illustrations—double and single page—by famous artists.

The same high average of complete, double book-length novels in each and every issue.

Also the fine assortment of novelettes and short stories you are accustomed to reading in the *Blue Band* periodicals.

Put your order in now with your nearest newsdealer. The October issue will be on the newsstands the latter part of August.

RACKETEER STORIES, like GANGSTER STORIES, believes that crime does not pay, but it also believes that these stories are not only entertaining to an immense audience but packed with knowledge. Knowledge, after all, of conditions in the Underworld, should and does help us to guard against dangers.

Faithfully yours,
HAROLD HERSEY

Gangland Stories, August-September 1930

A Page from the Publisher's Notebook

YOU CAN'T WIN.

That notice has been printed in every street car, subway, and elevated train for the past three years. For the criminal, from the big diamond in the shirt kind down to the little petty larceny crook, finds that in the parlance of the upper world that "Business is falling off." That it is true. YOU CAN'T WIN.

At first the police did not know how to cope with these new rackets.

They were used to two-story men and safe crackers, not the kind of people that had the guts to work rackets that would tax the finest of brains, to say nothing of brawn—men that had gangs and worked with machine guns. But now all that is changed. The police of every town, large and small, knows how to cope with these people, and so today the pickings are not easy, for every place is guarded and for every machine gun that the gangster has, the police have three.

A great deal has to be said in regard to the gangster cooking his own goose and spoiling what might have been a swell feed for him. He fought with his partners in crime, they murdered right and left. Taking a life was nothing more to them after a while than licking a postage stamp. They fought among themselves and killed each other. The ones that they killed off were generally the ones with the brains, and, as it happens in every game that is not on the up and up, they began by losing ground. The minute that happened the police, always on the jump for a break, came in, and the gangster, the racketeer and the petty crook found that the little subway signs were right.

YOU CAN'T WIN.

Faithfully yours,
HAROLD HERSEY

The "Eyes" Have It

By CHUCK WRIGLEY

No one even saw the draw. All anyone could remember was that a flat ugly weapon seemed to sprout from the palm of the Chi Kid's hand. "Dogs" sighed and fell to the floor, two bullets in his skull through the eye sockets.

"DOGS" MILLER, FIRST LIEUTENANT TO MARTIN FARRELL, overlord of New York racketeers, was strutting his stuff before the big crowd gathered in Fat Siler's speakeasy on Eleventh avenue.

"Dogs," thus nicknamed because his were the largest feet in Gangland, was both drunk and disorderly. But therein lay one of the reasons for the existence of Fat's place. Fat was unofficial fixer between the underworld and the powers that be. In return it was agreed between gang leaders and officialdom that his speakeasy should be recognized as neutral ground. It was the unwritten law that there should be no gunplay there and that the area for a block in each direction must be kept free of ambushings and stand-up gun fights.

It followed, then, that Dogs was "putting one on" in a place where even the bitterest enemies parked their grouches outside.

The liquor had been flowing freely for hours. Now, with the hands of the clock standing at 11:30, Dogs was becoming both maudlin and boastful. Sober, he was quiet and retiring, a man who possessed the respect and friendship of even his rivals.

He flipped his gun from its holster and pointed it waveringly at one or another of the patrons, meanwhile mouthing bloodcurdling threats of what he might do if the notion struck him.

The others, secure under the house rule of "No shooting," grinned cheerfully as they turned negligent shoulders toward him. Even guns must have their play-times and Dogs, one of the squarest and best of them all, was merely letting the booze talk.

The buzzer at the door shrilled its call. Parker, head bartender, flipped open a slot and held a low-toned conversation with the newcomer. Those nearest him heard the words: "Wait a minute." He turned to a speaking tube connected with Fat's private office and blew a shrill blast.

"Bimbo callin' himself 'Chi Kid' is here t' see youse," he bellowed. A low mumble came in response. Turning, Parker released the magnetic door catch and admitted the stranger.

"Fat'll see youse in a few minutes," he said. "Got somebody wit' him right now. What'll youse have?"

The stranger chose Scotch, ginger ale and a strip of lemon peel. For a few moments he stood sipping his drink, oblivious to the curious glances of the other patrons. They saw a man of less than medium height, slight, well dressed, and wearing a derby hat and spats.

Only a predatory beak of a nose and deep-set, Indian black eyes, marked him as different from ten thousand others of the same description.

Presently, his drink consumed, the stranger hooked his stick and one arm over the edge of the bar, turning an inquiring eye on his fellow patrons.

It was fated that Dogs Miller should be the one to attract his attention, for at the moment he was bellowing at the top of his voice and had his gun out.

Their eyes locked, the vacuous, bleary ones of the drunk and the burning, black ones of the visitor.

"Well, look (hic) whosh here!" Dogs ejaculated. "Li'l Lor' Faunl'roy himshelf—ankle awnin's, cane 'n ev'thing. Whass shay fellersh—wan' me shoot hish spats off?"

It was the Chi Kid who answered for them. He turned and barked a single word—

"Don't!"

It was a command, not an appeal. Dogs' eyes hardened at the tone. There was no one to tell him that the Chi Kid was a congenital killer—that the gunmen of Chicago and Cicero feared the brittle temper of this little man as they feared neither their fellows nor the police.

"Whazzis?" Dogs demanded blankly. "Li'l squirt givin' orders (hic) 'roun' here, huh? Aw-ww-wright! Now watch 'em spats!"

With the words the muzzle of his weapon wavered toward the visitor's feet. The others, recognizing it for one of Dogs' "sandys," looked on smilingly. In another moment he would burst into drunken laughter and order a drink for the house.

No one's eyes saw the draw.

All that anyone remembered afterward was that a flat ugly weapon seemed to sprout out of the palm of the Chi Kid's right hand.

It barked twice, one report blending into the other. Dogs sighed wearily and collapsed to the floor. Had he lived, he would have been blinded—for each of the heavy bullets had entered his skull through an eye socket.

The Chi Kid, feet outspread, froze in a posture of defense. His eyes darted from face to face, alert for possible reprisals. No one moved. A thin film of smoke drifted upward, level with the top of the bar.

The killer's hand stole behind him and caught at the door handle. Then, as Fat Siler, bellowing angry protests, leaped from his private office at the end of the bar, Chi Kid slid through the door and out to the street.

Thus it was written that, for the first time in years, the officers of the homicide squad and newspaper reporters were summoned to Fat's Place for the story of a killing. An armistice had been violated.

The police investigation profited little. No one would admit knowing anything about the slayer or the cause of the killing. Out of the welter of internationally opposed descriptions, the police chose one which flung wide the dragnet for a roughly dressed stranger, taller than medium—probably a Swede or Norwegian.

But over the mysterious grapevine telegraph of the underworld went the news:

"A cannon calling himself Chi Kid knocked off Dogs Miller in Fat's Place tonight. Mart Farrell will want him."

"Hey, Mart! I want off tomorruh aft'noon an' night. Me an' de twist's goin' to Coney. Oke wit' youse?"

Paddy Bowers flung down his cards as he spoke and turned to Mart Farrell—"The square guy who never broke a promise." Paddy was Mart's chauffeur, and for the last hour he had been losing steadily "throwing jacks" with Chimp Janos, Mart's wrestler bodyguard.

The racketeer chief nodded absently but did not look up. His finely chiseled features seemed worn and lines of worry showed between his usually placid eyes.

Speck Thompson, the red-haired and befreckled liaison man of the gang, turned anxiously to Chimp and Paddy. The three exchanged worried glances. Finally Speck, after a period of silence, said:

"What's the matter, Big Shot, still got th' hunch?"

Mart's eyes came up slowly from contemplation of his well kept hands—caught and held Speck's glance levelly.

"Yes," he replied slowly. "Still with me. Remember, you chaps, I've been in this game eight years, principally because I always play my hunches. There's black trouble coming now, and it isn't so far away."

"Got a name for it?"

"Yes—'Chicago.' Ever since we ran their Big Noise off last fall they've been trying to cook up a new racket here."

" 'At's easy," Chimp broke in crisply. "Let 'em start it an' 'en knock 'em off."

Mart lost himself in frowning thought for a moment before he replied.

"Maybe you're right, Chimp, but there's enough lads going for one way rides without sacrificing a lot of our best guns just because the Big Noise in Chicago thinks he's fast enough to cut in here. Damn it all! For a plugged nickel I'd hop a rattler for Chicago tonight, hunt this troublemaker up and shoot it out with him on his own dunghill."

"Let's go!" Chimp roared. "I'll take a stack wit' youse."

Then the telephone tinkled its summons. Mart, his features still an angry red, reached out for the receiver.

"Yes?" he said. "Fat?—Yes—Who? Dogs Miller!—In your place just now?—What about the rule? Who did it?—Stranger, eh?—Who? Chi Kid? Yes, I know him. A rod for the Big Noise.—Call Campbell to take the body.—I'll be right down. Thanks. Goodbye!"

He snapped the receiver back on the hook.

"Put the word out," he snapped in tones choked with anger. "A cannon named Chi Kid just burned Dogs Miller down in Fat's Place. *I want him!*"

The others were on their feet, cursing, burying him under a flood of questions.

"Maybe Dogs was wrong," he said, "but he was my pal and that makes him right. Fat says he made one of his cockeyed gun plays and the fellow—a stranger—croaked him."

Then, for the first time in their long association, the three men closest to the Big Fellow saw his veneer of coldness and self control crack like thin glass. Hands shaking in anger, teeth bared in a snarl, he whirled to Speck and gritted:

"You're top cutter now. Get the word out everywhere. Five to the man who turns Chi Kid in to me before night—alive. Ten grand if it's before noon. Snap into it. He don't know how hot this killing is. He'll stick around."

"Everybody? Anybody?" Speck asked. "All the gangs?"

Mart flared back at him bitterly:

"Anybody in the world—even a lousy dick. You know what a friend Dogs was to me, and whoever turns Chi Kid in can lift my bankroll Come on, you guns—maybe we can get him yet tonight."

Speck already was busy at the telephone as they clattered down the stairs and into Mart's big Lincoln roadster.

Only once did Mart break silence on the fast trip along Broadway and down the Eighth Avenue short cut. Then he said:

"I knew the lid was going to blow off with us standing on it. Now watch me put it back on."

Fifteen minutes after they had left the house, Paddy piloted the big roadster up to Fat's Place and snapped on the parking lights. A solitary dark figure detached itself from the shadows and whispered:

"Fat's closed now. It's Mr. Farrell, isn't it? He said to bring you in through the side door."

Then, as though obeying orders to hustle the visitors within as quickly as possible, the man shoved Paddy forward and motioned for Mart to follow. A black passageway yawned before them but Paddy, a regular patron, knew the way. Mart, lulled to security by the other's assured progress, stepped out briskly. The guide fell in behind him with Chimp bringing up the rear.

The events of the next ten seconds always were vague in Mart's mind. In his grief and anger over the death of Dogs he relaxed his vigilance for the moment. Suddenly through the daze, he sensed rather than heard a warning shout in Chimp's gruff voice.

Instinctively he threw himself to one side and the slungshot blow intended for his skull grazed his left shoulder. He heard Chimp's joyous battle cry as he leaped to grips with the attacker—the double roar of a pistol—Paddy's feet pounding back from the door. All of these items registered vaguely in Mart's mind as he tugged at the pistol which had jammed in the holster under his left arm.

At last the weapon worked loose. At the same moment a dark form appeared for a moment, shadowlike, in the entrance to the passageway, but Mart withheld his fire in the fear of hitting Paddy or Chimp.

A second later a powerful engine roared into life and gears clashed. Then came the sound of a car—his car—whizzing off down the street

Chimp was staggering to his feet, cursing. Paddy ran to the mouth of the passage and called back that the assailant had escaped; that Mart's car was gone. Someone opened the side door of Fat's place and a stream of light showed Chimp bleeding from a wound in the face.

Mart led the injured gunman inside, while Paddy borrowed a flashlight and searched the passageway. Suddenly he shouted and came rushing back with a seriously damaged derby hat.

Mart took it, studied the inside and went white with rage. His hands trembled as he fought back the words that leaped to his lips—for there stared back at him from within the crown the initials "C.K." and the address of a Chicago hatter.

Silently, striving to keep his face expressionless, Mart turned to study the faces before him. Carefully he kept the hat turned against his side so that the telltale markings could not be seen by the others.

It all was plain to him now, the Chi Kid had not gone to earth. Instead he had waited for the almost certain coming of Mart, his first victim's chief. Then, coolly, he had sought to kill him with one smashing blow on the skull. Even in his rage Mart could not repress a thrill of admiration for the gameness of one willing to take on the death gamble at odds of one to three. At least, here was an antagonist worthy of his own attention.

Resolutely putting the intruder out of his mind for the moment, Mart turned to ascertain the extent of Chimp's hurts. As usual that human ironclad had escaped without great damage. One bullet had struck a glancing blow on the jaw, tearing away the lobe of the ear in passing.

The impact over the main trunk nerve had served to stun the Chimp momentarily, but already he had tied a clean towel about his head and now was staring about the circle to surprise someone laughing at his odd appearance.

"No wonder they call him Chimp," Mart mused as he marked his bodyguard's resemblance to the jungle dweller whose nickname he bore. The bloodstained towel bandage set off his protruding jaw, red-rimmed slits of eyes and the huge hands hung on arms all too long for the height of the squat body.

Turning back to the group before him, Mart looked from one to another, waiting for one of them to open the way for him to start a line of inquiry suggested to him by the markings in the hat.

There was Fat Siler, the self-satisfied smirk wiped off his flabby face; "Red" Slater and Hymie Eltner, gang leaders in widely separated localities; Gus Banks, a racketeer who posed as a labor organizer; Albert Skillman, contact man with the agents of the controlling powers; Benny Kauffman, who owned the delicatessen and fruit store racket—and a number of lesser lights.

These, Mart knew, comprised the loosely organized group which endeavored to keep in effect a working agreement between the various gangs. All supposedly were friendly; certainly all acknowledged him as the Big Shot—yet as he studied them red lights of suspicion and rage danced in his eyes.

He centered his attention on Fat, who was squirming uneasily in his chair. Finally Fat broke the silence.

"I thought you'd like to have some of the boys here, Mart. This Chicago cannon sure shot a big hole in things when he turned Dogs off."

"He did!" Mart replied coldly. "Now what did you tell the dicks?"

"Usual thing—stranger—bum description. I knowed you'd want to tend to this guy yourself."

"Instead of which he nearly attended to me."

Mart snapped the words out angrily. He was watching Fat's expression closely. What he saw sent his nails digging into his palms. Fat knew! He was too ready with his apparently surprised query:

"Hey? You mean this Chicago gun was in th' scuffle out there just now?"

Mart favored him with a snarling grin; threw the smashed derby into his lap.

"That's what he left behind," he rasped. "Write your own ticket. He got me flat-footed. I was thinking about the way Dogs had been burned down. He pretended you'd sent him to bring us in through the side door, then got in behind me and tried to knock me off with a sap. Chimp crawled him, but he shot his way out and got away in my car."

Fat did not respond, but Mart saw that his hands were trembling. The air was electric with tension now and it seemed that every member of the group jumped when Mart turned suddenly and barked:

"The Chi Kid came here tonight, Fat; he came to see you. What did he want? You knew he was coming, I can prove that. Now, what was it for? What business could a Chicago gun have with you?"

Fat looked miserably from face to face. Everywhere, he met only hard eyes and seeming suspicion. He knew too well what this meant—he was on trial—and his next few words would clear or smash him.

"I—I don't know what he wanted, Mart," he said huskily. "I'd swear to that on a stack of bibles as high as the Chrysler building. I did know that somebody'd be along from Chi in a day or two—but that come to me roundabout and I wasn't sayin' nothin' until I could get all the dope."

"Quit stalling and spill it!" Mart demanded tersely. "As a matter of fact, you've been dickering with the Chicago outfit, haven't you?"

"Jeez no, Mart!" Fat wailed. "Here's what happened. See if you can make head or tail out of it.

"Babe Jordon come over from Newark a week ago; introduced a man as Bill Meadows from Philly. He said this bird was comin' in with a taxi racket and wanted some advice. We talked Philly for awhile and the feller sure knew the town and the big shots there.

"Anyhow I tol' him to keep out; told him everybody'd forget personal rows and gang up on him if he came in. I told him, 'New York's organized better'n Chi ever was.' "

"Well—" Mart demanded. "What then?"

"He kept on askin' a lotta questions, wantin' to be told why he couldn't edge in. When I'd tell him, he'd ask if this or that couldn't be done. He wanted to know if the cops could be got to, if anything went to city hall—an' he brought your name in. He said you was all that stood in his way.

"When he got up to go, he says, 'Think it over; a guy named "Kid" will see you in a few days.' That was all until tonight when Parker whistled back that Chi Kid wanted t' see me. Me an' Red and Hymie was talkin' so I said for him to wait.

"That's all, Mart; hope to Gawd I die this minute if they was anythin' else."

The circle of faces remained bleak, but no one saw fit to comment on Fat's story. Presently Mart motioned for Skillman to accompany him to a corner of the room. Then, one at a time they called Slater and Eltner, quizzing them about their presence in Fat's private office.

Both plainly were worried and lost no time in returning to the others at Mart's nod of dismissal. He chatted for a moment longer with Skillman, then both rejoined the others.

Fat was in a state of complete funk by now. His lips were working spasmodically and great drops of perspiration stood on his forehead. Unsteadily he reached for the whiskey bottle, but snatched it back as Mart snapped, crisply:

"Fat, you sold out to the Chicago gang. We've got it on you. You called Slater and Eltner in tonight; you said it was important business. Then you stalled for two hours.

"You were waiting, Fat, for Mister Chi Kid to come and lay his plan before you three. You figured that with Slater handling things in the Bronx and Eltner taking care of the East side, you could pull some more in with you, enough so that the Chicago lads could get a foothold."

"It's a lie!" Fat almost screamed the words. "Jees, Mart! Ain't I always shot square wit' you 'n everybody; I'm makin' good jack the way things is. Why should I turn up my pals?"

Mart leaned forward fixing him with a baleful glare as he said raspingly:

"Fat, for fifty grand—half of it—you'd sell your soul and the lives of your whole family. You were the pivot guy; I know it now. They tried to get to Skillman and when he balked, they dickered with some of the Brooklyn outfit. But they didn't get anywhere until they found you."

"It ain't so, I tell you," Fat chattered through bloodless lips. "I didn't have nothin' to do with it."

Mart was inexorable.

"Last chance, Fat, or a ride," he snapped. "Tonight wasn't the first time Chi Kid had been here. He was here once before—when?"

He barked the last word. It snapped like a pistol shot.

"Yester— He never was here before." Fat's voice rose to a scream.

But he knew that he had fumbled. Moaning, hiding his face behind his fingers as though to shut out the sight of the vengeance which was upon him, he rocked unsteadily in his seat.

Chimp came to his feet, gibbering horribly, his bony hands twitching toward the flabby bulk weaving before him.

"Lemme have him, Mart!" he husked. "Gimme him—the damned, lousy double crossin' rat."

"No! No!" Fat wailed, terrified. "Not that, Mart. Gimme a chanst!"

Mart motioned Chimp back.

"Wait," he commanded. "I'm going to count six. If Fat starts talking, it's off. If he doesn't, you can help yourself—and tear me off a chunk of white meat."

Fat uttered a moan of mortal anguish. Unnerved, broken, he slid to his knees. He raised his hands, pleadingly, to the others.

"Skill—" he mouthed droolingly. "Boys—make him gimme—a chanst. I ain't done nothin'—honest t' Gawd I ain't."

"One!"

Mart pitched his voice to rise over the tumult. The others continued to regard Fat stonily, faces set in grim refusal to interfere.

"Two!"—"Three!"—"Four!" It seemed to the others that an almost interminable period divided the count. Fat was on his face now, groping and grovelling in anguished terror.

"Five!"

Chimp leaped to his feet, kicking his chair halfway across the room.

The crash seemed to galvanize Fat into action. Hoisting himself to his hands and knees like a fallen boxer, his head rolling drunkenly, he muttered:

"I did it—I did it! They promised—protect me. The Big Noise—got something on me—made me help. It—it wasn't much—he wanted, Mart—

taxicab racket—"

The words broke the calm of the onlookers. Skillman and the others, accustomed as they were to the unmasking of double crossers, growled angrily at the spectacle of Fat, recipient of gangland and official bounty, turning on his own kind.

But over it all rose Chimp's voice. Bloody and horrible in his rage, he kept shouting over and over again his plea of:

"Gimme him, Mart. Lemme have him!"

Again Mart waved him back.

"Where did the Chi Kid go after he killed Dogs?" he demanded.

Fat groaned and slumped back to the floor again. Mart hooked his foot into the other's armpit and thrust him over on his back.

Then calmly, unhurriedly, he stooped and smashed downward with his open palm, putting all of the strength of his powerful shoulders into the blow. Blood leaped from Fat's nose and lips.

"Where did he go, I asked you?"

"Up-upstairs—to my room."

"And he was on the extension line when you 'phoned to me?"

"Yuh—yes."

"Where's his hideout?"

Fat moved his head from side to side wearily. All of the life seemed ebbing from his gross body. He gulped, blew a bloody froth from his lips.

"I don't—" he began miserably.

Mart's foot crashed against his ribs.

"You do know," he snarled through lips stiff with hate. "And you'll tell me—now. Where is it?"

"Ep—Eppsley Arms on Broadway—name of his moll, Vi Taylor."

"Tie him up," Mart commanded, turning to Paddy. "Maybe he's given us a bum steer. If it is, I'll work on him again. Put him up in his room and stay there with him."

Now he was the old Mart, the efficient, well poised leader. He continued to snap out his orders.

"You, Chimp," he said, "help Paddy put Fat upstairs. Then we'll go and make a call. I want the rest of you to stay here—and there'll be no telephone calls going out over this line. Get me? Somebody else besides Fat was in on his play and now that I've started hunting, I'm going to get all the rats."

One by one he caught and held the eyes of the others. They were stony hard, but all stared back defiantly except Red Slater and Hymie Eltner. They fought with all of their willpower to face the racketeer chief down, but each in turn lowered his gaze guiltily.

There was a bleak half-smile on Mart's lips as Chimp came down from upstairs. A moment later the door slammed behind them.

Mart and Chimp were "going calling."

"Where to, Mart?" Chimp asked as they reached the street. "We gotta chanst to corner dis Chi Kid tonight. Huh?"

"Home first," was the reply. "After that we'll take a crack at this slippery gay-cat. Keep your eyes open for a taxi."

A maroon Paramount solved that portion of their problem. Within a few minutes it had deposited them before Mart's headquarters flat.

As he unlocked the inner door, Mart heard the telephone bell. He picked up the instrument and answered with his customary inquiring "Yes?"

"Mart Farrell?" a crisp voice asked.

"Yes. Who is this?" Mart replied.

"I just want to tell you how lucky you are, but that your luck's gone sour now. You're a big sap—a nitwit."

"Yes? Then I presume this is the Chi Kid," Mart hazarded the guess, but his voice was cold and hard.

"Himself," the other said gloatingly. "I said you're a sap, and you are. Now here's some news for your thick head.

"Go back to Fat's place and you'll find him all tied up like you left him— but I slit his throat, the big stoolie. You'll find your fuzztailed guard beside him. He ain't so damn pretty neither. I moved the front of his face back an inch or two with a piece of pipe."

Chimp, standing beside Mart and listening to the voice coming through the loosely held transmitter, saw his muscles bulge and knot as he fought for self-control. Mart's voice was cold, and emotionless as he replied:

"Got your rod on you?"

"Surest thing you know. I'd feel half naked without it. Listen, saphead, don't fret about my rod. You'll see it plenty soon, and it'll be right in front of your eyes."

"Check!" Mart snapped. "I've passed out the word that there is five grand for whoever brings you in. That's off. If you've got the guts, it's you and me for it."

The taunt struck home as he hoped it would. Chi Kid's voice cracked as he yelled obscenities into the mouthpiece. Mart cut him short.

"Where are you talking from?" he demanded. There was a chance that surprise would make the answer truthfully.

"From Fat's," the other snarled—then cursed himself for the slip. But congenital killers are braggarts. Mart was not surprised when Chi Kid continued:

"I drove your car two blocks and beat it back so I could listen in on what was happening. I was back of the bed when your punks carried Fat in. After your ape left, I fixed the other two up—and now I'm pulling out.

"If you'd had anything in your head but mush you'd have searched the place for me before you left. I was waiting—wanted to show you that rod you're yelping about."

With the words "From Fat's," Mart heard a scuffle of feet behind him. Half turning he saw the door closing behind Chimp then a clatter of feet on the stairway and the bang of the outside door.

Chimp was on his way to trap the Chi Kid. Mart, tied to the telephone, had no choice but to remain and stall the other as long as possible.

"Yes, Kid," he replied in an unhurried, conversational tone, "I must see that rod. But do you know, I've an idea mine is better. I use dumdums—and while they tell me you have a face like a gutter rat, I know it won't be any prettier with one of my slugs in it."

"You big, fat-headed rumdum gay-cat—" Chi Kid bellowed, but Mart continued. He was talking now against time, wildly anxious to hold the killer on the line. Anything would do that would keep him from realizing the passage of time.

"I think you're short on guts, like all the rest of the Chicago mob," he taunted. "Here's a chance to prove I'm wrong. Any taxi driver will take you to the zoo in Prospect Park, Brooklyn. It's up a little hill, away from the road—a sweet place for a couple of men to show one another their rods. Do you get what I mean?"

"Hell, I ain't dumb," Chi Kid expostulated.

"No? Well, it's guts I'm talking about. Here's the lay. At the top of the hill there's a flat place about 200 yards long. You name the hour and come in at the north end, I'll come alone from the south. Each holds his rod in his right hand pocket; that's how we'll know each other.

"We'll walk toward the center and start shooting when we feel lucky. We can get our affair over with and the winner can make a lam before the cops get there. Are you game?"

"Fine simp you think I am!" Chi Kid growled. "You'd have the dump planted with cannons; you wouldn't even be taking a chance. All I'd get out of it would be a barrel of lead. Not me, Mister, I'm hep."

"Hep—also gutless!" Mart rejoined tauntingly. "There'd be no other guns there; they wouldn't be needed. Get this, Chi Kid—I want you, man to man. You croaked the best pal a man ever had and it's up to me now to get you. I wouldn't take a hundred grand for the pleasure of seeing you through the sights on my gun."

"Leave it at that then," Chi Kid snarled. "Just keep your eyes open and be ready to start smoking—I'll be in front of you, turning you down, before you know it."

"Did you say 'in front'?" Mart sneered. "Why, you filthy little ambusher, you wouldn't face even a rookie harness bull, let alone a good rod-man."

• • •

His eyes sought the clock on his desk. How long had he been talking? He must hold Chi Kid a few moments longer. He was hoping—almost praying—that Chimp would get there before Chi Kid could get away.

The latter was snarling curses and threats again. This time Mart did not interrupt. Every second was precious. When the mouthings ceased suddenly, Mart said, "Listen—when will you feel brave enough to take a chance?"

For a few long seconds there was no answer. Then the other said, "What's that?" but his voice was a half whisper now.

"You swear fine," Mart went on desperately, "but I still think you're a filthy coward. See here, skunk—I'll play any game you can think of—adjoining hotel rooms—meet on a corner—anything. I don't want to have to wait to ship your carcass back to Chi so they can be planting you while Dogs Miller is being put away."

"Ye-ah?" It was Chi Kid's turn to taunt now. "Don't forget your other curly-toothed bandit down here—the one with his face smashed in. He's going to need some burying too—and that's saying nothing of the nice funeral the boys'll frame up for you. That'll be something for th—"

The line went dead. Mart jiggled the hook, but the only result was a belated "Number, please?" from the operator.

Mart sank dispiritedly into his chair. Either through craft or accident, Chi Kid had sensed danger. Damn the luck! Now he'd be on his way to another hideout. The Windy City crook was getting all of the breaks. It wasn't humanly possible for Chimp to be anywhere near Fat's place yet.

He lifted his wrist and consulted the face of his watch. It was nearly four o'clock. He'd have to go back to Fat's and send Skillman and the others home, and too, he must find out if Chi Kid really had claimed two more victims.

He was exhausted, mentally and physically. It was the let-down which comes with failure even to men as iron as he. The thought of a reviving shower came to him like an inspiration. Five minutes later, rejuvenated, he was getting into clean linen and a light suit of neutral color.

He donned his shoulder holster and gun, his coat and a limp-brimmed Panama, then started for the door.

A telephone shrilled again. This time it was the mellow ring of his private line—a number known only to his aides. He picked up the receivers but listened for a moment before speaking.

A confused sound of men's voices made an overtone above the crackling on the line. "Probably from a speakeasy or night club," he reflected as he settled in his chair and said, "Yes?"

"Mart! Mart! Jeez, chief, I got him!"

It was Chimp's hoarse voice, shrill now with excitement.

"I got him down here at Fat's place—tied up—waitin' fer youse. Come on, Mart—hurry!"

"Chimp!" Mart shouted joyously. "Are you sure?"

"Soit'nly" the other replied. "W'en I run outta de house Eddie Moran was comin' along in his new cab—an' he jerked me down here in no time.

"We was two blocks fr'm Fat's w'en I seen a little guy wit'out a hat, doin' a lam. So I gotta hunch an' scrooched down in de cab, tellin' Eddie t' pick de guy up if he flagged him.

"Sure enough, dat's w'at happened—an' I folded him all up in a bundle w'en he started t' get in. Hot cats, Chief, but maybe that sucker isn't sore! Hey, when'r youse down?"

"Now, Chimp!" Mart exulted.

Dawn was breaking as he left the house.

Chimp, a transformed, joyous victor, opened the door as Mart leaped from his cab and ran along the passageway.

"Get a load of dat, Mart," he husked happily, pointing to what at first seemed a blood stained bundle of clothing lying in a corner.

The Chi Kid it was, in truth, but under the deft handling of the Chimp he had been metamorphosed from a natty, cold nerved gunman into a bloody, chattering Thing.

"I woiked 'im over some," Chimp confessed naively. "He socked me in de eye wit' his t'umb—an' 'en he needed it anyhow."

The Chi Kid's face was a mass of purple bruises; the beak of a nose puffed and patently broken at the bridge. His eyes were mere slits, and one of his ears was horribly cauliflowered. What Chimp lacked in science, he more than made up for in strength.

The final indignity was the manner in which the Chicago killer had been rendered helpless. Ankles and wrists were lashed together in such a way that the Chi Kid's body formed a painful "U." His agony must have been excruciating but as Mart approached he could hear the man gurgling curses in his throat.

"Hello, Chi Kid," Mart said in a casual tone. "Let me see that rod you were going to show me—you gutless punk!" The last words blazed from his lips as the face of Dogs Miller flashed into his memory.

"Well," the Chi Kid snarled. "It took a man to get me—not a white collar simp."

"When're yuh gonna croak him, Mart?"

Chimp, breathing heavily at his elbow, interrupted Mart's reply.

"Not for a little while," he said. "This punk's going to tell me a lot of things about the Chicago racket before he gets out of those ropes."

"An' then you'll gimme him?"

Mart smiled bitterly.

"I think not, Chimp," he said slowly. "You see, he killed my pal and I promised him over the telephone that we'd make it man to man. He told me too that he'd killed Paddy and Fat—know anything about that?"

With the words the others made a concerted rush for the stairs of the upper room, but Mart called them back.

"Just Skillman, please," he said, "I don't want any rummaging done up there until I see what papers Fat may have been keeping."

He was watching the faces of Red and Eltner as he spoke, and noted that both flinched and looked covertly at one another.

Skillman was back in a matter of seconds, whitefaced and nauseated. He nodded his head affirmatively.

"Both of them," he said. "He cut Fat's head nearly off and Paddy's face looks like a mule had kicked him."

A ghastly chuckling came from the bloody bundle which was the Chi Kid.

Mart leaped and caught Chimp from behind in a choking throat lock as the gangster threw himself forward intent on finishing the killer with his hands.

"Wait!" he commanded. "He'd rather be knocked off quick than to tell what he's going to tell before he goes. Quiet, I tell you!" His great muscles, a fair match for those of Chimp, were cutting off the latter's breath. Finally he felt Chimp's arms go lax at his sides and released the hold.

"Aw, cripes, Mart!" he wheezed. "I can't stand his gigglin' over killin' Dogs 'n Paddy. Hell wit' dose Chi mobs. Lemme pull him t' pieces!"

For answer Mart drew two tables together and with one lurching swing of his shoulders, lifted the Chi Kid from the corner and laid him on his side, while the others clustered around the improvised couch.

"Now Chi Kid," Mart said calmly, "here's a proposition for you. I told you over the telephone while I was stalling you an hour ago, that I'd make it man to man.

"You dirty louse, I mean just that!

"When you've told me what I want to know, I'll give you back your rod, give you time to get the kinks out—and then we'll shoot it out. If you get me, you walk out, a free man, but you won't get me, Kid—you're going to pay for Dogs and Paddy."

"Bunk!" the Chi Kid mumbled. "Kid somebody else, nitwit."

He had managed to force one puffed eyelid open and his beady, black eye was studying Mart's face venomously.

"No kidding about it," Mart replied. "Take it or leave it, Chi Kid, you can have that chance or I'll give you to Chimp."

• • •

Despite his iron nerves, the prisoner could not control the shudder which shook his frame.

"What do you want to know?" he mumbled.

"You came here to get me and to knock off my lieutenants, didn't you?"

"Yes—you know that anyhow."

"Why?"

"The Big Noise in Chi's cuttin' in here."

"What is the plan?"

Chi Kid remained silent. Mart did not press the question, waiting coldly until the other said:

"Listen. I ain't no stoolie, but flopped this game anyhow—so if you're on the square about givin' me a break with my rod, just you and me, I'll tell you the set-up."

"Everything?" Mart demanded.

"The works."

"All right. Now who was in on this with you and Fat?"

"Red Conley and Eltner, an' Izzy the Yid over in Brooklyn."

Mart raised his eyes accusingly at the two gang leaders. Eltner was brazenly defiant. "He's a damn liar," he said.

Red, however, was white with desperation. His right hand was stealing under his lapel toward the gun under his armpit. Mart's draw was like a flash of light. Before anyone realized it, the traitor's forehead was threatened by the unwavering muzzle of the racketeer's gun.

"Take him, Chimp!" Mart snapped.

The ex-wrestler needed no second bidding. Before Red could cry out for mercy, Chimp's hands had flashed upward. The left clutched Red's head high in the back. The right caught at his chin—then pulled suddenly in opposite directions.

There followed a grisly, muffled snap—a single groan—and Red, his neck broken at the axis, slumped to the floor.

The others stepped back from the body and all eyes turned to Eltner. Chimp, his hands still raised in the gesture of attack, nodded toward the other and said, "Him, too?"

Mart shook his head.

"Hymie's a rat," he said, "but we've got to have somebody to throw to the bulls so the reformers'll be quiet. We'll give him to the homicide squad and they'll figure out a nice little yarn that will send him to the hot-spot in Sing Sing for these three killings."

Already his gun had covered Eltner, and at a nod of command Chimp stepped forward to deprive the trembling victim of his weapons—a heavy automatic and a spring-knife. Then Mart turned again to the Chi Kid.

"There it is," he said. "An out for you if you win. All of the killings accounted for and a nice, easy case for the dicks. Now speak up. What was the plan?"

"I was to get you and that ape-guy, Doggie and the chauffeur. Then the Big Noise and two others was coming in to take over. It was all framed to get the gangs to fighting while the Big Noise got his claws on the alky and dope rackets. After that—well, you know the game."

"Anybody come with you?"

"Only my twist—Vi Taylor. She hasn't done anything yet. Leave her alone, will you?"

"Send her back to Chicago if I get you—make your own arrangements if you win," Mart snapped.

He nodded to Skillman and for a few moments they talked in a corner. Then Mart turned to the others and said:

"It's time to scatter now. I'll attend to what is to be done here. Everybody forgets what has happened during the night. Skillman will wait at the end of a telephone line to hear from me and when I give him the word he'll slip the dope to the dicks.

"Beat it now, boys."

"But Mart"—it was Kelly Martin speaking—"don't you want us to stick around if—if—" He motioned toward the Chi Kid.

Mart shrugged contemptuously.

"Hell no!" he said. "See you all tonight. Go out one at a time now, and forget what you've seen and heard."

They left as he had directed, but each stopped and clasped Mart's hand in friendly good wishes, before going.

While this was going on, Chimp saw to it that Eltner's wrists and ankles were tied and looked again to the Chi Kid's bonds to be certain they were secure.

When the last man was gone, Mart said:

"We'll go up and search Fat's room now, Chimp; probably there'll be some letters or telegrams to tell us more of the story."

With a last look at the prisoners, Chimp turned and followed Mart to the death room above.

The Chi Kid, listening for the sound of their feet upstairs, set his teeth in his lower lip to suppress a groan and forced one swollen hand backward and upward toward the other coatsleeve.

It was a gruesome task Mart and Chimp found awaiting them in the death chamber, but it was one they were forced to perform for the common good. Mart's leadership demanded that he go through to the end, so he turned resolutely from the ghastly bodies of Fat and Paddy, to search drawers and other hiding places for needed evidence of treachery.

The task required nearly an hour of reading, assorting and the final search for some concealed hiding place in the walls. Until now nothing had been found which had a bearing on the Chicago mob and its plots.

Mart, tapping the walls for hollow places came at last to the bed on which Fat's body lay. He pushed it out and instantly his eyes lighted. There, hidden behind the frame of the bed was an ordinary, built-in cupboard, secured by an ordinary tongue lock.

Fat's key-ring provided the proper key and Mart exclaimed in satisfaction as the door swung open and disclosed a steel cash box, a document folder and some bankbooks. He opened the steel box and there came to light several thousand dollars in large bills and a number of promissory notes.

What he sought was contained in the document folder. There were two compromising letters from the Big Noise in Chicago, several carefully worded telegrams, and the note of introduction Chi Kid had given Fat on the occasion of his first call.

Another paper bore a list of the gang leaders. Several were crossed out. Others had question marks after them, indicating to Mart that they had refused so far to join in the plot.

After the names of Red, Hymie, Izzy the Yid, and four other minor leaders, were crosses. Satisfied that here was the proof he sought, Mart put the folder in his pocket and returned the other articles to the cupboard. Then he snapped the lock shut and nodded to Chimp.

After one final look about the room, they went downstairs, passed through the rear of the bar and into the back room where they had left the prisoners.

Chimp walked in advance. As he entered the door, he leaped forward excitedly.

"Cripes, Chief—he's gone!" he barked.

Mart leaped past him toward the table where they had left the trussed-up Chi Kid.

The table was empty and the ropes with which he had been bound lay on the floor. Mart picked up one of them and examined it carefully. It had been cut, cleanly, with some keen instrument. Mart swore and flashed his hand to his gun, his eyes darting about the room in search of his resourceful enemy.

Nowhere was there trace of the Chi Kid.

Hymie Eltner still lay in the corner where Chimp had dumped him unceremoniously, after binding his hands and feet. Mart strode over, glowering blackly, and examined the bonds. They had not been tampered with.

Chimp was dashing about the place, seeking in closets, under the bar—anywhere—everywhere—for some trace of the vanished gunman.

Finally, satisfied that Chi Kid had gone from the building, Mart strode over to Eltner.

"Tell me," he rasped, "who turned him loose?"

"Nobody," Hymie replied. "He had a safety-razor blade stitched in his coatsleeve. You hadn't been gone five minutes before he's cut himself loose. And the lousy rat lammed without giving me a chance. He left a message for you, Mart—"

"What?"

"He said to tell you that he'd stick around—that he wanted to show you his rod, like he'd promised. Cripes, I hope you get him, Mart—even if you are giving me the works. No chance for me, Big Fellow?"

Mart glared at him for a full minute, then turned away dispiritedly.

"Cut him loose," he said to Chimp, "he's just a rat and there'd be another rat in his place. What do we care for all the Hymies and Reds and Izzys when there's a Chi Kid loose in the town?"

"Youse 'r th' doctor," Chimp said, "but kin I take a good sock at him before he goes."

Mart shrugged, nor did he give more than a casual glance a moment later when there was a thudding blow and Hymie, his face a gory mask, crashed into a corner.

"C'mon, Mart," Chimp said a moment later. "Let's get outta dis joint; it gives me de willies. Jees! An' t'ink of de times I been down here an' got cockeyed with the guns and frills!"

There was no reply. Mart, his head sunk in thought, walked out through the door and into the morning sunlight.

The Chi Kid was free—and Dogs Miller and Paddy were unavenged.

When they reached the street and found a cruising taxi, Mart directed the driver to circle about for several blocks. Search failed to reveal any trace of the car Chi Kid said he had abandoned and Mart was forced to the conclusion that it was his own motor which had provided the second getaway.

Wearily, disheartened by the ill luck which had pursued them, Mart and Chimp returned to the apartment. There was but one interruption of the silence when Chimp said:

"Dat's w'at youse get for playin' square wit' a sneak, Mart. You shoulda let me have 'im 'n den youse wouldn't be goin' aroun' wit' yer lower lip hangin' down like a wet towel."

"Oh, I'll get him!" Mart snapped. "I'd given him my word, Chimp—and that's something I've never broken yet."

"Yaaaah!" Chimp growled. "Dey calls youse De Square Guy—'n for dat youse'll mebbe get your noodle shot off. Bla-a-ah."

They found Speck drowsing in a sleepy hollow chair, but Mart left it to Chimp to tell him the incidents of the night. Without a word he walked to the rear and entered his bedroom.

Tired as he was, almost exhausted, he spent an hour spreading the call among gang leaders, hi-jackers, harbor mugs, anyone who might find a trace of a little crook with a broken nose and a bruised face.

"A grand to know where he is—I'll get him myself," was his set formula.

At last, with the hands of the clock pointing to 2 p.m. he literally fell into bed. His last thought was:

"The showdown with Chi Kid is coming. I'm ready for it."

Midnight! Mart's bedroom, where for ten hours he had slept without movement was black as the Pit. Not a ray of light filtered in about the curtains and the only sound was the sleeper's deep breathing.

But one of the jungle animals would have been watching the dark shape crouching in a corner back of a huge wing-chair. More, its night-seeing eyes would have witnessed the method of entrance.

For the dark form, ten minutes before, had swung down on a rope from the cornice, pausing at the bathroom window. There had been just the tiniest of scratching sounds to accompany the removal of an oval of glass, but there was no click, no rustle as the intruder pushed back the catch and raised the sash a sufficient distance to permit him to slip through.

In the next room Speck sat on guard, while Chimp, now thoroughly rested, had gone to a white-tile eating place on Broadway for a substitute for the three meals he had missed. Speck was playing his interminable games of solitaire. The only sound in the apartment was Mart's deep, regular breathing and the slap-slap of Speck's cards.

Now the intruder was moving. Crawling, snakelike, he neared the door, rose on hands and knees and grasped the key firmly. For what seemed an age he retained his hold, turning the wards by microscopic degrees until he felt the actuating spring take hold. Then, delicately, he reversed the pressure, holding back the tongue of the lock to prevent it snapping into place.

Finally the task was ended. The metal bar which meant safety to the intruder rested in the mortised stop. The fingers clung delicately to the key, releasing their pressure slowly to guard against even the slightest click.

Then the Chi Kid reversed his position and started creeping, ever so slowly, toward the sleeping racketeer, still so completely immersed in slumber.

He advanced his fingers an inch at a time, feeling lightly over the soft surface of the Chinese rug for any slight inequality which would indicate a hidden alarm contact. With each tiny inch of progress he was careful to test the floor ahead of him for creaking boards by putting part of his weight on his outspread hands.

Once Mart stirred as several fire engines, their sirens shrieking eerily, rushed past on West End avenue. Recoiling like a spring, the Chi Kid squatted on the balls of his feet, right hand on the butt of his gat. The shrieking died away and Mart's breathing became regular again.

Now the intruder was not more than three feet from the foot of the bed. He arose to his full height and took a cautious step forward. As he moved, his hand came forth and brought with it the rod he had retrieved when he escaped from Fat's.

Another step, he calculated, would bring him to the foot of the bed. Thence he would work to right or left and when he stood beside the sleeper there would be needed only the flash of his pencil battery lamp, one quick shot—and then the getaway while Speck was battering his way through the locked door.

Cautiously he swept the toes of his right foot back and forth across the carpet. It was soft and yielding. Apparently all was well. Slowly, firmly, he set the foot down and balanced himself with outflung hands, like a tight-rope walker, as he shifted his weight from his left foot to the right.

Too late he realized that something had shifted underfoot. Instantly he caught himself and tried to swing backward.

Too late.

Even as he executed the movement, a gong whirred above his head and two scorching, stunning rays of light leaped out of the wall above the bed.

Blinded by the intense light, off balance and with his gun hand pointed toward the side wall, the Chi Kid stood for a second like one stunned.

But one chance remained for him—he must force his eyes open and plant a pot shot into the place where Mart had laid but a moment before.

But even that was denied him, for, as the motor thought went to the muscles of his arm, a heavy automatic materialized in the light rays and covered him.

"Drop it!" Mart's voice was low and calm, but Chi Kid sensed the grim purpose behind it. With a grimace of disgust he opened his fingers and let the weapon drop to the floor.

Blows on the door behind him showed that Speck was in action. Then there was a pause and a splintering roar as the gunman sent a slug crashing through the lock. In another split second Chi Kid was covered from the rear and Speck's arm shot around his neck in a strangle hold.

Mart arose, stretched and smiled at the picture before him.

"I thought you'd come," he said quietly, "but I had the cards stacked on you. How do you like my system, Kid? Pretty hard to beat?"

Mart stooped and turned back, a corner of the rug.

"They'll carry you out of here," he said, "so I might as well show you. See these one-inch strips of wood between the flooring strips? Any one of them will throw a switch. That in turn drops down a projector box containing four 1000-watt lights. Behind these are reflectors and the light is shot out in crossed rays through lenses. The same operation starts the gong in the ceiling—and I always sleep with my gun in a holster strapped to the edge of the bed."

The Chi Kid tried to stare into the light rays, but was compelled to close his already weakened eyes.

"It's no use," Mart said as he noted the action. "Even I cannot stand their glare. They give me time to wake up and get the drop—like I got it on you. Now let me see"—he walked over and picked up the Chi Kid's gun—"this, I suppose, is the rod you've been wanting to show me so badly.

"It's been your worst friend, Chi Kid—but I'll send it back to Chicago with you. I'm going to ship you direct to the Big Noise himself, way-billed as a musical instrument."

"Hell with that," the gunman snarled. "Shoot your gun, stupid; I'm game."

"Sit down over there," Mart replied, indicating the wing chair. "You'll get all the shooting you want before the night is over. "Where's Chimp?" he continued, turning to Speck.

"Out for a bite to eat; be right back," the other replied without letting his eyes leave the form of Chi Kid. Almost with the words, however, a key turned in the lock and the door slammed. A second later, Chimp dashed into the room, blinking as the light rays stabbed at his eyes. Then he saw Mart in his pajamas, and lastly the Chi Kid guarded by Speck.

"Cripes, Mart!" he jubilated. "Youse gottim, hey? Now lissen, Big Fellow, don't play aroun' no more. Give it to him quick—like he give it to Dogs and Paddy."

Mart raised his hand for quiet. Actually he was responding to Chimp's suggestion, but his eyes bored into the Chi Kid's as he said:

"Three times is out. That's where you're going tonight. But I've made you a promise, Chi Kid—and I'm going to keep it. I told you that no one but I had a right to kill you; that I'd give you a break with a rod in your hand. I still agree to that even though you've lost the right to hold me to my promise."

"Jees, Mart—no!" Chimp and Speck shouted the words together.

"Yes!" Mart said and there was finality in his tone. "They say that Mart Farrell never broke his word after it once had been given. That won't be changed. I'm going to send this rat to stew in hell—but he's to have an equal chance at me."

"Yer nuts!" Chimp exploded disgustedly. "Burn him down an' call it a day."

Mart's reply was to turn back the rug from the polished floor and push two chairs into nearby corners. On one he laid the Chi Kid's rod. His own weapon he put down on the other. Then he said:

"Here's the rules. Speck keeps you covered. We both stand face to the wall. Chimp counts slowly *as long as he wants to*. When the time comes, whether at two or two hundred, he'll say 'Fire.' Then we each turn, grab a rod and turn loose. I hope you like it in hell."

Mart watched as the Chi Kid slipped from his chair and swaggered to the wall. He hated the ratty little killer as he never had hated anyone before, yet unwillingly he felt a surge of admiration for the businesslike manner in which Chi Kid accepted the duel.

Mart cast one last glance over the scene as his antagonist stood, facing in, against the wall; smiled grimly at Speck who stood out of the line of fire covering the Kid; then nodded to Chimp to begin the count. Then he too took his place.

"One!" Chimp's voice quavered. "Two!" He was calmer now. "Three!" A pause. "Four"—"Five." He was spacing the count properly now and Mart began swinging his body as he caught the cadence. "Six!" Still true to the time-beat!

"Seven!" The cadence had been lost and Mart caught the break between the syllables.

It was coming. Chimp, an inveterate crapshooter, believed in the luck of that numeral. The thoughts flashed like lightning but his muscles and nerves were coordinated—ready, balanced for the turn and slashing grasp for the gun butt—as Chimp barked "Fire!"

The following day a scarehead appeared in the press.

GANG LEADER KILLED

The most powerful leader in the city, Mart Farrell, was found, early this morning, lying dead. Near him was the body of a dangerous killer who recently arrived from Chicago and whose movements have been watched ever since. The police broke into Farrell's apartment when they heard shots. It was empty, except for the two bodies. The gunmen had evidently shot each other almost simultaneously. The eyes of both men had been shot out.

A few hours later Farrell's gang was rounded up.

Writer's Digest, September 1930

The NEW Gangster Story

By Joseph Lichtblau

When the Climax Comes and the Lights are Flashed on, the Racketeer Must Find His Wrists Encircled in Handcuffs, While the Law Pants and is Proud of its Catch

BEFORE MR. VOLSTEAD PUT OVER HIS CELEBRATED LAW, crook stories and yarns dealing with a criminal hero never ended happily for the members of the underworld. It was a rule among writers to have the law come out on top at all times in such stories.

There was a mighty good reason for this. Editors demanded such stories because the highly-organized mobsters, racketeers and crooks of today didn't exist before Prohibition; the public was accustomed to seeing the forces of law and order win over criminals in all stories where crime and the law were in conflict. And editors, being sound businessmen as well as judges of a good story, gave the public what it wanted.

But the coming of Prohibition changed that very quickly. Since booze was outlawed, and bootlegging made millionaires overnight of those who defied the law, highly-organized rackets of every conceivable type began to flourish as well.

Then a new type of crook story began to appear. The Big Time magazines featured them and the pulps soon followed suit. No longer did the crook or gangman inevitably "get his" in the climax! No longer did the forces of law and order "win out" in the denouement over the crooks, the criminals and thugs! The new type of crook story featured a mobster or a gang all through the tale, not only at odds with the public and with the law, but with other gangs or mobsters; and the crook hero or heroes of these tales won signal triumphs without being in any way punished for their lawlessness.

Mr. Harold Hersey published *Gangster Stories* and *Racketeer Stories* for a time with signal success. The authorities claimed that the stories in Mr. Hersey's two lurid periodicals gave added impetus to crime and fostered criminals, and in New York City, particularly, his magazines were forbidden on the stands until he agreed to change them radically.

Hence Mr. Hersey's new crook story periodicals will not feature gangs and crime triumphant in the future. The mobmen and criminals will not be permitted to come "out on top" any more!

And take *Black Mask* for example also: Erle Stanley Gardner, a very skillful and well-known writer of this type of fiction, had been exploiting a crook hero in a series in this magazine for a long time—"Ed Jenkins, the Phantom Crook." Now Mr. Jenkins, if you will notice, is aiding the law in Mr. Gardner's stories, and is aligned with it against mobmen and gangsters!

Some time ago, when it was *au fait* for the criminal to triumph over the law, I wrote a yarn of this type, in which my crook hero sensationally came out on top in the finish. It was submitted to *Prize Detective Magazine* and came back with a polite note from the editor. Mr. Mann stated: "In our stories, the crook *can never win*, therefore we can't use your story in its present form." So I made a simple revision of the climax, with a bit of a twist to it in which a member of the crook hero's mob turned out unexpectedly to be a "dick," and the crook hero "got his" plenty, instead of triumphing! And Mr. Mann took that story.

Fashions in fiction change with the times. When Prohibition came into being, it was orthodox and accepted technique to have crime punished in the ending of any story dealing with criminal leading protagonists. Then the wave of crime all over the country following the bootlegging racket exploitation by gunmen gave writers nifty new ideas for crook yarns, and a flood of sensational gangster stories swept these United States.

The kids who used to read dime novels seized on the new type of magazine with whoops of joy. The stories far exceeded in danger, suspense, thrills and excitement the most gory dime novel yarns they had ever read! But they grew up, these youngsters; they became adolescents and young men, and many of them got dangerous ideas from the racketeer and gangster stories. Many a prison warden can tell you, grimly, that plenty of his "cons" are in "stir" now because they got the idea of becoming gangmen and racketeers solely from these stories, which pictured crime and organized rackets and mobs so alluringly.

Naturally, clergymen, the Police, civic bodies, and so on, all protested against the type of crook and gangster story in which crime was pictured so attractively, with the law getting a "sock in the eye" in the finish instead of the criminals. So editors were forced to change fashions in fiction of this type again.

Hence, if you are ambitious to write the gangster story, make sure that your crook hero, your gang chief, your mobs, your racketeers, never beat the law in the climax of your stories. This type of yarn commands one of the juiciest markets today, now that the air magazines and the Western story magazines are not as "hot" as they were in their demands for material.

Practically every detective magazine can use a fast-moving gangster story in which the criminal leading protagonist or protagonists are engaged in a duel of wits with a detective or detectives, and in which the detective or detectives finally triumph. If your gangster or gang has a feud with another mobster or mob, and the law is after both and wins out in the end, that's an even better bet for the detective magazines.

You don't have to follow the usual formula for a detective story at any time. No murder need be the mystery in the beginning of the tale which a detective sets out to solve in the orthodox way. The gangster story depends on its thrills, its suspense and its fast-moving action for its punch, and there need be no mystery in it whatever. Clever and unusual stuff pulled by both the criminals and the detectives is what counts tremendously in these yarns. If you have the Erle Stanley Gardner flair for making masterly criminal minds do their stuff until some cleverer gent representing the law outwits them in the end, you can write your own ticket with editors right now!

Stereotyped yarns will not sell. Your racketeers and gangsters must be as clever as Satan. They must have the most devilish and ingenious and devious minds you can create out of an imagination running riot, in addition to their deadly skill with lethal weapons. For example, in my gangster story one gang chief had a feud with another one. He visited the enemy in his lair. He gave him fifty "grand" notes in a wager that he'd walk out of his gambling hell with the stolen "ice" he'd been gypped out of by his rival. The latter had him covered by the invisible machine guns of four mobmen in a spy gallery, in addition to menacing him with his own automatic pistol. The first gang chief seemed to have no chance whatever to walk out alive from that gambling hell. Suddenly, as his enemy sneeringly counted the fifty "grand" notes, he slumped unconscious to the floor, also the four mobmen in the spy gallery! The notes had been sprinkled with a deadly, invisible poison which engendered a lethal gas, and the crook who had invented that formula had also invented a tiny gas mask so small it didn't even bulge out a coat pocket. The first gang chief whipped out the mask from his pocket and as the five mobsters passed out, he donned it, got the "ice" for which he had come, and coolly sauntered from the gambling hell!

If you think this is fairly clever, however, you should read the gifted Mr. Gardner's stories. He invents things in his yarns which would make your hair acquire a permanent wave! The point is, though, you can't simply depend on stickups, hijacking, machine-gun play, and stereotyped stuff like that in your gangster stories. These may enter incidentally into your plots, of course, but they should be merely trifles, a part of your atmosphere. Your mobster and racketeer "heroes" must continually put over totally unexpected things of the cleverest kind—fast ones that will make the reader fairly gasp with their satanic ingenuity.

Did you ever read one of Mr. Gardner's yarns in *Black Mask* where the villain had a pocket flask with a trick compartment for poisoned booze and another trick one for the right stuff? If a guy drank from the wrong side of that flask—good night! And how about that fountain pen which is really a deadly pistol that shoots tear gas bullets? I used that one in my story very effectively in the climax, and I got the idea from a newspaper account of a Chinaman in real life who sold those cute toys by the gross to gangsters.

The cleverer and more Machiavellian your gangsters are the more chance you'll have to put these stories over. It is not enough to make your mobmen mere roughnecks who depend on their gats and machine guns alone; you must give them brains of the most cunning sort, too—minds which will continually invent the trickiest stuff with which to outwit the law or their rivals. Then if your detective hero is even cleverer than the criminals he's after, and if he wins out in the climax in a most unexpected, stupefying way, your yarn will be according to present-day demands, provided, of course, that the plot and the action are equally clever and move at top speed.

Suspense! That's what you need more than anything else in this type of story, too. Mr. Gardner's yarns are masterly chiefly because of this element, in addition to their cleverness. *Every incident, every situation, every crisis and complication must pack a wallop, must hold the reader breathless with uncertainty as to what the next development will bring. Thrill the reader all the time! Keep him gasping! Don't let his interest flag for a moment! Not only physical action alone will do the trick for you, remember. It must be brains against brains—deadly ruthless cunning against equally deadly ruthless cunning—the gangster, or gangsters pitting their wits and rattlesnake minds against a "dick" who is wise to every fast one the underworld "can pull." Combine powerful suspensive mental action with equally gripping physical action, and do it without a moment's let-down, and you'll have a real gangster story.*

Read these stories for inspiration. And above all, if you want to get new stunts for your gangster stories, read the papers! Truth is always stranger than fiction, and the news stories every day prove this overwhelmingly. A coal truck is sent out by a bank with twenty-one thousand dollars hidden under a pile of coal to throw gangmen off the scent! A mysterious murderer "bumps off" two different men who had been petting in lovers' lanes with their sweeties; sends notes to the police saying he's going to bump off sixteen more male petters, and defying the police to prevent him from doing so!

The newspapers are a gold mine for the writer of gangster stories. They will provide you with stunts of the most ingenious and diabolically clever variety to amaze your readers. Not only are the detective magazines eager for clever gangster yarns, but also out-and-out action magazines like *Short Stories*, *Adventure*, and so on, welcome them. And, if you can write artistically enough, the pulps are not your only market. The slick-paper lads will take your gangster yarns too. *The Saturday Evening Post, Collier's,* and *American Magazine* can be favorably impressed if you've got the goods they like.

If you're wondering what to write next, if that's the burning question in your mind, make a stab at the gangster story. It's one of the most promising and lucrative markets to try for right now. It bids fair to be so for several years to come. Following are some of the magazines that use the new gangster story:

Black Mask, 587 Madison Ave., New York City. Editor, Joseph T. Shaw. Uses shorts of 4000 to 8000 words, and novelettes 10,000 to 15,000 words. One of the very finest markets for the gangster story there is, and Mr. Shaw will give you a square deal and a very prompt decision always. He pays around 1¢ a word, on acceptance. But don't try to wish any mediocre stuff on this editor—you've got to be good! Simple, clipped style preferred to fine writing, so don't use any fancy language. Your detectives and gangsters, above all, must sound *authentic*; their dialogue *must ring the gong.* Study the magazine—*hard*—before you aim at it!

Blue Book, 230 Park Ave., New York City. Editor, Edwin Balmer. Uses short stories of all lengths, novelettes and novels. Many big names in this one, so if you've got real confidence in yourself, go to it, but your chances of landing here are not so "hot" unless you're better than the big shots in the periodical. Anyway, if you land, rates are 2¢ up, acceptance. But decisions are darned slow if you're unknown, and very rarely will you get any friendly comments with the rejection slip!

Clues, 80 Lafayette St., New York City. Editor, Carl Happel. Shorts, 3000 to 6000; novelettes, 20,000 to 30,000; serials, 40,000 to 60,000. Gangster stories must move fast as lightning for this one, be packed full of mob atmosphere and characterization, contain oodles of suspense and thrills, and if your dick in each yarn is the sort of smart guy who solves a mysterious mob stunt cleverly, all the better. If you make a hit with the editor of this magazine, you're in soft. Rates, 2¢ up, acceptance.

Complete Detective Novel Magazine, 381 4th Ave., New York City. H.A. Keller, Editor. Try this fellow with shorts of around 5000 words, or true tales of detective work, 1000 to 2500. 1¢ per word on acceptance. A careful study of the magazine recommended beforehand.

Detective Fiction Weekly, 280 Broadway, New York City.

Howard V. Bloomfield, Editor. The gifted Mr. Gardner appears in this magazine regularly, so unless you can put over your stuff with a bang, as he does, better expect thumbs down! However, you've got plenty of chances of landing here if your plots are "naturals," so don't be afraid to try. 1½¢ up, acceptance. Shorts, novelettes, serials, standard lengths.

Detective Story Magazine, 79 7th Ave., New York City. F.E. Blackwell, Editor. Same as above, Shorts up to 5000, novelettes up to 25,000, serials up to 80,000—12,000-word installments. 2¢ up, acceptance. Decisions fairly fast—around three weeks to a month.

And here are Mr. Hersey's magazines, grouped together for your benefit. Address 'em all to Mr. Hersey, Good Story Publishing Co., 25 W. 43rd St., New York City. He's rather peculiar when he sends you back a yarn—he doesn't use rejection slips of any kind! But don't imagine your story hasn't been read thoroughly nevertheless, even if you do get it back in your return envelope with nothing but the script. Mr. and Mrs. Hersey both read every yarn carefully, and you'll get fast decisions. A wonderful market for the clever unknown writer—Mr. Hersey doesn't give a darn about big names—it's the *story* that counts with him, first, last and always. The wise scribe will study the following periodicals first, then go after 'em like a tiger! Here they are:

Gangland Stories. Gang and racketeer fiction, indefinite lengths.
Gangster Stories. Crime short stories, detective novelettes and serials, indefinite lengths.
Mobs. Gangland and racketeer fiction, indefinite lengths.
Racketeer Stories. Gangland and racket fiction, all lengths.

All paying 1¢ a word on acceptance. Mr. Hersey used to pay on publication until recently, and I can't recommend this group for your offerings highly enough!

Real Detective Tales, 1050 N. LaSalle St., Chicago, Ill. Edwin Baird, Editor. Mr. Baird doesn't care for the common or garden variety of gangster stuff; he wants stories with the very cleverest plots, in which the gangsters and racketeers have relations with the higher-ups, public officials; stories that move cleverly in unexpected twists, chock-full of suspense and with dramatic fireworks in the climax. At present, he is overstocked, and he is continually slamming back stereotyped gangster yarns, so he's a doubtful prospect at best. However, if you think you have a gangster story that is decidedly novel, unusual and extraordinary, make a stab at Mr. Baird anyway—and if you're lucky, you'll get from 1¢ to 2¢ per word, on acceptance!

Detective-Dragnet, 67 W. 44th St., New York City. A.A. Wyn, Editor. Shorts, indefinite length; novelettes up to 20,000. Very slow on decisions, and pays 1¢ to 2¢ on publication. The slow decisions may be due to the fact that Mr. Wyn has just replaced a former editor. His magazine is on the stands; study it!

A final word: The slick paper magazines and book publishers are flirting coyly with the gangster story. If you have a book-length gangster novel of genuine merit and artistry, try 'em with it. If, though, it's only a short or a novelette, the pulps are your best bets always. You all know the requirements of magazines like *The Saturday Evening Post*, *Collier's*, *Liberty*, *American*. If you believe you write distinctively enough for these fellows, submit your short gangster yarns and novelettes to 'em.

Two out-and-out action magazines that are also worth trying with your gangster stories are *Short Stories*, Garden City, L.I., and *Adventure*, 233 Spring St., New York City. *Adventure*, A.A. Proctor, editor, demands a very high literary standard and pays 2¢ a word on acceptance; and *Short Stories*, Roy de S. Horn, editor, is also keen for good writing and pays the same rate on acceptance.

In addition, H.S. Goldsmith, formerly with *Detective-Dragnet*, and Harry Steeger, ex-editor of the Dell Publishing Co., have formed a corporation entitled Popular Publications, Inc., 220 E. 42nd St., New York City, and one of their projected magazines, *Gang World*, will be a gangster periodical.

The Singing Kid
By DAN YOUNG

*A pair of hot bennies, a packet of ice, and a three way
double-cross from Frisco to L.A. that ended
just where it started!*

THE SINGING KID HAD A HUNCH!

For once there was no song on his lips as he looked ahead from the ferry to the Oakland shore line, showing faintly through the enveloping fog. His eyes narrowed in thoughtful anxiety, and his hand tightly gripped the package in his overcoat. The Kid was sure enough worried!

He felt a prickly feeling between his shoulder-blades, and almost unconsciously, his right shoulder tensed itself against the anticipated touch which would again place him within the arms of the law.

With an assured air of nonchalance, he strolled casually to the rail, his eyes roving from side to side in as wide an arc as was possible, without moving his head and betraying his solicitude to an onlooker. Leaning carelessly against the rail, he closely scanned the faces of his fellow passengers, resting his glance for but a brief second on each face, yet missing no detail of facial or bodily appearance.

His look dwelt no longer on the face of Detective Sergeant Morey than upon any other, yet his heart missed a beat as he recognized his nemesis, while doubt of mind was changed to certainty.

What a break for Morey! The green covered package tightly held in clenched hand would mean added prestige and possibly promotion to the detective, but would also mean good-by for the Kid. A four time loser in Folsom can expect only a back gate parole, and the Kid was not yet forty.

His face showed no change of expression, but his brain was racing madly. He must find some way out.

Of course he could toss the package overboard and trust to lack of evidence, but his rep was bad, and anyway, the Kid hated to definitely cut loose from his chance to get something out of the previous night's ten grand prowl.

As the boat neared the dock he slowly edged himself into the crowd of passengers crowding together for disembarkment, but from the tail of his eye he noted that Morey was trying to keep closely behind him. He hummed absently to himself.

"There's danger in your eye, Morey,
Here's danger in your eye for the—"

A sudden lurch of the boat caused by the stopping of the screw threw the Kid against a man standing in front of him, and he noticed that this man was holding a travelling bag in hand, a bag which bore on the end towards the Kid the inscription:

M.H. PRITCHARD
Emeryville, Calif.

He next noted that the object of his scrutiny was wearing a topcoat of vivid plaid, one whose bulging side pockets bore witness of frequent and rough usage.

But the Kid failed to notice that next to this man stood another, wearing almost a duplicate of this coat, which had evidently come from the same maker.

There was a jostling of the crowd as the gangplank was lowered, and in the same moment the Singing Kid felt the anticipated touch on his shoulder. His hand, still cunning despite his fear, made a quick movement, and the green covered package dropped within the pocket of an unsuspecting recipient.

"All right, Kid," said Morey softly, "let's go."

"Yeah?" replied the Kid sneeringly. "Where and why? What's the rap?"

"We'll talk that over when we reach the hall," responded Morey. "Don't make any funny moves or you may learn something sooner."

Knowing he was clear of anything incriminating, and that resistance was futile, Puggy O'Conner, the Singing Kid, walked arm in arm down the gangplank with his captor and within thirty minutes was being booked at the City Hall.

The Goddess of Chance, whom some call Old Lady Luck, decreed that the wearers of the twin coats should enter the same train together, and sit side by side. The stranger glanced casually at Pritchard, noted his coat and started to speak, but refrained, and, opening a paper, was soon buried in its contents.

Pritchard, however, was not so reticent.

"These are sure hot bennies," he smiled.

His companion looked up inquiringly, then seeing at what the remark aimed, laughed.

"In more ways than one. Mine nearly baked me today, and I'm sure going to ditch it tonight for the summer. I'm firing on the S.P. to Stockton, and I sure don't need it there."

"I'll have to do the same, I guess," said Pritchard. "It's getting pretty warm now for one."

The train slowed down for San Pablo stop in Emeryville, and Pritchard rose from his seat.

"Well so long," he said to his seat mate. "Drop in and see me sometime. We may have more than bennies in common," and he handed a card from his pocket. The stranger glanced at it, and handed him one in return, as the train pulled to a stop.

On the sidewalk, Pritchard set down his bag and removed his coat which he threw carelessly over one arm. As he stooped for his bag, however, the coat fell to the walk and he reached for it with a muttered curse. He missed the collar and lifted it by the bottom, but as he did so, he heard the soft tinkle of coins hitting the pavement. A glance showed him they were small so he left them laying and strode down the street to a building whose sign showed it to be a combination pool-room and cigar stand.

With a brief word of greeting to the inmates, he entered the back room, mounted a stairway, and disappeared from sight.

His late train companion looked at the card left him in casual curiosity, but whistled softly to himself as he read the inscription.

"Big Mike himself," he murmured. "Believe me, I'll sure look him up."

His coat becoming too warm, he arose, took it off and threw it carelessly across the back of his seat. Immersed in his paper, he almost missed leaving the train at his destination, but as he realized where he was, he leaped to his feet and was just in time to get out before the conductor closed the door.

His forgotten coat still remained on the back of his seat, since there were no passengers left to call his attention to his forgetfulness.

About that time there was another party sweating, and that was Puggy O'Connor, alias the Singing Kid. Seated in a straight backed uncomfortable chair, faced by a phalanx of detectives, Puggy was undergoing the "third." His hair was somewhat rumpled and he had lost his accustomed jauntiness of demeanor.

"You ain't got nothing on me," he snarled. "I been going straight since I was sprung. I'm through with the old game for I don't want no body-snatcher's parole for mine."

"You should have thought of that before you cracked that crib at the Lake," said Morey coldly. "You didn't feel that way when you were copping that bunch of ice there."

"I ain't been by the Lake in years," shouted Puggy, "and I never copped no ice there or anywhere else. You've got the wrong guy, but I suppose you Dicks will frame me, because you're so dumb you can't pick up the right one. You have to have a fall guy some place, so you elected me."

"Yes?" answered Morey smoothly. "Then where did you get the ice you were trying to put over the fence at Ikey's on Fourth Street in San Francisco this afternoon? I suppose you found them."

The Kid froze into silence for a moment, his worst fears confirmed. Then Morey had seen him there. Evidently he had been tailed.

"This is a frameup," he muttered, "and I want a mouthpiece. If I put anything over the fence, you've probably got it, and if I had it and didn't, it must be on me."

Further questioning being useless, Morey gestured to a uniformed patrolman.

"Take him away, and book him as a vag," he said.

When they had left, Morey turned to his fellows.

"He's a wise one and knows his back is to the wall, for another conviction means life for him under the habitual criminal act. I really haven't anything on him but if Ikey hadn't looked out of the window this afternoon and seen me, Puggy would have put it over.

"If we can't break him we'll have to let him go, but I was certain we'd find some stones on him. I watched him closely, and he had no chance to ditch anything. I'm darned if I know how he did it. That Lake job had every appearance of being his, and I still believe it was."

When the Kid was regretfully released after two days in the hold-over, his first thought was to get in touch with the man Pritchard of Emeryville. His incarceration had scared him for he feared the club of the four-time loser which hung over his head, so he resolved to secure what cash he could on the stones and leave for parts where he would not be so well known.

In Emeryville he had little trouble in locating his man, but was surprised to find that Pritchard was what might be called "the Big Shot" of the night life there.

Big Mike's interests were many and varied, so Puggy studied for a long time to find the best angle of approach. He could not go to him direct with his story. He would have to become acquainted with him first, so with small difficulty, Puggy secured a job singing in one of Big Mike's night clubs.

The Kid was an immediate success and as such was soon taken in as a welcome member of the night life. The inconspicuous dish on top of the piano was filled more often than not, and it was not seldom that bills nestled there amid the silver coins. Puggy was making a good living, but was not satisfied. He could not forget the diamonds.

He occasionally came into contact with Big Mike and a mutual liking sprang up between them, but Puggy was no fool, and he realized that Mike would not let go of what he once had his hands on.

It was nearly a month later the Kid had the opportunity of broaching the subject that was always on his mind, for one night Big Mike sauntered up to the piano and stood talking with the Kid before the crowds had started to arrive.

"Say, Mike," Puggy began, "will you do something for me?"

"Sure, kid," Big Mike laughed as he reached into his pocket. "How much?"

"Not that," repudiated the Kid. "It's something more. Say—what did you ever do with that load of ice you found in your overcoat pocket about a month ago?"

Mike looked at him in surprise. "What's the matter, Kid, been taking nose candy? You don't look like a snow bird. What ice are you talking about?"

"Oh, you know all right," replied the Kid suspiciously. "I mean that bunch that was wrapped up in a cloth that someone dropped in the pocket of your benny on the ferryboat. I need the coin, Mike, and I'll put it over the fence and split with you, or you can do it and split with me. It's fifty-fifty."

"You must be hopped up," said Big Mike coldly. "I never had no ice slipped to me."

The Kid jumped from the stool angrily and turned towards the door.

"All right then," he cried, "if you're that sort. I thought you was a square shooter, but you're just a dirty rat like the rest of them."

Big Mike uttered a strong oath and sprang forward, grasping the arm of the smaller man tightly above the elbow. He savagely whirled him around, and his fist drew back to punish the man who dared to doubt his squareness.

But he had not gained his supremacy in the underworld without learning to control himself, and his cupidity was aroused at mention of the ice. He hesitated a moment, then released the futilely struggling Kid.

"Wait a moment, Kid," he said slowly. "There's something more behind all this. Let's get to the bottom of it. Spill the works."

Puggy was too wise to incriminate himself even to Big Mike so he thought for a moment before answering.

"I had a pal who saw he was going to be gloomed on the ferryboat coming over from Frisco, so just before he was pinched he stuck a green covered package of sparklers in your overcoat pocket. He wants me to get them so he can beat the rap. That's all the story."

"That's right in part," said Mike thoughtfully. "I was across the bay about a month ago and wore my benny, but I'll swear I never found anything in the pockets. I haven't worn it since, either. Let's go to my rooms and take a look."

Once in his rooms, Mike opened a closet and took a coat from a hangar.

"That's the one," exclaimed the Kid excitedly. "Look in the pockets."

With eager hands Big Mike explored the pockets, turning them inside out as he did so, then handed the coat to Puggy who also searched vainly. They looked at each other in silence. The Kid could not help but believe that Mike was playing fair, was ignorant of any package, for he could not be such a good actor, nor would there be any necessity for his so doing. Who could have got the stones?"

Big Mike cursed suddenly and the Kid looked at him inquiringly.

"I remember dropping the damned thing on the walk, and I picked it up by the bottom. A few coins dropped out. Maybe the ice dropped out with them and I never noticed it. I was in a hurry."

"Then it's gone," said the Kid despondently. "Whoever picked it up has cashed in and beat it. Damn such luck!"

Big Mike knitted his brows in thought and then again searched the pockets. His hand brought forth a card, and he looked at it, his face lightened.

"Maybe you stuck it in the wrong coat, Kid," he offered. "This guy had on a coat just like mine, and was on the same boat. That's how we got acquainted. He gave me his card. Let's hunt him up."

They got into Mike's car and at the address on the card were fortunate enough to catch the fireman, Harrison, home between runs. Big Mike recalled himself to the fireman's memory and introduced Puggy.

"The Kid here is nuts about my benny," said Mike, "and I won't sell it to him. I remembered you had one like it and thought you might want to make a good deal. He's offered me seventy-five smackers for it, and they only cost fifty. How about it?"

Harrison looked at them smilingly.

"Don't know as I blame him at that," he said. "I like it myself, but I haven't got it here. I left it on the train the day I met you and never went back after it. I phoned the Lost and Found Department and they said they would hold it for ninety days, so I knew there was no hurry. Tell you what I'll do. I'm on the board for a call in an hour, but I'll be back day after tomorrow, so I'll get it then and leave it at your place. How about that?"

The Singing Kid saw immense possibilities in that statement so replied:

"That's O.K. with me. I'm sure nuts about that plaid and I want one like it. I'll leave the money with Mike and you can get it when you leave the coat."

Puggy and Big Mike parted at his place, both agreeing to be on hand when Harrison returned, but both knew the other would not keep the appointment. Mike was sure that the opening of the Lost department in the morning would find the Kid waiting at the door, so he resolved to pull a fast one himself.

Also Mike was cursing himself for the break he had made in letting the Kid know about Harrison. Otherwise he would have had it all to himself with no trouble. He decided to call on one of his henchmen, Docky Wilder, for aid, so he would not appear personally in the matter.

So it was that the following morning when the elated Kid left the railroad office, the prized coat over his arm, he softly patted the coat which contained a small green covered parcel. He laughed to himself as he remembered the assurance he had that he had ditched it with Pritchard.

Some coincidence! But a lucky break for him at that. Now he was set for a quick getaway. To hell with Pritchard! He didn't owe him anything!

Puggy stepped towards the curb and his elation vanished like air from a toy balloon punctured with a pin. He cursed silently as a soft voice met his ears.

"Morning, Kid," said Docky softly. "Goin' somewhere?"

"Not in particular," replied the Kid, sensing the menace beneath the soft tones.

"You don't know it, but you are," responded Docky. "I'd shake hands wit' you only I gotta keep my gat hid, I suppose."

Puggy looked down and noted that Wilder's hand was concealed within his coat pocket, and that a lump appeared against his side, a menace against any sudden action.

"You'd never dare use it here," said the Kid shortly.

"Maybe not," Docky murmured, "but how'd it be for me to holler to that bull comin' and ask him to frisk you?"

The Kid's heart dropped. Docky had him dead to rights, for if he were picked up with the ice in his possession it would be the finish for him. Going with Docky was the least of the two evils, and anyway, he might brazen it out with Pritchard.

"All right, you win now," he conceded. "Where do we go?"

"My boat's parked right here. Jump in and we'll take a ride."

The Kid felt safe, for "taking a ride," or being "put on the spot" was not common in Oakland. The risk was too great, but mentally he kissed the sparklers good-by that he had in his pocket. He climbed in the front seat of the indicated car, noting that the back seat held a moll who had been lately playing around with Docky. The driver turned to her as he started the car:

"Your gat's got a silencer. Use it if he starts anything."

That was that! No chance to grab the wheel and make a getaway. Puggy was out of luck. The car picked up speed and was soon out of the business district, and the Kid noted with some surprise that it was not headed for Emeryville, but for the open country beyond the Tunnel Road. He kept silent, but watched for some clue to his prospective destination. At once the answer came to him!

Docky was double-crossing Big Mike!

The car left the eastern portal of the tunnel and made its way between the hills until it reached a road which was evidently little travelled. In fact it was more of a country lane, not even a gravelled roadbed to show of occasional use. Docky drove down this road for about five miles, then stopped his car.

"All right Kid," he said cheerfully. "End of the line! All change! Don't forget your parcels!"

His gun emphasized his orders, so the Kid climbed down. His face was black with anger but he knew they had him cold, and a struggle was useless. Maybe his chance would come later! But Docky had another sudden idea!

"Slip off the boats, Puggy, bare dogs for you!"

The Kid cursingly tore off his shoes which Docky threw into the back of the car. With a farewell gesture of derision he regained the driver's seat, turned the car around and disappeared in the dusty distance. The Singing Kid was left alone, miles from anywhere, bare of foot—robbed of his spoils— facing a long weary walk back to the main travelled highway.

It was nearly dark before a truck driver took pity on him and gave him the coveted lift into town. Puggy was disgusted, was entirely through with the town which gave him such bad breaks. He would pack up his belongings and take the boat the following day to Los Angeles, where a man had a chance, if not too well known.

Meanwhile, as day grew towards night, Big Mike was becoming worried.

He had trusted Docky, but one could never tell—the double-cross was the usual thing in the underworld, despite that reputed "honor among thieves."

He felt that he had been a sap to let anyone handle the deal but himself. When night-time arrived he was certain he had been two-timed, and his wrath was great.

He drove to the small hotel where Docky had been living with his moll, Belle, and a few questions to the landlady, who knew him and was desirous of ingratiating herself with him, made him bite his lips in anger.

Belle had been unable to entirely keep her mouth closed, and had intimated that they would take the boat the following day to San Diego, and in the meanwhile would visit friends in San Francisco. Big Mike realized the futility of trying to find them in that city, and knew he could not make a scene at the boat, so resolved to also take passage on the same ship.

Big Mike got to his stateroom early the next day, and remained hidden as the boat backed out from the pier and turned her nose towards the Golden Gate. He kept his cabin door open an inch or so, his ears keenly alert for the possibility of his quarry passing his door, although with the three decks and numerous passageways, he knew the odds were against it.

But luck favored him, and at last he heard Docky's deep voice. Cautiously peering out he saw the pair following a cabin steward down the passageway to a stateroom. The door closed behind them, and he quickly and noiselessly stole past, noting their number to avoid any possibility of mistake.

Satisfied, he returned to his stateroom where a flask and a magazine engaged him until he heard the call for dinner. He again fixed his door open a crack and finally heard the voices of the pair as they passed his door.

"I'm hungry enough to eat a horse," said Docky. "I guess we've earned our chuck today, haven't we?"

Belle laughed in reply. "I'll say so, and the best of all is that we're in the clear tonight, anyway."

Waiting until sufficient time had elapsed for them to gain the dining salon and secure their seats at a table, Mike walked again towards their door. He was at a loss, for he had keys which would fit it, but brightened as he saw a steward approaching. He decided to take a chance.

"Just open this door for me, will you steward?" he asked smoothly. "My wife has our key up on deck."

The steward hesitated a moment, but being in a hurry took a master key and opened the door. Big Mike handed him a coin, and with a word of thanks the steward disappeared. Time was short, but Mike made a close search of all their belongings, being careful not to disarrange anything which might give them an inkling that a search had been made.

But he was unsuccessful, so decided the stones he sought were on their persons, probably in the somewhat large handbag that Belle was carrying. He carefully opened the door, saw the passageway was evidently clear, and returned to his room.

Yet in his caution and haste to avoid observation, he failed to note that the entrance of another stateroom stood ajar, and that a man stepped hurriedly back out of sight as he passed. Had he noted this and recognized his watcher, he would have felt much less optimistic regarding the stones.

He decided to keep under cover, so he had a steward bring him something to eat in his cabin, complaining of not feeling very well. He dared not show his face on deck or in the dining salon.

It was after midnight when Docky and Belle became tired of watching the sea and were ready to retire. They walked down to their stateroom, tired but happy, and the soft carpets muffled the sound of the trailing footsteps in their rear. Docky opened the door, reached in and turned on the light, while Belle followed him.

A startled scream broke from her lips, and a curse from Docky's as the door closed behind them and Big Mike stood carelessly against it, the gun in his unshaking hand menacing them both.

"Not a move or sound, rats," said Mike coldly. "Thought you'd put something over, didn't you?"

Belle sank down on the side of the berth, half swooning in terror, while Docky stood wordlessly, his shifty eyes widening in fear.

"Lie down on your faces on the floor, both of you," commanded Mike tonelessly.

He rolled them over on their backs, so they could see him as he copped the stones, enjoying their expressions as they saw their fortune leaving them. The eyes of Belle glittered malevolently as she saw Mike lift up her handbag, carelessly throw its contents out on the floor and take up a covered parcel.

He ripped it open at one end, and a small cascade of glistening diamonds fell into his avid hand. He toyed with them absently a moment, then replaced them in the packet, put it in his pocket and turned to the two.

"You won't dare squawk about this," he said fiercely. "If you do, even if they do get me, someone will get you right. You'd better report when they find you in the morning that someone you didn't know stuck you up and left you. Otherwise it'll be just too bad for you."

Big Mike stepped to the door, turned out the light and stepped into the corridor. He had a flashing glimpse of an upraised arm holding something bright and shiny—a sudden feeling of intense pain just above the right ear, and blackness engulfed him. He was dragged into the darkened stateroom, deft fingers went through his pockets and again the green covered parcel changed hands.

The two prone bound figures, lying in the dark, tried vainly to gain an idea of what was going on. Muffled sounds came from them, and the Singing Kid switched on the light. He laughed outright at the sight that met his eyes, and ignored the mute looks of appeal on the face of Docky and Belle. He tore a sheet into strips and bound Big Mike tightly, then stood gazing at his handiwork. His lips opened in a soft low song.

"Just give yourself a pat on the back,
You've had a good day today."

The following afternoon, before the boat docked, Puggy saw a steward knocking at the stateroom door wherein lay his bound antagonists, ready to take their baggage up to the deck. The Kid thought quickly.

"No chance there, steward. They just beat it themselves, with their own baggage. I know them and they're so cheap they'll save your tip. You won't get anything from them."

The steward cursed feelingly and hurried on. Puggy got himself ready for disembarkation. His bag had gone up, and he followed it, waiting alongside the rail until the gangplank was out. He walked slowly into the barn-like structure where baggage was reclaimed, singing softly to himself.

"Happy is the man
who keeps out the mill."

The Singing kid was happy. He had put the lug on those who had tried to double-cross him—had a fortune in jewels in his pocket and knew where he could dispose of them without too much of a cut. The warm Southern California sun was shining. All was peaceful. It was a good old world after all!

"Well, well, if it isn't the Singing Kid! Welcome to our city! This is a surprise! I flew down here to pick up Docky Wilder who was making a getaway, but so long as I find you I may as well take you, too. Maybe this time we'll find something on you."

Puggy, the Singing Kid, gave up. It was no use. Morey again had him, and he had the ice on him this time. Quick light hands tapped his pockets, and once again that green covered parcel came to view, this time in the hands of the law!

Ahead of him Puggy could see long dreary years wherein he moved, a fellow automaton amongst hosts of others who had also transgressed the law and who were also paying the penalty. He hummed a parody softly to himself:

"When it's Springtime in old Folsom,
I'll be looking out at you.
Where the meals at least are wholesome,
And we're black-jacked by a screw.
It is then I will remember,
All the things I used to do,
When it's Springtime in old Folsom,
I'm not coming back to you."

Glycerined Gangsters

By HENRY LEVERAGE

The Big Guy wanted The Spider, so he sent Indian Chick to find him. It sure takes an Indian to uncover a hide away—but it takes the brains of a Class A broad to blast 'em to hell!

WHEN THE BIG-SHOT SENT FOR CHICK CHESTER he knew that gangster had Indian blood in his veins.

It would take an Indian to find the whereabouts of the surviving members of The Spider's gang. They had vanished after a battle royal in one of Chinatown's narrow streets, leaving their dead piled on top of some of the Big-Shot's best men.

The Big-Shot ruled the Rose Hill Gang with a rod of steel. He swiveled back in his chair when Chick Chester was announced. Between drags at a huge Cuban cigar Big-Shot Morphy gave Chick Chester the gist of what he wanted him to do:

"See me pay-off man. Get five 'leaves' from him. Duck tu Pop Griffith's road-house an' work from there 'till y'u locate wot's left ov them guys ov Th' Spider's mob. I want tu know where they're under cover. Y'u ken do it—'cause it'll take an Apache. They're sure hid!"

Chick resembled a dark-haired, black-eyed Sheik in his tailor-made suit and custom-built shoes. His long features ended in a square jaw.

"Griffith's?" he questioned the Big-Shot.

"Yeah! Out Moundville way. He used tu be Th' Spider's armorer. Now he belongs tu me. See? A young moll out there mixes th' nitro fer his bombs. Name's Gabby. She'll help y'u locate Th' Spider's push."

"Want 'em bumped-off, boss?"

Big-Shot Morphy let his cigar recoil in his mouth. He drew it out and flecked the ashes.

"I want th' coppers tu do th' dirty work if I can arrange it, widout belchin' on 'em. If th' coppers won't—I will. 'Cause if I don't get 'em they'll get me."

Chester went directly to Moundville. He entered Griffith's Road House and introduced himself to the owner, a thin man with a tired air. A blond broad, not more than eighteen years of age, sidled up to her father. Chick noticed her hands were stained yellow in spots. He told Griffith what the Big-Shot wanted. Griffith shook his head.

"That Spider is a tough egg. He's running a gambling house now, just opened one I heard. It's a 'scatter' for his gang who're wearing dress suits now. They got some of the rods an' gats with them that they used in that Chinatown shootin'."

Chick stared boldly at the moll. She dropped her eyes.

"Where's his gambling-house located?"

"Search me. Somewhere in Windville. If you find his joint and the Big-Shot wants to get hunk, look out for a military machine-gun. I furnished 'em it, before I blew that mob. You remember the one I mean, Gabby?"

The moll shivered slightly. Then she threw back her chin and laughed:

"It's a regular cannon. That Spider's crazy lugging it around—when he could pull off a job better with the new sub-caliber air-cooled ones. He always was too rough to suit me, y'u know."

Chick Chester, otherwise Chickasaw Long-Wolf, so called before he became a gangster, drawled "ye—s?" He had noticed that Gabby was the brains behind her father. She made the bombs and he peddled them for someone to throw.

"Y'u know," repeated Gabby, "it's the thing now for a gang to pretend they were chased out or bumped-off and wait for their chance. The Spider must look like hell running a stuss-house, in a dress-suit, y'u know."

Again Chester regarded Gabby while Pop Griffith corrected her:

"He ain't runnin' a stuss-house, from wot I've heard. It's a come-on joint in a brown-stone mansion. Faro, stud, draw poker and roulette. A place where suckers are steered, trimmed and taken for a ride if they squawk hard enough."

Gabby placed her hands on her rounded hips.

"I'd go see Captain Jack if I was you," she told Chester. "He's got charge of Ward No. Nine, where The Spider must be in hiding. He'll know the new night-clubs and gambling joints. He oughto, y'u know. He collects the gravy."

"Ye—s," said Chester. "Well I won't do that, baby. Not me. Captain Jack and th' rest of the coppers would give their shields to put their nippers on these." Chick held out his dark wrists, exposing silk cuffs and diamond-studded links. "I'll scout through his ward and get an earful from some wise underdog."

Chick Chester gave a backward glance at Gabby when he left Griffith's Tavern. She waved her hand. He went on with his heart thumping. What a moll to pal with! Just his type—blond and talkative. No squeal in her.

He rather thought he could use Gabby in the search for The Spider's mob. It was going to be no small job finding an unknown gambling house in Windville. The Big-Shot, with all the gangsters he needed under his thumb, had evidently failed to locate the gang he wanted wiped out completely.

Chick Chester spent a day and a night running down every clue. He was forced to be careful on account of the police. His record as a bad man with a rod was enough to send him away for life.

Two ex-gamblers and a handbook tout, whom Chick knew, were skeptical regarding The Spider's gang. The tout gave Chester a long list of houses he knew. "Some's just started up," he sniffled. "Take a chance, I'm takin' 'em every day. Pick up a taxi-bucker that's hip an' have him make th' rounds. Try that fellow over there. He'd kill a guy for ten bucks."

Chester rather favored the suggestion. The driver over there was an ex-pug with a pock-marked chin. He confessed ignorance to The Spider's hang-out but he offered to let Chick ride for a week, free, if he couldn't find it.

"Ye—s?" said Chester. "Here's an X. Start her up and let me look around the town."

The thug-ugly chauffeur grinned at the crinkling bill.

"You're part Indian, ain't youse?"

"It's none of your damn business what I am!" Chester retorted. "As long as I got jack I'm a prince in this burg."

• • •

Chick visited six houses, without results, and began to doubt if The Spider was in that section of the city. The yellow gangleader may have spread his web somewhere else. The color of Chester's features grew darker and more determined. He had talked with housemen, croupiers, faro-dealers, proprietors and runners. He lost fifty dollars wandering from table to table. No one could give him the slightest clue concerning the Big-Shot's worst enemies.

He phoned Morphy who shot back:

"Keep movin', y'u! See th' pay-guy if youse need more kale."

The overworked taxi-driver began to think his fare was goofy. "Wot t'ell y'us lookin' fer?" he asked Chick.

"A sneaking welcher named Gronto. Spider Gronto."

He continued:

"I want to locate a new come-on joint, brown-stone front house, somewhere in Captain Jack's ward. It's probably got a back entrance."

"Th' Spider's."

"Ye—s?"

The driver scratched his head. "Wot's he look like?"

"Thin—thin as I am. Bent over. Grayish brown hair, a nick on the lobe of his right ear—a gash across his chin. Bad actor."

A light began to dawn in the depths of the driver's eyes.

"Say, cull, I saw that baby onct—last week. Sure I piped him, good an' plenty. Why didn't youse tell me y'u wuz lookin' fer him?"

Chester gripped the driver's muscular arm.

"Come clean!"

"Oh, all right." The chauffeur drew away from Chester's intense stare. He recognized the steel beneath his passenger's velvet manners. Getting out a map of the city, from a side-pocket, he ran a grimy thumb over it. "Say, cull, I saw that guy—or a ringer fer him, in Prospect Square. I had two fares from there. I knew the dump they came out ov wuz queer. How did I know? By the squawk a sucker put up about losing a lousy ninety bucks. Th' other guy, th' one wid evening clothes an' a gash on his chin, got rid of th' squealer by payin' him off. Wot a dirty look he gave him. Then this guy had me take him back tu th' square. He looked like a killer who didn't want tu smear things up fer that little kale."

"Ye—s? What number Prospect Square?"

"No. 6."

"Did you hear this man's name?"

"Th' sucker, who wuz trimmed, called him every name that ain't fit tu print. Funny how them honest guys ken beat us regulars when it comes tu cussin'."

Chick Chester looked at his platinum watch.

"Make for the nearest coffee house. We'll feed, on me. Then stop at a garage and fill up with gas. I want to take a look at that house before they put the blinds up."

"I'm on, cull."

The driver hurtled Chick northward, swung corners on two wheels and beat the red-set semaphores at the narrowest margins. He stopped at one corner of a green Square and said out of the side of his mouth:

"All th' numbers run on one side ov th' street. Y'u ken mooch along, while I wait here."

With a long, lanky stride, like an Apache after a scalp, Chick glided up the street, pretending to be looking at nothing in particular. His black eyes saw everything—the marks on the asphalt where many taxis had stopped, the cigarette-butts in the gutter thrown by waiting chauffeurs, spots of oil that stretched along for half a block. A slight feeling of doubt came to him when he noticed the doors of No. 6. These were frail looking, unlike any kind The Spider would order. That gangleader favored boiler plate and ax-proof protection.

The windows of No. 6 were shaded with green blinds. The steps leading upward had been scrubbed until they shone. A big 6 was painted on a transom.

Crossing the asphalt to a wall that fenced in the Square, Chick studied the row of houses intently. It was an aristocratic-looking neighborhood. Just the place no one would look for The Spider. Behind the houses were private garages, on an alley.

Springing over the stone fence Chick Chester detoured through the Square and came out by the side of the waiting taxi.

"How about it, cull?" queried the chauffeur.

"Looks good. Get me to the nearest drug-store."

Chester entered a sound-proof telephone-booth and called up Griffith's. He was connected with Gabby. "I've got two 'yards' for you," he promised her. "I need a swell broad for a job. One that can stall for me."

"I'm cooking some pineapples," chortled the moll.

Chester insisted: "Put the cooking away for a day. The Big-Shot wants certain information you can get for us. Meet me near Hadden Towers, early this evening."

She consented, saying she would drive in and take a load of stuff back to the tavern on her return. "Stuff off a boat," she laughed. "Y'u know, Dad sells it."

It was after six when Chester finished his preparations. He greeted the taxi-bucker and ordered him to rush to Hadden Towers. Gabby was already parked near the building. She sprang out of a long, black touring car." Chester shook his head.

"You see, I'm here with my bus," said Gabby.

"Yes? Say, sweetie, I wouldn't drive that machine much if I were you. Every hooch runner uses that brand. You ought to know better."

The moll bent down and adjusted a garter. "Gimme th' two 'yards.' Two centuries, I gotta have clothes."

Chick peeled two one-hundred dollar bills from his bank-roll. He folded them up and handed them to Gabby. "Now, come along with me," he said. "You needn't worry about glad rags. You better worry about that wreck you're driving."

Gabby dove again for her garter, where she concealed the two bills. She straightened a youthful back and swung on one high heel toward the parked phaeton.

"That's a stall," she explained. "A throw-off, y'u know. I never had any glycerin or hooch in it. I use taxis loaded to the axles. They trail that wagon, and if some sap copper stops it, the taxi turns around and beats it."

The Indian blood in Chick recognized a ruse, remarkably effective. Brains were better than bullets.

"Say," said Gabby, "if y'u stand there looking like that much longer, I'll fall for you. Y'ur a swell looker, but y'ur cheek-bones are too high. Maybe you don't fall for me. We might not mix any more than fulminate an' nitroglycerine!"

Chester gripped the moll's round brown arm. "Come along, kid. I've located The Spider, or think I have. We'll both stand aces with the Big Shot if it's true. We've got to check up and make sure. That's a trick I've planned for you. The Spider is so shifty he'll beat it at the first rumble."

"Do you want me to vamp him?"

"No! He's so tough he wouldn't fall for ten joy-broads. I want you to identify him without exciting suspicion. Do you know what he looks like?"

"Dad told me, y'u know."

Gabby's catching little "y'u know" fascinated Chick Chester. He felt himself falling for the moll. He drew her toward the taxi. "The Big-Shot," he explained, "has called on most of the gangster talent of this city to find out what The Spider is scheming. It's the fear of not knowing what he is doing or planning, or where he is in hiding, that gets the Big-Fellow's goat. Morphy is Czar of Windville."

"Yes, I know. Them Czars are easy marks with an army smoke-wagon like The Spider lugs around."

Chester felt the red-hot presence of a live aid as the taxi rolled toward Prospect Square. He got out two blocks from No. 6. To the chauffeur he whispered: "The street is slippery. Go on and make a good job of skidding in front of the house. Crash a lamppost. Smear things up. Then lug the dame up the steps and ring the bell. Don't take no for an answer when the doorman comes."

The taxi-driver squinted at the street, then at Chester. "How tu hell did th' street get so wet? It ain't been rainin'."

"Ye—s? Well, somebody high up ordered it sprinkled about an hour ago. Just a little idea of mine."

Gabby sank back on the cushions and set her eyes in front of her when the taxi started. Chick, after a look around for gangmen, strolled after the cab. He saw the driver slide toward the wall of the Square, strike it, rebound, and skid over the wet asphalt toward a lamppost in front of the brown-stone house.

The smash that followed seemed a natural one. Glass showered to the pavement. The taxi's lamps and mudguards were bent. Gabby fell staggeringly, out an open door, to the curb. She lay still, with her blond hair covering most of her face.

A white-whiskered granddaddy came running up. He recoiled, and dropped his cane when the chauffeur muscled him away, lifted Gabby and marched up the steps. A small crowd gathered. Balefully glaring back, like a gorilla with a prize maiden, the driver jabbed at the vestibule button. The inner door opened revealing an English butler.

Chester sauntered along in time to see the driver and Gabby disappear inside. The door was shut with a click.

It came to Chick that The Spider was rather overdoing things. An English butler, who looked honest, was a strange guardian for a mob of killers.

Believing that he would soon learn something from the clever moll concerning The Spider, Chick moved on to a corner east of the wrecked taxi. He saw the driver come out of No. 6, without Gabby. A doctor's coupé arrived. Soon after it came an emergency ambulance.

Chick began to worry about Gabby. The rouge the moll daubed on her cheeks and chin, to resemble blood, would hardly deceive a good physician. Gabby might come out of the house, with The Spider wise that a spy had visited him.

Walking toward the house Chick put on a pair of "cheaters," with thick tortoise-rims. The gangsters inside the house might be watching through the windows, he thought. The clothes were unlike those he usually wore. Dark in hue, they were a throw-off from his usual ones.

An altercation between a cop and the taxi-driver, caused Chester to pause near the wrecked machine.

"What happened?" asked the cop.

The harness-bull ignored the question and charged up the steps of No. 6.

"Want tu use her as a witness against me fer reckless drivin'," spat the chauffeur. "Ken y'u beat that?"

"She'll be a good witness—for you." Chester started, stepped rapidly to a railing and placed his back against it, with his hand on his hip. The door of the old brown-stone house had opened in the face of the officer. Out through it came Gabby, followed by an indignant doctor and the staid butler. They started explaining something when the moll reached Chester.

"Come! Blow!" she pleaded.

Chester was stoic as any Indian. He did not ask what had happened, in No. 6.

"Run across the street," he suggested. "Climb that fence. Go through the Square and wait at the entrance, under the arch. I'll tail an' croak any gangster who follows you."

"There is no gang—"

Gabby gathered up her skirts and ran for the wall. Chester waited. He saw the chauffeur motion for him to make a get-away. Searching for Gabby, after he leaped the fence, like an agile cougar, he reached the high, stone arch at the entrance. Gabby was rubbing her red-stained chin with a handkerchief.

"Ye—s?" asked Chick.

"It's all right, y'u know," the moll giggled. "Swell stuff, pal. Y'u sent me on a bum steer. I got a good eye-full before that croaker came. He touched the rouge and spilled the beans."

"Ye—s? And The Spider?"

"Doesn't hang out there. It isn't the kind of house you think it is, y'u know. It's respectable as hell. Woman there named Ambrose. Husband's a big guy in the coffee business, downtown."

"Ambrose?"

"Yes."

"Are you sure, kid?"

"Take a look in the telephone-book." Gabby finished removing the blood-like stains from her face. She arranged her clothes and sent a spiteful glance across the Square, in the direction of No. 6. "I ought to have another 'leaf'!" she suggested. "For damage to personal property."

They walked toward a drug-store. "That driver," said Chester, "gave me the dope about a man resembling The Spider steering a sucker away from No. 6. That, taken in connection with the information I have about The Spider's scatter being a come-on joint, caused all this trouble. The taxi-bucker was so sure—too sure. He said there was a big 6 on the transom. There is."

Gabby suggested: "Why don't you stall around a while and see if The Spider comes out of there."

"A coffee merchant, named Ambrose, wouldn't be shielding gunmen."

"Say, sweetheart, anybody will do anythin' in Windville for enough jack, y'u know."

"Ye—s? Come on in this drug-store."

Chester consulted a telephone-book while Gabby stalled. He read aloud: "Ambrose, J.J. No. 6. Prospect Square. Asia 7598."

Then below:

"Ambrose and Cunningham. Coffee Importers. No. 45 West Street. Garden 7320."

Lifting the receiver Chick dropped a nickel in a slot. He asked the operator for Asia 7598. "Hello?" he drawled.

He swung his lithe form toward Gabby after asking a single question and receiving an answer. "I'm going back and crown that taxi-bucker. I'm beat, so far. Ambrose is not covering up The Spider's mob. He's real."

"Well, y'u know, I thought so when they sent for a regular croaker. It didn't look like a come-on dump to me."

Gabby sprung an idea:

"Couldn't that pock-marked driver been wrong about the house, y'u know? There's a row of them that look alike to me."

"It's a slim chance, kid, but—"

"Shoot it. But what, Chick?"

"One worth a gamble. Nobody will make me, with these cheaters on. I'm going back to No. 6."

Gabby had learned to think as gangsters reason. She had encountered some of the sharpest brains of the underworld, while helping make bombs in her father's tavern.

"Go on, Chick," she urged. "I'll stall round, out of sight. That driver is either crooked or straight, y'u know. Beat him up an' find out which way he leans."

Trailing Chick, with the stone fence between them, Gabby swished the grass of the Square with her skirts. She saw that the wrecked taxi had been towed away.

Nearing the fence she leaned over it and beckoned to Chester. "Come here a minute," she whispered when he strode over the street.

"Ye—s?" he asked her.

"Take a look. Why did they sweep the broken glass up the gutter, over there? See it, y'u know. And that lamppost has been moved."

Chick's Indian-dark eyes flashed along the row of brown-stone fronts. He saw details Gabby overlooked. The lamppost had not been moved. The windshield glass was in the same spot. No. 6 was on the transom of Ambrose's mansion. There was also another No. 6 three doors away. The light through that transom was reddish, baleful.

"I get yeh!" Chick exclaimed. "Notice the blinds at the other No. 6. All drawn down, like a gambling house. They're expecting a sucker, or going to get rid of one. The taxi-bucker was right, Gabby, when he stated he left a man resembling The Spider at No. 6."

"Easy, kid. Swell stall. That transom on the other number 6 can be swung around to read No. 9, its right number."

Gabby bobbed her head. "You're a clever brain-worker, Chick. We better blow. Climb over the fence before they spot us."

He crossed the Square with her. "I'll phone the Big-Shot, kid. I'll collect a couple yards for you when I see the pay-off man. You take your big phaeton home and get back as quick as you can with a couple of pineapples. Just strong enough to blast the doors in of No. 9. Those doors are probably steel-lined."

"Sure, if The Spider's mob hang out there."

"Two bombs," repeated Chick. "I'll gather a bunch of killers. We'll lay in a car we have, near the alley, going north. We'll block the south end with an old wagon."

"I don't get you yet," said the puzzled Gabby.

"Easy. The Spider and his yellow curs will beat it in the car they have planted in their garage. We'll give them the works when they come out the north end of the alley."

"Maybe they'll stick in the house, y'u know. Even if the doors are blown to pieces."

"Have you any tear-gas at the tavern?"

"Dad can get some from the station house. The captain in charge has a bunch of tear-gas bombs. And he's crookeder than hell."

"That's set then, kid. Beat it and meet me where the wagon is blocking the south end of the alley. I'll have two more centuries for you. How long will it take you?"

A gold wrist-watch flashed from Gabby's shapely wrist.

"A couple of—three hours, sharp."

Chick Chester sensed a note of doubt in Gabby's voice. "Three hours, ye—s? What's the matter, kid? Don't you want to do it?"

"I want to do it! Sure. But I don't want to see you croaked in one of them dog-fights. The Spider will lug along that machine-gun, y'u know. The one Dad copped from some arsenal. It's a hell of a thing, and ain't sub-caliber."

"We'll get the drop on them and—that's all there will be to it. If we don't get that bunch of snakes tonight, they're going to get us an' get the Big-Shot. He knows what they're planning."

"I wouldn't have them croak you before you can croak them, y'u know. Give me a kiss and I'll go after the stuff."

Chick watched the moll glide through the dark shrubbery of the Square. "Best ever," he said to himself. Out came his watch. He marked the hour hand with his polished finger-nail.

"Three a.m. is The Spider's time to get the works," he said with Indian grimness.

Connecting with the Big-Shot and getting his permission to wipe out The Spider's gang was a delicate matter, which Chick knew best how to do. Morphy was under-cover so deeply it took him fifteen minutes before he heard his voice on a private, relayed wire. "Hol' on," grunted the Big-Shot, "before goin' ahead. I'll get th' low-down on No. 9, through me own channels."

Chester waited. The word came back to work fast and hard and go the limit. "Unleash the Rose Hill rodmen."

A bunch of gangmen, crowded in a hundred-horse-power sedan that had a steel shutter at the rear, met Chick by appointment. The pay-off man attended to blocking the alley with a junk-wagon. A beer truck was moved to the cross street above No. 9 and backed to the curb so that any escaping gangsters from the alley should turn in an easterly direction. A runabout, containing a driver and a "thrower," were waiting to blast out The Spider.

The moll, driving her phaeton like an expert, appeared sooner than she had promised. Chick aided her with a quick arm when she finished parking and sprang from the seat. She reached back and lifted up a package.

"Don't drop this," she warned him. "There's enough soup in it to blow up the block, y'u know."

"Wait," said Chester. He crossed the street and handed the package to the "thrower" in a runabout. "Blast goes off at three-forty-five. Circle at the corner of Prospect Square and give No. 9 the tear-bomb on the way back. Nine is three doors from the lamppost. They've got a changeable number on the transom. It may read 6, but it'll be 9."

The car rolled from the curb. Chick went back to Gabby. He saw her hastily conceal something under her skirt. The object appeared to be larger than a gat.

"What's the idea, kid?" he asked her.

"Nothing. That is, not much. I'm in on this too, y'u know."

"What do y'u mean?" Chester's black eyes searched the girl's form. There was an unusual bulge on her right hip. She quickly covered it with her coat.

"Come clean, kid."

"Say, who do'y'u think I am? A rummy? You come clean—with the jack. I'm going to do a little private work of my own on this job. Where's the two C's?"

Chester handed her the money. Again he looked intently at the moll. He gripped her arm. "We're going to start in a few minutes," he said evenly. "I can't drag you along when The Spider's mob get what's coming to them. Sure you're not going to gum things up?"

"I'm going to stay right here. I'll be sitting in that old bus of mine when you come back—if you do come back." Gabby averted her head. "Be careful," she whispered. "I've fallen hard for you. Don't get croaked!"

He walked away from her with a soft feeling in his heart. This feeling changed when he slipped up to the waiting sedan and instructed the driver: "Keep the front, right hand seat for me. I'll be back when I give the job the once over."

The net drawn around The Spider's lair was tighter than a French "fly-trap." Chester saw with satisfaction that the junk wagon effectively blocked the south alley. The beer-truck, laden with near-beer in kegs, apparently had broken down across a respectable street. A Rose Hill gangster, in greasy overalls and cap, was taking off a double-tired wheel. He nodded curtly when Chick went by him, coughing that everything was O.K.

Avoiding No. 9, Chick detoured for three blocks and came up to the rear of the waiting sedan. Its curtains were drawn. Two rodmen had their sub-caliber machine-guns ready to run out the side windows. The steel shutter protected the rear of the car.

Swinging beside the driver Chester pulled out his watch. He looked up and down the dark, deserted street. "Start your engine," he drawled. "Listen, pals. It's time—it's overtime—for—"

A roar and the reverberations of the roar came crackling through the misty air. A second roar sounded. The "pineapples" manufactured by Gabby had not been duds. Chester gripped the driver's arm.

"Wait. Now, there they go. No. 9 is one hell's mess now. It's full of gas."

The black runabout had flashed over the asphalt and swung at the Square's stone arch.

Chester ordered. "Step on it. Round the corner. Now up to the next. Slow down. Wait. You heard me. What do you see by the beer-truck?"

"Nothin' at tall. Yeah, that them. Comin' out dat alley. Wot tu hell. They're crashin' th' truck. No—say, they took th' sidewalk, chief! See Th' Spider's car? It's turned at th' Square. They ain't comin' dis way."

The cunning brain of The Spider had sensed a trap after he retreated to the garage in the rear of No. 9 and started his car. He acted contrary to the route framed for him.

The snarls from the gangmen at the machine-guns rang in Chester's ears. "Beat it through—same way they went!" he told the driver. "Keep 'em in sight. We got the fastest car."

The roaring sedan avoided a fireplug, scraped an iron railing, swerved with its right wheels on the sidewalk, tore off the bumper of the truck, and spun the corner at full speed. Ahead two blocks, The Spider's phaeton was speeding, with open muffler.

"Der's a guy behind a cannon, pointin' at us," gritted the driver at Chester's side.

"Forget it. Go through, an' we'll give 'em the works. There must be ten in that car. Pass them so they can't use that army gun."

The chase was short. The hundred-horse-power sedan gained on the rocking, overloaded phaeton. Chester ducked his head and drew out his gat. He stared around the windshield.

"Why don't they turn that buzz-saw loose?" protested the Rose Hill driver. "I gotta have me guts full ov lead before I get mad."

"Duck, it's coming," said Chester. "Get a death grip on that wheel."

An evil-visaged gangster rose in the rear of the touring-car. He pointed the army machine-gun at the front of the sedan. The Spider shouted something from the front of the car. The gangster drew back on the automobile trigger, behind the oil-cooled barrel. To Chester, crouched and watching with his dark eyes afire, there should have come a hail of hot fire.

Instead yellow and flamingo and purple light burst all around the phaeton. A ball of incandescence was in front of the sedan. A gust of wind and smoke blotted out everything. Through this acrid smoke the sedan plunged, struck an obstruction, turned partly over and righted itself when the driver twisted the wheel.

Looking back, Chick saw the remains of The Spider's get-away phaeton strewn about the street. Torsos, heads, quivering limbs and blood smeared the curbs. Again Chester looked when the driver slowed the sedan to a legal limit.

"Cripes!" he heard one of his pals say. "There ain't any ov 'em left!"

Intuition told Chester what had happened—what had probably saved his life. The machine-gun had exploded with all its big-caliber ammunition.

"Stop at this corner," he instructed the driver. "Right there. I'm going back—you go on and get under cover."

A north-bound taxi swung around at Chester's hand-signal. He sprung in and said to the bucker, "Take me south, along Prospect Square, to the arch. Make it snappy."

The driver started up, after adjusting the meter. He turned his head.

"I can't go through by th' Square, sir. Been an accident."

"Ye—s? What kind?"

"A hell ov a big touring-car blew up. Five killed an' two are dyin'. Tore a hole in everythin'. Must have been luggin' dynamite. Guess they were gangsters."

"Was one of them a man with a nick in his ear, scar across his chin?"

"Sure. Friend ov yours? All that wuz left ov him wuz not worth pickin' up."

"Take me to Hadden Towers," smiled Chester. "I've changed my mind."

Knowing The Spider had been effaced, Chick's stride was buoyant when he approached Gabby's ancient phaeton. She perched at the steering wheel. Chick got in and clutched her arm.

"They got th' works, kid. All of them. The Big-Shot will be tickled to death. He'll be—"

An innocent roguish smile curled the moll's red lips.

"Did something explode? I thought I heard a blast, y'u know?"

"You heard one, kid. And you turned the trick for us. What was that you hid under your skirt when I left you?"

"Quart of nitroglycerine. M' own brand."

"Ye—s?"

"I didn't want tu see you shoot it out with The Spider's gang. I sneaked up the alley, before the pineapples went off, and pried a window open in the garage, at No. 9. I crawled in, y'u know. The army machine-gun was in a big car. I'd seen it before, when Dad had it. I—I unscrewed the lower drain-plug of th' cooling chamber."

"Ye—s?" Chick's black eyes snapped.

"That let the commercial glycerin out. It was a shame to leave the chamber empty, so I pours m' quart of nitro in. Anybody firing that cannon would set it off, an' blooey for them!"

Chester looked at Gabby's inviting lips. His face neared hers.

"Gimme a kiss, kid. You're one swell pal."

A harness bull strolled past the phaeton. He rapped the hood with his night stick. "No petting parties allowed!" he said gruffly. "Move on!"

"I can't move," gurgled Gabby. "He's holding both my arms!"

OFF-TRAIL PUBLICATIONS
Specializing in the era of American pulp fiction

The Weird Detective Adventures of Wade Hammond: Vols 1-3
by Paul Chadwick
each with 10 stories from *Detective-Dragnet* and *Ten Detective Aces*
180 pages, $18 each

The City of Baal
by Charles Beadle
introduction by John Locke
7 stories of African adventure
from *Adventure* and *The Frontier*
240 pages, $20

Pulpwood Days
Volume One: Editors You Want To Know
edited by John Locke
Writers' magazine articles by and about pulp
editors; with ample biographical info
180 pages, $16

Doctor Coffin: The Living Dead Man
by Perley Poore Sheehan
introduction by John Wooley
8 novelettes of Hollywood detection
from *Thrilling Detective*
174 pages, $16

Shipping: $3.00 media mail; $5.00 priority
Check or MO to:
Off-Trail Publications
2036 Elkhorn Road, Castroville, CA 95012
Paypal: offtrail@redshift.com